I forced myself down Madison Avenue, over to Park, up to Ninety-sixth, over to the candy store and back along Madison. I walked quickly, scanning the streets, making sure I did not see a small figure with red curls, a green T-shirt and jeans. As though in front of me, I could see underneath those curls Randy's square face, scrunched up as though he was about to go into a tantrum. Even though it was in my mind, the sight made me want to cry. And I was dogged by the feeling that my search was useless, and worse, a waste of time. He was in that house. Randy was in that house and he had to be found before it was too late....

Fawcett Books
by Isabelle Holland:

Moncreiff   23089 $1.50
Darcourt   23224 $1.75
The deMaury Papers   23606 $1.75
Tower Abbey   24044 $1.95

THE MARCHINGTON INHERITANCE

Isabelle Holland

FAWCETT CREST • NEW YORK

For
JANE LUCAS
with many thanks for her help

THE MARCHINGTON INHERITANCE

THIS BOOK CONTAINS THE COMPLETE TEXT OF THE
ORIGINAL HARDCOVER EDITION

Published by Fawcett Crest Books, a unit of CBS Publications, the Consumer Publishing Division of CBS Inc., by arrangement with Rawson, Wade Publishers, Inc.

ISBN: 0-449-24339-7

Printed in the United States of America

First Fawcett Crest Printing: October 1980

10 9 8 7 6 5 4 3 2 1

CHAPTER 1

I didn't know it at the time, of course, but the part I was to play in the terror that was to grip the city three weeks later started quite innocently the second week in May. And it began with Aunt Ginevra doing something she'd been doing every day for a month: complaining about the noise from the playground under her window.

"Avril, I cannot endure that noise. There must be *something* we can do! Have you spoken to Julian?" My aunt—or, to be accurate, great aunt—Ginevra's voice came from behind me, managing to be both imperious and plaintive.

I glanced back. Aunt Ginevra's ample form was stretched out on the white lawn cover of her four-poster, her head and shoulders resting on several pillows and her right hand gripping—somewhat dramatically, I thought—her forehead. "I have not been able to get a wink of sleep since those wretched and neglected children burst into that . . . that *yard*, last month. Something must be done!"

That something had to be done had been the leitmotiv of Aunt Ginevra's outcry sounding every afternoon, quite punctually, at three o'clock, when two events converged: Aunt Ginevra repaired to her bedroom for her afternoon nap, and, at almost the same moment, somewhere between six and a dozen children were precipitated into the back garden—or what had once been a back garden—of the brownstone house next door to ours on a street between Madison and Park in Manhattan's East Eighties. But what had once been a garden was now covered with cement, and on the cemented ground stood a steel frame holding swings, a slide, a miniature jungle gym, a sandpit, a couple of wagons and assorted other toys. This children's heaven was immediately beneath my aunt's bedroom window, my bedroom window, and the windows of my studio two floors above.

"Darling Aunt," I said, "I've asked it before and I'll ask it again. Why don't you lie down on the sofa in the living room?"

"And I'll give you the same answer as before. I've never, in seventy-nine years, lain down in my living room. I don't intend to now. And I don't see why I should be driven from my bedroom by a so-called school that obviously doesn't know the first thing about the management of children! Have you spoken to Julian?" Julian Demarest was our cousin and Aunt Ginevra's lawyer.

"No, Aunt, I haven't. I called a couple of times, but he was away on business. So I left a message for him to call us when he gets back. That's the best I can do."

"I don't think you have the smallest sympathy," Aunt Ginevra said crossly.

"We can close the other window," I suggested.

"On a beautiful spring day? I will not sleep in a stuffy room."

"You could put on the air conditioner."

"It's cool enough. And you know I only put those wretched things on when it's boiling hot. Have you no feeling for the country's energy problem?"

"If we'd stop driving cars the size of schooners and riding in them two blocks for a loaf of bread—"

"There you go again," Aunt Ginevra said. "I should have thought that after all that happened, you would have got over that nonsense by now."

"—then we'd not only have more gas, we'd have less poundage," I finished, determined not to be sidetracked.

"You're quite thin enough."

That much was true. I gazed at the rather angular woman reflected in the shadowy window glass in front of me. The ten pounds that I'd been trying for two years

6

to put on would have softened those cheekbones and added a touch of curve here and there. And then, as though to underline the irony, I had a sudden mental image of myself as I had been at seventeen, plump, bursting out of my T-shirt and jeans, a trial to myself and to my father and a humiliating contrast to my slender and beautiful older sister. In between that younger self and now lay fourteen years, and the devastations of some of those years had apparently done something permanent to my metabolism.

"It is really most unfair," Aunt Ginevra said.

I knew what she meant and smiled a little. The wages of sin and rebellion should not have been the welcome loss of my early and traumatic weight problem. Given everything I had done, I should now (according to Aunt Ginevra's scale of justice) be gross and unhappy.

Well, I thought, I might now be spare rather than gross, but could I call myself happy? As the question idled through my mind there flickered within me, like the touch of remembered fire, an old pain. No, not happy. Content, perhaps...

There was a piercing shriek from below, followed by another even louder. As the two voices rose I glanced down to the playground. One little darling was trying to push another little darling off one of the swings. For the moment, the aggressor won, and two sets of tiny arms flailed at each other as the voices, undimmed and undaunted, reached new decible heights. A young woman in skirt and T-shirt, seated on a bench, gazed at them, hand cupped in chin, and made not one move to lessen the noise. Evidently she believed in self-expression. Well, so, for that matter, did I, and my attitude towards the children was undoubtedly more permissive than my aunt's. But I had to be fair. I was not seventy-nine. I was not trying to take a nap, and although my studio also looked down on the bedlam, I seemed to be oblivious to that and every other noise when I painted. It *was* trying for Aunt Ginevra. She had, according to her indignant comments, been taking her peaceful nap for thirty years. The opening of the school, a month before, had torn a hole right in the middle of that pleasant habit.

"I'll call the school and see if they can keep the noise down to a dull roar," I said.

"Thank you, dear," Aunt Ginevra said faintly. "That would be helpful."

I left her bedroom and went into the study that faced the front of the house and the street. But, after looking fruitlessly in the Manhattan directory, I realized that the school would have opened too recently to be listed. I then called the operator and tried new listings. But, since I had no idea what the school—if indeed it were a school—was named, the operator couldn't help me. Well, I thought, I could always walk next door to the front of the school and see if it sported a plate or sign of any kind. On the other hand, that would eat into my afternoon painting time, which was as sacred to me as Aunt Ginevra's nap was to her. But if Aunt Ginevra was going to lie there and fuss, I wouldn't get much painting done anyway. For one thing she would be on my conscience. For another, she would not endure sleeplessness long without sounding the buzzer that had been especially set up so she could reach me two floors above in my attic studio, and Jessie two floors below in the kitchen, without having to put her arthritic legs to the stairs.

Temporizing, I decided to go back past her bedroom to see if, despite the worst the playground could do, she had surprised herself and dropped off.

Tiptoeing across the hall, I glanced through her doorway. Aunt Ginevra's eyes were closed, and her imperious, aquiline nose was pointed to the ceiling. But there was a frown between her eyes which told me that she was still awake. At that moment a spine-tingling scream sounded from the playground outside. I wondered if it was too much to hope that one little darling was successfully murdering another little darling.

"From ghoulies and ghosties and short-legged beasties," I paraphrased quickly, "and things that go bump in the night (or day), Good Lord, deliver us."

Running upstairs to my bedroom, which, in this tall, narrow house was immediately above Aunt Ginevra's, I picked up a jacket to wear over my paint-stained shirt and jeans and was coming down the stairs again when the phone rang.

In the faint hope that my aunt might have dropped off despite the Beasties outside, I tore down the remaining steps and into the study and snatched off the receiver. "Hello."

"Hello, Avril," Julian Demarest said in his casual, uninflected voice. "You wanted me for something?"

Julian and I have never been friends. As the youngest partner in my father's law firm, he frequently acted as general aide and boy-Friday to my father when he first joined Turner, Baker, Marchington and Brooke. This meant that since my father never hesitated to express his irritation at me in the presence of whoever happened to be around, Julian was a witness to some of my more humiliating moments. And even though those moments went back a decade and a half, their memory formed in my mind—however foolishly—a sort of dimly felt backdrop to every conversation I had with Julian, whether it was on the phone or in person. Besides which, he had never once stuck up for me. Perhaps it was that that I still had not forgiven him for . . .

"Aunt Ginevra would like to talk to you about the nursery school or day-care center or whatever it is that has opened up next door."

"Is the noise bothering her?" Julian asked. One thing I always had to hand to him: he was not slow on the uptake.

"Yes. They've built a playground in the garden, and the Beasties scream their heads off under Aunt Ginevra's window just when she's used to taking her nap."

"Beasties?"

"Yes. As in ghoulies and ghosties."

"I see." His tone was dry.

"I am sure your two would be far too well behaved

for you to understand what I'm talking about," I said, inserting the needle.

"Absolutely. Marjory and I always beat them soundly twice a day to discourage any raised voices." Marjory was Julian's wife. They were, at the moment, undergoing one of their periodic separations. But since this had happened several times in the past few years, no one thought it permanent.

"Where are the boys now?" I asked.

"In school."

"Boarding school, I assume."

"That's right. Boarding school."

It was a curious ritual that we went through at least once every three or four times we had occasion to talk, rather like boxers exchanging automatic jabs. None of it was real. I was no longer the irresponsible dropout his barbs usually implied. And while I thought him an authoritarian stuffed shirt and an inadequate father, he was now a senior partner in his law firm, and no longer had to play apple-polishing sycophant, gofer to the great, the role I frequently ascribed to him in our exchanges.

"What's the name of the school that is destroying Cousin Ginevra's peace?" he asked.

"I don't know. I asked information to get their telephone number, but since I don't know what the school is called they couldn't give it to me. So I was about to go around and see if the school has a name and possibly talk to whoever is in charge."

"Maybe they'll be sympathetic and helpful," he said.

"Maybe."

"If not, give a shout and I'll see what the voice of the law can do."

"Thanks so much." But he had hung up.

Feeling somewhat stimulated by our brisk exchange, I left the house, ran down the steps of the stoop, turned right, and stood in front of another brownstone identical to ours. Sure enough, beside the door was a large white plaque on which was printed in black bold type: *THE LITTLE WORLD FOR LITTLE PEOPLE*.

10

"Yuch!" I said aloud.

Underneath that overcute title smaller print informed the world that fully licensed and trained teachers supervised the creative work, play and rest of children from three to seven from the hours of eight-thirty A.M. to six P.M. The final sentence stated simply: *Playground facilities.* It was the last, of course, that was distressing Aunt Ginevra. But as I stood there, rereading the sign, I realized that almost certainly the playground facilities were the main attraction of the school.

With the enormous increase in the numbers of working mothers, there was a matching upsurge in private school cum all-day care centers of one kind or another dotted over Manhattan's Upper East Side. In most of them, from what I had heard, the children either stayed inside or were chaperoned to Central Park. Any school that could boast its own playground would be considerably ahead of those that could not and would go far towards allaying the consciences of the Upper East Side working mothers as they hurried off in their Calvin Klein dresses, clutching their Gucci handbags and their Channel 13 totes.

Well, I thought, I would return to my quarters and ask the telephone operator to give me the number of The Little World for Little People so I could call them up and ask them to keep their little people quiet. And even as I turned to go back knew that my natural tendency to avoid confrontations with other people had won yet another round. What you should do, Avril Marchington, I told myself, is march up those steps, ring the bell and announce yourself as a neighbor and lover of little people everywhere, but explain that you and your aged aunt would like a little peace and quiet.

At that moment, the matter was at least partly resolved. The front door of the school opened and a dark, stocky young woman in a white shirt and wraparound flowered skirt appeared. The straight black hair was cut in a Dutch-boy bob over a short nose and rather heavy jaw. The woman, who looked about thirty, hes-

11

itated at the top step. Then her lips parted, showing a mouthful of prominent teeth. "May I help you?" She came down the steps, still smiling. "Is there anything I can do?"

"My name is Avril Marchington," I said. "My aunt— great aunt actually—and I live next door there." I waved a hand towards our house. "Our back windows look down on your play yard." Was I reading something into nothing at all, or did that large, toothy smile seem to freeze in place a trifle? "I realize that children are children," I ploughed on, "but my aunt, who is quite old, is used to taking her nap just about the time your kids come out into the playground, so I was wondering if you could maybe keep the noise down a little?"

The smile was now definitely gone. I was fairly sure that the quick, dark eyes had taken in my jeans, jacket and shirt, and, before I had spoken, had placed me as a parent desperate to find a dumping ground for her child. Instead, I had turned out to be that most obnoxious of human beings, a complaining neighbor.

"As you say," the slightly strident voice said, "children will be children. And their rights must be respected, too."

So there was to be no insincere nonsense of pretending courtesy. The woman, who had not introduced herself, had not conceded an inch in the rights of the school children to make as much noise as they wished regardless of any pain or inconvenience they caused an old lady. And then, as I looked back into those almond-shaped black eyes, I experienced that sense of psychological or metal double vision that had marked my more recent years: at one and the same time I could see both sides of a question, not only intellectually but emotionally. A dozen years before I would not only have given very much the same answer as this woman, I would have done so with the same poorly concealed sense of triumph. In my young days out on the West Coast, it was known as sending up the establishment, showing up the middle class with its idiot and hypocritical emphasis on good manners, quiet voices, law-abiding behavior, and general civic virtue. "They're all good Germans," one of my early radical boyfriends had said. "Underneath that well-bred garbage they're fascists," he continued, as enthusiastic an indoctrinator as I was an eager novice. "And our job is to prod them into showing what they're really like. Make the pigs mad. Then the sweetness and light will peel off and the racial and ethnic and class insults—which is the way they really think—will come out and all the people who haven't committed themselves will see what they're like." Oh, how eager I was to believe him! And how much I enjoyed carrying out this particular lesson in political theater. But time and tragedy had turned me around. I knew to my nerve endings how this woman facing me was feeling. She was hoping I would puff up and start talking about neighborly behavior. Instead, amused at us both, I started to laugh.

That shook her. She started to say something. Then the door above her opened and another young woman came out. The contrast between them was startling. The striking woman standing above us, pulling the front door closed, was tall, considerably taller than my five foot five. Her waving black hair fell to her shoulders. Blue eyes stared down at us. Her slacks, open-neck shirt and tweed jacket were the height of chic. Her features were strong but perfectly balanced. Altogether she was one of the most startlingly good-looking young women I had ever seen.

"There's our principal," the teacher standing next to me said. "Perhaps you'd better speak to her."

"May I help you," the principal said, coming down the steps.

It was odd and ironic, I thought. Those were the same words used by her predecessor. But with what a difference! This time the smile had spontaneity, and a well-shaped, long-fingered hand was held out to me. "I'm Janet Sutherland," she said in her pleasant alto, welcome to my ears after the shrillness of her associate.

I shook her hand. "Avril Marchington. I was just explaining to Miss... Miss..."

13

"Miss Gales," Janet Sutherland said.

"Miss Gales," I repeated, "that my great aunt, who is quite old and not well, is used to taking her much needed nap in the afternoon. Her window is immediately above your playground. And she finds that some of the noise—the children screaming, for instance—keeps her from sleeping. So I was wondering if the screams could be cut down, or even out." I would love to have added, *and your assistant here, in effect, told me to go and fly a kite*. But strategy prevented me. There was no need to put this obviously intelligent principal in the position of having to stick up for a member of her staff who was plainly in the wrong.

"You didn't tell me that your aunt was in poor health," Miss Gales said to me, her eyes spitting dislike. "What I said was," she explained, turning towards her chief, "that children would be children."

"True," Miss Sutherland said. "I'm sure Miss Marchington realizes that and wouldn't want to be unreasonable. But there's no question that children will take every advantage if they think they can get away with it. Some discipline is all to the good." The brilliant blue eyes smiled at me. "I'd be delighted to show you over the school. Won't you come inside?"

"You were on your way out," I said quickly. I shrank from being in close quarters with the children. "I don't want to stop you."

"You won't. Showing the school takes a bare ten minutes, and we're very proud of it."

Without being rude, even hostile, there was no getting out of it, particularly since I had come to ask a favor. I marched up the stone steps beside my recent opponent, who, I would have been willing to lay a bet, was no more pleased at this sudden access of harmony than I was.

"As you can see," Miss Sutherland said, unlocking the front door and pushing it open, "we've just about left the old brownstone as is. It was so perfect for a day care school."

14

As she said that I remembered the plaque outside the building and the rather nauseating name given the school. Such a piece of banal sentimentality went ill with this bright, obviously sophisticated young woman now leading me through the square hall into what must have been the original dining room, identical in layout, size and height of ceiling to the dining room in Aunt Ginevra's house.

But here the lofty room was painted a sunny color, with large Winnie-the-Pooh illustrations around the lower part of the wall, drawings from the children themselves above that, small chairs and desks, posters on low easels, stuffed animals, toys, wooden blocks, two aquariums of goldfish and, running around the middle of the wall, a blackboard.

"The children are all out in the playground in the back, preventing your aunt from sleeping, I'm afraid," Miss Sutherland said. "Come along and meet them."

But I knew suddenly that I could not cope with meeting the children.

"Thank you. But I must get back while the light is still strong." It was a feeble excuse, but I snatched at it.

Janet Sutherland's dark, slim brows rose. "You paint?"

"Yes. Some commercial work. I do the art work for children's books and book jackets, but I also do work of my own—mostly portraits." I felt like a fool babbling away when they could not possibly be interested. But I was overcome with the feeling of wanting to get out of that house.

"I don't suppose you'd be interested in teaching the children," Miss Gales astonished me by saying. "Some of them have talent."

"I don't have any teaching certificate," I said, working my way towards the door.

"That doesn't matter. This isn't a public school. Don't you think the children could benefit by some art lessons, Janet?"

"Of course. But we mustn't impose on Miss Marchington."

I had reached the front door and managed to open it. "Perhaps later," I said.

"So many of our children are poor," Miss Gales offered accusingly as she followed me out. "I think it's important to give them everything we can."

"True." Miss Sutherland pulled the door closed behind all three of us. "But let's face it. As far as I can see there are no budding Rembrandts in the present class. And for them to have a professional artist teaching them at this age would be a waste of Miss Marchinton's time. Come along, Lucy. We'll have to take the subway, or we'll be late. It was nice to meet you, Miss Marchington. And we'll do our best about the noise." The principal gave me a swift smile as they turned.

The two teachers, one tall and limber, like an athlete, and the other looking almost squat by comparison, set off towards the nearest subway stop. I turned in the opposite direction, and back up into our house. Well, I thought, at least I had learned the name of the school and registered our problem with them. Whether they could—or would—do something about the noise was another matter. Curiously, for all Miss Sutherland's dazzling smile and charm of manner and air of cooperation, I had serious doubts. Quite why, I didn't know.

Tiptoeing back up the stairs, I hoped that Aunt Ginevra had been able to drop off, although I could hear the squeak and squawk of tiny voices from the playground before I got to the head of the stairs.

But Aunt Ginevra was not only not asleep, she was up, her handsome form encased in her red silk dressing gown, and her eyes snapping with excitement.

"Avril, where have you been? The most marvelous thing has happened. I looked for you everywhere. Why did you go out?"

"I went next door to the school to ask them to be quiet, Aunt Ginevra," I said, coming to the top of the stairs.

"Yes, well, thank you. That was very kind. But now

16

wait until you hear this. I just got a cablegram from George and Suzanne. They're coming home. All four—that is, Suzanne, George and the two children—are landing at Kennedy this evening. Isn't it marvelous? I haven't seen them for at least eleven years..."

I smiled a little as I listened to her rattle on. As gregarious as she was imperious, Aunt Ginevra doted on having friends and relations from all over the world dropping in on her. Age, inflation and declining income now prevented her from throwing open an entire floor to various guests for an unlimited time as she once did. And an added deterrent to her dwindling resources was the growing frailty of Jessie, her maid for some years. Once, Jessie was merely one among four servants. Now she was the only one, and while the three of us rattled around the big house like small peas in an overlarge pod, Aunt Ginevra was reluctant to put an added burden on her old servant for anyone but family.

I suddenly became aware, through a slight change in her voice, that Aunt Ginevra had brought her meandering monologue around to me, and I hastily refocused my attention.

"It's even more than eleven years since you've seen them, isn't it?" Aunt Ginevra asked. "I've always thought it so strange that you and a sister so close in age should not have been closer and seen more of each other, but, of course, she and George have lived abroad ever since they married. I do wonder if they'll find it hot... Where's Jessie? Do you think I should give Suzanne and George the room next to the dining room, or should I give them the study? They can use the sofa in there, of course, the bed pulls out... Now about the sheets—"

"Aunt Ginevra," I said loudly. "Whoa!"

Aunt Ginevra drew her head back in a characteristic gesture, so that she looked a little like an enraged eagle. "Yes, my dear," she said with ominous calm.

I knew she did not like to be stopped in mid flight, so to speak, that she considered my interruption impertinent (and wanted me to know it), and on some deep level was a little afraid that I would put a spoke in her wheel. The only reason I was living with her at all was because she was given to occasional fainting "spells" and because her doctor had put his foot down stating she had to do one of three things: go to a posh nursing home; hire a companion who was strong enough to move her if she fell (which Jessie, being half her size, was not); or have some younger and stronger relative to live with her. All the choices were, to Aunt Ginevra, unpalatable. She loved her independence all the more dearly for having survived a crushed and crushing girlhood. But I had returned East at about that time, and since she had had a soft spot for the family rebel (although she violently disapproved of the various forms my rebellion had taken) she asked me if I would be interested in sharing the house with her. I, too, cherished my independence, but, despite some success, I was low on money and still in debt from the costs incurred during the fruitless two-year search for my child. So, four years before, I came to live in the tall brownstone in the East Eighties, assuring myself it was on a temporary basis, and had been there ever since. The fact that I could have the entire attic for my studio was a strong incitement to remain. Besides that, I had become fond of the old lady and had been able to distract her attention when she was about to embark on some of her more eccentric flights, which would lead, inevitably, to her overextending her strength and bringing on the collapses that the doctor had warned her about. Most of the time, Great Aunt Ginevra thought of herself as around fifty and acted accordingly, and had to be reminded that a seventy-nine-year-old body had a way of stating its limitations. On other occasions—such as the matter of the sacredness of her afternoon nap—she needed no reminding at all.

But I could see that with her passionate clan instinct she was enormously exhilarated at the thought of having four more members of the family rattling around the house—my sister, her husband and their two children. And that eagle look she was now bending on me meant that she was afraid I would put my foot down and refuse to allow it—which, to be honest, was exactly what I would have liked to do. My sister and I had never got on, and I found her husband an impossible snob. And while I had never met either of their offspring, I still shied away from the presence of children and would be much happier not to have them underfoot.

"They'll be an awful lot of extra trouble, Aunt Ginevra," I said. "And you know how the doctor feels about your overtaxing yourself."

"I don't see how they will tax me at all. Suzanne and George will look after their own children, Jessie will cook the meals and if you don't want to have anything to do with them you can stay up in your studio."

"Remember when you wanted to take in those Cambodian refugees?"

"That was different. And this is *family*, Avril. After all, you're here. And I think sharing this house for a short while until they find their feet and a new apartment is the least you can do for your own sister."

I recognized that ploy for what it was: the guilt game, and I refused to let her get away with it.

"You know perfectly well, Aunt Ginevra, I have no family feeling whatsoever. Suzanne and George and their children can quite well afford to go to a hotel."

The eagle look grew more fierce. I had an uneasy feeling she was about to burst into tears like a disappointed child. And I felt mean. A large part of my protest on this occasion was personal. I really didn't want my sister and her obnoxious husband in close proximity. And Aunt Ginevra needed diversion, even at the expense of a little overexertion.

Reluctantly, I relented. "I think," I said, "you should give Suzanne and George the old bedroom behind the living room. The children can have the study, or they can have the bedroom next to mine upstairs."

The fierce look vanished. "Yes, I was just thinking that. Of course, the children are of different sexes..."

"The girl is about ten, I know. How old is the boy?"

19

"Nine. I don't really know how you can avoid knowing. Heaven knows they sent out notices enough. But, as you say, you have no family feeling, and I know you never write letters."

"Never," I said amiably. "I probably got the notice and promptly forgot. What are their names?"

"Michelle and Toby." Aunt Ginevra glanced at me. As though it were print that I could read, I could see her pondering the advisability of asking me about the rift between my sister, Suzanne, and me. She had often been on the point of asking that question and drawn back, and I was fairly sure she would now. Aunt Ginevra might be imperious and demanding, but she had an old-fashioned dislike of probing questions. Instead, she commented, "Nine and ten years old. That's all right then. They can share that room."

Ten, I thought. Even now, after a decade, it hurt. My daughter would have been ten. Would be now, if she were alive somewhere. If. I gave myself a mental shake. "Well, they're obviously still young enough to have a room together. And there are two beds in that room. Whereas it would take rearranging to make the study over into a bedroom."

Aunt Ginevra gave me a warm smile that even now, when she was nearing eighty, had a childlike quality. "You're absolutely right. I'll just speak to Jessie." And she moved towards one of the bells near the head of her bed.

"How long are they going to stay?" I asked.

"They didn't actually say," Aunt Ginevra replied. She pushed the bell connected with the lower portion of the house and I could hear the buzzer sounding two floors below.

"Did they say *why* they are coming home?"

Aunt Ginevra put on her half spectacles and examined the long cablegram in her hands. "George says he feels it's more than time for the children to go to American schools and grow up in an American background. So he'll be touching base with some of his connections in New York," she read.

20

"That means he's out of a job and probably out of money," I said cynically.

"All the more reason why we should offer them food and shelter," Aunt Ginevra said.

I was rather touched by the "we." It was, after all, Aunt Ginevra's house and her money that ran the house. After a pitched battle that had lasted a week and had made Aunt Ginevra refuse to speak to me for three days afterwards, I had won the right to pay her a nominal sum—thirty-five dollars a week for room, board and the use of the attic as a studio. And she had only given in on that sum when I said I would not live with her if I couldn't pay her something and then she would have to hire a companion. The latter thought was sufficiently terrifying to her to make her surrender. When I explained to her that I could not feel reasonably independent otherwise, she was mollified. Independence was a big word with her. But her enormous sense of family was nevertheless wounded, which explained the eagerness with which she was about to welcome the descent of four human beings, two of whom she had never seen, and the other two of whom she had not seen for eleven or more years.

My sister, Suzanne, a Marchington beauty like our mother—and like Aunt Ginevra herself when she was young—was two years older than I and was one of those blessed females who sailed through adolescence without a spot, an extra pound or any other of the blots and blights that can make the years from about thirteen to about seventeen a living torture. If she had been stupid or lazy or frivolous, I would have felt better. But she was an A student, a leader in a variety of extracurricular activities, president of the student body in her private school, and a graduate of the Sorbonne. It was all too much and it was an impossible act to follow. Not only did I have the usual quota of teenage woes, I had the ones she didn't: acne, pudginess, shyness and unpopularity. Our mother died when I was twelve. She was a vague, distant, kind woman of whom Suzanne and I saw relatively little, partly because she spent years in and out of various expensive sanatoriums as a result of a series of nervous breakdowns. If she had lived, she might have insisted that I attend a different private school from the distinguished one Suzanne (and Mother herself) had gone to. During the times when she was more or less well, Mother had a kindness and perception that never troubled or halted our father's dynamic forward drive. But when the time came for me to change from the junior private school to the senior one, Mother was dead and, with the—to him—logical idea that Suzanne could keep an eye on me, my father sent me to the one she was still attending.

As might have been expected, it was a disaster from the beginning. A few teachers had the good sense not to mention the relationship between Suzanne and me, nor to refer to her commendable record. But there were others who seemed to take delight in throwing it in my face. I was too proud and timid to make an open fight about it. Instead, I seethed with an inner anger that I nourished and fed in secrecy and silence. It was only after Suzanne had graduated (with honors) and I came to see that getting into the college of my choice would demand a much better scholastic performance than I had so far displayed that I buckled down and worked. I, too, then made straight A's and developed enough outside activities to enable me to enter the University of California at Berkeley at just the right moment to become part of the radical movement. A born rebel, an injustice collector and a sulky teenager with giant resentments, I was made for the Movement, and it was made for me. And I went all the way with it. I marched, protested, occupied buildings, fought with the police, spent nights in jail and, when my grades inevitably plummeted, declared studying to be the final irrelevance and dropped out.

After that I moved into Haight-Ashbury and took the pot-and-pill road to a better society. It took pregnancy, illness, the loss of my daughter and a long hospitalization for me to come to see something that almost

22

any observer could have told me from the beginning: that my indignation over the much touted ills of society had its roots not in any genuine passion for social justice but in a desire to pay back my well-to-do, upper-middle-class family as a quid pro quo for all the intangibles they hadn't given me.

When, with the aid of a wise and kindly therapist, I finally saw that, my personal devastation was complete. I had placed my entire justification for everything I had done during my politicized college years and immediately afterwards on righteous indignation over what the world had done to me and others. When, at twenty-four, I saw that my life was in ruins over what I had done to myself, I reached some kind of bottom. The only decision left was whether I would live or die. I was never actually conscious of making such a choice. But a year later I realized I had. I was alive and wanted to stay that way.

To my astonishment, the painting I had begun as an act of despair and an alternative to opting out of reality altogether had become an absorbing interest. Even more surprising, I had achieved some small recognition. Curiously, the development of my style reversed the usual order. I had started out with abstract paintings. Then, out of idle curiosity and nothing much to do, I had studied drawing and portraiture and found I had stumbled on my métier. Art critics called me a neo-realist and compared my portraits to the seventeenth- and eighteenth-century Dutch and English schools. Certain critics, those who found my style philosophically unacceptable, ignored me. But they themselves were now being called passé.

So, at the age of thirty-one, I had a modest degree of fame and was making a good living as a successful painter and illustrator of children's books. Those wild days out on the West Coast were rarely, if ever, referred to and seemed far behind.

I turned now to Aunt Ginevra. "When exactly are they all arriving?"

"They get into Kennedy at six, which means they'll be here around seven. I wonder if I ought to meet them?"

Considering that my aunt disliked both cars and airports, her question was not only rhetorical, it was a device we both recognized.

"You mean you would like me to meet them?"

"Well, dear, it *is* past the best light of the day for your painting"—(Cunning old fox! I thought affectionately, bringing that in)—"and you know what a dreadful muddle that airport is. With two children—"

"Darling Aunt. I will, of, course, meet them if you want me to. But you can't expect me to believe in this poignant picture you're drawing of four bewildered refugees standing on the brink of the unknown. Hour for hour, Suzanne, George and company have probably spent more time in the air than they have on the ground."

"Very well, dear, just as you think best."

I went over and kissed her cheek. "I said I was going."

By this time Jessie was slowly mounting the last of the steps leading up to the second story. "You called me, ma'am." The words were all that nineteenth-century propriety could have demanded. But the undertone was pure Clydeside. Jessie MacTaggart may have been born on a croft in western Scotland, but she grew up in the shadow of the great docks on the Clyde, where her father had finally sought work. And she was as tough as any of the nails used by the shipbuilders.

"Yes, Jessie. My niece and her husband, Mr. and Mrs. George Petersen, and their two children, Michelle and Toby, will be arriving this evening and will be staying with us. I thought . . . Miss Avril and I thought the old bedroom downstairs behind the dining room could be made up for Mr. and Mrs. Petersen, and the front bedroom upstairs opposite Miss Avril's would do well for the children."

"I'll no be carrying meals up and down the stairs," Jessie said ruggedly.

"Of course not. I see no reason why there should be any carrying of meals at all. If one of the children should be ill, their mother or . . ." Aunt Ginevra eyed me cautiously, "or their aunt, Miss Avril, would be glad to help out."

"Oh, would they!" I was amused and exasperated. "Aunt Ginevra, every instinct tells me that you should put a definite time limit on this visit, and I will be glad to inform them of same when I meet them at the arrival building."

"It seems so ungenerous and inhospitable to say thus far shalt thou stay and no further, when they are coming to us in trouble—"

"Who said anything about trouble? George Petersen has gone from one multinational giant to another, first in Europe and then the Middle East, gathering more perks and large expense accounts, to say nothing of a higher salary with each move. They've lived off the fat of the land with layers of servants. If they can't afford a luxury suite in a hotel, you can bet your last dollar that George will find some company or person who will afford it for them."

"An' tha's the truth," Jessie said, wiping her hands on a dishtowel she had been carrying.

"This is my house . . ." Aunt Ginevra began, sounding her most imperious.

"And you have the right to do as you want. I'll agree to that. But I'll tell them myself to go if it looks as though it were going to be too much for you, and it's no use arguing with me, that's what Dr. Forster wants me here for."

Aunt Ginevra swept back into her room and I turned to go downstairs. But suddenly my aunt was back in the hall. "I forgot to ask. What did the school say when you asked them to be quiet?"

"Basically, not very much. One teacher, a dour type, seemed to think any effort to reduce the noise would represent despotic repression. The principal seemed more amenable to the idea that neighbors, too, have rights. And yet, I don't know that anything's going to change." I looked at the imposing woman standing in front of me. "Perhaps if you went and stated your own case," I said, half joking.

"I really would prefer not to. However, if things get bad enough I shall certainly not shrink from an unpleasant encounter."

"Why unpleasant? The principal, anyway, seemed cooperative enough."

"Is she tall and dark with very blue eyes and rather stylish?"

"That's right. Yes. That fairly describes her. I didn't realize you'd met. I should have waited until you waked up and made you go with me."

Aunt Ginevra's own blue eyes almost seemed to be looking at something over my shoulder. "Agatha Lacey's car dropped me off at the corner of Madison the other day. It seemed so much easier than going all the way around the block that I insisted on it, and this young woman was coming along just as I was saying good-bye to Agatha. Apparently Agatha has met her somewhere, so she greeted her and introduced me. I'm afraid I didn't make much sense."

"Why?"

"Because I had the odd feeling that I'd met her somewhere before, but can't for the life of me think where."

"How tantalizing."

"Yes. It's my age. All kinds of things suddenly disappear when I want them. It's annoying, and a little embarrassing."

"Never mind, you'll remember sometime."

"Yes. I know. But I'm afraid at the time I must have seemed rather haughty."

"It won't hurt if you did. Perhaps that's why she seemed more receptive to the idea of keeping a lid on the noise. She wouldn't want to cross anyone as imposing as you."

"Perhaps."

Aunt Ginevra seemed uncharacteristically abstracted. However much she might act the *grande dame,* she had a rich sense of humor, and I expected her to rise to my comment. But she merely said, "Hadn't you better be getting on your way, my dear? You know what traffic to Kennedy is like."

I sighed. "I've already left," I said, and went back down the stairs. The whole thought of this impending visit filled me with foreboding.

CHAPTER 2

Suzanne, her blonde head held high, came through the customs shed first. Immediately behind her were two smaller figures, and behind them came George. When anyone saw Suzanne and George for the first time the almost invariable and unoriginal response was "What a handsome couple!" They looked hand-picked, as though for a TV series on the upper crust: Suzanne—tall, slender, naturally fair, blue-eyed; George—tall, slender, brown-haired, and wearing the best Côte d'Azur tan. They looked like any photograph from *Town & Country*, the very social magazine in whose pages they had, as a matter of fact, often appeared: *"Mr. and Mrs. George Petersen of Southampton and Paris,"* the caption would almost always begin, varying only as to the last location, *"of Southampton and Madrid; of Southampton and Beirut; of Southampton and Cairo . . ."* But the house in Southampton that Suzanne and I had inherited from our mother had been sold several years before and my share of the money had gone, partly for medical expenses, partly to pay the investigators I had hired for as long as I could afford them.

"Hello, Suzanne," I said as my sister came towards me and kissed the air somewhere near my ear.

"Hello, darling. How nice of you to meet us." Close up she looked tired and seemed to be wearing an extraordinary amount of makeup.

"George?" I said, and held out my hand. But he kissed me anyway, smelling rather strongly of aftershave lotion.

I had been putting off meeting the children but there

was no postponing it any further. "So this is Michelle and Toby?" I said inanely.

Thin, light-haired, with patrician features and level gray eyes, Toby, like his mother, was all Marchington. "How do you do?" he said gravely, his European manners in startling contrast to anything that would have been bred on this side of the Atlantic.

"And you're Michelle," I said. She too, inherited a family appearance, although not with such happy results. My father's dark eyes and square face scowled back at me. "Hello," she said, almost glaring at me through thick glasses. I felt a beat of sympathy. It could not be easy for such an ungainly child to be brought up by a beautiful mother.

"I'm glad to meet you, Michelle," I said. "You look like your grandfather."

"She used to look like him much more than she does now," George said quickly. "She's growing more and more like Suzanne."

The straight black brows descended on the child's face. "No, I'm not."

"Don't contradict your father, Michelle," Suzanne said absently. "You have my chin and nose."

Only the eyes of love, I thought, could imagine that. "Come along out here," I said, "I managed to park beside the building. Do you have all your baggage?"

Considering that they were supposed to be moving back to the States permanently, they had very little. George was carrying two large suitcases, Suzanne had one small one, and each of the children had a small bag.

"The rest will follow us," Suzanne said vaguely.

By yak, burro or slow freight? I thought. And then reproached myself for cynicism and meanness of spirit.

"Here we are," I said cheerfully as we reached the car, to make up for unkind thinking. "Why don't you sit in front, Suzanne," I said, "and George and the kids can fill up the back."

"I want to sit in the front," Michelle said, and climbed into the front seat.

29

"Come out of there at once," Suzanne ordered.

I tried for peace. "It's all right. Michelle can sit between us."

"No, she cannot. I will not have this kind of behavior. American children have a deservedly bad reputation in Europe, but Michelle has been brought up there and knows better. Now do as I say, Michelle, or your father will drag you out."

I opened my mouth to say that it was, after all, my car. But then closed it again. For one thing, it was not my car, it was Aunt Ginevra's. For another, this was a battle I would do well, for everyone's sake, to stay out of.

"Come along out, Michelle," George said in a curiously flat voice.

Michelle glared mutinously at her parents and me, then grudgingly wiggled out. George and I put the bags in the trunk, then he got into the back between his two offspring, and I slid into the driver's seat next to Suzanne.

It was not the most comfortable ride.

"How's Aunt Ginevra?" Suzanne asked, after we had driven for a while in silence.

"Doughty as ever. She's got a new annoyance to keep her irritation up and her arteries young. I call them the Beasties. They are a clutch of young kids—three to seven—of great lung power who gambol around a playground right under Aunt Ginevra's window just as she lies down for her nap."

"A playground? On East Eighty-eighth?" George sounded amused. "What's happened to the old city? We've heard of its plight, of course. All over the continent, and even in parts of the Middle East, it's everyone's favorite subject."

I glanced at his face in the rearview mirror. He looked more like his old self, I thought, and only at that moment realized how, despite his tan, unlike his usual sleek presentation he seemed. I had never been his greatest admirer, but I was now almost glad to see that arrogant, mocking look on his handsome face.

"In the style of 'how are the mighty fallen,' I suppose," I said.

"Precisely. Good old *Schadenfreude.* There's nothing so cheering as somebody else's downfall."

"George is exaggerating, as usual," Suzanne drawled. "But he's right. What on earth is a playground doing on East Eighty-eighth Street?"

"It's not a public playground. But the brownstone next door has been turned into an all-day nursery plus primary grade school. They've cemented over the garden and put up swings and a slide and a sandpit and other delights, and according to at least one of their teachers, they feel that any attempt to keep the darlings quiet would do permanent damage to their little psyches."

"They're right," Michelle said.

"You are *not* psychologically damaged," Suzanne said, with a strange, repressed anger. "You're just spoiled."

"Easy," George put in from the back.

I glanced again in the rearview, this time at Toby. I wondered how he reacted to the internecine warfare between Michelle and her mother. But Toby was staring out the window. "When can you see the skyline?" he asked.

"In about five minutes, when we cross the Triboro. By the way," I said, as if the idea had only just occurred to me, "how long do you plan staying?"

Silence.

"We're thinking of buying an apartment in the city," Suzanne said.

"The lawyer said we had to pay all our bills first," Michelle stated from the back seat.

Her mother swung around. "If you ever say that again, in public or private," she said in a voice like cold iron, "you will be punished severely." Pause. "Do you understand me, Michelle?"

"Yes," the child said. I looked quickly at her image in the mirror. The corners of her mouth, which was big, had turned down. But I thought I caught a glint of

31

satisfaction from behind the thick lenses. Not a pleasant child, I thought, and, curiously, felt more relaxed. It was the child who appealed to me, who touched that angry, desolate nerve within me, whom I feared.

"Julian might be of some help in finding an apartment," I said. "His law firm seems to have a finger in an astonishing number of pies."

"Julian Demarest?" George said. "I'm supposed to see him about something."

"Lucky you," I said dryly.

Suzanne gave me a sidelong glance. "Still on the outs, you two?"

"It's a permanent condition, I'm afraid. He doesn't like revolutionaries and I don't like sleek lawyers in club ties."

"Your political views don't seem to have altered much," Suzanne said dryly.

"Yes, they have. I no longer want to blow up the establishment. I'm just willing to see it drop of its own weight—a weight supplied by people and corporations such as Julian and his partners."

"I should have thought one family member's involvement with the People's Revolutionary Army would be enough," Suzanne said.

"Who are you talking about? Look, Toby, there's the skyline, all laid out for you." And I felt the surge of pride that I always feel when I come into my native city. New York might have fallen on evil days, it might be broke, dirty, crime-ridden and deep in debt, but I still felt like the pilgrim returning to Mecca every time I came back.

Toby's thin, athletic body sat forward. "Super," he said, sounding rather English.

"It stinks," Michelle contributed.

"Speak for yourself," I spoke rather sharply.

"I always do," Michelle said.

Suzanne swung around. Glancing into the mirror, I saw Michelle shrink back a little.

"Okay," George said. "It's a free country, thank God." Curiously, his voice sounded moved when he said that. "Everybody is entitled to his or her opinion. But, Michelle, I think you're going to have to learn how to be more tactful."

"Why?" his unpleasant daughter asked.

"Because I'm suggesting it."

Michelle lapsed into sulky silence.

"What family member were you talking about?" I asked Suzanne.

"What?" Suzanne, who was gazing out at Manhattan State Hospital as we passed on the bridge, said vaguely.

"You said something about some member of the family being part of the People's Revolutionary Army."

"Oh. You know, Charles Carteret."

"The kidnapped kid? He was such a remote cousin it hardly counts."

"It may not to you, but the New York papers certainly used it. We saw them in Europe. Remember the headline? *Marchington Cousin Kidnapped by PRA?*"

"What's PRA?" Toby asked.

"People's Revolutionary Army."

"I'd like to join," Michelle said, and raised a clenched fist.

"You seem to have a chapter in your own house," I said to Suzanne, hoping that she'd take it lightly. She said nothing.

"I think Michelle's permanent sorrow is that she's too young to join it." And George smiled down at the little girl. For the first time I saw something other than a scowl or a pout on her rather unattractive face. A pudgy hand went out and touched his sleeve. Huge behind their distorting lenses, her eyes looked anxious.

"What's the first thing you'd like to do, Toby?" Suzanne asked.

"Go to the top of the World Trade Center Towers," he said.

"It shall be arranged." I turned off the drive into Ninety-sixth Street and headed west. "And what would you like to do first, Michelle?" I asked, feeling guilty that I'd forgotten her.

"Have a chocolate ice cream sundae with fudge, nuts and whipped cream."

"Have you forgotten that you're on a diet?" Suzanne asked.

Oh, my God, I thought, with another stab of sympathy for my unprepossessing niece. So she has that to cope with.

"I'm going to drop you off," I said quickly. "And then I'll park the car.".

"I'll go with you," Michelle said.

"You can just stay with us and get your own bag upstairs," her mother said.

"Let her park the car with Avril if she wants," George said. He was looking out the window, but not as though anything he saw interested him.

I saw a bewildered look come over Suzanne's face restoring, for a moment, the soft beauty that I remembered. With an abrupt gesture she turned and reached a tentative hand towards her daughter in the back seat. "Sorry, darling, I didn't mean to snap. Jet lag, I guess."

Scrunched back against the seat, wide mouth set, Michelle made no answering gesture in return. The large dark eyes stared hostilely.

What a pleasant family gathering, I thought and wished I had followed my instincts and fought Aunt Ginevra's congenital generosity down to the wire. The peaceable kingdom would be far more peaceful, I reflected if the four Petersens were ensconced in a hotel where they could carry on their skirmishing in privacy, without engaging others.

"All right, Michelle," I said. "You can come with me while I park the car. The garage is just down the block."

I had not really expected a smile by way of reward, so I was not too cast down when I didn't get one. I watched the child's face in the driving mirror. Just before her mother spoke, something flickered in the dark eyes and her mouth seemed—for a second—to lose

34

some of its rigidity. Maybe, I thought, she will say something ordinary, something that does not sound like a glove across the face or, conversely, a plea to be punished.

"Thank you," she muttered after a few seconds. Whatever expression her face might have shown was gone; banished after her mother's interjection.

I drew the car up outside the brownstone and helped George and Suzanne unload the trunk. Michelle, I noticed, loitered around the car until a glance from her mother pushed her into picking up her suitcase and taking it up the stoop.

"Okay, back in," I said to her, watching the others surge through the front door into Aunt Ginevra's embrace.

Instead of backing the car down the block to the garage that was next to and owned by a large new apartment house, I drove over to Fifth Avenue, down Fifth, back across to Park Avenue, up Park, around again to our block. I had no idea why Michelle wanted to come with me to park the car, but if she wanted a short holiday from her parents and brother, I was perfectly willing to give her a little longer than was actually necessary. Glancing once at her profile, I noticed that it was surprisingly good, the forehead a sharp rectangle to the strong, jutting nose.

"You have a nice profile, Michelle," I said idly.

"You don't have to flatter me."

Irritation went through me. "And you don't have to be so spiky. You can't expect people to like you if you go around being disagreeable."

"They don't like me anyway, so why should I bother to be nice."

I opened my mouth and then closed it, shocked that I, of all people, should be indulging in such conventional blather. Avril the enlightened, Avril the rebel-dropout could surely do better than handing this sullen child the old bromide about not being liked if you don't make yourself likable. I didn't dispute its truth. But it was such an inadequate comment to make to this particular child. On the other hand, there was the other extreme: to encourage a child to cop out, to believe that because she has been mishandled she is not responsible for what she does was a dogma that had created a generation of people who were only now sorting out the wreckage. Happy or not, like it or not, I had learned the hard way that one is accountable for what one does. And as that thought occurred, a shaft of bleak unhappiness shot through me for a second. The price I had paid for that bit of wisdom was extortionately high. I suddenly came to when the car behind me honked. "Okay, okay," I muttered, and then realized that Michelle had asked me a question, not one word of which had registered.

"What did you say?" I asked.

"I said what's the matter?"

Curious, the last person who said anything to me like that was Julian, and it had not been a friendly inquiry.

"Nothing. Why do you ask?" Which was like putting my hand in the child's face and pushing her backwards.

"Because there is. You just don't want to say. I don't care. Don't say."

"Sometimes I think of sad things," I said.

"So do I."

I certainly wasn't going to argue that one with her. "What makes *you* sad?" I asked.

She didn't answer for a minute. Mother? I thought. Father? Brother Toby?

"Bijou died."

"Who was Bijou?"

"My parakeet. One morning I got up and went over to his cage and he was lying on his back. Dead."

"I'm sorry, Michelle."

I nosed the car around to the side street. "Was that your only pet?"

"Yes. We couldn't have animals because we moved around too much. Only one of Daddy's friends who worked in his company left in a hurry and there was nothing to do with the bird. So they said I could keep

36

it if I fed it and cleaned out the cage and so on." Michelle, I noticed, like her brother, had a slightly English accent.

"Maybe," I said rashly, knowing I was courting trouble, "now that you'll be back here permanently, you'll be allowed to have another bird or a dog or cat. Here we are."

I parked the car. After a minute Michelle wiggled out her side and I got out mine. Slowly we walked up to street level.

"Speaking of animals," I said, as the garage's mangy, beaten-up stray streaked past, almost on its stomach.

"What was that?" Michelle asked, stopping.

"That was Joseph's guard cat. You've heard of a guard dog, well this is a guard cat, chiefly, I think against mice and rats."

"Who's Joseph?"

"Joseph used to manage the garage. He's dead now. There's a new manager."

"That cat doesn't look at all well taken care of."

"It probably isn't. But I'd appreciate it if you wouldn't say so to the new manager. We're not supposed to put our car in this garage. And if I'm rude to him he'll probably decide to go by the rules."

For the first time Michelle looked squarely at me. "I think that's terrible. Not to care about the cat just because you can garage your old car here."

"Maybe it is." I was stung all the more for having my own bad conscience about it. "But having had my car towed away three times has blunted my conscience."

We walked up the block to the house in silence.

Julian Demarest showed up just before dinner. He walked in when we were having drinks.

"Julian!" Aunt Ginevra said with pleasure. She was sitting bolt upright in her favorite chair, one with a high stiff back that everyone else found extremely uncomfortable.

"Hello, Cousin Ginevra, how are you?"

Julian is tall and thin with a slightly crooked aquiline nose and cold gray eyes. I have seen those eyes light up with either anger or malice, but seldom with anything warmer. Walking with his uneven gait across the room—he had been wounded in Vietnam—he stooped and kissed Aunt Ginevra's cheek. She blushed with pleasure.

"So glad you could come," she murmured, and I realized then that she must have called him up and invited him. "Isn't it wonderful that Suzanne and George are going to be in New York for a while?"

"Delightful," Julian said, and I grinned. For once he and I shared the same feeling on the subject—a rare thing.

"All right, Julian," Suzanne said cheerfully, "don't fall over yourself with delight. It wouldn't be like you."

"No, it wouldn't, would it?" Julian asked. "How are you? Good trip?" His eyes went past her to George, sitting in the huge wing chair that belonged to Aunt Ginevra's father. Somehow, just as Suzanne sat upright, as though she were, momentarily, prepared to levitate, so George, although sitting in a perfectly ordinary position, looked as though he were slumped. "How are you, George?" Julian asked.

"Fine," George replied.

"Aunt Ginevra tells me that you're thinking of finding a place here."

"I thought I'd look around," George said.

"How's Marjory?" Suzanne asked.

"She's well," Julian replied. He went over to a side table that served as a small bar and helped himself to some Scotch. "Also the boys," he said, sitting down on the corner of the sofa.

"How old are they now?" Suzanne sipped at her drink.

"Eleven and nine."

"Where are they in school? Buckley?" Suzanne idly twisted the stem of her sherry glass.

"Not a bit of it," I put in from my place at the other

end of the sofa. "They're in boarding school—a no-non-sense pukka upbringing right from the beginning."

"There is something about me," Julian drawled, "that brings out the lurking revolutionary in Avril. Whenever I'm around, she almost visibly regresses by about fifteen years."

Suzanne made a face. "Let's not bring up old sore points. There's nothing wrong with boarding school. I—George and I—are considering sending Michelle and Toby to one. Toby would love it and it would do Michelle a world of good."

"But she'd hate it," I said, astonished at my conviction on this subject.

"We're only thinking about it," George said. "I don't think it's right for Michelle either"—he glanced up and caught his wife's cool blue stare—"at least not the ones we've talked about."

"I went to boarding school," Aunt Ginevra said unexpectedly. "We used to have midnight feasts. It was considered very daring."

"Did you join in?" Julian said, with one of his rare warm smiles.

Aunt Ginevra sighed. "No. I wanted to. But I was never asked because I was thought of as too good. I would love to have been ungood. But if I had been caught—and I was always caught whenever I did anything out of the way—my parents would have been so angry and, what was worse, *hurt,* I didn't think I could bear it."

It was moments like that that made me realize how much I cared for the doughty old lady. All the various revolutions had come along two generations too late to benefit her. During her childhood and youth, she was, in her way, as much a prisoner as any convict, however luxurious her prison might be. I think it was because I did all the things she didn't dare to do that she has always retained a soft spot for me.

"Well, if all that repression led to your being here now among us," Julian said, "then from our point of view it was worth it."

What a handsomely polished apple, I thought. But I had to admit that her fine blue eyes sparkled. Perhaps—even probably—he might have his mind on her will (which, as her lawyer, he must have drawn up), but he certainly gave her morale a boost that no one else did.

"Maybe," Julian continued, "Suzanne and George's children will be able to do all the wicked things that you were denied."

"Not, I trust, a midnight feast," Suzanne said.

"Michelle's a square little body," Aunt Ginevra said. She glanced at me. "Avril had the same trouble when she was younger. And then she got thinner as I'm sure Michelle will, too."

"But, one hopes, at less cost," Suzanne murmured.

How easy it was for her, I thought, to drop into the role of cool, amused, somewhat superior older sister. Julian had spoken of me regressing to childhood when he was around. I knew well what he meant, because I was hanging on to my present self with both hands to keep from doing the same thing in front of Suzanne.

Quietly, to myself, I muttered, *I am a fairly well known professional painter with several showings and a respectable sale among my works.* Why am I sitting here waiting to be sent into the corner?

Since I neither opened my mouth nor moved my lips, it was impossible that anyone could have heard me. Yet Julian, with one of his satyr looks said, "You're an up-and-coming painter, Avril, so that Cinderella-among-the-ashes expression is a little unrealistic and misleading."

"Sometimes one's childhood comes up and grabs one from the rear," Aunt Ginevra said. "By the way, Julian, did you know that Avril went over to that noisy school and bearded the principal? I think it was very brave of her."

It was Aunt Ginevra's way of turning the subject, but I had to say, "Not really, darling. Miss . . . er . . . Gales, or whatever her name is, looked sulky, but the principal couldn't have been more gracious."

"I take it 'bearded' is merely a metaphor," Julian said. "The principal is a lady?"

"Yes, and in the old-fashioned sense of the word. Yet I have the feeling that once she made up her mind to something she would be hard to stop." I stared down at my glass. "Now I wonder why I said that? She was nothing but nice. A lot nicer than her sidekick."

"And what is the name of the place?"

"Brace yourself," I said. "The Little World for Little People."

Julian made a face. "Your glowing opinion of the principal seems unfounded if she thought that up."

"It does seem unlike her. Anyway, let's see if the noise abates."

Michelle and Toby came in.

"Hello, darlings," Suzanne said, her eyes on Toby.

He had wandered over to the window and was staring out into the twilight street. "I thought you said there was a playground," he said. "Filled with . . . with Beasties."

Everyone laughed.

"That's the front of the house you're looking at, Toby," I said. "The Beasties in their playground are at the back."

He walked the length of the room and stared through the rear side windows. "I don't hear anything, and I don't see anything either."

"The last scream dies around six, at which point all the employed mothers rush in, snatch their offspring and rush out." I glanced at my watch. "It's now six-thirty-five."

"I think it's mean of you to call them Beasties," Michelle said. "How would you like it if somebody called you that?"

I reflected that living with Michelle would take every bit of good temper and patience I had. "It's a joke," I explained carefully. "I took it from the old prayer, 'From ghoulies and ghosties and long-leggety beasties/And things that go bump in the night/Good Lord, deliver us!'"

Michelle produced an unexpected, urchin grin. "Only they go bump in the afternoon and wake up Aunt Geneva."

"Ginevra, darling. Not Geneva," Suzanne said.

"I don't mind being called Geneva," Aunt Ginevra said. "I think Ginevra sounds pretty silly, like something out of one of those dreadful Valentines."

"It's a lovely name," Suzanne stated firmly. "And there's no excuse in the world for Michelle not to have it right. After all, it's her middle name."

"No, it isn't," Michelle contradicted. "I unadopted it."

"You can't unadopt a name," her mother said. "It's on your birth certificate."

"If I could have got away with unadopting it, I would have," Aunt Ginevra said. "Michelle darling, it is incredible how much you look like your grandfather."

"But everyone said he was ugly. At least that's what they usually start to say as I come in the room. Then they stop."

"He wasn't pretty," Aunt Ginevra admitted. "But there was a lot of character and power in his face."

"Like a bull," I said.

Aunt Ginevra looked at me silently.

"I don't want to be like anybody," Michelle said belligerently.

Aunt Ginevra was staring at her. Then a faint smile touched her mouth. "What a little rebel you are," she said. "Well, that's in the family tradition, too. Look at Avril."

Michelle scowled at me. "You're not a real revolutionary."

"What makes you say that?" I asked quickly, before anyone commented.

"You give in to everybody."

"Only lately," Julian drawled. "There was a time when she must have been the leading bomb thrower of her cell."

"Why don't you be quiet," I said to Julian, taking out on him some of the irritation I felt at Michelle.

42

Suddenly Aunt Ginevra spoke. "What happened to little Charles, Charles Carteret's son? Has he been found?"

It was one of those sudden hops in sequence that she had been given to more and more in the past year, as though an event that had happened long in the past had occurred the day before, and the time in between swallowed completely.

"No, Aunt," I said. "He hasn't been."

"What made you ask that?" Julian said.

"I don't know," Aunt Ginevra said. "I just saw him suddenly in my head, only in some way he was *different*."

"I should imagine he might be," George put in. "If he's not dead."

"Oh, no," Aunt Ginevra cried. "Not dead." She looked at her lawyer. "You don't think so, Julian? You don't think he's dead?" It was a question.

"Cousin Ginevra, I have no idea. Ten years with that guerrilla group seems a little implausible." He hesitated. "I know he was a cousin of yours. I didn't realize how fond of him you were."

"I'm not especially. Not of young Charles. But I felt so sorry for his mother."

"She's dead, isn't she?" Suzanne said.

Aunt Ginevra sighed. "Yes. Both his parents are. His father—Charles Senior—died of a stroke a year ago. His mother . . . " her voice faltered, "his mother had a nervous breakdown about a year after the kidnapping, brought on, I'm sure, by all those promises and notes and disappointments. She died in the sanatorium."

"Poor Cousin Louise," Suzanne said.

"All that money should ease the pain. A posh sanitarium. Nurses around the clock." I heard my own voice with surprise. It was as though someone else had said that.

"That was an appalling thing to say, Avril," Aunt Ginevra said. "It makes me ashamed of you."

There was a cold silence. I could feel the shaking

43

beginning inside me. If I had had all the Carteret money to continue my search, would I have found my child? I knew the logic of my attitude—my resentment—was unreasonable. And there suddenly swam in front of my eyes a picture of Louise Carteret as it had appeared in the newspaper. How could I have forgotten that haunted face, those desperate eyes? Louise, too, had lost a child, in a far worse way than I. "I'm sorry," I said.

"That's quite all right," Aunt Ginevra said. But I knew she was still shocked and grieved. After all, as I should have remembered, she knew nothing of my daughter. No one in the room did.

There was a difficult silence.

Then Suzanne said, "Really, Avril—"

Fortunately for us all, Jessie heaved herself up the stairs and into the living room at that point. "Dinner's served," she growled.

The party broke up soon after dinner. Coffee was served in the sitting room, but Julian and I were the only ones to take it. Aunt Ginevra never had any coffee after midday lunch. Both George and Suzanne refused.

Julian handed me my cup. "I take it you don't fear insomnia."

"Coffee puts me to sleep," I said.

"How marvelous to have such steady unflappable nerves," Suzanne said. "It must go with all that cynicism."

One or two apt replies slid to the tip of my tongue. But honesty forced me to admit that I had lain myself open for that. So I held my silence.

Shortly after Jessie took out the coffee, Aunt Ginevra went to sleep sitting up in her chair. In a few minutes she waked up, blinked once or twice. Then said, "I'm going to bed. I'm an old woman and I'm sure I snore, so it's best."

Julian showed her to the foot of the stairs. When he came back in he said, "I ought to be going soon."

Suzanne gave him an oddly flirtatious smile that

44

put my teeth on edge. She'd always had a mild crush on him. "You certainly can't plead advanced age."

"No, Suzanne. Just an advanced state of being behind in my work. I have to go back to the office."

"Can I come with you?" George asked. He'd been sitting very quietly, his hands folded, as though he were waiting for something. "There are one or two things I'd like to talk over with you." Looking the way he did, the successful executive, par excellence, and given his list of high and distinguished positions—European vice-president of one of the world's biggest oil companies, Middle Eastern director of a multinational computer giant, first vice-president of a half a dozen combines—the pleading note in his voice seemed odd.

"How about tomorrow?" Julian said. "What I'm working on tonight has to be finished and ready by morning. Three o'clock okay?"

"Sure," George said.

I glanced at George's face and felt an unexpected pang of sympathy. "Come on, Julian. You can do better than that. I can't believe that you have back-to-back appointments until three."

"Yes, my dear Avril, I know you can't believe it. But that doesn't affect the fact that I do indeed have appointments booked solid until three."

My natural combativeness rose to the challenge. "Well—" I started.

"Why don't you say it all to me as you're showing me out?" Julian said, in a great good humor.

"You do try and get my goat, don't you?" I said as we went out into the hall.

"It's not hard."

I decided not to be drawn. He watched me for a minute and then gave his sardonic smile. "All right. I won't tease you. If the Beasties give you—or Cousin Ginevra—any more trouble, let me know."

"What good would that do? Unless you think that your charm with the good-looking headmistress or principal or whatever she is might carry the day for you."

"There is that, of course. Loath as I would be to try it on."

"Liar."

Julian picked up the briefcase he'd put on the hall table. "Actually, we carry a large stick as far as that school is concerned."

"What do you mean?"

"After you called I looked up some old papers on the house. As I was pretty sure, the house next door is similar. We could, probably and if we pushed hard enough, close the school. By New York law, all schools have to have two fire exits. As far as I can make out they have only one. Their first is through their own front door. Their second would be through the door in the wall between your gardens that would let them escape through your house."

He glanced at my astonished face and grinned. "Ciao," he said, and walked out the door.

CHAPTER 3

I got up at five-thirty the next morning, fumbled my way down to the kitchen and fixed my coffee, toast and orange juice before even Jessie emerged from her lair in the basement apartment. After I had finished, I cleared it all away, and took a second steaming cup up to my attic studio and closed the door. Then I sat on the window seat, sipped my coffee and stared at the blazing pink, rose and gold of the rising sun. After a while I put my hand up to my face and found it was wet. I had been crying.

This happened every few months, as though an old wound that never really healed would fester and erupt.

"Accept it," the shrink had said all those years before. "She is adopted now and undoubtedly in a good and loving home. Try and be happy for her."

"But you don't *know*," I said. "Any more than I do."

"No," he admitted. "But surely your father would not have given her to anything but a good home."

"My father would have given her to Jack the Ripper or the cannibal king if it would have saved the family name."

"He shouldn't have done it without your permission," the doctor admitted. "I really can't understand how he got away with it."

"He got away with it because he was rich and powerful, and the rich and powerful can do anything."

"That is a favorite theme of yours."

"You don't think it's true?"

"You can't get much more powerful than a President, but powerful as he was, President Lyndon Johnson was prevented from running for a second term by public pressure. I'm not saying the rich don't have clout and
47

get away with a lot. But you're not here to discuss abstract political or economic philosophy. I have a feeling that that is for you a tried-and-true device for moving the conversation away from yourself."

The nine-year-old scene unrolled in my head as clearly as though it were a movie, the dialogue complete.

"What do you mean?" I asked him angrily.

"It's a defense mechanism you've had for so long that you don't even recognize it as such. What it amounts to is, 'My father and his world are so powerful that I am powerless. And being powerless, I'm not responsible.'"

I walked out of his office then, sick with rage. I, responsible? Responsible for my infant daughter's being taken from me within a few hours of her birth, before I had ever seen her, so that by the time I had waked up from the fever and illness and many complications surrounding her birth, she had vanished? Given out for adoption by my father, who had been summoned by the police.

Eventually I went back to the psychiatrist, partly because the desire to live had outgrown my desire to die and I knew that I could not fully make it back without his help; and partly because my release from the psychiatric institution had been predicated on my assurance of continuing psychiatric care. I did not wish to be put back behind locked doors for my own good once again, lest I make another, and this time successful, attempt on my life.

"How could I be held responsible for my own illness?" I finally asked him.

"You tell me."

"I refused that jump for a long time, until, eventually, I could endure to look at it: I became ill through playing with drugs, self-neglect and the arrogant arrogation of rudimentary medical precautions and care to the category of outworn middle-class values. Casting medicine in the same area as big business, I took great pride in defying it. True, in the latter part of my preg-

48

nancy, frightened for my child, I tried to reverse myself and make up for lost care by a total change of lifestyle. But it was too late. I was hospitalized with an infection aggravated by malnutrition. My father was sent for. When he arrived and took in the situation he promptly moved me to a small private hospital where, half out of my head with fever, I went into labor. It was weeks later before I was more than dimly conscious of what was going on. I was told by a sympathetic nurse that I had asked frequently to see my baby, though I did not even know what sex it was. It was she who told me it was a girl, and who also told me that my father had said I had asked for it to be put up for adoption immediately after birth, and produced papers, signed by me, to prove it. The signature was, of course, a forgery.

It was not easy to catch up with my father. As soon as I was on my feet I borrowed some money and flew back to New York. But Father was then in London. Almost penniless, I did not have the money to follow him. Instead, I stormed into his splendid, paneled office. Not even his secretary of twenty years recognized in the gaunt, washed-out hippy standing in front of her the plump-well-dressed young woman of good family who had gone west to Berkeley to gain a liberal education and save the world. Tired, still weak, I burst into tears. She took me into my father's magnificent office and listened while I tumbled out the whole story.

"He had no right," I cried. "I want my child." I looked at her. "Tell me where she is!"

"I don't know, Avril," she said.

"I don't believe you."

"Don't you? Then you should know your father better. He does not confide secrets to anyone. Certainly not family secrets, and even less secrets that he considers would disgrace his name. Do you think, given the facts as you have stated them—that he forged your signature and put your baby up for adoption—that he would tell a soul on the East Coast about this? It's not even a question of trust, but of his pride."

And the moment she said that I knew she was telling

49

the truth. I would have given anything to be able to believe that there would be someone in whom he would confide.

"Julian," I said suddenly. "Julian Demarest."

"My dear, he's in a hospital in Vietnam."

Defeated, I just sat there. The family that had once been large had dwindled to a few. Aunt Ginevra, who, at the time, I considered the personification of family starch, was up in Maine. My sister, Suzanne, and her husband were in Austria. Both my parents had been only children and there were no first cousins and such second cousins as there might be were scattered far.

After a few minutes, the secretary, who had left the room, came back and put an envelope in my hands. "Your father left you this."

I stared at the white rectangle. Typed on the front was my full name Avril Mary Brooke-Marchington. The hyphen was a piece of added swank by my father, whose name was Brooke, but who became so infatuated with the Marchington clan he married into that he hyphenated the names à la English and had the change legalized. I dropped the hyphen, but discovered that to call myself Brooke caused so much confusion on government forms and driving licenses that I simply used the last name, Marchington.

"How did he know I'd be here? I suppose he guessed."

"Perhaps. I had instructions to hold it for a certain length of time."

"And if I didn't show up? How could he be so certain I would?"

"If the envelope was still here when he got back, then he'd give me further instructions."

I would have liked to hand it back to her. But, desperate for any clue as to the whereabouts of the baby he had taken from me, I tore it open. There was a check. That was all. No letter.

I stared at it in the gathering silence. Then I looked up and caught on the secretary's face a look of sympathy. "Did you know that that was all there was in it?"

She shook her head. "No." Then, after a minute. "He's . . . a hard man."

"Why have you stayed?" I asked.

She sighed. "He's a hard man, but a just one and a good boss. I'm a widow with three children. He pays well."

Everything in me wanted to tear up that check and leave the pieces for him to find. But I didn't. I needed the money to look for my daughter.

I went back to California convinced that the secret lay there, and for two years lived on as little as was humanly possible while I searched up and down the state and through every record office for some clue as to what had happened to my daughter.

The city hospital to which I had first been taken had, of course, no record of my daughter's birth, since I had been moved by my father to a private hospital before she was born. When I went back to the private hospital, I found it no longer in existence. It had closed, the building had been renovated and was now filled with offices. No one knew where the records of that hospital, if they still existed, could be located.

I hired a detective to track down all the personnel who could in any way help me. None of them could. My father had produced all the necessary papers for putting my child up for adoption, and he had walked out with her. That was all they knew. "Was it legal?" I asked a lawyer. Hardly, if my father had forged my signature. Given that the hospital asked no questions about the signature, believing, presumably, that it was mine, was my father's taking the child while I was still too ill to know what was going on legal? The lawyer tapped his pencil and speculated a little. A larger, more established hospital would most likely have insisted that I be conscious and aware of what was going on. But the hospital to which I had been moved was small, in debt and badly in need of funds.

I pounced on that. "If Father had paid them a hunk of money . . . ?"

The lawyer shrugged. "You'll have to have proof," he said.

To discover proof that a rich and powerful man had bribed a hospital to turn its head while he (in effect) kidnapped his grandchild would require the time and effort of an investigative reporter, well supported by an equally powerful newspaper.

I had run out of money, and something within me said that I had run out of time. I looked up an old acquaintance and got hold of some pills, the easiest thing in the world to do in the underworld of which I had been part. With what was left I acquired a bottle of vodka. The combination of pills and alcohol I knew to be lethal and I was taking no chances. It was supremely ironic that by making doubly sure with the alcohol, I foiled my own pupose. I had never been a successful drinker. Long before I was drunk I got sick. Somehow I had forgotten that. It was the unattractive sounds of me being vilely sick that awakened my light-sleeping and irritated neighbor. Then she heard the crash as I fell and knocked over a table and its contents. Outraged, she stormed to my room, kicked open the door (which was not locked) and found me. And for the second time in my life the California police took me, with sirens screaming, to the nearest city hospital. After my stomach had been pumped out and I awoke, I found myself in the psychiatric ward. A few weeks later I met the psychiatrist whom I continued to see after I had been released.

"Accept it," he said, and with all my soul I had tried. "Your own sanity comes first," he explained patiently, and I knew he was right. I started painting. One day, sometime later, I knew I would not try again to kill myself. Success came and money. Finally, I was given a showing in a small New York gallery and came East once again. My father had died while I was in the hospital a second time. I was not mentioned in his will, nor had I expected to be, or wanted to be. If he had been alive I would not have crossed the Mississippi. Since he was dead I felt that New York no longer held any dangers for me. So, I was not totally surprised when I felt that I had, in every good sense of the word, come home. When Aunt Ginevra's doctor issued his dictum about her not living alone, I found that my mind had made itself up and I moved into her house.

I didn't really come to accept the loss of my daughter. What I finally accepted was that I would never completely accept it. I avoided children en masse, although, ironically, it was children that had brought me both money and a modest fame. It was painful for me to paint them, and each time a portrait was finished I would make a vow to myself that it would be my last. But sooner or later, either I would succumb to the pleading of some parent, or the child him- or herself would seem to appear, and protesting inwardly and outwardly, I would pick up my brush.

I was working on one such portrait now and had been for some time, turning to it when I wasn't busy on a jacket or book illustrations. The fair-haired, gray-eyed child stared at me from the canvas, the look of bleak desolation reminding me of the original—a little girl I had glimpsed in a department store, sitting on a chair while her fashionably dressed mother went through rack after rack of clothes and snapped at her when she spoke. She was about ten and had a look about her both of my mother and Suzanne. Somewhere there was a ten-year-old child who had the same look. Would she have the same expression? Would her adoptive mother, having made the one gesture, ignore her?

I don't remember getting out of the store. I do remember finding myself on the chilly sidewalk drenched with perspiration. The next day I had begun the portrait. But somehow I couldn't get it right, so I would paint and repaint. I was doing so now as the morning light broke over Manhattan and I finished my coffee. But some essential reality about the child in the portrait eluded me.

"Damnation!" I said aloud, took the canvas off the

easel and placed it far behind some other canvases used and unused that were lying around.

Then I picked up the watercolor of a jacket I had started and calmed myself down by working on that. I don't know how long I'd been working before it was borne in on me that the children in the playground below were making even more of a racket than usual.

Going to the window, I looked down. My friend with the black hair and teeth was sitting on a chair apparently reading to one child while about ten others milled around pushing, yelling, screaming and generally enjoying themselves. I glanced at my watch. Time had passed quickly. It was now nearly noon.

I was about to turn away from the window when a thin, orange strip appeared on the piece of wall between us and the school. It was the late Joseph's ginger cat on one of his exploratory safaris in the gardens back of us. Evidently he had been behind the bushes in our garden and had jumped up on the wall we shared with the school. There, under the illusion he was safe, he sat down and started to wash.

One of nature's little noblemen underneath picked something off the playground floor and hurled it. The cat made a noise, half snarl, half scream, and headed back towards the wall that ran behind all the gardens and led back to the garage. But another missile came flying, and the cat, trying to dodge, lost his balance and was forced to jump down into the schoolyard. With shrieks of delight, the children closed in. Then there was a human yelp of pain.

"It scratched me," a little boy shouted angrily. It was, I noticed, the same red-haired child who threw the stone.

The teacher, whose name, I now recalled, was Gales, put down her book and, pushing her way between the children, faced the trapped and terrified animal. It was clearly a mistake. For the year since his late owner's death, Joseph's cat had virtually lived on the streets, and he had plainly been well schooled in the martial arts. I saw Miss Gales's hand go out slowly and be

54

snatched back. I was too far away to see if the cat had left his mark on her, but by the way she looked at her hand it seemed likely.

Why doesn't the idiot pull the children away and leave the cat space to escape? I thought irritatedly. She couldn't want to get rid of it any more than it wanted to leave. But either she didn't know much about animals or felt it presented a real danger to the children—probably both. She disappeared from the ring of children for a moment, reached a hand around a door that led to the school's first floor, and reappeared with a long broom.

At that point something in me took over. Without even thinking, I raised the window. Even so, I was not the first. I heard Michelle's voice.

"Leave that cat alone. It doesn't belong to you. If you do anything to that cat I shall tell on you to the RSPCA. Don't you touch it! I'll come and get it."

I glanced down. Michelle's head was sticking out of the hall window on the fourth floor right below me.

Miss Gales glanced up and raised a powerful voice. "This is a savage cat and shouldn't be allowed out where it can attack people."

Without thinking I joined the fight. "It only defends itself, like any other creature, when it is attacked. Those children should not be allowed to torment animals. For one thing it's inhumane. For another, it's against the law." Whether it was or not, I didn't know, but I was banking on the fact that she didn't know either. "Now if you and the children would just back off, the poor cat can get away."

She obviously didn't want to, because she stood, the broom poised, without saying anything. "Come, Miss Gales," I said, making a deliberate effort to soften my voice. "No good can come out of cornering the animal. Get the children away and let the cat jump on the wall."

She didn't like getting orders from me. But as one of her charges suddenly yelled "Shoo!" at the cat, she pulled him back. "You'd better get him back there right away before I call the police," she yelled at me, saving face.

"Michelle," I said.

The head below turned and glanced up.

"There's a door in the wall at the end of the garden. It's probably covered with creeper because nobody's used it for I don't know how long. But do you want to see if you can get through and rescue the cat?"

I heard Michelle's footsteps running down the stairs inside the house. Then I saw her stout form moving with surprising speed toward the door in the back wall of the garden. Yanking it open, she pulled aside the creeper and went through.

I don't know what she said to the children. I could hear her voice but not her words. But whatever she said, it was effective. They backed off still chattering a little, and the teacher took up guard behind them.

Walking a step or two towards the cat, Michelle lowered herself into a squatting position. Then slowly she held out her hand with the fingers extended. Gingerly, the cat relaxed its tense crouch, lowered its haunches to the ground and slowly and tentatively stretched its neck so that its nose was almost on her fingers.

"Brrrrrrr-r-r-r-r-r!" One of the children—the original stone thrower—effectively imitated a loud rattle ending in a screech.

The cat tried to spring. But by this time Michelle had hold of it. Clutching the clawing, frightened animal to her shoulder, she rose to her feet, then turned and aimed a well-placed kick at the child.

"She kicked me," he yelled at the top of his voice. "Did you see that, Miss Gales? She kicked me."

"I wish I had killed you," Michelle yelled back. "After *hours* of torture." She went back through the door slamming it behind her.

Miss Gales stared up at me. "I hope you saw how your ... your child—"

"She's not my child," I said. "She's my niece." We were ourselves behaving like two nasty children.

56

"Your niece, then, assaulted Randy here. We could sue you for that."

"Go ahead and try." I glared back down at her. "Michelle had the cat relaxed and soothed and would have been able to remove it in peace if that boy—the same one who tormented the cat in the first place—hadn't made that disgusting noise. Your children should be taught not to abuse animals."

"That's a dangerous cat, probably diseased. If Randy's mother insists *we'll* have to take it to the ASPCA—"

I did not plan to bring out our big gun at that unstrategic moment (expecially, as I was well aware, I was behaving as childishly as the hostile teacher below). Further, I could just hear Julian's scorn at our wasting our best ammunition on behalf of a fleabitten, battle-scarred stray.

But I heard myself shout back, "Not if you don't want the school closed, you won't take it to the ASPCA."

"Close the school? What are you talking about?"

All of a sudden there seemed to me, even at the distance of several floors, to be an anxious as well as angry look on the toothy face.

"I mean that according to New York law, you have to have two fire exits. One of them is through the door in our wall there, the one Michelle went through. That is your second fire exit. If we locked it and dropped a hint with one of the housing authorities, they'd come in and close up your school. So just cool it."

Feeling exhilarated by having had the satisfaction of the last word, I pulled down the window, went back towards my easel and picked up my brush. I was working on a delicate watercolor featuring a pool, some trees and a family of raccoons, one of several illustrations for a children's book. Gingerly, I put a touch of color on the raccoon's tail.

"I'm bleeding all over, Aunt Avril."

I jumped and jerked my hand. The raccoon's tail, to which I had been trying to give a particularly soft and furry look, was ruined. Unlike oils, where you simply scrape and start over, water colors ruin easily.

"Damn it, Michelle. Don't creep up on me like that!"

I caught one look of her wet face and bloody arm and shoulder before she turned and started to run downstairs.

"Just a minute. Now don't go. I'm sorry!" But I was talking to Michelle's broad back as she ran down the stairs.

"Michelle! Turn around at once!"

Slowly she complied, and turned a tear-stained face towards me. I then saw that the blood all over her arm was also down her front.

"I'm sorry I snapped. You startled me and I spoiled a picture. Come on back here."

With a sulkiness that I found exasperating, she climbed back up.

I put my hand on her unwounded shoulder, "Let's go to my bathroom up here."

I got her blouse off and examined the damage. The frightened cat had really used its claws, badly on top of Michelle's left shoulder where she had held the animal, but far worse farther down her back, where the claws on the cat's back legs had dug in for leverage. There the flesh was torn. I washed off the blood with soap and water and the wounds with water and alcohol.

"Michelle, do you know if you've ever had a tetanus shot?"

"Yes," she said quickly.

If she hadn't said it so fast I might have believed her. As it was, she sounded as though she were trying to ward off something.

I turned her around. "This is serious, Michelle. Tetanus is a terrible and possibly fatal disease. But if you get a shot now you won't be in danger. Heaven knows where that cat has been or what animal refuse has been on its claws."

"Cats are *clean*."

"I dare say they are. But that doesn't mean anything.

58

It would be the same with any animal. You haven't had a shot, have you?"

"Yes I have. Truly."

"When?"

Silence.

"When, Michelle?"

"You'll tell Mother." There was an awful note of despair in her voice.

"You mean I'll tell her you need a tetanus shot?"

"Yes."

"Well, so what?"

"I want to adopt that cat, but if she thinks its got a disease she won't let me."

"It isn't that the cat has a disease . . . And, Michelle, that's far too wild a cat for you to want to adopt. It's now a stray, and—"

"But don't you see? Nobody wants a cat like that. Anybody likes a kitten. Nobody will take a beat-up old stray like that, except me. But if you tell Mother he scratched me and I had to go to the doctor, she'll never let me have him."

"That doesn't make sense, Michelle. Your mother—"

"Yes, it does, Aunt Avril. You know it does. You've seen what she's like. She doesn't *like* me."

"Of course she likes you, Michelle. You mustn't say such things."

"Why not, if they're true."

Across ten years I could hear the voice of my father's secretary:

"You mustn't say such things, Avril."

"Why not, if they're true?"

This was the second time around for that particular piece of dialogue. Perhaps the Eastern religions were right: time was circular, not linear . . .

"Please, Aunt Avril—"

I looked down into the square face with it glasses and frame of thick, straight, untidy dark hair.

"All right, Michelle, But tell me, when did you last have a shot."

"About two years ago. I was talking to a dog that

59

had been tied up. It didn't mean to bite me, but some-body in a car blew his horn and scared the dog. It wasn't his fault."

"Then you're going to have to have another one." Sitting there on the side of the tub, I stared into her face, which was almost on a level with mine. "Go down and put on another blouse or sweater or something. I'll take you to the doctor. And bring your bloody clothes back here. I'll wash them out."

"And you won't tell Mother?"

It was wrong, of course. But I had seen the hard look on Suzanne's face when she spoke to Michelle.

"No. I won't tell your mother."

Dr. Tyler, Aunt Ginevra's doctor, fitted us in between patients.

"What were you doing?" he said. "Pulling the cat's tail?"

"Of course not," Michelle spoke with scorn. "I was stopping some horrible children from hurting it. I told them I'd tell the RSPCA on them."

The doctor held up the syringe, pushing the air out of it. "I know what the ASPCA stands for. What's the R?"

"Royal Society for the Prevention of Cruelty to An-imals. We have it in England."

He shoved the needle into her plump arm and emp-tied the syringe. "You obviously lived in England," he said amiably. "Did you like it?"

"It was all right," Michelle said indifferently.

"You must like animals," the doctor said, swabbing her arm with some disinfectant.

"Yes."

"What's your favorite sport?" He asked the question so innocently that I wondered what he was up to.

Michelle evidently wondered the same because the now familiar scowl appeared on her face. "Animals."

The doctor went over to a wash basin and washed his hands. "Animals are nice for a hobby, but I wouldn't call them a sport."

"I would." Michelle put on her blouse. The doctor had put fresh bandages on her shoulder, arm and back. I wondered what she would tell her mother when the latter saw them.

"Well, if I were you, young lady, I'd get interested in some real sport, like tennis or running. You need to get off some of that fat."

"Who asked you?" Michelle said rudely. As though I had slid into her body I could feel her humiliation, her sense of being belittled. Couldn't he have gone about it another way? I wondered.

"You came to me because I'm a doctor, and I'm telling you as a doctor that you'd better lose weight, or you'll have that problem dogging you the rest of your life."

I heard my own voice speak up. "Not necessarily, I was just as fat as Michelle. If not fatter."

"And you found losing it easy?" he asked with blatant sarcasm.

Belatedly, I remembered that Michelle hadn't wanted her mother to know that she had been scratched. The doctor probably didn't know Suzanne, but he was on very close terms with Aunt Ginevra. It was not a good idea to alienate him. On the other hand, now was not the moment to tell him that Michelle's mother didn't know about her mishap. He would probably delight in climbing into his starchiest form on the subject of the minor child and medical ethics.

"The method I chose," I said, thinking of the drugs I had taken, "was not one I would advise." I hesitated. Then, "Michelle," I said. "I know how you feel about weight and being nagged about it. I was nagged about it all during my childhood and adolescence, and I think it was the basic cause behind the terrible relationship I had with my father. But the fact is, you were rude to Dr. Tyler. Maybe he wasn't tactful, but you were rude."

The stubborn, cemented look that I knew so well settled around her mouth. I stared at her. She stared back at me. The doctor picked up his notes and pretended to be reading them.

"All right," she said surlily, "I'm sorry. But I'm tired
61

of people thinking that weight is the only thing about me that's important."

I looked up into the doctor's chilly blue eyes, trying to will him to understand. It had never been my experience that doctors were either sensitive or perceptive. Still, I thought, like Alice in Wonderland's concession about the treacle well, there might be one.

If so, I still hadn't found him. "I'm only giving you my opinion as a medical man," he said huffily. "Naturally the child will do what her mother thinks best."

"Naturally," I said dryly. "Come along, Michelle."

"I didn't like him at all," Michelle said before the front door to his office was even closed.

"*Ça va sans dire.* But for your own sake you might try to show it less."

"It's no use thinking you can say something I don't understand just because it's French," the not very appealing child next to me said. "I understand French."

"Then what did I say?"

"You said 'That goes without saying.'"

"Right."

"I know several languages," she boasted. And I suddenly realized why and how she sounded different from other girls her age I had known. Michelle, unlike most Americans, children or adults, but especially children, talked in full sentences. "You know you talk very well, Michelle. And you have a lovely voice—that is, when you're not growling."

To my surprise, she giggled. "Yes, I know." Then she sighed. "But it doesn't help. The other kids don't like it. They think I talk funny."

"Where? In England?"

"No, in American schools abroad. There are quite a lot, you know, in London, and Paris and Berlin, Egypt and other places. Most of the kids in them had gone to American schools back here and talked like the rest of the kids. But I didn't. They used to make fun of me...about the way I talked, and about...about—" And there, on Park Avenue and Eighty-third Street, she burst into tears. Some children—like women—are blessed with crying prettily. The fair, gray-eyed child of my haunted dreams was one. This uncomely dark hulk standing squarely in front of me, sobbing noisily and drawing to us a great deal of amused attention, was not one.

"Hush, Michelle. People are looking at us."

The drenched eyes looked up at me. Then the sobs abated. Michelle wiped her runny nose on the sleeve of her blouse.

"Here," I said, and took some tissues out of my blazer pocket. "Use these."

She blew her nose noisily and handed me back the damp ball of tissue.

"Put it in there," I said, waving towards the litter basket on the corner. Turning, she threw the wet ball towards the basket. It fell just short. Then she shrugged and turned back.

"Pick it up, Michelle. We're trying to keep the city a little cleaner."

"I don't care about the city."

I stared down at the child, resisting the impulse to take her by the collar and make her pick it up.

The brown eyes stared up at me. "You're like Mother," Michelle said. "You're ashamed of me and you don't like me. I thought you did."

I let her go, picked up the sodden tissue and threw it in the litter basket. "When you behave like this you make me ashamed of you. You seem to have a marked talent, Michelle, for acting in such a way that people will automatically reject you. You don't make liking you easy."

I turned and walked back home, not looking around to see if Michelle were following me, aware as I did so that I would be in a fine pickle if she took off and I had to explain (a) what I was doing with her at the doctor's in the first place, without first consulting her parents, and (b) why I had left her to stalk home by myself.

But I knew she was just behind me, pattering along, taking two steps to my one. Blast the child, I thought. She's right. I am ashamed of her and I don't like her.

63

By the time this truth had finally trickled into my consciousness, we were at home. Without further ado, I headed towards my attic.

Having had enough distraction for one day and possessed of a devout wish not to see anyone else for several hours, I had lunch up in my attic where I had installed a small refrigerator and kept milk, cheese, yogurt and fruit.

After working on the raccoon's tail for a while, I realized that it wasn't ruined. And probably, I thought, dabbling my brush in water, I knew it at the time, but used the excuse to snap at Michelle.

But thinking about Michelle did nothing for my peace of mind. The child disturbed me in an uncomfortable and unpleasant way. The more I thought about her, and I seemed unable to turn her off in my head, the less well the raccoons in their pastoral setting went. After a while, I put the watercolor away and retrieved from behind the stacks of canvases the portrait of the fair child.

That didn't go well either. Nothing I could do seemed to make the face alive. I had just put it back when Jessie's voice growled from the door.

"This just came for ye. Did ye no hear yur bell?"

I swung around. "No. Did you ring it?"

"Aye. Not once, but twice. Ye must be far away."

It had happened occasionally before—that my bell had sounded without my hearing it. "Sorry," I said. "What's up?"

"A body left this for you."

I took the envelope she was holding. "What kind of a body?"

"A wee one. A little lad."

I looked on the front of the white rectangle: *Ms. Avril Marchington.* Then I tore it open.

Dear Ms. Marchington:

We hope very much that Randy Ferris will not suffer any ill effects from the scratches acquired from your cat.

64

If he does, and if his parents insist, we will, of course, have to ask for some compensation. Nor will we be turned from what we consider legitimate action by your threat to close an integrated school. You can be very sure that we will bring any such attempt to the attention of the public.

Yours truly,

Lucy Gales, Assistant Principal

As easily as Ms. Gales could I read the headline: *Rich Eastsider Tries to Close Integrated School.* It might not make the *New York Times,* but it took no great imagination to see it on the cover of the *News,* the *Post,* the *Voice* and our own East Side give away newspaper placed in the lobby of every building. From there it could escalate.

"Oh, hell," I said and went over to the window. Vaguely I had noticed minority children among the cluster five floors down. But after all my years out on the coast in the student and dropout underground, I would be more liable to notice a group that was monochromatic.

As I looked down on the schoolyard the children were fanning out from the door leading to the school building and were sounding like the arrival of the Apaches in an old-fashioned, Grade B, late-late-show soldiers-and-Indians movie. And behind, like a shepherd, was Ms. Gales.

Driving sweet buds like flocks to feed in air, I thought irrelevantly. And, indeed, at least half of them were black or brown.

At that moment, the woman glanced up. Our eyes met. It seemed incredible that I should be able to read malicious triumph so far away, but I could have sworn that that was just what I did see.

"Your round," I muttered.

CHAPTER 4

I had to concede that the Petersens settled into the household with remarkably little fuss. They came to meals on time, were out a great deal during the day, and returned to their own quarters in the evening after dinner. Considering how much I had resented their coming, I was also forced to admit that an unexpected good had come out of it: I had managed to get an extraordinary amount of work done. This was not because of a great boost in inspiration, but because avoiding my sister and brother-in-law and children had become so essential to me that I had, perforce, to spend hours in my attic studio. The illustrations for the raccoon book were finished and turned in ahead of deadline, which sent the editor, used to pleading with writers and illustrators for the overdue delivery of text and drawings, into shock. I had another commission to fulfill, but the manuscript hadn't yet arrived, so I couldn't even start to plan the illustrations. That left me with old, uncompleted paintings, including the one of the fair-haired gray-eyed child. But tinkering with it removed what little life there was from the child's face. The pale oval stared back at me, a mask, a haunt, not a child.

"It looks like Toby, or at least a female version of him," Suzanne's voice said behind me early one morning several days after the arrival of Ms. Gale's note.

I jumped and turned quickly.

"Sorry," Suzanne said, "did I startle you?"

"You and your daughter, Michelle, are geniuses at quiet arrivals," I said. "Or maybe my hearing is not what it used to be."

"I apologize for us both," Suzanne said. And then

66

added with strange intensity, "She can be an aggravating child."

Suddenly I remembered Michelle's *"She doesn't like me,"* and how I had tried to squash her just as Father's secretary squashed me when I said the same of Father.

"She annoys you a lot, doesn't she?" I said.

Suzanne got out a cigarette. "As I pointed out, she's an irritating child. Even George—" She looked around vaguely.

"Ashtray?" I asked.

"Yes. Do you have one?"

"Here's the one and only." I gave her a round white china ashtray lying on a nearby window seat. "Even George what?"

Suzanne blew out her match. "Nothing important."

I knew of old Suzanne's evasive tactics, so I tried a frontal approach. "George seems to like and understand Michelle better than you do."

"Dear George," Suzanne murmured. "Always so understanding with the fragile female. Although I'd hardly call Michelle fragile."

"You haven't changed, have you? We've been over this ground before, you and I. As I've pointed out before, there's more than just the physical kind of fragility."

"Yes, I seem to remember your saying something like that to me about thirteen years ago. It all comes back, even to the filthy and malodorous T-shirt you were wearing. I think that was the summer you were home from Berkeley and told us that bathing was an expression of middle-class decadence."

Suddenly I saw myself as I was then, home after my first year at Berkeley, the compleat revolutionary, possessed at last of a cause in whose name I could spit in the eye of all those who had ever (in my opinion) ill used me. That meant just about everyone, but most especially my father.

He had liked—almost worshipped, in fact—tall, pretty, delicately made women like his wife, my mother, and Suzanne, his older daughter. The Marchington Inheritance he called it with pride. I had got none of it. For a man to whom well-bred beauty in the female was the one all-important attribute, I was a total flop and he let me know it. A supreme irony lay in the fact that the short, dark, square-faced looks he so denigrated I'd inherited from him. But I was too wounded and rebellious over his thinly veiled distaste of everything about me to appreciate the irony or to look beneath his aversion to what it might tell me about the man himself. If I had, so much anguish might have been saved for at least three people, and our lives might have been different.

But I, no more than he, was gifted with self-knowledge. If the women's liberation movement had been off the ground at that point, I would have delighted in calling my sire a sexist pig. But The Movement was the force of the hour, and I had to satisfy myself with yelling "Fascist!" at every opportunity, waving a permanently clenched fist and refusing to wear what my father considered suitable clothes.

I came back to the present with a thump and glanced down at the paint-smeared shirt I kept in the studio and was wearing over my sweater. "Yes, I remember that T-shirt. Nice of you to remind me. I trust this shirt doesn't offend you."

Suzanne looked up at me. "Do you really care?"

"No. Not really."

"I didn't think so."

"Then why the digs? It's true I no longer care. But Michelle does. What are you trying to do? Just keep your hand—or rather your tongue—in practice? If so, then you're welcome to practice on me. I don't mind. But Michelle's a pretty defenseless target."

She didn't say anything. But stared down at the slender, shapely hands in her lap, one of them holding a cigarette. Then, "You're not so bad yourself at dirty fighting." Suzanne got up. "I came up to say that George may be out to dinner."

"You'd better tell Jessie." I wanted her to go so I could go back to finding out what I had done wrong with the painting of the child.

"Jessie appears to be out grocery shopping, and I am going out myself."

"All right. I'll tell her. Or at least I'll try to remember to. By the way—"

Suzanne, who was beginning to stroll out, stopped. "Yes?"

"Didn't you say that the bulk of your baggage was being forwarded? Is it liable to turn up any day? Because if so, I must try and find a place in the basement. I don't want a couple of sweating men to bring it all the way up here, only for me to send it back down to the basement."

"Your studio is sacred, I take it."

"The holy of holies."

"Doesn't Jessie have her quarters in the basement?"

"There's a cellar below that."

"I see. Well, the stuff is coming by freighter. That seemed the cheapest way, and you know how long that takes."

I glanced at her. "You really must be broke. You were never willing to travel before without several wardrobes."

"I don't think making reasonable economies indicates bankruptcy."

She said it with so much of her old arrogance that I succumbed to the unworthy impulse to murmur, "Not to speak of all the bills Michelle mentioned." As I saw the pink stain Suzanne's cheeks I felt a little sorry.

"Now you can see why we—I—find her difficult."

"Michelle said you didn't like her. I snapped her head off for that, but I shouldn't have. It's true, isn't it?"

As I should have remembered, however, having a really honest conversation with Suzanne was impossible. Style, rather than content, was her preoccupation. And according to the style of her world, one just didn't say that kind of thing.

"Of course it isn't true. What an idiotic thing to say."

"Not idiotic, Sue. My father didn't like me."

Suzanne came back, stubbed out her cigarette and

walked once again to the door. Hooray, I thought. She's going to leave me alone. But, as I should have known, not before she had placed her parting shot. "It may interest you to know I love Michelle very much. And she loves me." Suzanne glanced at the painting. "If you want to do a good job on that rather pedestrian head you're staring at, why don't you get Toby to sit for you. It's meant to be the dead spit of him anyway, isn't it?"

"Of course not," I almost shouted.

Suzanne smiled a superior little smile, then trod lightly down the stairs leading to the fourth floor.

Just to prove how wrong Suzanne was, I concentrated on the painting with such ferocity that several hours later I surfaced to realize that Aunt Ginevra was standing there and had been speaking to me for some minutes. I turned.

"Aunt Ginevra!" I glanced at the cane in her hand and saw instantly that she was feeling sorry for herself. Her aging bones were stiff, but she used her cane largely as a psychological weapon.

"What's the matter, darling?" I said, feeling guilty already. "You know you shouldn't struggle up those awful stairs."

"If you would deign to answer your bell, or even shouts, I wouldn't have to. What on earth are you doing up here? Going into a trance? You've never ignored my bell before."

I pushed a chair towards her.

"It's quite all right. I'd rather stand," she said grandly, laying it on thicker.

"But I wouldn't rather you'd stand," I said firmly. "Come along, Aunt. I already feel terrible. Please sit down."

With the air of one doing me an enormous favor, she lowered her majestic figure onto the small canvas chair I had put behind her. "I don't see how you can *not* hear them," she said plaintively. "Even up here they sound like banshees wailing the dead, Avril, dear—are you sure you don't have some kind of hearing difficulty? Somewhere I heard that on your father's side of the family there was deafness. Although I can't imagine where I heard that from—he was always so close-mouthed about his relatives. Now on our side—"

I decided to head her off at the pass. Family was a subject on which she could expatiate for hours.

"No, Aunt. I'm not in the least deaf. What are you—"

And then, of course, I heard them: the shrieks of uninhibited little children at play in their playground. I glanced at my windows, which were closed. It really was astonishing, I thought, that small children could achieve such decible strength. "You're talking of the Beasties," I said, going over to the window to look down.

"Yes, dear, the children. I have been trying for an hour to get my nap. I even closed my window, which, as you know, I dislike. I thought you said their head-mistress or principal or whatever she is was going to be cooperative?"

The shrieks had been replaced by some kind of a chant, delivered at full voice. I recognized the black head of Miss Gales, sitting on a bench at the side. As I looked a little girl pushed the child next to her. There was a pause in the noise, and then a wail that rose like a siren.

At that moment Miss Gales looked straight up at my window. Then she went and picked up the screaming child, who sat on her lap, mouth open, still screaming. If she spoke to the child or attempted to soothe her I could not see it from where I stood. Certainly it had no effect. The wail had now turned to a steady, piercing shriek.

"I really cannot stand it, Avril," Aunt Ginevra said suddenly behind me, "Julian must *do* something. I know I'm an old woman and to be old today is considered not only unfashionable but the height of bad taste. But no matter how tired I am I can no longer sleep a full night through. So my afternoon nap is what makes life worth living."

There was a note of strain to her voice that was not, I was quite sure, part of her playacting. I glanced at her handsome beaky face. There were puffs under her

71

eyes and the lines around her mouth and nostrils appeared deeper than usual.

"I'm sorry, Aunt," I said. "I'm afraid I'm a little responsible. There was an...an incident the other day...Anyway, I brought out our big weapon at the wrong place and the wrong time and it undoubtedly should have been Julian who first brought it up—"

"My dear, what on earth are you talking about? What big gun? What is your fault?"

I took a deep breath. "Julian looked up the papers regarding the house, which is exactly like ours. It seems that we could, if we wanted to get nasty, close the school. By law they have to have two fire exits, and the second one is through our garden gate. All we would have to do is lock that and call up the fire department to make an inspection. The school would have a summons issued to them in no time and a judge would very likely revoke their license. In other words, put them out of business. Technically we could hold that over their heads as a negotiating device to get them to keep the children quieter."

"But how wonderful! What is stopping us from calling the fire department?"

"This." I took Miss Gales's letter out of the drawer and showed it to Aunt Ginevra.

She fumbled for the half glasses that hung around her neck on a ribbon. Then she put them on her nose and read the letter.

"What scratches is she talking about? Who is...er ..." she picked up the letter and gazed at it, "Randy Ferris? What have his scratches to do with us and the noise they are making?"

"You know that orange cat that used to belong to Joseph at the garage down the block?"

"Poor thing! I don't suppose it belongs to anyone now. Not that Joseph did much for it. I feel sorry for it."

"So did Michelle. The cat got up on the wall. One of the kids threw something and knocked it off into the playground where they all surrounded it, and one of the boys—this Randy Ferris—tried to get at him. Out of sheer self-defense, the cat scratched him. It also scratched Miss Gales, the teacher, who came after it with a broom. At that point Michelle took over, instigated, I'm afraid, by me. She hurled herself through the door in the wall and was getting the animal quieted so she could pick it up—and I must say I really admired the way she went about it—when this Randy made a noise like a Bronx cheer and scared the cat out of its wits. By that time Michelle was holding it and in its panic it tore her arm and shoulder to ribbons, but she hung on and got the cat out. But not before she'd kicked the wretched Randy."

"Quite right," Aunt Ginevra said. "How brave she is! I shall tell her so."

"Yes, but not in front of Suzanne."

"Why ever not?"

I explained about the tetanus shot and Michelle's ambition to adopt the cat. "Anyway," I went on, "when Miss Gales and I were exchanging pleasantries over the whole incident, and she was threatening to call the ASPCA and have the law on us, I lost my temper and shouted out what Julian called our big stick: I told her to go ahead and call the ASPCA and we'd close the school on her. That's what produced this note. Unfortunately for us, she's no fool. If she went to any of the papers—especially the tabloids—I can just see the headline they'd use: *Rich Eastsider Tries to Close Integrated School.* I'm sorry, darling, but the deck is stacked on their side."

Aunt Ginevra was no fool either. She sat there for a moment, her face still. Then she sighed. "In my day, the headline would have been *Noisy Children Rob Old Lady of Sleep.* I wonder if it was better our way or this way. But I do feel it's unfair," she said emphatically, getting slowly to her feet, "that I should have been repressed when I was a child because that was what you were supposed to do with children then. And now, when it's my turn and children should be repressed for my benefit, the whole thing's turned around."

73

"S'n'outrage." I said, using an old family joke word.

"I'll talk to Julian," she said.

"I don't see what good that will do."

"You probably don't, but then you have always been prejudiced against him. I don't know why."

"Because I've always believed he . . ."

"He what?" The blue eyes above the high-bridged nose seemed to probe into me.

"Nothing. Let's just say that Julian and I are temperamentally incompatible. Besides which, I don't think he treats his wife and children at all well."

"Oh? What makes you so sure? You've lived in the family with them?"

"All right. No, I haven't. But I don't approve of sending little boys off to boarding school just so they won't be underfoot."

"Are you certain it would be better for them to be at home? And anyway, who insists that they go? Did it ever occur to you that it might be his wife?" Aunt Ginevra was doing what she ordinarily did not do— backing me into a corner.

"No, frankly, it didn't."

"Have you met his wife?"

"Of course."

"And how would you describe her?"

"Very pretty, very social, very wifely."

Aunt Ginevra stared at me. "Humph!" she said.

"Isn't that true?" I said, going on the aggressive.

Aunt Ginevra turned to go down the narrow stairs rather like a battle cruiser maneuvering in close waters.

"Depends on what you mean by truth," she said.

"Oh, don't go around sounding like Pontius Pilate. Every word I said about her is true, isn't it?"

"That's right," my aunt said, taking one cautious step at a time. "Every word."

Considering that she admitted that, it was irritating that I felt unsatisfied. "Well, then—" I started.

"And you don't seem in the least concerned about MY NAP. Which is why I'm going to call Julian. He

74

may not be able to do anything, though obviously I have far more faith in him than you do. But he will CARE."

"Aunt Ginevra," I said penitently, as she got to the bottom. "I'm sorry. I truly am. And I'm sorry about your nap."

She stared up at me. "You know, if you have a suspicion about someone it's much fairer to the person to take it out into the open and confront him with it. Instead of hugging it the way you do."

"What are you talking about?" I asked slowly. If Aunt Ginevra knew about my baby—My heart started to pound. "Aunt—" I started.

"I mean that a backward child could tell you're nurturing some grudge against Julian. And I think you're being most unjust."

"Just because you have a crush on him—"

"I do not have a crush on him and I will not be spoken to by you in this way. This is an outrage. No—" she almost shouted as I started down the stairs. "I do not want you to come down. I came all the way up to you because you're so self-absorbed you don't listen when other people need you, and you don't listen to what they say, and you don't care what happens to them. NO! I wish to be left ALONE!"

For emphasis she brought her cane down on the floor with a loud thump. Then, walking far more agilely than she had when she arrived in my attic, she stumped off.

I really was sorry I hadn't shown my concern over her lost nap, and I saw how oblivious—self-absorbed?—I had been in not seeing immediately that she was seriously upset. "Damn!" I said to myself. I wondered what Julian would say. Something soothing, I had no doubt. Well, I thought, going back to the easel and picking up the brush. So much the better. She deserved a sympathetic ear.

It was about fifteen minutes later that the phone rang.

75

"Aunt Ginevra seems seriously disturbed," he said abruptly, without preamble.

"Yes. And I wasn't much good, I'm afraid. Did she tell you I blew our biggest argument?"

"Yes. I wish you'd saved it, but it's done, so there's no use in recriminations."

"Thank you."

"You don't deserve it. Couldn't you show a little more understanding to the old lady? An afternoon nap may not mean much to you. But it makes all the difference in the way she feels."

"Yes. All right. Your criticism is fully earned, I'm afraid. But I'm not a child, so don't lecture me." I took a deep breath. With no one else did I have this trigger reaction. "You know," I said conversationally, "you might be interested to hear that you're the only one who provokes this instant hostility in me. I'm sure there must be some probably squalid underlying reason."

"More like a dozen. And it's mutual."

I was astonished at how astonished I was. For some reason, the possibility that Julian might be hostile to me had never occurred to me. "Why do you hate *me*?" I asked, diverted.

"Why shouldn't I?" he said in his pleasant, detached voice. "You've never been anything but a pest and a sorehead. You seem to think that your going to Berkeley and becoming a dropout is an honor that entitles you to be as obnoxious as your fancy dictates. You take potshots at me, you needle me in and out of public, you criticize me, my family, the schools we send our children to, and what you suppose our reason to be for sending them there. You seem to think that you have direct revelations about our reasons for everything we do and that those reasons are as unpleasant and self-serving as it is as important to you to think they are. Anything else?" he went on in a musing voice. "No, that will do for the moment. Now, as to our problem school. I know various people on the board of education and elsewhere. I'll ask around and see if I can find out

76

anything about them. It might help if you swallowed your pride enough to go around and explain about Aunt Ginevra's nap. But I guess—"

I answered automatically. "I already went over." Julian couldn't know it, but I was in a state of shock at what he had said. I felt as though one of the paintings on the wall had suddenly bitten me.

"I see," he said. "Well, there's nothing further to be done until I do some investigating to see if I can come up with something that will give us some clout. I'll be in touch." And he hung up.

I stood and stared at the telephone for a while. It was true that in my mind I had denied him all right to have any retaliatory feelings: I could say what I wanted, but his role was to receive it without response because, being guilty, he deserved it.

Guilty of what?

Like a steel shaving to a magnet, my mind went back nearly a decade before to the agonizing week between my talk with my father's secretary and my journey back to California.

Julian Demarest, she had said, was in Vietnam.

But three days later, walking down Lexington Avenue, I had seen him. Not only was he not in Vietnam, he wasn't even in uniform.

It was a crowded part of Lexington, near Bloomingdale's and the subway stop. He was across the street, staring at something to his right.

"Julian," I had called. But at exactly that moment the light changed and one of New York's impatient motorists had leaned on his horn. My voice disappeared inside the noise. The crowd surged across the street with me in the middle. When I got to the opposite corner, Julian was gone. I searched along all the adjacent streets and down the subway. I tore into Bloomingdale's, looking, I'm sure, like a wild thing. If Julian were here, in New York, when he was supposed to be halfway across the world in the middle of a jungle or rice paddy, then that meant he was involved in some-

77

thing he shouldn't be—most likely the kidnapping of my child.

I never located him.

I called immediately to tell the secretary. She was patient with me, as one used to dealing with loonies and children. But she was adamant.

"I'm sorry, Miss Marchington, if I sound like a broken record. I heard from Mr. Demarest less than a week ago. He was wounded and is in a hospital in Guam."

"He couldn't have been. I saw him on Lexington Avenue."

"Don't you think it's possible, Miss Marchington, that you were mistaken?" As I hesitated, she continued. "You know you have, in the past few months, been given to . . . fancies, imaginations."

"You must have heard that from Father."

"The hospital kept him informed, regularly."

I was quiet for a moment. It was true that all the drugs I had taken had produced, for months after I stopped taking them, some very odd results. Once, when I was in my hospital bed, I thought I saw an old friend from Berkeley come in the door, and I started having a conversation with her. The next thing I knew two nurses had come up beside the bed and I had been given a shot of some kind. When I woke up I asked when the friend left. They gave me a funny look. It was then I remembered: the friend had been dead for four months. Another time it was the magnificent black cat I'd had as a child, Rattle, that jumped up on my bed and sat purring and washing itself beside me. This time when I woke up I said to the nurse, "Did you see that cat?"

The nurse shook her head and gave me a suspicious look.

There were two more such episodes and then they went away. The doctor said it was possible that I would have another one and not to be upset.

"You are absolutely certain Julian is in a hospital in Guam."

"If he's not, then he and the army and the hospital are all lying."

As an ardent antiwar activist I was quite ready to believe that the government and the military establishment lied on principle. But I could see no reason why such an elaborate lie should be promulgated for no reason. And, as I thought back about it, Julian's appearance on the corner opposite to me, followed by his total disappearance later, had much of the quality of the previous hallucinations.

"All right," I said, and accepted it.

Now, with Aunt Ginevra's reproaches ringing in my head, I wondered if I had merely temporarily complied but, at a deeper level, hung on to my suspicion that Julian was involved in my father's abduction of my daughter. It would certainly account for the anger at him that seemed to burst out from some subterranean depth within me and could not really be justified by my general dislike. I stared out the window down at the playground.

Poor Aunt Ginevra, I thought; the noise was indeed deafening.

About eight or nine children were at the swings, tearing around the playground and chasing each other up the back and down the front of a slide, with a great deal of pushing and shoving. They were rough youngsters, shrieking with laughter and screaming with general excitement as they slid down, legs first. As far as I could see from my fifth-floor height, there were oriental kids as well as black, but the red-haired Randy Ferris won the noise prize hands down. He also won the rough prize. As I watched, he scrambled up the rungs of the ladder behind the slide and deliberately pushed the little girl who was before him in line so that she had to jump down to keep herself from falling.

My attention caught, I waited to see if the teacher in charge, a young woman with long brown hair, would do something about Randy's aggressive instincts. But she was busy talking to another adult, and only when the little girl picked herself up, discovered she was not injured and gave vent to a loud yell of protest did she turn around. By this time the triumphant Randy had come down the slide once more and was agilely getting up the ladder again.

The teacher was comforting the vanquished little girl pushed off the ladder. Then she went over and spoke to Randy. He put out his tongue. At that, with my full approval, she hauled him off the ladder, legs flailing, and spanked his bottom. His protests were deafening.

I found myself staring at the back of the huge apartment house opposite. When I was young and growing up in New York that space had been occupied by several rather run-down brownstones. Since then, they had been bought, the buildings themselves torn down, and a high rise put in their place to the distress of Aunt Ginevra and her neighbors.

But surely, I thought, behind all those windows rising some thirty stories, there must be residents who also were bothered by the children. Perhaps a few fellow sufferers would strengthen our hand. Julian could find out. I went over to the phone and hesitated, my hand above the receiver. What did I really believe about Julian? I didn't know. This is stupid, I thought, and dialed his number.

"Hello," he said when he came on.

The words that tumbled out of my own mouth astonished me. They had nothing to do with Aunt Ginevra or the schoolchildren or the apartment house opposite and might have been spoken by another creature living in my head. "Did you know that I had a baby ten years ago, a girl, and that my father conned his way into the hospital and took her away and had her put up for adoption?" I heard my own voice with a kind of curious detachment. For ten years I had spoken to no one about this. It was like pulling the lid off some terrible cavern.

"Yes. I did."

"And you helped him." It was an accusation, not a statement.

"No. I did not."

"But you know whom he gave my baby to."

Pause. "He didn't confide that to me."

"You're lying," I said. But I knew he was telling the truth. Quite how I knew I wasn't sure. But I knew. As the certainty of that came over me, I burst into tears. Slamming down the phone I walked to the window and stared down, trying, without much success, to control my shaking. After what felt like a long time I calmed down, and as I did so became aware again of the shrieks and screams and yells from below. Poor Aunt Ginevra, I thought. I still hadn't done anything to help her. I hadn't even, as I intended when I picked up the receiver, talked to Julian.

Turning, I stared at the phone. I found myself, after my outburst, strangely reluctant to call Julian again. But, reluctant or no, I had to. I owed Aunt Ginevra at least that.

But Julian had gone out, his secretary informed me. "Did I have a message?" she inquired.

"No," I said, and put the receiver down again.

I stood for a moment and stared at the lifeless painting in front of me. Aunt Ginevra was right to call me self-absorbed. The trouble with that admission was that it brought a wave of other realizations with it, the chief being that while Aunt Ginevra might be indebted to me for being a supportive presence in her house and life, I owed her much more. She had given me something I had not had in a long time—a home. There was something I knew I could do for her, and though I was appalled at the thought, I had at least to try it. Sighing, I walked down the stairs, picked up my jacket from my bedroom, and left the house.

Except for the sound of singing, The Little World for Little People was quiet when I rang the bell. A tall young woman in jeans and plaid shirt and with long blonde hair opened the door.

"Is Miss Sutherland in?" I inquired.

"No. She's away."

Well, it would have to be the disagreeable Miss Gales. Pushing the door slightly so that I was inside before the young woman had had a chance either to invite me in or—as she might—shut the door in my face, I said, "Then I would like to speak to Miss Gales."

The girl eyed me. "Who shall I say?"

If I gave her my name it was at least possible that Miss Gales would refuse to see me. "I want to see her about a child," I temporized.

Evidently prospective customers were still very much wanted. The young woman's face relaxed. She smiled. "Just wait in here," she said, pushing open a door to what looked like a small office and might have been a cloakroom. "I'll get her."

I walked around the room. The singing I had heard when I was outside was now louder and clearer and remarkably good. I had no trouble in recognizing the tune of a French folk song I had grown up with, though, I thought, listening carefully, the words seemed to be English.

A minute or two later the door opened and Miss Gales came in. When she saw me her welcoming smile vanished.

"Miss Gales," I said, and then had an inspiration. "I came to ask about Randy Ferris." Such an inquiry might make me slightly more acceptable to Miss Gales and would, technically, keep me from having told a lie when I said I had come about a child.

Her face became a shade less hostile. "He seems to be all right. His mother took him to the doctor for a tetanus shot."

I managed not to say that, more than just all right, Randy seemed his usual bouncing aggressive self. Instead, taking a breath, I said, "I'm terribly sorry it happened. And I'm sorry about my sharpness yesterday." It galled me to produce those words, and would gall me even more to go on. But if Aunt Ginevra was to have any peace, then I would have to eat dirt. "As I told you," I said, hating every word, "I'm a painter,

82

and as I'm sure you know, we sometimes get so frustrated when work isn't going well that we really don't know what to say."

It was such arrant rubbish that I wondered the words didn't make me retch. But evidently I had hit the right note. The anger that had set Miss Gales's face in a mold retreated a little. But her eyes narrowed. She didn't (quite rightly) trust me.

"That cat should go to the ASPCA," she repeated, as though testing me.

Aunt Ginevra, I told myself, is more important than the cat. If the cat had to go to the ASPCA to appease this witch, then he would have to go. I opened my mouth, but no words came. Instead, I suddenly saw Michelle's huge dark eyes magnified by her oversized glasses. No, I'd have to find some other way to placate this woman.

"We're going to try to find him a good home," I said, making it up on the spot. "He used to be a very nice cat, when he had a place of his own and somebody to care for him. So we're going to find him another." I hurried on. "You asked me if I would be willing to give art lessons to your pupils." I heard my words with horror, but there was no backing out now. "Perhaps something could be arranged."

Someone opened the door across the hall and I was suddenly aware that the singing had stopped. Then there was a rush of noise in the hall behind the closed door, as though about twenty bodies had fallen downstairs, the noise partly drowned out by shrieks, screams, yells and giggles.

"What's that?" I asked, jumping.

"The singing rehearsal is over and Alice Hurd is taking the group out to the playground."

"They sing very well."

It was the right thing to say. The toothy grin appeared. "Yes, they do. They should! We've been working hard on them. We want them to be as near perfect as possible at their performance in three weeks."

"They're going to give a concert?"

83

"They're going to sing at a reception at the UN," she said proudly. "Miss Sutherland was asked to bring them and have them sing songs from different nations."

"How wonderful! Some special occasion?"

The black eyes sparkled. "Yes, it's going to be in three weeks, on the sixth, right after the meeting in Washington between the Israeli prime minister and the Arab chief of state. In celebration of their signing a peace treaty."

"Well, it certainly deserves all the celebration anyone can lay on," I said devoutly. "Peace in that area would be a triumph."

"That's why we're so pleased our children have been asked to sing. It's a terrific honor."

Honored or not, the young singers were not sufficiently overwhelmed to restrain their self-expression. The noise continued unabated. "Go down the steps *slowly,*" shrieked a female voice. "Deirdre, do *not* push Boopie. I've told you once before. If you push him I'm going to spank you."

A smart-aleck comment about the self-expressive approach to education rose to my overready tongue, but I suppressed it, clamping my teeth together so hard my gums hurt.

"Miss Hurd is one of our stricter, more conservative teachers," Miss Gales said, giving me the impression that she knew exactly what frustration I was going through. "Of course she never carries out her threat, but we are sure that she will be able to achieve the same results with love and understanding."

"I'm sure she will," I croaked, felling a pang of sympathy for Benedict Arnold. Perhaps traitors had their higher motives, too.

"When could you begin?" Miss Gales asked.

"Any time. What would suit you best?"

"Mornings," she said, thus destroying my best hours. "Twice a week, perhaps. We have four groups, four-, five-, six-, and seven-year-olds. You could give them each two one hour classes."

"Do you think it might help to keep them quieter?

I'm worried about my aunt's health. She needs her rest desperately, and is unable to sleep at night."

Greek eyed Greek. "We could see what we can do," she said finally. "And, of course, if you would like to help also with the playground, then you could keep them as quiet as you find it possible."

Was there the suggestion of a grin? Was she saying, in effect, just see how successful you are? I felt my familiar impulse to withdraw from anything to do with children. But pushed it away.

"It would be interesting to try," I said. Then another thought struck me. "How do you think Miss Sutherland would feel about this?"

The faint pleasantness that had begun to touch Miss Gales's unattractive features vanished. "I'm sure I don't know. If you would prefer to wait..."

"Oh, no," I said. If this didn't help the noise, I thought desperately, then I could always stop giving art lessons to the Beasties. "When would you like me to begin?"

"Tomorrow."

When I got back up to my studio I was dumbfounded to see Julian standing there staring at the canvas.

"It looks like Toby," he said.

"So Suzanne commented. She suggested that it would be improved if I asked him to sit for me."

He turned away. "You don't sound as though you want to."

"Not much. I don't particularly like him." Until I said it, I hadn't realized that it was true.

"Why?"

"I'm not sure. I have a feeling that he makes life harder for Michelle. He's thin and perfect and good-looking and provides some horrible kind of contrast to Michelle without even trying."

"You sound as though you were describing yourself and Suzanne, some twenty years ago."

I stared at Julian. I had moved past him to the window, so that the light was on his face and head. I hadn't realized, I found myself thinking, how much gray there was in his black hair, giving him a salt-and-pepper look. And at the same time I was acknowledging that he was right. Suzanne had always been the perfect one, which probably had a great deal to do with the way I felt about her and acted in general.

"How old are you, Julian?" I asked.

"Forty-four."

"That's a lot of gray in your hair for forty-four."

"The results of a care-filled life," he said lightly.

"What nonsense you talk," I said, and eyed him. "You know I've always hated you."

"So you said over the phone."

"And you told me it was mutual."

"That's right."

"Well, I know why I hate you. I always thought you were the apple-polisher of all time, toadying to Father, not sticking up for me when he attacked me—"

"You were doing a good job of sticking up for yourself, at least when I was around. This vision of yourself that you seem to cherish of the timid mouse, the fragile, helpless victim easily bullied and crushed by the tyrant's heel is straight out of soap opera. You were exactly like your father. He was a brilliant, tactless, domineering man who loved you in his own way, but every time he opened his mouth you shoved your fist in it. I wasn't about to get myself into that family quarrel."

This was such a novel view of my early life and experience with my father that I had to think about it. "Oh," I said.

"Yes, 'Oh.'" He moved with his odd, dragging step to the window. "But you were about to ask me why I disliked you."

"Yes."

"I thought I told you that. You were a pain—always on the defensive, always convinced that the world was out to get you, always making trouble for your father when he least needed it. You've accused me of toadying to your father. I liked and admired him. He had his weaknesses and blind spots, his silly snobbery and idolatry about the Marchingtons' being a leading example of the latter. But he taught me more about the law than I learned from all the professors. And he didn't have an easy life of it. Maybe he was hard on you. But you weren't exactly easy on him. With a constantly sick wife—"

"He drove her into her nervous breakdowns."

"Rubbish! He knew she was given to so-called spells when he married her. The one thoroughly impetuous and emotional thing he did was to marry her. But he was in love with her and forgot everything else. It's true I often thought—?"

"What?"

"Never mind."

"Come on, Julian. You can't leave it there. It's not fair."

"All right. I often thought that the glory of the Marchington name had a lot to do with his infatuation. He idealized the whole family, with its lawyers and judges and Supreme Court Justices and New England governors and senators—all going back to the colonial days. There was a streak of Celtic mystic in your father—the Brookes came from Northern Ireland—and he endowed the Marchingtons with some near-royal aura. But all that is beside the fact that I did not engineer the kidnapping or adoption of your baby."

"Yes, all right," I said grudgingly. "I shouldn't have accused you." I paused. "I gather you didn't have the slightest hint as to what he did with her?"

"Your father simply asserted that you had had a baby and had put it up for adoption."

"He forged my name to documents saying I wanted to have her adopted, then, before she was born, moved me to a small private hospital which was so deeply in debt to him that they wouldn't question what he said or did, and walked out with her. There is no trace, nothing—" I beat my fist on the side of the window. "I'll never find her!"

"Can't you just accept the fact that she's in a good home being loved and cared for?"

"Could you? Yes," I said, quite in my old combative style, "I guess you could." Then, when he didn't say anything, "I shouldn't have said that. I'll try not to take any more potshots at you."

"That would be a change," he said dryly. Then, "Anyway, I'm sorry."

"Thanks." I stared out the window. I'd heard a shriek, but other than that, the noise was considerably abated. And, as if to answer my thought, I heard the teacher say, "Now just stop making that noise, Dora. You mustn't shriek so loud."

"It seems to have worked," I said.

"What?"

"I went next door and offered them my fair, white body as a price for keeping their little beasts quiet. To be precise, Miss Gales, the toothy one who isn't out there at the moment, asked me the other day if I would teach the little dears some art or drawing. I was not enthusiastic, but it occurred to me if I contributed to their offering for the children, they might cooperate about Aunt Ginevra's nap. It may not work, and if it doesn't, I can always leave."

"That was nice of you. I hope it won't be too much of a bore."

"No. The manuscript for the next book I'm about to work on hasn't turned up. I don't have that much to do except that"—I waved a hand at the canvas—"and as you can see, the more I work on it, the worse it gets."

He walked over. "If it was not supposed to be Toby in the first place, then who is it supposed to be?"

"Just from imagination," I said casually.

"I don't want to arouse your wrath again. But does it occur to you that it does look a little like Suzanne?"

It was as though, as he spoke, there was a tremor, and everything fell out of alignment for a moment and then went back in. Because all of a sudden I saw that the painting did, indeed, look like Suzanne—a Suzanne without vitality or even life, but a Suzanne. What was disturbing was that I had not seen before something that was now so obvious: all this time I had been painting the perfect child, Suzanne.

Without even thinking, I walked over to the easel, plunged the brush into whatever was on the palate and was about to strike it through the picture when I felt my hand gripped.

"Take it easy," Julian said. "I only said it was *like* Suzanne, not that it was Suzanne. Never in her life did your sister look that haunted."

That stopped me. It was true. And even if it weren't . . . I dropped the brush. "By the way," I said, "do I remember correctly or not, but weren't you once in love with Suzanne?"

"I'd say it was more of an infatuation, and it didn't last long. How did you know?"

"I discovered that little item on my last full vacation at home, at the end of my sophomore year. That was in nineteen sixty-seven. Suzanne had just had a late coming-out party and for all that you were married, you spent a large part of your time mooning around our house in white tie and tails." Some devil prompted me to add, "What did Marjory think of that?"

Julian took out a cigarette and lit it with a match.

"I thought you'd given up smoking," I said. "Aunt Ginevra, who adores you, said so."

"Cousin Ginevra is an excellent woman with superlative taste, especially in men. And of course she's right. I have given it up."

"Then what's that in your hand?"

"A momentary backslide." He paused. "You asked how Marjory liked my calf love episode over Suzanne. The summer I followed Suzanne around like a sheep coincided with Marjory's first hospitalization."

"What do you mean? What was the matter?"

"That time it was pills."

I digested this for a while. "I take it from the way you talk that there have been other times."

"In the twelve years in between there've been about seven hospitalizations, not counting periodic visits to health farms and recreation places."

"All for pills?"

"She got off pills and went onto alcohol for a while. Then she's tried suicide three times."

Having been hospitalized myself, I knew a little about it and about people's reasons for being there. "Is it all real?" I asked. "Or is this her way of not having to cope with something she doesn't want to cope with?"

He stared down at the cigarette in his hand. "Nobody seems to know. Both, I think. At different times. I don't think there is any doubt that she has severe depressions. I also think she enjoys the fancy sanitariums she visits. On one famous occasion her own doctor was away and his place was taken by another one. When she went into one of her withdrawals, this doctor sent her to the state hospital before she knew what he was up to. It was very different from the places she was used to, where she had had her private room, and white-coated attendants to call for her and take her to her daily session with her therapist. The state hospital gave her a tattered blue robe and paper slippers, and she slept in a room with four others, two of whom were senile and incontinent. She recovered in record time. On the other hand, I've visited her when she has seemed to have gone somewhere and left her body behind to go through the motions of living. And she wasn't faking. It was frightening. That was why—" He stopped.

"Why what?"

"Why I probably seemed to you to be so unsympathetic to you and sympathetic to your father. We had that in common. Our wives were always going off to sanitariums. When your wife is away most of the time you have a choice. You have a girl friend or friends, or live celibate. Your father, who was a puritan, chose celibacy. It probably would have been less moral but easier on the rest of you if he hadn't. Celibacy doesn't come easily to most men, especially to men who have deliberately chosen to be married."

"Oh," I said, as this sank in.

Julian got up and put out his cigarette. "You just

thought your old man was a natural born son of a bitch whose preferred sport was persecuting you."

"Yes, I did. And I'm still not sure he wasn't."

Julian laughed. "I told you you were like him. Stubborn."

"By the way," I said, as he went towards the door, "when were you wounded?"

"Nineteen-seventy-two. Why?"

"And where were you in October of nineteen sixtynine?"

"What is this? Are you playing district attorney?"

"Sort of." He was right when he said I was stubborn. I was quite determined not to tell him that I thought I had seen him on Lexington Avenue. But I wasn't quite sure of my reason for my determination.

"Why is October sixty-nine so important to you?"

I didn't answer.

"That was the year, if I remember, that your child was born and given up for adoption."

"Yes."

"But you're not going to tell me anything more than that?"

"No." It was foolish the way I clutched that secret. Yet I did.

"Well, I see no reason why I should go scrabbling back to try to put together what I was doing in a given month just so you can play games."

"Father's secretary—I've blanked out her name—said you were in the hospital."

"Her name was Miss Briggs, and she was a compulsively truthful woman. Why did you doubt her?"

I looked into his light gray eyes that seemed curiously devoid of expression. An odd little shiver ran over me.

"I had my reasons," I said.

CHAPTER 5

Having decided to offer myself as a sacrifice, I found it almost annoying that teaching what could loosely—very loosely—be called art to the four-, five-, six-, and seven-year-olds at The Little World for Little People did not turn out to be the calamity I expected. They were noisy, or at least most of them were noisy. But I could see why the school thought we were making a fuss over very little when we complained. It was no noisier right in the middle of the yard than it was listening from above, and being in the middle of the scene, where the children had faces and names and reasons for doing what they were doing, made it far less objectionable than the mindless din that floated up, caught in the tunnel of buildings surrounding the yard.

Most of the time I was there, of course, I was inside one of the school and play rooms, but occasionally I was pressed into service in the playground, and did my best for poor Aunt Ginevra's nap. And there was no doubt about it, the other teachers made much more of an effort to keep them quiet. By common consent neither Miss Gales nor I mentioned our exchange of threats.

It was an interesting nursery school and all-day care center. The children were a thoroughly international mix. Many of them were the offspring of various people attached to the United Nations missions or to foreign business concerns. Every race was represented, and a variety of ethnic groups as well. The Americans, who also came in three colors—black, yellow/brown and more or less white—were by far the noisiest, regardless of race or group. The quietest were two little Swiss boys, twins, who, scrubbed and obedient, did what they were told without fuss. Their names were Boopie and Hans Schlegel.

"Boopie!" I said, when Miss Gales showed me the list. "That poor kid, imagine going through life with a name like that!"

"I think it means, literally, 'little boy' in Swiss German. I mean, if you yelled 'Boopie' on any street in Basel, every little boy within hearing would look up. Or so their mother explained."

"I see."

Miss Sutherland appeared to be right about one thing: there were no budding Rembrandts or Picassos among my young charges. But they were all vigorous and energetic about smearing large blobs of watercolor over everything in sight. And then, on my third day there, I had Randy Ferris in my class.

Seen from ground level he looked like an ordinary, pug-nosed little boy with widely spaced green eyes and a mop of magnificent red-gold curls. But he was what used to be called a limb of Satan or, in more modern parlance, hyperactive.

The morning he was in the class I arrived to find that he had thrown every other child's paint book across the room. All the children were wailing, mouths wide open, while he stood there and looked pleased with himself. In the course of the rest of the class he poured his paint water over Sylvia Rosenthal's blonde hair, kicked Pedro Valdez and Oojima Wachita in the behind, stuck out his tongue at Miss Gales and, I gather, gone through the playground like a junior terrorist. After he quieted down he went around crooning to everyone, "I know something you don't know, I know something you don't know..."

"Stop it. I can't paint," Mimi Townsend, a black child, said.

"And it's right here in the house," Randy said, dancing around. "Right here, but I'm not going to say where."

"Ignore him," I counseled Mimi, who, as far as I

could see at that point, had the nearest thing that could be called talent in the class.

Because of his general obstreperousness and carrying on, I had not seen Randy's work until he finally settled down. And then I stood in front of his easel with astonishment. He had done a scene of rocks and caverns well drawn and painted with an eye to eeriness. It was, in fact, so well done that I wondered if his mother had sketched the drawing in before he had left home that morning. Yet, the moment I thought about it, I knew that couldn't be. I had given him a fresh paint book out of the cupboard.

"That's very good indeed, Randy," I said, trying to put out of my mind the picture of him throwing something at the cat. After all, I thought, children have to be *taught* kindness. I wasn't entirely sure I believed this, but I would hang on to it for the time being.

"It stinks," Randy said.

"No, it doesn't. Why don't you draw me something else?"

"What d'ya want?"

"Anything. Why not do me a cat?"

The handsome little face scowled. "I don't like cats."

"Why not?"

"Because they scratch."

"They only scratch when they think somebody is going to hurt them. Don't you try and defend yourself?"

Randy's light skin turned red. He tore the painting out of the book, put the book back on the easel, and with about three strokes of his pencil created a very catlike cat. Then he painted it a bright orange with two flaming green eyes not unlike his own.

"That's extremely good!"

It was obviously the wrong thing to say. With an expression af absolute fury, Randy tore it out of the book and threw it on the floor. "I don't want to paint any old cat," he yelled. Then, before I could stop him, he ran over to Mimi's easel and stared at the black, orange-and-white blob that she was painting with great care.

94

"That stinks."

"No, it doesn't. Yours stinks."

"Miss Match said it was good." Miss Match was the closest he would come to my name.

"She only said that to keep you quiet."

"That's not true," I started to say, and then flew to Mimi's aid. Randy had stuck his knee up against her stomach and was pulling one of her several pigtails. Mimi was screaming, for which I could hardly blame her.

After trying to get his hand unclutched from her hair without success, I picked him up bodily and landed a huge whack on his behind. He let go of Mimi's pigtail. A great bellow burst from his mouth. The door flew open. Miss Gales came in.

Randy stopped yelling and said loudly, "She attacked me. She hit me. Mom will sue the school."

"What happened, Miss Marchington? I thought I told you we do not allow corporal punishment in this school. And it's against the law."

"It was the only way I could get him to let go of Mimi's pigtail. Wasn't it, Mimi?" Mimi had her hands over her head and was crying. "He almost pulled my hair out. My head hurts."

"Good!" yelled Randy.

"I thought I told you, Randy, that if you can't behave you can't come to school," Miss Gales said to the boy.

He stuck his tongue out, crossed his eyes and wiggled his ears. Then he said a four-letter word.

"Now Randy—" Miss Gales said.

He said another one. I grinned. I saw his leg go back. "If you think you're so smart, why don't you paint me another picture?" I said. "Here, here's your book."

I fully expected him to throw it at my head. But he didn't. He glared first at me and then at the book. Then the angry red receded from his face and he picked up his pencil.

"Mimi," Miss Gales said, "would you like to come with me and let me put something cool and soothing on your head, or would you rather stay?"

"I'll stay," Mimi said. "I was painting my dog and I want to do it again."

"That's no—" Randy yelled.

"One more word out of you," I said, "and I won't *let* you paint."

It was a trial balloon, and I didn't expect it to work. But after glaring at me belligerently for a moment, Randy turned back and went on drawing. That, as much as his considerable talent, made me realize that I had a weapon in what I could clearly foresee was going to be a war.

Miss Gales gave him an odd look and then left. At the door she turned, "By the way, Miss Sutherland's coming back some time today. I haven't told her about your being here, so if she walks in you'll have to explain."

Leaving Randy alone, I went over to Mimi to see if there was any way I could help her to turn her blob into a recognizable dog.

"What's his name?" I asked.

"Smoky," she said. "Daddy gave him to me for my birthday. I take him out, with Mom, every day when I get home from school. He likes me best. I feed him and give him fresh water. My head still hurts." Tentatively she put her hand up.

"If it continues to hurt then I think Miss Gales will have to see what she can do to help with the pain."

But Mimi, like Randy, but without Randy's uncanny ability, wanted to paint. "Let's try a line here," I said. Putting my hand around hers, I guided it to create the semblance of a head and two ears. "See? Now why don't you try to give him a properly shaped back, somewhere here like this."

After a few more lines, with my hand guiding hers, the blob turned into an approximate beagle. "There he is. There's Smoky!" she said excitedly. "Miss Match, can I take it home and show Daddy and Mom?"

"Of course, Mimi. Now—" Something made me turn. Randy, his eyes wrinkled and slanted in a scowl, was just about to throw his paint water at Mimi's artistic endeavor. I stepped in front, and got a shirt full of chilly colored water. "All right, Randy. You know what I told you. You can just leave the room."

"I won't," he yelled with astonishing strength. "I WON'T! My picture's better than hers. It's better than anybody's here."

"It doesn't matter," I said. But I went over anyway to look, curious as to what he might have done. Then I stood and stared. He really was incredibly gifted. There was the ginger cat, sitting in the clearly recognizable stance of the Egyptian cat, looking down from an almost leonine dignity at a calico cat curled on the floor, a few little fat blobs feeding at her middle. Forming a protective circle around her were shapes that might be cartons. On the wall behind was a squiggle that seemed to be two wavy lines with something that looked like balloons at either end.

"Randy, that is terribly good," I said, the painter in me easily winning over the teacher and disciplinarian. "So you do like cats after all!" I glanced down at the sulky face. "Don't you?"

There was a bare nod.

"Then why did you throw a stone at the ginger cat?"

"'Cos he wouldn't pay attention to me."

"I see," I said. "But you know sometimes you don't listen to people, do you, because you have things of your own on your mind. And you wouldn't like somebody to throw a stone at you." Randy continued to scowl at me. I gave this message a few seconds to sink in, then put my hand on his shoulder. "But you paint very well indeed." I peered at the squiggle on the wall behind the cats, and then pointed to it. "But I can't make out what that—"

"Miss Marchington!"

I looked up. Janet Sutherland stood in the open doorway. I saw the clearly marked jaw and nose. But what held my attention were the ice-blue eyes, eyes that for a second filled me with a strange dread. Fear shot through me and some other feeling or sensation that I couldn't put a name to. Then everything changed.

97

Her eyes shifted from the painting and her expression altered. She was once again the attractive woman I had been introduced to.

"So Miss Gales won you over, Miss Marchington!" Somehow her beautiful voice gave an especial richness and grace to my name. "Randy, that's a splendid painting. Did you do it all from memory?"

As I looked at Randy my admiration for the principal soared. Without apparent effort she had tamed the savage beast. He stood there, his eyes down, his scowl gone, one pudgy hand picking at his stained red T-shirt. Miss Sutherland, good-looking and chic in her tan slacks and shirt and tweed jacket, came over and stood beside me. "Randy, you made a liar out of me, I'm afraid. I said we had no budding Rembrandts. But I can see I was wrong." She put her hand on his curls and tousled them. "Now let's see what the others have done."

It was easy to see why the school was a success. Miss Gales and the other assistants were pleasant and competent run-off-the-mill watchdogs of the young. But it was Miss Sutherland who made the difference between this school and others. A quiet seemed to fall on them when she was around, as though, I thought, some demigod had stepped among them. The multicolored faces turned up towards her like little stars, all except Randy's, which continued to examine the floor. Moving among them, she commented on each child's painting: "That's lovely, Dora, such beautiful colors! I like the freedom in it. And yours, too, Oojima. It soars, no binding lines, all bursting color..."

I, too, was mesmerized, looking with new eyes at Dora's and Oojima's paintings. I had seen them merely as blotches of color, something to keep the young busy so they wouldn't occupy themselves with more destructive pastimes. The only ones who had any talent—I had thought—were Mimi, a small amount, and Randy with his extraordinary gifts. But as I listened to her I found myself changing my mind. Randy's watercolors no longer looked like swift and fluid studies of motion and color. In Miss Sutherland's eyes they were bound and traditional, and I found myself thinking that she was right, that I had been too conventional, too preoccupied with my own style, to see the others clearly.

"It's an honor to have you," Miss Sutherland said after she had finished commenting on the paintings, only Miss didn't seem the right title. I had never had any particular feelings—for or against—about the feminist insistence on Ms. Yet that, too, I saw now, was appropriate, as appropriate as Miss was wrong.

"Thanks," I said, trying not to succumb to some power that seemed to be pouring out of her. And then said, whether under her influence or not, I couldn't be sure, "I like being here."

Suddenly her eyes went past me. "No, Randy, don't throw that on the floor. Give it to me and I'll put it in the wastepaper basket."

She held out a long supple-looking hand. Meekly he went and put the crushed paper in her hand. I came out of my somewhat dazed state with a slight start. "Please, Ms. Sutherland. Don't throw that away. It's good. It may not be the style you admire, but I think Randy should keep it."

The brilliant blue eyes turned towards me, and I was visited with the same sensation I had before, without, still, being able to identify it. Then she turned back to Randy. "Randy, do you want this drawing? You can do so much better."

Randy looked up. "Yes," he croaked.

"Very well then. I'll take it outside and put it with the drawings we save. You can collect it there at the end of the term. But I want you to express your*self*, not what you've been taught."

"I haven't taught him anything, Ms. Sutherland," I said, trying to recover my own reality and put her right. "I haven't had time. Anyway, Randy has had his own encounters with cats."

"Oh? When was that, Randy?"

There was a long silence. I wondered why Randy didn't air his grievance about the ginger cat scratching him and Michelle following this with a kick. End of art teaching, I thought to myself.

But something seemed to have mesmerized the child. "A cat scratched my hand," was all he said. The vinyl floor seemed to fascinate him.

"I see." Janet Sutherland put the crumpled-up ball of paper on the desk and smoothed it out. "No wonder you drew cats. The calico one was the one that bit you?"

"Not bit," I said hastily. "Scratched. And it was the ginger one. It belonged to the garage down the street, but its owner has died and it's become a semi-stray."

"And where did the calico come in?"

"We have a cat that just had kittens," Boopie Schlegel suddenly put it. The two little boys were so quiet that people were inclined to forget they were there.

"And she looked just like that," Hans added.

"And you told Randy about her?"

I suppose that's what makes her a good teacher, I found myself thinking. No detail, however small, that one of her charges records is too petty to interest her. "Is that the way you keep track of what is going on in their little minds?" I asked with a smile.

"It's important, you know. Does a child get something out of his head or has he seen it? Is he copying or is he fantasizing?"

I was tremendously impressed, without knowing quite why. My own memory of art classes in the small, rigidly correct private school I went to was that whatever I did was crossed out, and the art teacher painted it over on another piece of paper to show me how it should be done. "There," she would say, admiring her own handiwork, "that's giood," from which, around the school, she acquired the name, Miss Giood.

"Why are you smiling?" Ms. Sutherland said to me.

"I was remembering my own art teacher." And I told her about Miss Giood.

Janet Sutherland laughed, "That's exactly what I'm trying to avoid. This way I know that Randy paints as much from his imagination as from life, and that the Schlegel boys are better with the word than with the brush. Aren't you boys?" she said, looking at their art offering.

If she liked free, untrammeled paintings, the Schlegel boys certainly offered it. They had painted not only the paper in front of them, but their arms, shirts, faces and the wall besides.

The bell rang immediately after Ms. Sutherland left. My teaching chore for the day was over. I cleaned up as quickly as possible and went home.

Our first crisis since the arrival of the Petersens came up at dinner. I looked around the table. Aunt Ginevra was at one end and George at the other. Suzanne was on Aunt Ginevra's right, with Toby next to her, and I was on her left. The place next to me was empty.

"Where's Michelle?" I asked.

"Upstairs in her room," Suzanne replied. She helped herself to some peas and mushrooms that Jessie was offering.

"Isn't she well? Would she like some soup or something?" Aunt Ginevra said. "Now, I always think that if you're feeling a little under the weather—"

"She's being punished," Toby said.

I couldn't help it. I said, "That doesn't seem to make you unduly unhappy."

"What Toby is saying is true," Suzanne said. "Michelle defied me and I told her to stay in her room until she was ready to apologize."

"Is depriving her of a meal the right way?"

"I don't think . . ." George started.

"We agreed that I would handle this," Suzanne said. George shut up.

Aunt Ginevra's attention seemed to be on her roast chicken, which she was cutting with great care. But I noticed the flare of her black brows.

"It was full of fleas anyway," Toby said.

I almost dropped my fork. "What was?"

"That dirty cat she wanted to adopt."

"A ginger one?" I asked.

"Yes, but Mummy said—"

101

"Never mind, Toby darling. I think we've really exhausted the subject."

"Look," I said, "that cat needs a home. It used to belong to the garage manager before he died. It doesn't have a home now. One of the school kids threw a stone at it the other day. God knows what will happen to it if it doesn't get adopted."

"It should be taken to the ASPCA," Suzanne said. "That's the humane thing to do with it. If Michelle wants a pet we can quite easily get her a good one from one of the proper breeders—"

I put down my knife and fork. "Come on, Suzanne, surely your snobbery doesn't extend to animals!"

George gave a laugh which he tried to turn into a cough. Suzanne glared at him, then said, "The subject is closed."

"Oh, no it isn't," I countered. "If you won't let Michelle adopt that stray, then I will. I've been thinking of doing it anyway."

"Good!" Aunt Ginevra said. "I remember that cat of Joseph's. He rescued it from the shelter when it was a kitten. Perhaps you ought to take it to the vet and let him give it all the right shots."

It was Napoleon who said that God was on the side with the biggest battalions, and I felt like a huge battalion had just come in to help me. I waited for Suzanne to look crushed. Which showed how long it had been since we had lived together, and how short memory could be. Suzanne never looked or acted crushed. She just shifted her troops a little.

"Well, Toby darling," she said, leaning to one side to allow Jessie to take up her plate, "that means that you're the one who will have to stay in the bedroom. We can't afford to let your allergy act up. Not after what the doctor said."

George, who had been staring at his plate, looked up. "What allergy?"

Suzanne refused Jessie's dessert. "Darling, how many times have I told you that the pediatrician in England said Toby had a tendency towards asthma? If

102

he was around that cat and there was no one near with the right antidote he could suffocate."

"First I've heard of it," George said.

Aunt Ginevra's brows were pointed towards the bridge of her nose again.

"Oh, that's all right," I said. "I'll keep him in my room or upstairs in the studio. Michelle can visit him and me any time. All Toby has to do is to stay in his room or below his floor."

As if by magic, Aunt Ginevra's brow cleared. "Good idea!"

"I was rather thinking you might want to paint Toby's head," Suzanne said.

"Or Michelle's," George offered.

"What a good idea!" Aunt Ginevra exclaimed.

"I might," I said. "I've been thinking of it."

Suzanne turned to George. "How did your interviews go today, darling?"

The words were so innocent: a question that might be asked by any wife of any husband or vice versa. Yet something happened to the tanned, handsome face at the end of the table. For a second he looked stricken. Then he said, "Fine."

There was a moment of prickling silence.

Aunt Ginevra rose to her feet. "We'll have coffee in the living room, Jessie, please."

I decided I didn't want any coffee, so I excused myself, went upstairs and knocked softly on Michelle's door.

There was an odd scuffling sound inside. Then the door opened about four inches. "Who is it? Oh, it's you." Michelle seemed her usual gracious self. "I've gone to bed."

"Do you usually go to bed fully dressed?"

She glanced down. "I mean I'm just going to bed."

"Hungry?"

A bleak look flickered lightly across her face. "No."

"I can get you—"

"It's all right, I don't want any."

"Suit yourself. I just thought—"

103

A muffled howl came from inside the room.

"I have to go now," Michelle said hurriedly, starting to close the door.

"You have that cat there," I said.

"What cat? I don't know what you're talking about."

"Michelle!" Suzanne's voice sounded behind me. "I ordered you not to bring that cat in the house. Now take it downstairs immediately."

Michelle stood in the doorway. "I won't. It's hurt. It's got a cut where that awful boy threw the stone."

"I'm sorry it's hurt, but—"

"Suzanne," I said. "May I speak to you a minute? Downstairs?"

She swung on me. "This is between my daughter and myself."

"You're forgetting the cat. It affects him, too."

"I'm not a monster and I don't wish to figure as one. But that was the cat that scratched Michelle all over her arm and shoulder. Yes, I know all about that. Dr. Tyler told me when I went to him about another matter. He strongly advised getting rid of the cat."

"Maybe he wants to give it to some lab to cut up," Michelle said.

"Well put," I commented without thinking, and then saw, from Michelle's and the cat's point of view, how stupid I had been. "Look, I'll take the cat now and carry it to the vet. If he thinks the cat is all right, then there's no reason why it should be destroyed or not given a home. You know," I added more slowly, letting the words sink in, "Aunt Ginevra is an enthusiastic contributor to the animal medical center. I think not to give it a fair chance would not please her at all. And then we can ask her how she feels about having the cat here."

"After you've briefed her," Suzanne said dryly.

"I don't have to brief her. She feels that way anyway."

"Then isn't it odd that she doesn't have an animal—at least one—of her own?"

"She did. She had Pluto. If you think this ginger one

is plebeian-looking you should have seen Pluto. He was an ugly black stray from the Brooklyn docks. Aunt Ginevra scooped him up one night when he ran in front of her taxi. She was on her way back from seeing friends in Park Slope. I think the taxi driver thought she was raving mad. Pluto had six toes on each front paw and one ear mostly chewed off. But he died two years ago at the age of nineteen, and whenever I suggested her having another animal, Aunt Ginevra always said that she thought Pluto's presence was still in the house and he wouldn't like it."

"You're perfectly capable of thinking that whole thing up," Suzanne said.

"True. But I haven't."

"Please, Mummy," Michelle said.

The dark eyes were enormous, and the full, indented mouth looked absurdly vulnerable. As though a spring had relaxed, Suzanne let out a sigh. "I'm sometimes horrid to you, baby, aren't I?" Reaching out a hand she rubbed Michelle's dark, smooth head. "I don't mean to be. It's just that things . . . But that's no excuse, is it?" She turned to me. "All right, Avril. Take the wretched cat to the animal medical center and see if they'll give it a general bill of health. But if they don't, out it goes. Okay, everybody?"

"Thank you, Mummy, thank you so much." She took a tentative step forward, a square hand reaching out. Unfortunately, a dark red scratch showed against her palm. Hastily the child snatched it back. "Do you have a carrier?" she asked me quickly, obviously not wanting to push her good luck.

I was watching Suzanne. Those few seconds before she saw the scratch had she moved imperceptibly away from her daughter? I thought she had. And immediately there sprang to my mind an old picture. It flashed and was gone, some swift break in the smooth continuum of time: Once my father gave me a present. I went towards him, arms out. And he moved back. A second later he said he was late for his appointment.

105

"Yes," I said now. "There's a carrier around some-where. I'll get it."

"Are you taking him tonight?" Michelle called eagerly.

"Yes. Might as well. They have twenty-four-hour service."

"Can I go with her, Mummy? Please."

"No, Michelle, I want you to go to bed. Now, I've done the best I could for you about the cat. Please don't nag me for something else."

Michelle hesitated. That child had no sense of when to go and when to stop. "That's right, Michelle. Do as your mother says. I'll take the cat and report to you tomorrow. Now I'll get the carrier."

A few minutes later, I was back upstairs with Pluto's old traveling case. The angry terrified animal was hiding at the back of Michelle's closet. It tried to dart past me, but I managed to pick it up, put it in the carrier and slap the lid on before it knew what lay in store.

"Back later," I said, and went downstairs.

"About three years old," the young doctor said at the medical center.

"What kind of shape is he in?"

The young man turned the big ginger around, felt his ribs and abdomen and looked into his mouth and ears.

"He's got some ear mites which are easily fixed. And there's the cut on his neck. I'll give him a shot, which should take care of any infection, and, of course, a distemper shot, plus a couple of vitamin injections. Just hold him."

"That might be easier said than done," I muttered.

"Talk to him."

"What shall I say?"

"Just reassure him."

So, feeling like an idiot, I told the cat that everything was going to be fine, that he was descended from the gods and that succulent feasts would await him on his return. And—perhaps it was magic—I could feel the taut muscles of the cat relax. The young vet grinned. "What's his name?"

The name literally fell out of my mouth. "Clancy?" I said on a questioning note. The cat looked up and, out of some coincidence of timing, let out a loud, mournful cry.

"It suits him," the doctor said. "Goes with his red hair."

What with the rides there and back, and waiting when we arrived at the medical center, it was late when Clancy and I got back and I was burdened down. Not only did I have Clancy in the carrier, I had managed to stop at a small all-night deli and pick up some canned cat food, a bag of kitty litter and a collapsible cardboard litter pan.

"All right, Clancy," I said, struggling up the stairs. "I hope this is going to work."

Once in my bedroom, I opened the carrier. Clancy leaped out, spat and disappeared under my bed.

"Okay. If that's the way you feel about it."

I put the box and litter in my bathroom, hoping that Clancy would find his way there. Then I took a bath and went to bed.

Some time later I awoke to feel something round and warm in the middle of my back. A soft rumble vibrated the quiet night air. Smiling, I went back to sleep.

I have a wide bed, which was just as well. Just before morning I was awakened once again. Clancy was in the middle of the bed. Sound asleep with her arm around him was Michelle, her face, in sleep, looking considerably less formidable and square.

By tacit consent, the matter of Toby's alleged allergy was not mentioned. Partly to keep the peace and assuage Suzanne's feelings, I invited Toby up to have his portrait done, figuring that it would not be too difficult after apparently (and unconsciously) using his face when trying to paint the face that seemed to live in my head.

I was right. The charcoal sketches that I started with went swiftly. Toby was a lot easier to deal with than his sister. His personality was less abrasive. He did not seem to be as whipped and tossed about by emotion and his interest in things outside himself seemed greater. He was a handsome little boy, with his cool gray eyes and well-shaped head of thick blond hair.

"Are you going to paint me in oils?" he asked and reached up to scratch his head.

"Don't move if you can manage not to," I said. "Just for a minute hold that pose, I think it's a good one. Yes, I'm going to do you in oils."

"What's the difference between them and water-color?"

I stared at the sketch under my hand. It was good, and it caught Toby in both a characteristic and an attractive pose. Yet I didn't feel satisfied with it. "What did you say?" I asked.

He repeated his question.

I tore the sheet off and started another in very much the same pose.

"The difference is what it sounds," I said absently, making a long sweep with the charcoal. "Oil is color based in oils, and water is color based in water. Oils are better for some things and watercolor for others."

"What makes you choose?"

I put in a line and didn't like it. "Look, Toby, we can talk later when I'm close to knowing what I want to do. But right now I want to concentrate."

"All right," he said.

Five sketches and an hour and a half later I had come no nearer to finding exactly what I wanted, and, furthermore, I did not know what I wanted, which was strange and unusual in itself. This was the first time that after an hour or so of sketching I did not have the pose and the feel of what I was going to do. It was odd and it was unsettling, especially after such a good beginning. I stared at the sketch, then decided that perhaps this was simply not my morning. In some way and for some reason I did not understand, I was off my stride. The fact that this had not happened before was nothing to go on.

"Toby," I said, "this does not appear to be my day. How about trying it again tomorrow? I'm sorry. I'm sure it's nothing to do with you."

"Can I look at it?"

"There's nothing to look at except a bunch of sketches that I don't much like."

"Can I look at them anyway?"

I didn't want to say yes, but I had no good reason for saying no. "All right. Here they are." And I indicated the various pages lying around on the floor.

Jumping down from the high stool I had placed him on, he came over, reminding me once more how well he moved. Like Suzanne.

Bending down on one knee on the floor, he slowly turned over all the sketches and half sketches I had tried. After a while he said, "They look like me, but they don't feel like me. Maybe it's because I'm not used to looking at pictures of myself."

"Maybe," I said dampingly. What he had said was remarkably perceptive, but I was not prepared to talk about it.

I arrived at the school the following morning to find Randy, covered with paint to his elbows and all down his front, furiously painting two more portraits of the cats he had painted previously.

"I *will* paint the cats, I will, I *will!*" he shouted, wielding a brush that in his square hand looked almost like a monkey wrench.

"Of course you can, Randy," Miss Gales was saying soothingly, but with an odd note of desperation in her voice. "It's just that you should develop your *own* style—"

"He is," I said coming in. "Why all the fuss about his cats?"

"It's just that Miss Sutherland feels that—"

"But Miss Sutherland is not teaching this class. I am."

"Of course you are," Miss Sutherland said behind me.

I turned, and found myself wondering if by chance she had been waiting for my arrival. Today her slender, athletic body was encased in well-cut corduroy slacks and another tweed jacket over a tan turtleneck. The dark, waving hair lay in thick folds around her collar. She bent down and put her arm around the little boy. "You shall paint as many cats as you like," she said. I stared at the top of her head. She straightened up and looked at the picture.

In his general rage and perturbation, Randy had made the calico mother cat much larger than the orange, and the six blobs, suspended at her nipples, somewhat resembled dumbbells.

"That's that same wonderful cat, Randy," Miss Sutherland said, her head against the little boy's red curls. Randy's face was screwed up, as though he were in mortal pain.

"You must love her very much," Miss Sutherland murmured.

Randy's face went even redder than it already was. He opened his generous mouth wide. "Stink!" he yelled.

The principal pulled her head away, and turned up a laughing face. "Oh, dear," she said, "I wonder if it's my perfume he objects to. I've changed my mind," she went on, "I think Randy should go on and do his cats." With another warm smile Miss Sutherland withdrew, followed by Miss Gales.

"There you are, Randy," I said, "you can paint your cats as much as you want."

Randy scowled at me. Then he stood, brush in hand, and stared at his picture. The easels for the children were child-sized, but there were only half a dozen of them. The rest of the young artists had to work at their desks.

I devoted some attention to the other children, all of whom seemed to have taken Miss Sutherland's praise of the nonobjective approach to heart. Mimi Townsend was putting large pink blots in the middle of a sky-blue plain.

"Did you show your mother your picture of Smoky?" I asked her.

"Yes. She put it on the wall," Mimi said proudly.

"Wonderful!" I stared at her composition. "I see you're just doing color studies."

Mimi turned large reproachful brown eyes at me.

"Those are seagulls, Miss Match."

At the end of the hour I went back to look at Randy Rembrandt's offering. Two more pages produced two more cats, one black, one orange.

"You seem to be in a bit of a rut, Randy. Why not try something else?"

"Wanna do cats." He painted livid green eyes in his newest black cat. Then he said, "Want other painting."

"What other painting?"

"She threw it on the floor and then she took it away."

After a minute or two I decoded this. "Why do you want it?"

"I just do."

"All right," I said. "I'll see if I can find it."

After the hour was over, Randy's class went with a roar out to the playground, and the younger children came in. Here, all pretense at being an art class vanished. It was just a matter of finger, water and paint. My main job was to see that as much got on paper as on their faces, hair and clothes. No matter what Miss Sutherland said, I thought the children ought to have an idea that painting and drawing occasionally related to something else—such as a story. So one activity that I started, usually twenty minutes before the hour was over, was to tell the children a story, and paint the main events and characters as I went along, allowing the children to choose such variables as color of hair and eyes and color and shape of clothes. It was enormously successful.

At the end of that hour one of the younger teachers, Ginny Stevenson, came in to collect the children to take them to a rest period. For five minutes she stood grinning while the children screeched at the top of their voices. "A blue dress, Miss Match. Blue. Not brown. Nobody wants brown. Blue."

I painted the blue dress onto my young heroine. "And her hair was..." I started.

"Blonde," came a full-throated roar.

"You had blonde last time," an oriental child said. "It's the turn for black."

"I think you're right, Anita," I said. "Black it is."

As they all put away their paint papers and filed past me, she said, "I think you've hit on the success game of the school."

"I dreamed it up to keep them going just about the time I'm winded," I said, emptying paint water into a large jar. "By the way, where does Miss Sutherland keep the kids' paintings?"

"In those cupboards," Ginny said, pointing to the slide-door cupboards that lined the walls of the classroom at floor level. "She keeps them for parents who want them to put up at home. I think she's also planning some kind of art exhibit later on."

"Okay, I'll look there."

An hour later I had shuffled through stacks of paint-covered pages. Randy's unmistakable cats were not there. Maybe, I thought, forcing myself to remember the incident in detail, it was because the principal had crumpled up the page. Perhaps she thought that the painting was damaged beyond repair. Yet I really believed that Randy was entitled to his art endeavor. No matter what the principal's preferences and philosophy of art, Randy showed a remarkable grasp of design. And there were places in the art world for those who had such a talent and enjoyed using it. Once more I looked through the paintings. Most definitely, it was not there.

By this time the painting had become a mild obsession. I abandoned the idea of going through the sheets for a third time, encouraged in this by the fact that the youngest group of all was about to be brought in, this time not to paint, but to play with blocks and other educational devices. I liked four-year-olds, but I did not want Miss Sutherland and Miss Gales to think they could co-opt my services into longer and more frequent hours. Firmly I left the room and went in search of the principal. But she was not out in the playground, nor was she in any of the other rooms on the first floor.

I paused at the foot of the steps. I had not been upstairs, and hesitated to go, feeling that that might be private territory.

"Miss Sutherland," I called out tentatively.

There were footsteps above my head and down the first few steps of the double-jointed flight. Miss Gales's black head suddenly appeared. "She just left for the coast. Did you want her?"

"The coast? I saw her a couple of hours ago."

"That's right. She left immediately afterwards. Can I help you?"

I found myself possessed of an enormous curiosity as to where she had gone. "Where did she go?" I asked, realizing, as I did so, how nosy it sounded. "I mean, she travels a lot, doesn't she?"

"She's much in demand for talks," Miss Gales said proudly and a little reprovingly. "Day-care centers and nursery schools are always asking for her."

"Oh."

"This isn't the first school she's headed," Miss Gales went on, sounding very like the advance flack for a prominent movie star.

"I guess not. Oh well . . ."

"What is it you wanted?" Miss Gales said. "Can I help?" She came down the rest of the stairs.

"I was just looking for Randy Ferris's first painting. The one of the cats. His mother wants it. And it was good, however uninventive it may be of me to respect good drawing."

"Well, you know how Miss Sutherland feels," Miss Gales said.

"Yes, I do. But I would like to remind her that ability in drawing and design is a talent, too. There are many

113

other things—such as children's book illustrations—that someone talented in art can get both a living out of and gratification in doing. Not everybody has to end up hanging in the Museum of Modern Art."

To my surprise, the usually humorless Miss Gales gave me a dry smile. "As a matter of fact, I agree with you. I think it's just one of her things. Everyone is entitled to them. You'll find Randy's painting in one of the cupboards—the third one facing the door—in the room back of you."

"I just looked there. Randy's painting isn't there."

"It has to be. I put it there myself."

I stared at her. "But it isn't."

CHAPTER 6

Two nights later I found myself going to a philharmonic concert with Julian. Both of us were guests of Aunt Ginevra, who took season tickets.

"Why don't you offer the seats to Suzanne and George?" I asked my aunt, ungraciously, when she told me she'd invited Julian to take me. "I really don't find myself thrilled at spending an evening sparring with Julian."

"You'll be spending the evening listening to Beethoven and Mozart. After those two, if you find yourself sparring, as you put it, it will be entirely your own fault."

I grinned a little. "I suppose it goes without saying that it won't be Julian's fault. The way you favor him is disgusting. Haven't you ever heard of women's lib?"

"I'll have you know I marched in some of the suffragette parades of the nineteen twenties, so you may just keep a civil tongue in your head, miss."

I thought back to what her parents had been like, and to the luxurious cage that had been virtually her prison when she was growing up.

"I wonder your parents let you. March, I mean."

"They didn't know until some of their friends went into shock seeing me, shivering in the cold, striding along in the front line of the parade, going up Fifth Avenue."

"That was very brave, Aunt Ginevra. Did you catch hell?"

We were having an early breakfast before what I had come to think of as "the horde" descended.

Aunt Ginevra poured herself some more of the strong Indian tea that she favored for breakfast. She had bought the sturdy, ugly china pot somewhere on Fulham Road in London when she was a girl and had used it ever since. The tea was made up for her, as it had been for her father, by an English tea importer off Jermyn Street, also in London.

"You should drink tea, my dear, instead of that coffee. Your insides are quite brown by now, I'm sure. Tea would be much better for you."

"Given the strength of your tea, I'm sure your insides are just as brown if not browner. Did you know that strength for strength tea has just as much caffeine—if not more—than coffee?"

"That's not what my dear father always said."

"Your father would never hesitate to change a fact or so here and there if it made a point, or supported his argument. You told me so yourself. Anyway, I asked you a question. Did you catch hell when you marched up Fifth Avenue for women's votes and rights?"

Aunt Ginevra helped herself liberally to sugar. "I don't suppose most people would call it hell." She stirred her tea meditatively. "They said nothing about it at all, which relieved me enormously. If I hadn't been so young and innocent I would have realized that that was an indication of how deeply worried they were. The next thing I knew they were outlining a perfectly marvelous trip to Europe that any seventeen-year-old girl would adore. They had friends in every capital and in most of the embassies, and I was taken from dances to balls to spas to receptions and *thé dansants*." Aunt Ginevra took a swallow of hot tea and blinked. "I don't suppose there was an eligible man that I wasn't paraded in front of."

Suddenly, I saw the picture of the tall, gangling girl as it hung on a wall in our house. In the traditional long white dress with the three feathers of the Prince of Wales fixed at the back of her head by a narrow circlet, there was the eighteen-year-old Ginevra Marchington, robed for her Presentation by the American Ambassador at the Court of St. James's. In addition to her being uncomfortably tall and lanky, her upper lip

116

was pushed out a little by crossed and slightly protruding front teeth. Her white gloved hands clenched a fan. The eyes were wide and a little frightened. She looked out of place and unhappy. What was it my mother had said to me when she caught me staring at the picture? "Ginevra always looked better in riding clothes." Even as a child I could see that that was probably true. In Ginevra the characteristic Marchington looks had not added up to beauty.

"Did you hate it all?" I said now. "You looked as though you did in that photograph when you were presented at court."

"Yes, I did," Aunt Ginevra said. "I was too tall and I couldn't dance very well and I had no small talk. Those were the days before it was common for young people to go out together by themselves. Dutiful young men would call. Trying to talk to me was probably as painful for them as trying to think of something to say was for me. I know that now. I didn't then."

"Wasn't there anybody you liked?"

"Not at that time. Once or twice I did think one or two of them were rather nice. One in particular sent me flowers almost every day and we used to go riding in Hyde Park together."

"What happened to him?"

"My father pointed out, as he did with almost any young man who showed an interest in me, that he was after my money."

I digested this. "Your father sounds almost as good as mine. Did you believe him?"

"Of course. All I had to do was to look at the other girls and then look in the mirror."

"Wasn't there anybody you ever really liked?"

"Oh, yes. Unfortunately, he was unsuitable. He had no money. He was younger than I was. And he came from Mexico."

"Why didn't you just take off with him?"

"He did ask me to. I suppose I was afraid. I find that harder to forgive than anything my father ever said. And now, dear, are you or are you not going to this

117

concert with Julian, because if you're not then I'll ask someone else to go."

But I liked both Beethoven and Mozart. Besides, the thought of having a brisk little set-to with Julian—which I was almost certain would occur—gave me a pleasant sense of stimulation.

"I'll be happy to go. I take it Julian and Marjory are at the moment separated."

"Of course."

"Well, they've gone back together so often that I assumed either state could be considered temporary."

There was a silence. "How long has it been since you saw Marjory?"

"Years. I never actually knew her. She was Suzanne's age. What really is the matter with her?"

"Too many pills over too long a time. Besides, she enjoys going to luxurious rest places. At some point a long time ago Marjory took one look at reality and decided she didn't like it."

"Why hasn't Julian divorced her?"

"I should think for several reasons. One, I know, is that there is a strain of mental illness in her family, and he was never sure how much this was genuine illness and how much a successful device for not having to cope. Another is that he would not leave the custody of the children to her, and until fairly recently, judges had the strong habit of preferring an unfit mother to a fit father. And I suppose also, he's not had any strong motive for unlatching himself."

"You mean he hadn't fallen violently in love with anyone else." I paused thinking over that picture. "Although I'm bound to say that it's hard to imagine Julian in the grip of a major passion. Infatuation, yes. He followed Suzanne in a wan and palely loitering manner when she came out. But that was different."

"Keats," Aunt Ginevra said, gathering up her various scarves.

"Right. Considering that you never went to school and were educated by a bunch of half-dippy governesses, you're amazingly well read."

118

"Perhaps that's why." She rose to her feet and stood, her powerful nose in the air, looking like a benevolent hawk. "I'm thinking," she said. "Why don't you and Julian have dinner here?"

"Thanks," I said, also getting up. "I'll ask him."

But Julian didn't want to come to the house.

"I thought you were crazy about Aunt Ginevra," I said. "And after all, she's treating us to these tickets."

"I am fond of her. But not of all the kith and kin that seem to be around."

"What a liar you are! I thought we discussed your calf love for Suzanne of some years ago."

"That was years ago, and it was calf love."

"All right. Where shall we meet?"

He named a restaurant over on the West Side. "I'll reserve a table for six-thirty."

It turned out to be quiet, expensive and excellent.

"Sorry not to pick you up," Julian said, lifting the back bone out of his broiled trout. "But I didn't want to run into George."

"I feel sorry for George," I said. "No one seems to want to run into him, including Suzanne."

"I know."

"Did he have that appointment with you he was talking about?"

Julian helped himself to some more garlic bread. "I feel profoundly sorry for anyone sitting within smelling distance of our seats," he said.

"But not sorry enough not to eat garlic bread."

"I'm afraid not."

I grinned at him and then remembered my question. "You haven't told me, did he keep that appointment with you?"

"Who?"

"George, you idiot, who else were we discussing?"

Julian closed his mouth over some of the buttery, garlicky dough. "Ummmmm!" he said ecstatically.

"All right. Don't answer. What are you doing? Playing CIA?"

"Just sunk in pure self-indulgence. I love good food."

119

I looked at his flat waist and hollow cheeks. "That just confirms me in my belief that there is no cosmic justice."

"You still moaning about weight? Aren't you skinny enough?"

"No poet could have said it better."

He wiped his fingers on his napkin. "How are you getting on with the Beasties? Cousin Ginevra seems to think you've worked some kind of miracle. Her afternoon siesta is saved."

"I suppose I have to admit that it's not quite as terrible as I thought it would be. I was rather fancying myself in the role of sacrificing martyr. Actually, I enjoy it. But I was surprised to discover the principal, Miss Sutherland, whom I would have described as a rather spit-and-polish type unconfused by faddy ideas, coming out rather strongly for the nonobjective school of painting."

"Aren't your students a little young for any school of painting? I thought that the main idea was to keep them occupied and as quiet as possible. Surely just to get the paint on the paper would be a triumph."

"Well, it is with most. But we have one genius—I'm not kidding, if that child stays out of jail he'll be a great painter—and one of moderate talent. But the genius, a terrible-tempered brat named Randy Ferris, who is responsible for wounding Clancy, has a passion for drawing cats, and drawing them brilliantly, particularly considering he's only seven. But Miss Sutherland took one look at his painting and reproved both of us—him for being too conventional and overinfluenced by me, and me for imposing my realistic style on a budding artist who should be liberated from all form."

Julian stared at me over his *mousse chocolat*. "Who's Clancy?"

"That large yellow cat that used to belong to Joseph. You know," I said, at Julian's blank expression, "the manager of the garage who died."

"Oh."

"Well, anyway, nobody took his cat, who became a

stray. One day when it got on the wall above the playground, Randy picked up a stone or toy or something and threw it at the wretched cat and cut it badly. Michelle went to the rescue, getting herself well scratched, and what with one thing and another, it is now ours, patched up and minus ear mites, and named Clancy."

"And your boy genius painted Clancy?"

"Yes, plus another cat, a calico, with kittens."

"Who was the mother?"

"Who knows?"

Julian spooned up the last of his mousse. "I could easily eat another of those."

"Why don't you? I'm sure the management would oblige."

"And you'd sit and glare at me as you have while I've eaten this. No thanks. I'll get the check." He looked around and nodded to the waiter who hovered a few feet away. While we waited for the change Julian said, "As the father of two boys, each of whom has, at one time, been seven, I find it extraordinary that a child of that age could paint a recognizable portrait of two cats plus kittens."

"I didn't say they were Wyeths. The remarkable part is that they are obviously cats of identifiable colors, with green eyes, like the dog who was remarkable because he could speak, even if he couldn't speak very well. It was incredible that a boy of seven could draw and paint anything and make it that clear. Also," I said, arguing my case, "he didn't do too badly with the brown cartons or packing cases in the background, or that funny squiggle on the wall poster behind."

"What squiggle?"

"Nothing. It wasn't important."

The waiter brought Julian his change. Julian then helped me on with my raincoat. "Everything you say is important," he said.

I turned around. "I thought you found me a pain in the rear end. You said you did."

"That was in the past."

"And now you find me a treasure and a joy?"

"We're going to be late for the concert."

Mozart's Fortieth Symphony rolled over me, promising a world of sweetness and order.

"I know someone who said she believed in God because of Mozart," I said, when the audience had clapped itself sore.

"I've heard of a lot of reasons. That's one of the better ones."

"Do you believe in God?" I asked watching the maestro beginning to stride back on stage.

"Yes."

"Why?"

"Because of Mozart."

The maestro raised his baton and glared at the violins. Then he did a little lift with his heels and the music started.

"After a while I whispered, "That's not Mozart."

"Schubert," Julian muttered between his teeth.

"But they said—"

"There was a notice outside about the substitution," Julian, still muttering, barely moved his lips.

"Shhhhh!" people behind and in front hissed. One woman turned around with an outraged look. I gave her my best smile.

"That last symphony was incredible," I said, during the intermission. "I've never heard it before. I felt like levitating."

"Yes, there's something angelic about Schubert."

I stared down at the drink that Julian had bought for me at the bar. "If Schubert's an angel, then what is Mozart, the one who had led you to God?"

Julian took a swallow. "An archangel."

"And Beethoven?"

"A titan."

I thought about it for a while. "I believe you're right."

*　　*　　*

After the concert we strolled towards Central Park West. At the park we turned north and walked in silence along the pavement bounding the park, encountering no one except a hand-holding couple whom we passed. After a while I turned and looked at Julian and became aware that though I had known him all my life, I had not, for a long time, looked closely at him. What had been my idea of him? A tall, slender young man with thick, curly dark hair whose total personality—for me—was expressed in his trailing after my father, briefcase in hand. I stole another look at him. He was still tall and slight. He was walking, his hands in his pockets, head down, the streetlights, as we passed them, showing up the crooked nose, the gray streaks in his hair, the high cheekbones. But either the rest had changed, or I had not seen it right. There was a tensile strength there, a quality of stilled power, a waiting.

"Julian," I said.

"Yes," he replied without looking at me.

I couldn't put into words whatever it was that I wanted to say. Instead, "I intended to have a fight with you tonight."

"We can still have a fight." He stopped, and I stopped with him. Then he turned around, facing me. "What would you like to fight about?"

"I don't know. But in a funny way I feel cheated."

"Because we haven't had a fight?"

"Yes."

In the semidark I could see him smiling. "For a girl who's been through what you have, you still have a curious innocence."

"What do you mean?"

He glanced up and paused, staring over my shoulder. Then he said, "I mean you went down some strange and terrible paths to find out what life and other people were about, and how to love them and make them love

123

you. And after years of drugs and hospitalizations and protests and marches and having an illegitimate child and losing her, you're still using the same tactics you did as a teenager when you wanted somebody to notice and love you. You attacked them, the way you did your father."

We had stopped walking and were standing. Except for that couple still holding hands behind us, the street seemed deserted. On one side the trees of Central Park rustled in the night breeze. Opposite reared the huge, ugly Museum of Natural History. It was all very peaceful. Yet his words, spoken so calmly, had infuriated me. "I'm not aware of having tried to attack you. But if you see it that way, so be it. You are now, as you have always been, a pompous idiot."

"See what I mean, Avril?"

"I take it you were saying that in the past I was trying to jump up and down to get your notice and affection."

"Something like that. You can't just be, or let others just be. You have to have a confrontation. It never seems to occur to you that anyone else might have emotions and sensibilities every bit as tender as yours, and just as much in need of careful handling. You scream if anyone touches you the wrong way, but wear climbing boots when you walk over other people. May I put you in a taxi? I think I'll walk some more."

And I was in a taxi crossing the park before I knew what had happened to me.

To my unspeakable relief there was no one up and waiting around when I got in, although I knew I would probably not have bothered speaking if there were. Going up the steps two at a time, I could hardly wait to get to my room to be alone, although I did not have any very clear idea what I would do when I got there. But my room was not empty. Clancy, who had been curled in a huge orange ball on my bed, looked up and leered at me. Then he gave a tremendous yawn, and sharpened his claws on my quilt.

"Help yourself," I said angrily.

124

He gave a low, cushiony growl that became a loud purr. Then he got up, padded slowly across the bed towards me and rubbed his big head against my stomach.

At least somebody loves me, I thought. And burst into tears.

"How was the concert, dear?" Aunt Ginevra asked the next morning.

"Wonderful," I said, without enthusiasm. What with one thing and another Clancy and I had spent a restless night.

"Apparently they put in the Schubert C major," she said, glancing at the music page of the *New York Times* in front of her. "Did they do a good job of it?"

"I've never heard it before to my knowledge so I can't judge. It sounded wonderful to me."

"Yes," she said slowly. "The *Times* seems to think it was good, too. How was Julian?"

"I don't know and I don't care. I think he's crazy, among other things. He accused me of attacking him, which I did not do, and then attacked me."

"He must have had a good reason, dear."

I put down my butter knife. "If you want to take his side, that's okay with me. I'll move out and he can have my room when he isn't playing round and round the mulberry bush with Marjory. Whatever her megrims are, she's entitled to them."

"Methinks you do protest too much. Julian is a complex man. He probably had a reason for doing whatever it was that has upset you."

"I didn't say he didn't have a reason. But I don't have to like it, whatever it is. Hello, Suzanne."

My sister, looking somewhat less beautiful than her usual self, sat down and held out her cup to me for coffee. I poured her some and added more for myself. "How are you?"

"All right," she replied. "May I have part of that paper, Aunt Ginevra?"

Aunt Ginevra, who would prefer to be robbed of her

jewels than part with pieces of her morning paper, slowly and gingerly detached a few sheets. "Here you are, dear. Try not to get them too messed."

"Ummmm," Suzanne said.

Since it was fairly plain that Suzanne didn't want to be talked to, I returned to my eggs and private sulks. The noise of Suzanne trying to turn a page made me look up. Her head down, Suzanne was staring at an article. A pot of orange marmalade plus a sugar bowl and milk jug with a napkin across the top prevented me from seeing what was absorbing her attention, so I stared at the top of her bent head. A natural blonde for many years of her life, Suzanne's hair had obviously begun to darken, because it showed several shades darker at the part than on the rest. Tut, I thought. If there was anything I found tacky it was colored hair that was growing out. But there was something about it that tugged at my mind. Where had I seen dark roots before that seemed to have some special significance? Trying to figure that out took me through the remainder of my eggs and toast. Rising, I put my napkin in its ring. "Bye, everybody. No, no, no protestations. I really must go!"

"Good-bye dear," Aunt Ginevra said absently, her head over the book review. "I really do feel that Mr. Lehmann-Haupt has missed the point of this book."

"Who?" Suzanne asked, raising her head.

"The book critic, dear. New since you were here."

Suzanne looked at me. "Did you hear George leave?" she asked. "You seem to have been down early."

"No. Not a sound. Since I was here by a quarter to seven, he must have been early indeed. Where was he going?"

Suzanne looked down at the paper again. "I don't know. I woke up and he wasn't there."

"Perhaps he had to meet whoever was calling him at such a late hour last night," Aunt Ginevra said reproachfully.

"He didn't say anything about it if it was. He just

126

said it was a businessman he'd known in Lebanon. However, you're probably right."

I went up to my studio and was busy working on Toby's portrait when I remembered where and when someone's hair parting had bothered me: It was in the schoolroom when Miss Sutherland was talking to Randy, her face down on a level with his. Only that time it wasn't dark roots. The rest of her hair was dark. Her roots were very light. White, undoubtedly. I rolled the table that held my paints over to me. Janet Sutherland was pretty young to have white hair, even yellowish white hair. But then I'd known people to start growing gray in their early twenties.

At nine-thirty Toby himself appeared, wiggled onto the high stool, and, without apparent effort, fell into the right pose. He was oddly silent for a nine-year-old, something for which I was profoundly grateful, but which seemed almost unnatural. Anyone more different from his sibling, Michelle, was impossible to imagine. I stared at the painting. Technically, it was one of the best I had ever done. Yet it seemed without life almost as though it were a painting of a painting. I looked up at the boy. He seemed to be staring out the window. It occurred to me that while I could have written half a book about Michelle, I knew nothing of Toby.

"Toby," I said, "do you like New York?"

"Yes. It's interesting."

I wondered how many of the nine-year-old brothers and sisters of the kids next door in my art class would put together words like that: *"Yes. It's interesting."* Toby was like a little foreigner who had learned correct English but had to speak it slowly.

"What do you like about it?" I asked.

He shrugged. "Lots of things."

"Such as?"

"I like the Staten Island ferry. It's really super going over and back on that. You can see the ships all over the harbor." There was a tinge of color in the pale cheeks. Suddenly his face was alive.

I looked back at the painting. At that moment it

127

didn't even much resemble him, even though the painted face was handsomer than the child sitting across from me. For the first time since he'd arrived, Toby looked all boy instead of some curious androgynous figure out of myth. He looked, I thought, as though, with a little freedom, he might just as easily be as dirty as Randy Ferris next door.

"Just stay there a minute," I said. I worked swiftly, wondering if I could make the changes necessary, or if it would be better to start from scratch.

"You should have come over on one of the ocean liners," I said, "instead of a plane."

"Yes. I wanted to. But Mummy and Daddy said it was a ridiculous waste of time and also expensive. Besides, Daddy and Michelle get seasick."

"Have you been much on the water?" I decided recklessly that I would start again from scratch.

"One summer, when I was in school in England, one of my friends' family had a boat that they sailed off the coast of Scotland and he invited me along."

"Was it good?" I asked, working swiftly with another canvas. I was taking a risk with no sketch, but I now knew what I wanted to do, and I had a feeling I might not be able to capture this look on Toby's face again.

"It was terrific. Really terrific. The best summer I've ever had. I hated coming home."

Unexpectedly, and for the first time in my life, I felt sympathy for Suzanne and George. How awful to have children neither of whom wishes to be with their parents.

"That's much better," Suzanne's voice said from the door. "That's really like you, Toby."

I wondered how she knew. In the moment her voice sounded his face had gone back to where it had been before. But when I picked up the old canvas and glanced at it, I saw that though the small-boy enthusiasm had gone from his face, the first painting was still some kind of abstract of the way he looked. Nevertheless, I didn't want Suzanne there while I painted her son.

"Suzanne," I said, mixing colors, "it's probably stupid, but I can't paint if anyone other than myself and the person I'm painting is around. It's somehow a one-to-one thing. So I'm afraid I'm going to have to toss you out."

I made it as kind as I could, partly because I felt guilty at wanting so intensely to get rid of her. But it was, still, a rebuff. She stood, looking lost and then irritated. "Very well. I certainly didn't mean to intrude. By the way, when do you think you'll be finished with that?"

"What's the hurry? Are you going somewhere?"

I hadn't meant to ask that question. I certainly hadn't meant to use that tone of voice. "Look—" I started.

"We are staying only until George is settled in a new ... new position. He's had several offered to him, but we have to decide which one he wishes to take."

Rubbish, I thought to myself. But I didn't say so.

"Come, Toby," she said. "You and I have to go downtown."

"I thought you wanted me to do his portrait?" I was really put out. "I haven't found it easy to do. And now, when I think I'm getting somewhere, you want to yank him away. It won't take much longer than this morning, but please leave him here."

"Very well, I'll leave him here now, but I really must insist that you hurry it up."

"What—" I began, deciding to pin her down as to what her rush was. Since I didn't think she was acting on anything but wounded dignity, I was out of patience with her bluff.

"We have to arrange for Toby's schooling next fall, get his clothes and find out where he stands on work."

I looked at her. "Where are you sending him to school?"

"St. Hubert's."

"You could buy a yacht for what that place costs."

"There are such things as scholarships."

"Do I have to sit for a scholarship exam, Mummy? You know I hate taking exams."

"Nevertheless you do very well at them, unlike Michelle, who seems to panic. After being educated in Europe it shouldn't be any problem for you at all."

"Does Daddy want me to go there?"

"Of course. I wouldn't have otherwise spoken to you about it."

"That's not true. Lots of times—"

"I will not be contradicted. I'll expect you downstairs in an hour. Don't be late."

When she left Toby giggled. "She is in a wax," he said.

"What's a wax?"

"You know, a temper."

"There's no need to sound happy about it. Your mother has problems of her own to contend with."

"Like Daddy," said Toby.

I didn't say anything. I couldn't deny what he'd just said, but I wished I had not spoken to Suzanne the way I did, at least not in front of her son.

"It's not easy to cross an ocean and try to find work on another continent," I said.

"Daddy's not looking for work," Toby said.

I glanced up at him. "How do you know?"

"I just know. At least I'm pretty sure." When I looked skeptically at him, he burst out, "Whenever he's been looking for a job before, he always comes home and talks about it for hours with Mummy. Now he's almost never at home and he never says anything at all."

I painted in silence for a while, quite sure that what Toby was saying was true, just as I knew perfectly well that Suzanne was ordering me to hurry over the portrait not because she had anything to do with it, or was planning to leave, but because it was important to her to have me think that she and George were bustling around, filled with activity. Was it just for morale purposes, or was there another reason?

"Toby," I said. "How do you like Michelle?"

"She's all right. She doesn't like me."

"Why not?"

"Because Mummy makes me her favorite."

130

"Don't you like that?"

"No. It's not fair, and anyway, I often like Daddy better."

Suzanne, the beautiful, Suzanne the all-conquering, I thought. And then paused, brush in hand, struck by the truth of something I had always considered a bromide imposed on my generation by all the con artists who preceded it.

"Beauty's not all that important," somebody had said in my hearing—I think it was the rector of our church in the course of a sermon. "By itself it cannot bring you either happiness or success," he intoned.

"Garbage!" I had stated flatly, safely outside the church.

"It is not garbage," my father said sternly.

Considering he led the parade of those who—in my opinion—had rejected me because of my lack of beauty, I considered this a shining example of the cant of the church and the hypocrisy of an entire generation and used it for years as an all-purpose justification. Now I was faced with the obvious fact that what the wretched cleric had said was true: Beauty does not necessarily bring happiness.

I worked silently on Toby's painting, watching it come to life under my hand, and the total absorption that envelopes me when things are going well shut out everything else.

Sometime later—how much I didn't know—I became aware that Toby was saying, "Can I go now, please? It's been *hours!*"

He had to repeat it before what he was saying sank in. Then I glanced at my watch. It was after twelve.

"I'm sorry, Toby. Yes, of course you can go. You've been wonderful."

"Do you want me again?"

I stared at the portrait. "No, I don't think so. There's just the background left and I don't need you for that. Run along. And thanks."

I stood staring at the head as his feet scampered downstairs. It was one of the best things I had done, and I knew it. Pushing the table away, I walked to the window seat and sat down. Until that moment, I hadn't realized how tired I was. But it was a good feeling.

Idly I watched the children. There was Mimi's dark pigtailed head and Anita's smooth black one. They were sitting side by side in the swings. And the Schlegel twins were following each other down the slide. Chasing an orange ball were Tom Hawkins and Shirley Roth. One by one I identified the others. When I had them all named and tagged, so to speak, I had an odd, unfinished feeling that I couldn't identify. Somebody must be missing, I thought. And then, of course, it struck me: Randy Ferris. How could I have forgotten his fiery curls and piercing shriek. Had he emptied an ink bottle over some blonde head and was being kept inside as punishment? Was he sick? Who was in charge of the kids? Whoever it was was just out of sight, standing in the doorway that was hidden behind a stone block. I was mildly astonished at how concerned I felt.

After a while the children went in for the long lunch period, and I went downstairs for lunch, which consisted of a solitary sandwich and coffee, everyone else being out.

After lunch I found myself at loose ends. I had done all the painting I wanted to do that day. I put some stuff away, turning on my little transistor radio as I often did when I was working. But after listening to four different announcements about the treaty being signed in Washington that day I felt I'd had it with Middle East affairs and turned it off. Enough was enough. After discarding various ideas for amusing myself I found I was walking the few steps next door to the school.

As I turned to go up the stoop a young man in jeans and zip jacket came down. Assuming him to be a parent, I wondered which child was his offspring and almost stopped him to ask. Since I had taught all the children and by this time knew most of them, I thought it might be interesting to talk to him. But he moved quickly past, his head turned in the opposite direction

132

as though looking for a taxi, and withdrawing his hand as he did so from some inside pocket of his jacket.

Ginny Stevenson was in the hall when I walked in. "Hi," I said, and then, noting her distracted expression, "What's the matter?"

"I'm sure there's a perfectly rational explanation," Ginny said in the tone of one who is frightened half out of her wits that there isn't. "But . . ." Her voice trailed off as other voices were heard from one of the schoolrooms.

"I've told and told you not to take Anita's pencil. Now I shall be very angry . . ."

Plus ça change, I murmured. "But what?"

"Randy Ferris is missing," she said, all in a burst. "We simply can't find him."

A cold feeling slid down my spine. It seemed inconceivable that I should become attached to that stone-throwing child, with his tantrums and four-letter words and never-ending demands for attention. But obviously I had. "When was the last time anyone saw him?" I said.

"This morning. Around eleven-thirty. Everyone is sure that he was in the class at that time because . . . well because there was a row."

"What about?"

"He was drawing cats again, when everyone was supposed to be rehearsing their songs—you know, for the concert tomorrow."

"I'd forgotten. Is it tomorrow?"

"Of course. Don't you ever listen to the news? They're signing the treaty today and then coming up to New York tomorrow for the celebration at the United Nations where the kids are going to sing. What a day for Randy to be lost! Anyway, he has such a loud voice that Miss Gales, who was running through the songs with the kids, finally missed him. So she looked around and then through the connecting door to the other classroom. And there he was slopping paint water all over everything and painting those wretched cats

133

again. Nobody knows how he got out of the rehearsal group and into the other classroom."

"So what happened?"

"She dragged him back to the others and told him—once again—that it was not creative at all to be doing the same thing over and over, and that he was to practice the songs with the other kids."

"And then what?"

"I don't know. Nobody knows. The song hour came to an end and they were all herded outside. When they came back into lunch, and I automatically counted heads—because I always do when they're sitting down—I discovered he was missing. I didn't think too much about it. Randy is independent and well able to get himself to the bathroom and back and I thought he'd gone there. But that was two hours ago. All the bathrooms were searched. He wasn't there. We looked over the entire house, in all the closets and cupboards. He's not here." Ginny looked on the verge of tears.

"Could he have tried to go home? How far does he live?"

"Only about four blocks away down Park Avenue. His mother, who's divorced, has an apartment just south of Eighty-sixth. The doorman there hasn't seen him."

I looked at her stricken face. "Have you told Mrs. Ferris?"

"We finally called her. But she works for a magazine and was out on some kind of assignment. Her secretary said she doesn't expect her back today. She said she'd probably go straight home from the assignment, which means, straight here."

The thought of confronting Mrs. Ferris with the news was obviously what was undoing Ginny.

"Cheer up," I said. "Either Miss Gales or Miss Sutherland will have the unpleasant task of telling Mrs. Ferris. Ginny, I know this sounds crazy, but are you sure you've looked everywhere? He's powerfully vocal, but he's small, and he could fit into a pretty small place."

"I tell you. There isn't a *drawer* we've left unsearched."

"Then he must have gone somewhere else."

"Yes, but where?"

"All right. Let's think." I paused. "While we're thinking, a couple of obvious questions: Is there a candy store around here that he might know about?"

"Yes, there is, about four blocks north on Madison. I suppose it's *possible* he went there. Although I don't know why he should suddenly take off. Since we have the playground here, we don't take the kids past there to the park, the way we used to do at the nursery school I was at before on Ninety-sixth Street. It was a regular thing, then, to come back from the park via the candy store. But he's never been there from here to my knowledge."

Suddenly there popped into my mind the picture of the young man coming down the steps of the stoop. "Did somebody come to the door this morning that you weren't expecting?" I asked.

"I don't know. Why?"

"No particular reason. But I saw this young man coming down the steps just as I came in. I suppose the reason I thought about him in connection with Randy is that children can sometimes be like cats or puppies. Somebody comes to the door and they slip out before anybody notices."

"I can see how a small animal could slip out, but I can't see how a child could. Anyway, I don't think . . ." She paused. "Yes, as a matter of fact, there was a young man. Miss Gales answered the door. She said he came to read the meter."

I tried to remember how the young man looked. As a painter of heads and faces, I could usually describe in some detail anyone I had ever met. Yet, if asked, I wasn't sure I could describe this man. Of course, he had his head turned away from me. But before he turned . . . A swift impression of dark, angry eyes slid through my mind. "A meter reader?" I said.

"Yes. Why?"

"I don't know. I suppose meter readers from Con Edison come in all shapes and sizes. But he didn't look like one to me."

"Well, that's what Miss Gales said, and, anyway, what on earth does it have to do with Randy Ferris?" Almost literally, she rang her hands.

"Is there a basement to the house? A cellar?"

"It's always locked. That's one of the unbreakable rules Miss Sutherland made. She said the stairs down to the basement or cellar or whatever were unsafe, especially for the children. She and Miss Gales are the only ones who have keys."

"I know Miss Sutherland is away. So has Miss Gales looked?"

"I don't know. It's such a rule that nobody goes down, I never thought to ask."

"Let's ask. If something or someone isn't where they should be, then let's try somewhere where they shouldn't be."

But Miss Gales was adamant that the keys were never out of her possession and that it would have been impossible for Randy to have gone down to the cellar. "He's slipped out somehow. I know that. It's just a question of waiting to see where he shows up."

"Have you notified the police?"

She paused a second. Then, "Not yet. I wanted to be absolutely sure that he hadn't shown up at the house of one of his playmates, or in the lobby of his own apartment house. There's no point in getting the police involved unless it's absolutely necessary. And he's only been missing a couple of hours."

It didn't take much imagination to realize that the poor woman was trying, in the absence of the principal, to protect the school. Suddenly I remembered Aunt Ginevra and her nap—the original reason why I became involved with the school in the first place. If the school went out of business, she—not to mention, possibly, other neighbors—would not be unhappy. But it was too late for me to feel that way. Without meaning

136

to, I had become involved with the school and its pupils, especially that missing limb of Satan, Randy.

"I'll tell you what. I'll walk around the neighborhood and see if I can find him or find anyone who's seen hide or hair of him."

"Would you?" breathed Ginny, almost embarrassingly grateful.

On Miss Gales's boxy, unattractive face a struggle was taking place. She, too, was grateful. She was also worried. Talking about a missing child around this area would, again, not do the school good.

"I'll be discreet," I promised.

"All right. Please let us know." She paused. "If you can't . . . well, I'll try to reach Miss Sutherland." It was odd, I found myself thinking. Janet Sutherland was younger than Miss Gales, not much older than Ginny Stevenson. Yet both women talked of her with the formality that would be less remarkable if she had been seventy.

"Before you talk to the police?" I asked.

"I'd never get in touch with any outside agency like that without her full knowledge and approval. Anyway, she'll be back tonight."

Funny, I thought. Surely in her absence, if she trusted the older woman enough to make her second in command (and again, "command" seemed an odd descriptive of a nursery and day-care school, even though it did not seem out of place when thinking of Janet Sutherland as the head of it) . . . I snatched my mind back . . . If Miss Sutherland thought highly enough of Miss Gales to place her in command during her absence, surely that would include calling the police over a missing child.

"Is there anything else?" Miss Gales asked.

I realized I had been standing there while my mind played back and forth.

"No, I'll be on my way, and will check back with you."

I was halfway out when I said, "What was he wearing?"

"Jeans, green T-shirt," Miss Gales replied.

"With his red hair that should certainly be colorful and outstanding," I said, and as I spoke, was swept with the overwhelming conviction that Randy was in serious danger. It was so strong that I stood, with my feet locked.

"Aren't you going?" Miss Gales said sharply, betraying her anxiety.

"Yes," I said.

I forced myself to go through the front door and down the steps. I have never in my life had anything that could remotely be called a premonition. When I had thought about such things as premonitions or previsions at all, I had envisioned them as rather romantic and pleasant. But what I was experiencing was neither. What I was feeling was terrible confusion and fear and unease amounting to nausea.

"Come on," I muttered to myself. "Snap out of it. Start walking."

Step by step I forced myself down Madison Avenue, over to Park, up to Ninety-sixth, over to the candy store and back along Madison. I walked quickly, my eyes scanning the streets, making sure I did not see a small figure with red curls, a green T-shirt and jeans. As though in front of me, I could see underneath those curls Randy's square face, scrunched up as though he was about to go into a tantrum. Even though it was in my mind the sight made me want to cry. And I was dogged by the feeling that my perambulations were useless and worse, a waste of time. He was in that house. As the words formed themselves in my head, I stopped. Randy was in that house, and he had to be found before it was too late. I stood stock-still and prayed. Surely Whoever and Whatever created the order and sweetness of Mozart would have some way to help me find Randy.

"Avril, the theologian," I said aloud to myself sarcastically.

I found myself staring at a public phone. Julian was the one who believed in God. Julian was a bastard of

138

the first fiefdom of bastardy, I reminded myself. But all of a sudden I knew he was also a rock. Somewhere in the back of my consciousness, as I all but ran towards the telephone, I acknowledged I had let go forever my picture of him as some kind of hanger-on of my father. Of all the people I knew, he was the one to call in an emergency.

While I waited for his office to answer the phone, I sent up another request that he be in.

"Hello?" his secretary's voice said. "Mr. Demarest's office."

"Please let me speak to Mr. Demarest."

"I'm sorry, he's in a meeting."

"Then get him out. This is an emergency. Tell him it's Avril Marchington."

"Well, I don't know, Miss Marchington—"

"Just get him."

In a minute he was on the phone. "What's the emergency?"

"Randy Ferris, one of the kids at school, is missing. The principal is away. Everybody at school seems to think he's run off somewhere. But I'm absolutely *convinced* he's in that house. I don't know why I'm so sure, but I am. I know you probably think I'm crazy to worry you about this..." How would I explain to him how strongly I felt without sounding a fool.

But he seemed to think it was only natural I should call him. "Where's the principal—what's her name?"

"Sutherland. Janet Sutherland. She's away. Naturally."

"Why naturally?"

"Isn't there some kind of natural law about it? On the weekend the baby comes or the appendix acts up, isn't that always the time the doctor is on vacation?"

He laughed. "Of course. Where are you?" he asked.

"On the corner of Madison and Ninety-third."

"Go on home and I'll meet you there in fifteen minutes."

This was far more than I had expected when I called.

"Thanks," I said. "I didn't mean to yank you out of your comfortable office."

"See you," he said, and hung up.

I left the phone booth and stood uncertainly for a moment, glancing up and down the streets and along the avenue to see if I could catch sight of a green shirt. But it was a *pro forma* act. I knew, beyond any question, that it was pointless, that Randy was in the school building somewhere. Turning, I walked rapidly down Madison and towards Eighty-eighth Street.

Julian arrived at the house five minutes after I did, and found me staring disconsolately out the living room window.

"I take it he hasn't turned up yet," Julian said without preamble.

"No."

The narrow gray eyes that I had always found so cold looked down at me. "Are you still convinced he's somewhere in the school?"

"Yes."

"And in danger?"

"At the risk of sounding as though I'm ready for a padded cell, yes."

"All right. Did you know that Cousin Ginevra's house—this one—and the one owned now by the school were once both owned by the Marchingtons?"

"No. When?"

"Back a generation or so ago. Cousin Ginevra's aunt, her father's sister, married a man on the West Coast. A man named Carteret. When the father died he left his daughter, Aunt Ginevra's aunt, the house. The aunt, or her family, must have sold it to the present owner."

"Janet Sutherland?"

"No. I don't think so. In fact, I know it isn't. It's a foundation or some kind of philanthropic outfit whose emphasis seems to be on children. They run a very good home for emotionally disturbed children in Oregon, and one for retardees in New Mexico. Apparently Miss Sutherland and her children are the other beneficiaries. Anyway, after we spoke, I looked up some old plans for the house that I knew were in our files and made a sketch of the cellar." He took a sheet of paper from his pocket and unfolded it, setting it flat on a nearby table.

"Why the cellar?"

"Because I remembered someone telling me once— it could have been your father, for all I know—that there was, or had been, a connecting door down there between the two houses in the cellar. It dates from the days when Marchingtons lived in both houses. The door was made for some domestic arrangement or other, so that their servants could get from one house to another without having to go outside, or they shared a furnace—something like that. Anyway, if the door's still there, and we can get it open, and it isn't blocked from the other side, we can go and look for your wandering boy without being too obvious."

"Julian, that's wonderful!"

"Wait, let's see! There are a hell of a lot of 'ifs' in that. Softly, softly catchee monkey." He bent over the paper.

I peered over his shoulder. "Is that the cellar?"

"Yes. Here's the door. Do you have any idea what's in your cellar?"

"None. I don't think I've even been down there."

"Well, now's the time to find out." He folded the plan again and put it in his pocket. "By the way, I think it would be a good idea if you don't mention this new discovery to anyone."

"Why? It's not as though we were building a secret passage. It's already there."

"Because ... well, for one thing, I don't think it's good for Cousin Ginevra's security for a lot of people to know about another and unguarded entrance to the house. For another ..." He frowned. "Put it in the category of your conviction that Randy's still in the school and in danger." He gave me a sardonic look. "Has it occurred to you to wonder why you didn't confide that

141

conviction to one of the staff members at the school and enlist her aid to go and look for your runaway?"

"No," I said. "It didn't occur to me to do so."

"Precisely."

I brooded over that. "Strange," I finally said.

"So, promise not to mention it?"

Again I hesitated, wondering if at any time Randy's safety might depend on my telling someone.

"Come on, Avril, don't be pigheaded. Don't dig your heels in just because I request it."

"It wasn't for that reason," I said indignantly. I stared at him.

That little shiver I had felt before flickered over my skin. Julian was looking at me steadily.

"There's more to this than you're telling me, isn't there, Julian?"

He hesitated, then said, "It's only a hunch, but I have a feeling there might be."

CHAPTER 7

"Just how," I said, "do you plan for us to go down into the cellar and go rooting around for a door without people knowing? The cellar steps are right next to the kitchen. If Jessie's not there, Suzanne could be."

"Why should they know? You're going to the cellar to get some old letters of your father's that you stored in a trunk, and I'm tagging along to help."

"I can't imagine anyone, knowing our family, who would believe either of those two. Any letters my father left would have gone straight into the incinerator if I had had anything to say about it. And your coming along to help me is even less credible. We're not exactly noted for our harmonious relationship."

"You might have kept business letters," Julian said, opening the door leading down to the basement floor, half below ground level, where Jessie had her quarters, and, through another door, to the cellar beneath that. "And I have suffered a change of heart. There is even a ludicrous rumor going around that I've fallen in love with you."

We were in the middle of the steps between the basement and the cellar when he said that. The stone treads were worn, the banister shaky and the light bad. Nevertheless, I turned on the narrow, dangerous stair and looked up at Julian coming down immediately behind me. "What did you say?"

"I said there was a rumor that I was in love with you."

I stared up at him, more than a little annoyed. "As anyone who has been in our company could witness, you and I can't be together for five minutes without being at each other's throats."

"Speak for yourself. Anyway, that was a while ago. Since then I've seen your true worth. But shyness, combined with low self-esteem—"

"—not to mention a present wife."

"—not to mention a present wife, have prevented me from speaking."

"Of all the garbage I've ever heard! There is nothing wrong with your self-esteem and never has been. And you've never been shy."

"Ah," Julian said. "That just shows how well I've hidden it."

"You're beginning to annoy me."

"That, alas, was ever my fate. Are we going to stand here forever? Might I point out that the longer we loiter here, chattering, the greater chance of people hearing us and coming to see what is up?"

I turned forward and clanked down the steps, making no effort whatsoever to soften my footsteps. When I got to the bottom, I could see how narrow the house really was. The cellar was open space above a cement floor. The light, which we had turned on by a switch at the top of the stairs, was a dim, naked light bulb hanging from the ceiling. A damp mouldy smell seemed to pervade the whole cellar. I stared down at the dark floor. "I wish we'd brought a flashlight," I said. "It occurs to me that there could be water bugs down here."

"Almost certainly there are water bugs," Julian said from behind me. "As it happens, having been a Scout in my early years, I came prepared." And from behind me there was a click and there flared a white powerful light that shone onto the ground.

"Where did you produce that from?" I asked, gratefully.

"My pocket. Do you want me to go first?"

Pride battled my dislike of water bugs. Pride lost. "Yes, please."

Julian stepped around me and turned his flashlight this way and that. We were facing the back of the house. Pipes of all kinds ran along the walls. Straight ahead were trunks, including two old-fashioned steamer trunks standing upended, and what looked like a Con Ed electric and gas meter. To our left was a huge furnace, its back against the wall that we shared with the school, an enormous aluminum pipe going up from its top to the ceiling.

Turning around, Julian shone the light towards the front of the house, to the longer part of the cellar. A first glance, as the light went from the floor to the ceiling and back and forth, produced an impression of ordered chaos. Chairs, small tables, larger tables, cabinets, bookshelves, stacked pictures in their frames, rolled-up carpets, chests and what looked like about fifty cartons were arranged and fitted together so that they covered that end of the cellar and the entire wall between the front of the house and the furnace.

"Where's the door, do you suppose?" I asked.

"Somewhere behind all that. I'd say probably about there." And he turned the round circle of light to a place a few feet from the furnace wall itself.

"Well," I said, my anxiety about Randy becoming more urgent. "Let's start clearing out the space there."

It took us less time than I would have supposed. Moving the furniture was fairly easy. It was the cartons, which were heavy and cumbersome, that took up the time.

"What on earth do you suppose is in there?" I asked.

"Books, probably."

"Hasn't any Marchingtons ever heard of thrift shops?"

"Waste not, want not," Julian said, hauling the last of the stacked cartons back to the middle of the floor. "Now," he said. "Let's have a look." He shone the bright white light onto the cleared wall space. The door was so filthy and scratched it barely showed up against the equally filthy wall. But it was definitely a door.

"Eureka!" Julian said, his voice louder than it had been.

There was a dim, muffled sound. Then an unmistakable voice. "Help! Help! It's me, Randy. I'm locked in."

"Your premonition was right," Julian said dryly. Taking a long step forward he reached the door and knocked on it. "Randy? We're coming to get you. Just hang on. Are you all right?"

"Get me out!" Randy's voice yelled. "I'm scared!"

I went up to the door. "Randy, it's me, Miss Match. You're going to be all right. Now just hang on another minute."

"Hold this," Julian said, thrusting the flashlight at me. "Now, shine it here."

I pointed the light towards something in his hand, and saw he was looking at two keys.

"Don't tell me you have a *key!*" I said, "that's too much."

"Our legal offices have handled the affairs of the Marchingtons for three generations. We have a fairly large box in our files, filled with keys to various parts of your house, closets, etcetera, all carefully marked. I zipped through them and found two labeled 'cellar door.'"

"Miss Match!" Randy yelled. "Are you still there? Why don't you come and get me? Right now!"

"I'm coming, Randy, as fast as I can. We have to get the door open."

"Okay," Julian said, "shine the light on the lock. I'm going to try this."

It was a Yale key that Julian fitted into the door. "Now pray," he said, and turned the key. There was the sound of a thunk. Julian took the doorknob, twisted and pushed. "There's something on the other side," he said pushing harder. "But I think it will move or fall over. Randy," he called. "Can you hear me?"

"Yes. Are you coming?"

"In a minute. Do you have any light in there?"

"It went out."

"Do you know where my voice is coming from?"

"Yes. Here." Randy's voice sounded much nearer.

"Okay. I'm standing in front of a door here. But there's something in front of the door on your side. Can you tell me what it is?"

146

"Bookshelves. Yes. It's bookshelves."

"Do they have books in them?"

"I can't remember. Let me feel. Ouch!"

"Are you okay?"

"Yeah. A book fell. But there's not a lot."

"I want you to stay way back and to one side. I'm going to push the shelves over, but I don't want them to fall on you. Do you understand, Randy? Av—" He glanced at me and grinned, "Miss... Miss Match... tells me you're very smart. Do you understand what I mean?"

"'Course I do. Okay. I'm going to the side so you can push."

There was a slight noise on the other side, as though Randy had stumbled over something.

"Okay, Randy?" Julian asked.

"Okay." His voice sounded much farther away. "You can push now."

Julian placed his shoulder against the door and shoved. There was the sound of things sliding and falling on the other side. "Shine the light where the door is opening," he said.

I directed the beam to the edge of the door and saw it widen. When it was about a foot across, Julian leaned over, took the light from me and shone it through the opening. "Okay," he called.

There was some slithering and then I saw red hair and a green T-shirt. Julian stood aside, and the next thing I knew, I had an armful of boy.

"Oh, Miss Match, I've been there for hours and hours and I was scared and the light went out and I had to go to the bathroom."

"Randy, you gave me the fright of my life, but it's all right. It's okay, it's all okay," I kept murmuring soothingly while the little boy clung to me, crying now, out of sheer relief. He was filthy, but it didn't matter. I kept my arms around him and hugged and talked to him, and cried a little myself.

After a few minutes I became aware that Julian was missing. But looking through the opening of the door,

I could see the light traveling around the room in there. "Randy, what's in that room?"

"Nothing, now, except the bookshelves and some books all over the floor. That was where the cat was with the kittens, but they aren't there now. Don't go in there, Miss Match. Maybe the door will slam like it did when I was in there. Don't go in."

He sounded so upset, I said, "You can hold my hand on this side, but I just want to look in."

With Randy gripping me on one side I poked my head through the door. "Is there anything interesting in there?" I asked Julian. All he was was a black shape on one side of the flashlight.

"No. Not now. But from clean spaces on the floor, I'd say some boxes, or something square, have been moved out of here fairly recently. The rest of the floor's pretty dirty. Right now there are all those books, the shelves I pushed aside and that's about it."

Randy, who was right behind me, pushed his head past my arm and said, "There were lots of boxes here. Lots and lots. I drew them in my picture. You 'member, Miss Match?"

"Yes, I remember. And you had the cats. I wonder what happened to them. And Clancy. The ginger cat. I wonder how he got in here."

"Through the hole in the grating, I'd say," Julian said, and shone his light up to show a broken grating that led up to a small areaway next to the outside wall of the house. "It's not large, but a cat could get through there very easily. And it leads into the garden."

"There were lots of kittens," Randy said sadly.

"Maybe the mother cat took them to safety," I said.

"How did you get down here, Randy?" Julian asked.

"Through that door up there," Randy said, waving towards something behind Julian's back.

Julian turned the light on a staircase very similar to the one in our house. Then he went up the stairs himself and tried the door. "Locked."

He seemed to examine the door with great care. "That's a lot sturdier than the door we have in our

148

house leading down to the cellar," he said conversationally. "Randy, did someone lock the door on you, or did it just slam behind you and lock automatically?"

"It locked by itself. You see, the first time I was here, when I saw the cats and the boxes and the pictures, I just looked in from the door up there, 'cos I knew I wasn't supposed to be there. Anyhow, the door upstairs, the one near the bathroom, was unlocked. It was always locked before, but it was unlocked. So I came down the first set of stairs. Then I found that door there, and looked in, but I didn't come down those stairs that time. I saw the cats and everything and went back upstairs. But today I wanted to see the cats again, so when everybody was eating lunch I said I wanted to go to the bathroom and tried the door again and it was unlocked so I came down the first set of stairs and then opened that door and looked in. But the cats weren't there. So I came down to look for them and the door closed. And I couldn't open it again and I yelled and yelled but nobody heard." His voice began to rise again in grievance.

"Yes, Randy, I know. It must have been awful."

"It was. And the cats had all gone and I didn't see any pictures and everything was different and then the light went out."

"What pictures, Randy?" Julian said, coming back to the open door and the light. We all backed into our cellar. "By the way, I'm Julian Demarest."

"Hi. Just pictures on big pieces of paper. This big." Randy held his grubby sleeved arms wide.

"Posters," Julian said.

"Like the ones of animals at school?" I asked.

"Yeah, just like that. Only it was snakes."

"Snakes?" Julian said.

"Yeah. Like they were lying down only twisted together. With fire."

"Fire where?" Julian asked.

"Coming out of their mouths, of course," Randy said.

"Oh," I said. "The squiggle."

149

"I seem to have heard of that squiggle before," Julian said. "What was it?"

"The squiggle in the painting Randy did. I thought they were wavy lines with balloons."

"They were snakes, Miss Match. Anybody could see that."

"You should be ashamed of yourself, Avril," Julian said. "Missing something like that. What happened to the painting?"

"It got lost," I said.

"Miss Sutherland didn't like it and took it away and when I wanted it back to show Mom it wasn't there."

"I seem to remember your telling me something like that at dinner before the concert," Julian said. "Miss Sutherland didn't approve of Randy's approach to painting."

"That's right. And when I went to look where she keeps the kids' paintings it wasn't there."

"She threw it away," Randy said, with a tone of strong grievance.

"That's wasn't right," Julian said. "Look, why don't you two go upstairs to Miss Mar—Miss Match's studio? And with Miss Match's help, Randy, maybe you could draw for me again the picture that Miss Sutherland threw away. Could you do that?"

Randy puffed his chest out a little. "I don't mind," he said grandly.

"And what are you going to be doing?" I said.

"I'm going to put the cellar next door back into as good a shape as it was before I knocked over the bookcases, or try to."

"How can you?" I asked. "Since you have to come back through this door?"

"I can put the books back on the shelves—Randy was right, there aren't too many of them—and I think as I close the door I can pull the shelves back with it."

"Why bother?"

"Why not ask me later when we're upstairs?" he said agreeably. "Now off you go."

It didn't please me at all to be dismissed in such

lordly fashion, but Randy settled the issue by saying, "I'm *hungry*, Miss Match."

"All right. I have some food in a little refrigerator in my studio." I took his hand but looked back at Julian. "What am I supposed to say if I meet someone?"

"I don't know. Maybe that you found Randy when you were out for a walk and that you were about to return him to the school."

"That's going to sound pretty funny if I'm bringing him up from the cellar."

"Then just pray you won't meet someone. I'll join you in a couple of minutes."

Luckily, we met no one. Once in my attic I closed the door behind us with a feeling of relief. "All right, Randy," I said. "Food." I went to the refrigerator I kept at the other end of the long attic and opened the door. "Milk, bread, cheese. And there's some fruit on the table."

"No candy or ice cream?" Randy asked in a disappointed voice.

"No candy or ice cream. What's here is better for you."

"It *stinks*," Randy said, sounding quite like his old self. He added in an ordinary voice, "But I'll eat it."

"After you've washed. Here's the bathroom."

"I don't have to—"

"Yes, you do. Come on now."

He emerged from the bathroom a few minutes later looking virtuous and with one layer of dirt removed. I poured him a glass of milk, found some peanut butter, which I put on a slice of bread, and made him a sandwich. He was polishing this off when Julian arrived up in the attic. I looked at his dusty hands and clothes. "I feel like sending you off to the bathroom to clean up, too."

"I'll go quietly," he said. And disappeared. When he came out, he strolled over to the table and said, "I don't suppose you have the makings of some instant coffee, do you?"

"I do. I'll make some."

"Randy," Julian said. "I want you to tell me all over again about your going down there the first time and then the second time and what you saw both times."

Randy, talking around and through a second peanut butter sandwich, and interrupted from time to time by questions from Julian, told pretty much the same story as he had told before: One day two weeks previously, when he had gone to the bathroom near the kitchen, he had passed a door he had gone by many times before, and many times had tried to open, for no particular reason except that it was there. But that time, instead of finding it locked, he had discovered that the door opened, and he found himself looking down a flight of steps. Without a moment's hesitation he had gone down, only to find himself in a narrow hall on a lower level on which were three more doors. Two of these were locked. The third opened, and he discovered yet another staircase leading down. A light switch beside the door, which he had turned on, had revealed the cellar in which he had seen the boxes, the cats, and a stack of posters, one of which, leaning against the wall, had borne the drawing of the two snakes with fire coming out of their mouths. But he had not left hold of the door, and, thinking that someone would be coming after him, he had retreated, closing the cellar door, and gone up the steps leading from the basement to the first floor.

But he had remembered the cats, and when his first painting had been taken from him, he was determined to go down and find them again, which he had tried to do today, with the difference that this time he had released the cellar door to go down the steps, and heard it slam behind him. After that he had yelled and screamed and kicked and stamped, but no one had come. And furthermore, there were no longer any cats, any boxes or any posters. And the whole thing wasn't fair, because now no one would believe him. But he did so see them...

Julian, his deep-set eyes on Randy's face, had listened to the whole thing in silence, sipping from the mug of coffee I had given him. Then he said, "That was a bad experience. I think you've weathered it very well."

Randy looked pleased with himself. "I'm still hungry," he said.

"Have some fruit." I passed the dish to him.

"Are you sure you don't have any ice cream?" he said.

"I'm sure."

Sighing, Randy took an apple and sank his teeth into it.

"You know," Julian said, "I'm surprised they didn't hear Randy, even through two floors. And especially with that grating giving onto the areaway."

"That's about the only thing I find normal," I said. "With the bedlam that goes on around there all the time I'm not even sure they'd hear a siren."

"I see. Well, you have a point." Julian finished his coffee. "I wonder why that door that was always locked was left open a couple of times."

"Somebody forgot to lock it. In a school with young kids any door leading to a staircase going down would be kept locked. Only someone went down there for something and forgot to lock it."

"Yes," Julian said slowly.

"I don't know why you seem to find that sinister," I said.

"I don't know that I do. But if Randy is not letting his imagination gallop away, there were once various items in that cellar that are no longer there. Which items, by the way, he portrayed in a painting that now also is missing."

"That's silly..." I started to say, and then found myself thinking that those two facts, when put together, sounded, if not sinister, at least strange.

"Was there anything else odd about the school today, when you went there? Anything at all?"

"Well, I don't know what you mean by odd. Miss Sutherland was away, but then she often is."

"Doing what?"

"According to Miss Gales, giving lectures on schools for the young or some such.

"Ummm. Anything else?"

"No . . . except for that man, the meter reader."

"What about him?"

"Nothing about him, except that I met him coming down the steps when I was going up. According to Ginny he came to read the meter, or she thought he had. She was so distraught over the loss of this young troublemaker that she didn't know what he was doing."

Julian turned to Randy. "Did you see him?"

Randy shook his head. "No."

"I wonder where the school meter is," Julian said musingly. He turned towards me. "We saw yours down in the cellar, didn't we?"

"Yes."

I looked at Julian and he looked back at me.

"At the time you saw the so-called meter reader," Julian said, "Randy was in the cellar trying to attract attention and had been there for a while, I take it."

"Yes, Miss Gales said he'd been missing an hour or so. The funny thing is . . ." I paused.

"Well, don't keep us in suspense. What was the funny thing?"

"I remember thinking at the time he didn't look like my idea of a meter reader."

"What do you mean?"

I tried to summon the young man's face again, but couldn't. All I had was an impression. I shook my head. "It's no use. I can't remember why I thought he didn't look like a meter reader—and don't ask me what I think somebody who reads meters should look like— but I just didn't."

"Helpful," Julian said dryly.

"I'm sorry," I said rather indignantly.

"Randy," Julian said. "Did you see a meter in the cellar before the light went out?"

"No." He shook his head.

"You mean it wasn't there, or you didn't notice?"

Randy considered the question. "I didn't notice."

154

"Would you know a meter if you saw one?" I asked.

"'Course. The super in our building showed me the meters in our building."

"Did you notice a meter when you were flashing your light around, Julian?"

"No, but I wasn't looking for one. I was concentrating more on the floor. Whether I would have automatically seen one if it had been there, I don't know. Since it was dark, the beam from my flashlight could have just missed it. Randy," he turned towards the little boy. "Did you tell anyone how you got down to the cellar the first time when you saw the cats?"

"No." And he showed what a firm, if young, grasp he had on human nature and tendency. "They'd say I couldn't go down."

"True. So you went down the second time to see the cats."

"Yes. 'Cause she took my picture away and people thought I made them up." I heard again the rising grievance.

"Well, I don't think you made them up, Randy. I know you saw them, along with the boxes and the posters. Did you see what was in the boxes that first time, or were they closed?"

"They were closed." I could tell by the set of Randy's shoulders and the expression on his face that he was thoroughly enjoying the position of having a grown-up take him seriously and ask him questions about something which before simply produced an order not to do whatever he was doing.

"Okay, Randy," Julian said. "Miss ... er ... Match says you're very good at drawing."

"Yes. I am." Randy was untroubled by false modesty.

"I want you to draw for me what you saw on that poster. The snakes with the fire coming out of their mouths."

"You do realize," I said to Julian, "that Randy's mother, who by this time I'm sure has been informed of his absence, is probably going out of her mind with worry and alerting the police, the FBI and the fire department, and has already hired a lawyer to sue the school."

"That might not be such a bad idea," Julian said. "However, I see what you mean. Randy, I know you can draw and paint well, but I want you to do this in about five minutes. It's important."

"I can't," Randy said. His face started to grow red. I recognized the signs of an oncoming tantrum.

"Of course you can," Julian said sternly. "Now start. All I need is an idea."

Once again I saw some kind of magic go to work. Mouth open, Randy stared over his shoulder at Julian looming behind. Then, "Okay," he said. "Can I have a pencil and paper?"

"That's pretty fascistic, isn't it?" I said to Julian, giving Randy his tools.

"It's called authority and it's not necessarily a bad thing," he said, watching Randy's hand.

The drawing that emerged looked like nothing on earth I'd ever seen before.

"There," Randy said.

Julian stared, his eyes narrowed and squinting. I wanted to laugh, because it was obvious Julian didn't know either.

"Clear as a bell," I commented.

"Be quiet," Julian said, "Randy, what color is . . . are the snakes?"

Randy ran over to my easel, took one of my brushes and attacked the paint tray, as though it were a particularly glorious mud pie. After a while a muddy gray appeared. "That's not the right color," he said, staring at it.

"Do you want it more blue or brown?" I said, not thinking for a minute he would know how to answer. But he did.

"Blue," he said.

I went over and took the brush out of his hand. "Here," I said. "Now tell me when it's right."

Feeling like someone in a television movie doing a police drawing from the description of a witness, I kept

156

mixing a little of this and a little of that until Randy yelled, "That's right. That's the one."

"Is that drawing exactly the way you remember it?" Julian asked.

"Well, not *exactly*," Randy said. "But nearly."

"What's different?"

"Well ..." Randy put his coppery head on one side. "That line's longer, and that piece is bigger."

"Can you add your talents, Avril?" Julian asked.

Between us we produced a colored drawing that Randy pronounced correct.

"Now," I said to Julian who was staring at it. "Do you know what it is?"

After a minute he said, "I may. A friend of mine will know better." He looked down at Randy. "You helped a lot, Randy. May I take it with me? I'll tell my friend you did it."

"Sure. I'll sign it," Randy said. "Just like real artists."

Julian opened his mouth and then closed it. "Good," he said. "You should."

Working carefully with his brush Randy signed the picture. When he got through the signature was bigger than the drawing. "There," he said. "Everybody'll know."

Julian picked the page up, took another page and placed it on top of the painting, then rolled them up and put them in his breast pocket.

"Will it smear?" Randy asked anxiously.

"No," Julian said. "I folded it carefully." He stood looking at Randy for a minute. "Randy, how would you like to tell a couple of large lies—for the good of the country?"

I thought Randy would embrace such an opportunity with enthusiasm. But he astonished me. "Mom says the gov'ment should tell the truth," he said virtuously. "She said that American people have too many lies told them."

"Argue yourself out of that one, maestro," I said.

Julian gave me an exasperated look.

157

"What particular lie do you want him to tell?" I asked.

"I want him to tell the truth about how he wanted to look at the cats, tried the basement and cellar doors, found them open and went down. Given his obsession about cats, no one will have any trouble believing that. Then he could say that the door to the cellar slammed on him—which it did. In fact, Randy, the only real truth I want you *not* to tell is how you got out. I don't want you to say that Miss Match and I came through the door between the two cellars, that you came up here with us, that you did a drawing for me, or that you ever met me. Got that?"

"Okay. But what'll I say instead?"

"Now listen carefully, Randy, and you, too, Avril. It's very important. I want you to say that the door slammed shut and you couldn't get it open at first. But after a while you thought about it and thought maybe you twisted the door handle the wrong way. So you tried it again and found that if you turned the knob in a special way, the door opened. Okay?"

Randy nodded.

"You got upstairs. But because you knew you weren't supposed to be in the cellar, you were afraid you'd be punished, so you waited until everybody was out of sight, then you ran out and started to walk home. But you decided to go to the park for a while to see if you could see any old friends, and there, at the Fifth Avenue and Ninetieth Street entrance, you bumped into Miss Match, who thought you might have tried to go to the park and was looking for you there. And she brought you back to the school. All that should account for any lapsed time. Have you got all that?"

"Sure," Randy said.

"Okay. Repeat it back to me."

Randy, a bright child with good memory and a well-developed sense of drama, repeated it perfectly.

"All right," Julian said. "And stick to that no matter what anyone says."

"Will they believe it?" I asked.

158

"Why shouldn't they? Randy's known to have a passion for cats and also to be given to doing more or less what he wants."

"I guess you're right," I said doubtfully.

"And you back him up," Julian said severely. "I have less worry about his ability to tell a believable tale than about yours. When you start a lie people twenty feet away can hear you stripping your mental and moral gears."

"Thank you," I said. "No one would guess that it's a compliment—sort of. What about the meter reader?"

"What about him? If he is, indeed, a meter reader, it's irrelevant. If he isn't . . . well, one thing at a time."

"Shouldn't we tell the police?"

"Tell them what? That an overimaginative, trouble-making child with an exaggerated fondness for cats got himself locked into a cellar and had a hard time getting out? And then got scared that he would be—quite justifiably—punished, and ran off?"

I peered at Julian. "Is that what you believe?"

"I'll turn the question around. Is that what *you* believe?"

"Well, what about all the things that disappeared from the cellar? The cats, the boxes, the posters?"

"That's Randy's story. Who'd believe him? They aren't there now."

"But you said—"

"Yes, well, never mind, for the moment, what I said. What I want is a plausible story that Randy can tell and which will be believed."

I stood there, wanting to ask Julian if he thought Randy was in danger. But with the little boy himself standing there, I knew I couldn't do it. If he thought he was in danger, he might well behave in such a way as to bring himself into danger. Which brought me back to my own strong hunches—that Randy was both in the school and in danger. And certainly one of those hunches had been vindicated. Which meant, perhaps, that the other would be, too. But I couldn't query Julian about it now.

159

"Well, *you* believe Randy," I said. "Why?"

Julian smiled a little. "For reasons I'm not ready to go into. Why do you believe him?"

"Because I do."

"That's reason enough. Will you do as I ask? Take him around a couple of blocks and then walk him back to the school? After all you've been out looking for him, haven't you?"

"Yes, all right." I paused. "I can see now why you didn't want to meet anybody coming in."

"Let's hope our luck holds."

But it didn't. We were all three walking as quietly as possible past the door of Toby's and Michelle's room, when it suddenly opened and Michelle appeared in the doorway. Instant warfare exploded. Both Michelle and Randy yelled at once.

"She KICKED me," Randy yelled.

"That MONSTER threw a rock at Clancy," Michelle shouted. Then the war parties hurtled towards each other, two minds with but a single impulse of mayhem.

"QUIET!" Julian thundered.

It was like magic. They both stopped in mid dash and mid shout.

"Now," Julian said in a businesslike way. "You can both come in here." And without further ado, he hauled the combatants into Michelle's room. I barely managed to get myself in before he closed the door.

"I need both your helps," he said.

"There's the ginger cat," Randy said, and started forward.

Clancy lay on the bed, his great amber eyes on his late assailant.

"He'll hurt him," Michelle shrieked, and started after Randy.

"No, he won't," Julian said. "Now all of you, lower your voices."

"I only wanted him to look at me," Randy said. "I didn't want to hurt him."

"Miss Marchington can give you both instructions on the care and treatment of animals. Right now we

160

both want your cooperation. Randy, are you listening? Michelle?"

Both looked up. Between them on the bed stretched Clancy. After a minute he lowered his unblinking stare and started thoughtfully to wash a paw.

"What do you want us to do?" Michelle asked ungraciously.

"I want you not to tell anyone, and I mean *anyone*, about having seen Randy here in this house."

"Why not?"

Randy said importantly, "It's for the good of the country."

"What country?" Michelle said. "That's what people always say when they want to do something bad. My father says..." She stopped.

"What does your father say, Michelle?"

"Nothing."

"Well," Julian said, "I'm not going to tell you it's for the good of the country or any other high-sounding reason. I'm just going to ask you not to mention seeing Randy here. I can't give you the reason, except that it does involve Randy's good."

"How?" Randy said.

Poor Julian, I thought, caught between different ages and sexes and having to struggle with the obvious fact that what would work with one would alienate the other, and vice versa. I decided to intervene. "Michelle," I said. "It's important. Really important."

"Well," Michelle said somewhat grudgingly, "you stuck up for Clancy and took him to the vet. And anyway"—she paused and turned bright red—"I like you," she burst out.

Randy scowled. "Big deal!"

"It is a big deal," I said, and put my arm around Michelle's shoulder. "And it's mutual. I like her." I bent and kissed her on the cheek.

"I thought you liked ME," Randy said.

"I do," I said. "Can't I like you both?"

"No," Randy said. "It doesn't count."

"Tell me, Randy. Do you like your mother?"

161

"Sure."

"Then how can you like me if you like your mother?"

"That's different."

"It's not different. You like your mother a lot but you also like me. I like Michelle a lot, and I also like you."

"But you like me *best*," Michelle said.

"There are in this room a great number of rampant egos," Julian said dryly. "Do I understand that everyone will keep silent about Randy being here this afternoon?"

"Okay," Michelle said.

"Sure," Randy said.

"Promise. Swear."

"Cross my heart and hope to die," Michelle said, suiting action to the words. Another shiver ran through me. "I'm not fond of that oath, Michelle. Just promise."

"Okay, I promise."

Julian looked at Randy. "Promise?"

"Promise."

Julian held out his hand and solemnly shook hands with Randy and with Michelle. "It's a pact. Now," he said, looking at me, "I'd like you to telephone the school and say you found Randy walking around near Central Park at Fifth Avenue. Randy, do you have any friends who play in Central Park in the afternoon?"

"Well, Don sometimes does on the weekend. Only little kids are there in the week." Randy spoke loftily from his seven-year superiority.

"True. Okay, you're just going to have to say you were aiming to take a walk in Central Park. Avril, here's a dime. Don't call until you're over on Fifth. Call from a phone booth, okay?"

"Why can't I call from here? It's easier. Half the time somebody's using the public phone for a long, intimate private conversation and the rest of the time it's been vandalized and doesn't work."

"Have faith. You'll find one. And I don't want them to be on the lookout for Randy here and see you both coming out of this house. *Compris?*"

162

"I guess so. Come on, Randy. Let's go out so we can play our parts properly."

Michelle watched us go down the stairs. "Can I come?" she called down suddenly.

"I don't think you'd fit into the plot, Michelle," I said mischievously.

"Oh, I don't know," Julian said surprisingly. "You could have run into Michelle on the way home, and she accompanied you. Or something. Come along, Micky."

"*Micky!*"

Julian smiled. "Do you mind?"

Michelle thought it over. "No. I like it."

"I bet you her parents won't think too highly of it," I said.

"As long as Micky likes it, that's all that matters."

I called the school from a phone booth on the corner of Fifth Avenue and Eighty-ninth Street.

"Thank God," Miss Gales said.

"Have you told his mother?"

"No. Luckily, she was unobtainable. So she hasn't had the worry. Where did you find him?"

Without too much difficulty, I slid into my part. "Not far from Central Park. He was going for a walk there to see if he could run into any of his old buddies."

"He must be told that he's never to do that again," Miss Gales said. I thought I could almost hear her battling with the impulse to say he must be given a spanking. But I decided that was my imagination. "What on earth made him take off like that?"

I took a breath. "He found your cellar door open so went down to see his adored cats. Then the door slammed on him and he thought he was accidentally locked in. But after an hour or so of being scared, he tried the door again and found it opened, so he just took off by himself."

Not only did the story sound full of holes, but if I were his mother I'd like to know a few things, such as why someone on the staff wasn't watching him.

My own lack of conviction about the lame story was

163

so overwhelming that I was astonished to hear Miss Gales pass it without more than a comment about the teacher who was in charge of his room when he made his exit. "I really must impress on Ginny and the others that they can't take their eyes off any one of the kids for as much as five minutes, and that they should count heads on an average of every fifteen. You're bringing him right back, aren't you?"

"Of course," I said.

"Well?" Julian asked, as I came out of the booth. "Any trouble?"

"Not a scrap, which I find strange, to say the least."

"All right. Take the two kids to the school, deposit our hero there, and come on back to the house. I'll be waiting there." At this point he bent down and said something to Randy in his ear. Then he gave him a hug.

"What did he say to you, Randy?" I asked, as I took his hand and headed him to the school.

"I can't say," Randy said airily. "He said it was a secret. Just between us men."

"That's sexist," Michelle said.

"It certainly is. Never mind, we don't want to know, do we?" I said to her.

When we rang the school bell Miss Gales opened the door.

"Randy!" she cried. "You gave us such a scare, you naughty boy! Never run away again!" Then she surprised me by bending down and giving Randy a tight bear hug.

"The door slammed," Randy yelled, not waiting for anyone to ask him the correct questions. "It slammed and I couldn't open it."

"Randy, what were you doing in the basement? You know you're not allowed down there."

"No, I don't. Nobody said I couldn't go. I just thought I'd go look at the mother cat, because everybody thought I was telling a lie about her, but I wasn't."

"All right, you're forgiven this time, but Randy, if you ever do that again, I'll . . . I'll be very upset. NEVER do that again. NEVER! When I think what might have happened if you hadn't found you could open the door ... and if we'd had to tell your mother ..." She shuddered. "Now go into the painting room and make us a picture we can put on the wall."

The words worked like magic. The future Rembrandt ran off with alacrity.

"I can't thank you enough," Miss Gales said to me, sounding almost tearful. "You really saved us." Her short-fingered, pudgy hand came out and patted me. "You've done your good deed for the day, week and month." She turned to Michelle, who had been standing to the side and in front of me looking like a gathering storm. "And this is the girl who rescued the cat."

Something made me powerfully aware that Michelle was about to make hostile reference to Miss Gales approaching Clancy with a broom. Quickly, I put my hand on Michelle's arm and squeezed.

"Yes, this is Michelle," I said fatuously. "By the way, we—Michelle and I—have adopted the ginger cat and given him a new name. He's now called Clancy and lives with us in our house."

"Isn't that nice. You know," Miss Gales went on, displaying more sensitivity to atmosphere and vibrations than I would have given her credit for, "I didn't want to hurt the ... to hurt Clancy that day in the playground. I was just afraid that he might go after Randy or one of the other children. I am delighted to hear that he now lives with you."

"He stays mostly with Aunt Avril," Michelle said. "He likes her a lot, but he likes me, too."

"Come on, Michelle, time for us to be home." I put my hand on her arm to draw her out.

"Will Julian be there?" she asked.

"Probably."

"Your brother?" Miss Gales inquired politely.

"No, my cousin. Mine and Aunt Ginevra's. He's a lawyer."

"Lawyer?" The question, a single word, snapped hard as a shot.

165

"Quite harmless, I assure you," I said. "He spends his time worrying about corporate mergers," I continued soothingly. Why, I wondered, was I being so reassuring about Julian? Why should she care whether or not he was a lawyer? Was she expecting me to sue?

"See you tomorrow," I said to Miss Gales, propelling Michelle through the front door. "And keep an eye on Randy."

"We will. I'm thinking seriously of putting a long string around his waist," Miss Gales said, demonstrating more humor than I gave her credit for.

Julian wasn't downstairs when we got back to the house.

"He isn't here," Michelle said disappointedly.

"He doesn't seem to be. Maybe he changed his mind." But I was surprised. Julian struck me strongly as one who would be where he said he would be if at all possible. So what could have made it impossible?

"Are you going to paint?" Michelle asked.

"Yes. Would you like to come and sit for me?"

The blush that came so readily to her cheeks stained them red again. She was, I was beginning to see, very subject to anyone's show of interest.

"Yes," she said. "But could I go and play with Clancy first? Can I look in your room and see if he's there?"

"Sure." I fluffed her hair. She touched my arm. "Let's go on up."

But at that moment, just as we were a few steps up the staircase, Suzanne came out of her room. "Avril, has George called?"

"No, Suzanne. We were out for a while, but he didn't call before that? Hasn't he been in touch all day?"

"No." Her face looked drained and pinched, and her skin had an almost yellow pallor. "I thought he was supposed to go and see Julian. I tried to call him at his office to see if George had been there, but his secretary said he was out."

The obvious thing would have been to tell Suzanne that Julian had been most of the afternoon in my studio. And yet I said nothing. Even more curious, Michelle said nothing. "Oh, well," she said. "I shouldn't fuss. After all, he's a grown man perfectly capable of taking care of himself." She started to go back in and then looked up at Michelle and me, as though the fact that the two of us were together had struck her for the first time. The anxious look left her face. The lines around her mouth hardened. "Where have you two been?"

I said quickly, "I had to look for a little boy who had taken French leave from the school next door, and Michelle very kindly offered to help me. I am most grateful to her."

Somehow I thought this would placate her and remove the rigid look from her face, but it seemed to have the opposite effect, almost as though she were jealous. "Well, I have things for Michelle to do, as she very well knows, so I wish you would check with me before you take her away from the house."

"I didn't know you wanted me for something, Mom."

I had the curious impression that, far from being dismayed by Suzanne's criticism, Michelle was pleased, as though Suzanne's displeasure amounted to a mark of affection. Perhaps it did, I thought, in this strange, tangled mother-daughter relationship.

"It doesn't matter," Suzanne said.

"Sorry," Michelle said, sounding it.

"Where are you going now?" Suzanne asked her.

"To my room. I want to go to the bathroom."

"All right."

With an odd shrug of her shoulders, Suzanne went back into the room she and George shared.

As we arrived in front of Michelle's door I asked, "Are you coming upstairs now or do you want to make it later?"

"I want to use the bathroom and I want to see if Clancy is in my room or yours and play with him for a minute."

I smiled. "Okay. Come on up later."

I went on upstairs to my studio, my mind full of the new way I would approach Toby's painting, and stopped

167

dead on the threshold. Julian was in the studio, his coat flung over a chair, while he was down on one knee apparently going through my various sketches and paintings.

I opened my mouth to say something when he spoke. "These are good, really good."

"Praise will get you almost anything."

He looked at me. "I mean that. Why should I flatter you? Have I ever?"

I thought. "No, I'm bound to say you haven't. As a matter of fact . . ."

"Yes."

"I'm glad you think they're good." I was a little surprised at how true that was.

He got up. "Why? Don't you think I have any taste?"

It was such a casual question, yet I found it a string that pulled open a whole flood of thought. I had never thought of Julian as someone who might, or might not, have taste in painting, or in anything else, for that matter. I had thought of him solely as someone who did, or did not, flatter my father; who did, or did not, know about the forced adoption of my daughter; who was, or was not, as far as I was concerned, The Enemy. In other words, I had never thought of him at all except in relationship to my need. My therapist would have called it narcissistic. My mother, long years before, would have called it self-centered.

"What's the matter? Cat got your tongue?"

"You know," I said, suddenly. "I've always thought of you as The Enemy."

"You don't say?" he said dryly.

"I wonder why," I said thoughtfully.

"Because you always thought of your father as The Enemy. And since I was his gofer, chief cook and bottle washer, dog Friday, etcetera, it followed that I was, too."

"Were you?"

"Back to the old war! Yes, I think I was. For a while, anyway. Because, for all your father's short stature, he had a giantlike quality. He made me feel he was a man

168

who took hold of destiny and shaped it the way he wanted. When he had a mind to, he could charm the birds out of the trees. As a lawyer, he had the facility for taking the most antagonistic opponents, and getting them somehow to the place where they could at least talk and come to some agreement. That was his genius. He wasn't that good a trial lawyer. His sense of corporate structure was poor. But he was a whiz at making the lion lie down with the lamb."

Julian had been talking reminiscently. At that moment he turned towards me. "All except you. You were the grain of sand in his shoe that he couldn't get rid of, absorb, melt or swallow. You irritated him almost to distraction. He had come so far on his own enormous power and drive. He had forced everything to go the way he wanted it to. He had accomplished the long climb from his modest beginning as the son of a drugstore manager. He had married a Marchington, and sired a daughter who in looks and manner displayed, par excellence, what he called obsessively, the Marchington Inheritance. His feelings about that amounted to idolatry. And then came you. Every time he looked at you, it was like looking at the part of himself that he wanted to forget—"

"You don't have to tell me that," I interrupted. "I'd been in therapy a couple of years before it finally came to me that Father's dislike of the way I looked meant that he must have been walking around with a mountain of self-hatred. If he hated what he saw in the mirror, he hated what he saw when he looked at me."

"Yes," Julian said slowly. "He did." There was a pause. I strolled to the window and stared down through the dusk to the brightly lit playground.

"Avril—" Julian said suddenly.

There was a burst of singing from the school, sounding, by this time, somewhat less ragged than when I first heard it.

"Isn't it late for them to be there?" Julian asked. "It's almost six o'clock."

169

"Not really. Parents pick them up from two o'clock on. But some working mothers just can't make it before six, or even, in some cases, six-thirty."

"I don't see Randy down there."

"He isn't. He usually gets picked up a little earlier, although there have been times when he's stayed there until six-thirty."

A parent opened the school door and came out onto the playground, releasing a crescendo of singing from the open door.

"What's that song?" Julian asked.

"One of the international songs they're all going to sing at the UN tomorrow."

He swung around. "The UN? Tomorrow?"

"Yes. There's going to be some sort of ceremony or reception in honor of the treaty being signed today in Washington. You must have heard about it on the radio. Apparently Miss Sutherland was asked to bring the kids. Some of them are from UN families, you know."

"Why on earth didn't you tell me sooner?"

"Why should I? I mean, I wasn't hiding it from you. I just didn't think to mention it. Why is it so important all of a sudden?"

He didn't answer that, just turned back to the window and stared out. What I could see of his face looked tense and strained. "Who's that?" he said suddenly.

I looked down. Janet Sutherland, in corduroy pants and tweed jacket, was in the playground. "Good heavens!" I said. "I thought she was away. Although I suppose if she was going to take the kids to the UN tomorrow she'd have to come back."

"Who?"

"Janet Sutherland. That's right. You've never seen her. Well, there she is, the tall woman in pants and jacket."

Julian was peering down intently. "I wish I could get a closer look at her." He was silent for a minute. "How old would you say she is?"

170

"I don't know. Thirty maybe. At least from her face and figure she seems around that. But then I have to remember she's already gray."

"Gray! Her hair's black."

"It's colored. The other day she was bending over one of the kids—it was when the whole painting thing blew up and she was expressing her approval of the nonobjective and so on—anyway I was quite close to her at that moment and saw that at her hair parting the gray roots had grown out. Gray or white." I looked at Julian's steady, concentrated stare with some amusement. "That doesn't make her the scarlet woman, you know—coloring her hair. It's now common. Especially for people who get gray early. Out at Berkeley, I knew a kid of twenty-four who was completely gray. It's genetic."

Julian frowned. "I suppose so."

There was a knock at the door.

I turned. "Is that you, Michelle? Come in."

The door opened. Jessie's bent, square figure appeared. For the first time since I'd known her, the rough little Scotswoman looked frightened. "Miss Avril, Miss Marchington wants you to come down right away. There are two men, police officers, in the sitting room." She swallowed.

"What's happened, Jessie?" Julian asked.

"Oh, Mr. Julian, it's terrible. Mr. Petersen, he's dead. They say . . ." Into her round blue eyes sprang tears. "They say somebody's killed him."

CHAPTER 8

The two men were standing facing Aunt Ginevra, their backs to the door. Aunt Ginevra's face was towards me as I came in. When I saw it clearly I gave a cry. My aunt's face was colorless and drawn, her eyes and mouth sunken. She looked something she had never looked before—her age, and more.

"Avril," she said, her voice shaking. "Julian ... These officers have told me that ... George ... George is dead."

The men were now facing us. I felt as I had once when somebody on the hockey field had catapulted into my stomach. The breath was knocked out of me. The only one who seemed relatively calm was Julian, standing beside me, although he, too, looked pale.

"I'm Julian Demarest," he said. "Cousin and family lawyer. How is he dead?"

The shorter man said, "I'm Detective Sergeant Stein, this is Officer Williams." The taller man, a light-colored black, nodded. Sergeant Stein said, "His body has been found in Central Park. He was beaten, probably with a club or bat."

Suddenly George's face was in my mind—good-looking, immature, of late, strained. I had never liked him much, but now I felt a painful pity. "I hope ... I hope he didn't suffer too much. I mean, I hope that whatever hit him knocked him out."

"When did you last see him?"

"I guess at dinner last night. Have you told my sister, his wife?"

"We came to see her. She doesn't appear to be in and Miss Marchington doesn't know where she is. Do you?"

I shook my head.

"When did you see her?"

172

"An hour ago." I thought a minute. "Her daughter, Michelle, and I had been out. She—my sister—came out of her room as Michelle and I went upstairs and asked if we'd heard from George. I said we hadn't. She must have gone out immediately after that."

"Did she say where she was going?"

"No."

I saw the officer glance towards the door. Michelle was standing there. I wondered how much she heard.

"Michelle—" I started.

"What's happened?" she asked.

I went over to her. "Darling, I'm very sorry . . ."

"It's Daddy, isn't it?"

"How do you know that—is it Michelle?" Sergeant Stein said. He sounded kind without being sentimental. I found myself thinking he probably had children of his own.

"I don't know why I know. I just know. I knew something was going to happen to him."

"Michelle—" I said.

"Just a minute, miss," Sergeant Stein said, and he went over and stood in front of Michelle. "Sometimes we think things have happened when they really haven't. Like if somebody plans a movie treat, and then your brother or sister gets sick, somebody nearly always says, 'I knew that would happen.' But they don't really. They just mean that it was such a nice treat to look forward to, they were *afraid* it would happen. Do you understand what I mean?"

"Of course I understand what you mean. I'm not a baby. Let me think."

We waited in silence.

"I was *afraid*," she said, after a minute. "But I also knew. At least I think I did."

"Why?"

"He's been different."

"How different?"

There was another pause. "Sadder. Is he dead?"

The sergeant nodded. "Yes. I'm afraid so."

Michelle started to cry.

173

I put my hand on her shoulder. "Michelle dear—"

"Leave me alone," she said and moved away. Her sobs were coming in a dry, desolate way. I hadn't realized, I thought, how fond of her father she had been. There was a step in the door. I looked up. Toby stood there. "What's happened?" he asked, sounding foreign and extraordinarily like Suzanne. A light from nearby the door fell on his head glistening almost silver on his fair hair. The sight brought back a flash of memory: Suzanne talking to our father, smiling up at him, the light on her hair gleaming pale so that it was almost silver, the fine, straight nose tilted up a little.

"What's happened?" Toby repeated. Beside him Michelle rubbed the heel of her hands in her eyes. "Daddy's dead," she said.

Toby didn't cry. He went white. "Mummy?" he said.

"She's all right, Toby," I said. "I saw her just an hour ago."

At that moment, almost as though on cue, I heard the sound of a key in the front door. Then I heard the door open. All of us waited. Even Michelle seemed to hold her breath. Then I saw Suzanne's pale head in the hall. She took off her raincoat and came towards the sitting room.

"Hello, kids," she said, and then she saw the two men.

"Suzanne—" I started.

"Just a minute," Sergeant Stein said. And then, "Mrs. Petersen?"

She came to the door, glanced down at the children and put her hand on Toby's shoulder. "Yes?"

"We're from the police. I'm Detective Sergeant Stein. I'm sorry to have to tell you that your husband has been killed."

Like a taller, older version of her son, Suzanne didn't cry out. The color went out of her face and the lines seemed to deepen. She was forty years younger than Aunt Ginevra, yet at that moment, what my father was given to calling the Marchington Inheritance was very evident in the three of them, Aunt Ginevra, Suz-

174

anne and Toby. Michelle and I seemed as much out-siders as the police.

Finally Suzanne said, "Where? How?"

"Central Park. Beaten, I'm afraid," the sergeant said.

"Oh, my God!" The cry broke from her.

"When did you last see him?"

"Last night. He left this morning before I was up."

"You have no idea where he went when he left early this morning? Or the hour he left?" the sergeant asked.

Suzanne, her face drawn, her hands clenched a little, shook her head.

She and the two men looked at each other for a moment.

"Suzanne dear," Aunt Ginevra said, "wouldn't you like to sit down?"

"No, I'm all right. I'd rather stand."

"You and your husband lived in the Middle East these past years, I gather," the sergeant said.

Suzanne nodded. "Yes."

"Did your husband come back here to take a new job?"

"No. Not exactly... He was, of course, considering several offers."

"Did he have any enemies that you know of?"

"No. Why should he?" Suzanne said. I knew at that moment that she was lying. Whether this was merely sisterly intuition, or whether the policemen would pick up what was obvious to me, I didn't know.

"Well, the answer to why should he, Mrs. Petersen, is that he had at least one enemy—the person, or may-be persons—who killed him."

"You say it was Central Park," Suzanne stated.

The sergeant nodded.

"Well it's hardly a secret—everybody in the world knows about Central Park—that people get mugged, stabbed, killed, assaulted there all the time."

There was a sob behind me. "Oh, poor Daddy, poor Daddy." The tears were rolling down Michelle's round face. Toby and Suzanne were both white-faced, but

175

tearless. Michelle gave a rather noisy sob. "Oh, poor Daddy," she repeated.

"Please, Michelle," Suzanne spoke sharply.

"Perhaps she loved her father." Aunt Ginevra's words carried an undertone that stopped Suzanne with her mouth half open.

Curiously, much as I was used to criticizing my sister, I understood that Suzanne's brusqueness sprang from taut nerves rather than cruelty. Aunt Ginevra's comment, with all its implication, obviously flicked her on the raw. I saw a blaze of something in Suzanne's eyes. Then it went out. She hesitated for a second, then went over to Michelle, put her arm around the thick shoulders and said in a much kinder voice, "I'm truly sorry, darling. I know how you feel."

Michelle took her hands away from her face, revealing wet, smudged cheeks. "No, you don't," she said. "You didn't love him at all. And Toby didn't. Just me."

Suzanne snatched her arm away as though it had been burned. "That's not true, and you have no right to say it!" She was going to go on but she caught herself and stood, silent, facing the policemen, who were watching the whole scene with absorbed interest.

Suzanne said to the sergeant, "You have absolutely no idea who did it?"

"None. Which is why we thought you could help us. I realize this is a bad time. But there's no question about it. The sooner we have some idea of who might be behind this, and what the motive is, the sooner we can catch him—or them."

"Well, surely motive is no great mystery. As I said before, people are robbed in Central Park all the time. It's thick with thieves."

"Unfortunately, that's true. But I don't think in this case it applies. Your husband had on him some eighty dollars in cash and was wearing a valuable watch and gold cuff links. Neither the money nor the jewelry was taken."

"Perhaps the thieves were surprised before they had a chance to rob him."

"Perhaps. It seems unlikely." The sergeant's voice was even and pleasant, but his dark eyes were watchful and rather hard. "But the person—a jogger—who came on your husband's body and who notified us said there was no one there."

"Someone else could have come across the people robbing George and scared them away."

"But why shouldn't that first person—that hypothetical first person—have notified us?"

"I have no idea. That really is your department, not mine, detective-sergeant."

Suzanne, I thought, with grudging admiration, had not only managed to wiggle out of the corner the sergeant had placed her in, she had succeeded in sounding like injured innocence and virtue while so doing.

But the sergeant was not stupid either. "Yes, it is, Mrs. Petersen, which is why I'm pretty certain that your husband's murder did not have robbery for a motive. Which leaves us with the question: What was the motive? I wonder if you would mind answering some questions about your more recent years abroad."

"Yes I would," Suzanne said. "I think that this moment, when I . . . when my children and I . . . have barely had time to absorb the dreadful news you have brought, is not the time to go probing into our family life. You'll excuse me, please. Michelle, Toby, I want us to go upstairs."

I thought for a minute the detective would object. An even harder look came into his eyes. But after a fraction of a second, he nodded. "Very well. We'll be in touch later. Please accept our most sincere regrets for what has happened."

Suzanne received his condolence with a slight nod. Then, a hand on the shoulder of each child, driving them in front of her, she started to leave the room.

"One last question, Mrs. Petersen."

Suzanne, at the door, half turned.

"You were out when we arrived. Yet, according to your sister, you'd been in an hour before that. Could you tell me where you were?"

177

"Certainly, sergeant. I went to a local drugstore to buy some shampoo."

"Couldn't you have had it sent?"

"I needed the air. Is there anything else?"

"Not at the moment."

When Suzanne left, shepherding her children, the sergeant glanced at the rest of us. Aunt Ginevra, looking unhappy, was sitting on the edge of her chair, her black shoes meeting at her toes, her hands folded on her lap.

"I'm very sorry, Miss Marchington," the sergeant said.

"Yes," Aunt Ginevra said. "Thank you."

He looked at me and said, "Could I ask you a few questions?"

"Sure." I sat down on the end of the sofa. "Go ahead."

"I gather from Miss Marchington that your sister and brother-in-law arrived recently from the Middle East."

I thought back, and was astonished to realize it was only twenty-six days. It felt like two months at least. "They arrived on the twelfth of last month." Hastily I counted once more on my fingers. That makes it twenty-six days.

"How did they seem?"

"What do you mean?"

"I mean, were they like always, like they've always been? Were they different in any way?"

"I'm a bad person to ask, Sergeant Stein," I said, a little more brusquely than I intended, reacting, I think, to his steady, probing gaze. "I hadn't seen my sister and brother-in-law for about twelve years. And even before that, my sister and I weren't really close."

"Maybe not. But you'd know if she looked different, wouldn't you?" He paused.

"Well..." I was seeing George's face, the day he arrived. He had always been handsome. But one reason I had never warmed to him was that his face had always, to me, borne the arrogant patina of the successful corporate executive. But this time that patina, except for brief flashes, was gone, and with it the assurance

178

that had so often set my teeth on edge. In fact, he had almost seemed in a daze... except that that also was not quite the right description.

"He was different," I said. "He'd always been very assured. This time, he... he seemed off in a world of his own half the time."

"In those twenty-six days, what did he do?"

"I assumed he looked for a job." I looked over towards Julian. "He seemed extremely anxious to see you, I remember."

"Yes." Julian's brows were drawn almost down over his nose. He glanced up at the sergeant. "We'd gone to the same school and knew a lot of the same people."

"What kind of work did he do?"

"He was in computers for a while, also in oil. But I'm not sure he wasn't about to try something else. He implied to me he was."

"So you saw him?"

"Yes, we had lunch together several days ago."

"Did he leave his job voluntarily or get fired?" The question had a sharp edge, like a slap.

"As I said before," Julian replied, his voice calm, "he was more than ready for a change. I think he and his family were tired of being in that part of the world and wanted to come home."

"I heard he was fired," the sergeant said.

Julian looked at him. "Who told you that?"

"I did," Aunt Ginevra said. "Before you came down."

Julian shrugged. "Why were you so anxious to hide it?" the sergeant asked Julian.

"I'm the family lawyer. It is part of my business to protect the family as much as possible from unpleasantness. To have it broadcast in the press that George had been let go would not help the family in any way, as far as I can see."

"What difference can it make?" I said. "Heaven knows all his ex-colleagues must know the facts."

"Exactly," the sergeant said, turning towards me. I could almost feel the warmth of his approval. "Why was he fired?"

179

"I don't know. I never asked."

"Not even your sister?"

"Least of all my sister. I told you. We are not close."

"What would your guess be?"

"I don't think I ought to guess on a thing like this. A man's reputation should *not* hang on a guess." I could feel the withdrawal of the sergeant's approval.

"So you have no idea why he was let go?" the sergeant questioned again.

Julian got up. "Since truth seems to be the order of the day, then I would say too great a dedication to the executive lunch, and not enough to the nitty-gritty of getting a job done."

"Do you mean he drank?"

"He was certainly not a teetotaller."

"Just where in the Middle East did he spend most of his time?" the sergeant said.

"I don't know," I said.

The sergeant turned towards Aunt Ginevra. She looked wretchedly unhappy. "I'm afraid I don't know either."

"He was all over." Julian shoved his hands in his pockets. "Arabia, Egypt, Iran, Syria, Lebanon—the works, even Turkey, I think."

"But his family didn't follow him to all those places."

"No. I think they were in Cairo."

The sergeant paused. Then he said slowly, "Your brother-in-law was not in any way connected with that big meeting taking place today in Washington, was he? I mean did he have any government or diplomatic status?"

I was astonished at his question. The meeting to sign the new treaty between Israel and a covey of Arab chieftains was something that diplomats from both sides, to say nothing of the U.S., had been scurrying around and arranging for more than six months. Each night on television news there was a breathless report as to whether peace was on or off and who was yielding what to whom. To imply that George's tiresome and

180

rather sad job problems could have anything to do with that seemed almost insulting.

"Good heavens, Sergeant Stein," I said. "That treaty is in a different league. I mean that's really important. The peace of the world could hang on it."

"I know that, Miss Marchington," the sergeant said dryly. "Officer Williams and I have many discussions about it."

The rather austere face of the tall black broke into a charming smile. "We have somewhat different views," he said.

"But we have exactly the same view that the security around that meeting should be perfect. If anything happened to the signers..."

If anything happened to the signers... No matter who got killed, I thought, it would be our fault for not preventing it. How happily our nonfriends would point out that the U.S. was a country of assassinations. Ten years before, when I was busy marching and making as much of a nuisance of myself as possible, how eager I would have been to point that out... And all of a sudden, I saw in my mind's screen, Randy Ferris, his little chest stuck out, promising, for the sake of the country, not to tell how he had been locked away ... Randy Ferris, now there was a mystery that was worthy of the detective's time and attention.

And wasn't George? A stab of pity for my brother-in-law went through me. But the drift of my thoughts made it plain to me that I agreed with Suzanne: Tragic as George's death was, I didn't think it very mysterious. He had fallen prey to an ordinary, if murderous, mugger who had been frightened away before he could take what he had killed to get.

Glancing up, I caught Julian's eye and found him staring at me in a rather intent way.

"All right," Sergeant Stein said. "I guess that will be all for the moment. I'll be by tomorrow to talk to Mrs. Petersen." He turned to Julian. "We need someone formally to identify the body. Could you?"

181

"Yes. Is he in the morgue?"

The sergeant nodded.

"I'll be there tomorrow morning."

To my surprise, Suzanne and her children came down to the dining room for dinner. And Julian had been asked to stay. Of the three Petersens, Toby seemed the least affected by what had occurred. Always quiet, he seemed little more subdued than usual, but kept glancing at his mother in a worried way. Suzanne had brushed her light hair and freshened her makeup, which, with her, was not a sign of indifference, but automatic. Around the carefully drawn blush strokes over her cheekbones, her skin was so colorless it was almost sallow—her one physical imperfection. And her lines were more pronounced, making her look her age instead of ten years younger, as she usually did. There was strain, tension, anxiety on her face, but, as far as I could see, no grief.

Grief in all its least winsome forms was all over Michelle's face—reddened nose and eyes, tear-blotched cheeks and a repetitive sniffle. Her square face behind the glasses looked even less attractive than usual. Yet in a way that had not happened before, something about her touched me and wrung my heart. Since she was across the table from me there was nothing I could do without calling attention to her, which I felt would be no kindness, so I kept my eyes on her until, a few minutes later, she looked up and our eyes met. I smiled. Her well-shaped lips wavered into a smile. Then her eyes brimmed over. It seemed strange that the only mourner for such a smooth, good-looking prep school product as George should be this cumbersome waif.

"My dear," Aunt Ginevra said suddenly. "I am so terribly sorry. It is so dreadful. Is there anything at all I can do? Anything any of us can do?"

Suzanne, who had barely touched her roast beef said, "Thank you, Aunt Ginevra. There's nothing, I'm afraid. It is tragic . . . Poor George . . . I do hope . . . never mind."

Michelle suddenly started to cry again.

Suzanne looked at her. Then got up, went over to Michelle and bent over her. "Would you rather be upstairs, darling, or do you want to stay here?" It was a kind gesture and meant to comfort. Yet it was not quite real. Which probably explained why Michelle suddenly pushed her chair back, shoving it against her mother, and, with another sob, ran from the room.

Suzanne stood there for a moment, watching her leave. Then she started after her.

Before I had even had time to think, out of my mouth there popped, "Why don't you leave her alone for a while? It will probably do her good just to let go and cry."

Suzanne stared at me, gathering anger on her face. "Anyone would think—" she started. Then she went back to her seat and sat down.

"Look," I said. "I didn't mean to interfere."

"Yes, you did," Suzanne said. "And just for the record, I find it intrusive and impertinent."

"It's jolly well none of your business." Toby's voice had suddenly taken on an English accent. I looked up in sudden surprise and encountered a hostile stare.

I could think of one or two answers, but I said, "Sorry," in my most noncommittal voice.

"I think Avril was just expressing her understanding of how Michelle feels," Aunt Ginevra said, looking both unhappy and a little indignant. Bless her loyal old heart, I thought.

"By the way," she said brightly, "I suddenly remembered who ... whom that headmistress—Miss Sutherland, isn't it?—made me think of. It's Louise Carteret. It's really quite strange and makes we wonder if there's any relationship there. Of course, our cousin—"

My mind slid away. Aunt Ginevra was obviously trying to keep the conversation off explosive and emotionally loaded areas and on the safe, even soporific, subject of family relationships where she could meander happily for hours. Blessed are the peacemakers, I thought, and felt my own tensions relax somewhat. But a minute or so later I was brought up sharp when I heard Julian say to Suzanne,

"I don't want to harry you at a time like this, but would you feel like talking a little about George?"

"Julian?" Aunt Ginevra started.

"No, Aunt, it's all right," Suzanne said. "I don't mind." She looked at Julian somewhat warily. "That is, within reason. What is it you want to know or talk about?"

"I gathered from George himself during the lunch we had together that you had some debts and so forth. But before he told me what happened to his job, somebody came up to the table who knew us both and sat down more or less uninvited, and that was that. I feel extremely remiss at not having seen him again, but of course I thought there was plenty of time. What did happen? About the job I mean."

"Oh, it was one of those political things, political within the firm, that is," she said very quickly. "George was a little too intelligent for some of the higher-ups back here, and the only way they could cover up their own idiocies was to get rid of him."

Now she's openly admitting he was fired, I thought, instead of the line about wanting to come back. However, I couldn't blame her for trying to put her best foot forward for her husband. Nevertheless, and with all the marks in the world for wifely partisanship, it didn't sound like the truth, anymore than George's lame reasons.

Julian looked at her thoughtfully.

"I have a feeling there's more to it than that."

"Why do you say that?"

"Because the man who rushed up at lunch and stuck around so long was a top man in the oil industry. There isn't anybody of any importance either here or in the Middle East that he doesn't know. He has plenty of money, holdings in key firms here and abroad, and a lot of clout. If he wanted to put himself on the line for George, there aren't many companies that would refuse him. Which is why I gave him such a big hello when

184

he rolled up. He and I usually exhaust everything we have to say to one another in the first three minutes of conversation, but I thought that Providence was really putting itself out for old George. But if George was grateful, he sure didn't show it. He was polite, but that was about all. When the oil guy clapped him on the back and said, 'Let's have lunch,' I thought George's problems were over. But all George said was, 'Sure, I'll call you.' It was the damnedest thing I ever saw. It was as though he were in some kind of a daze. The moment the guy left he said to me, 'When can I see you again?' I told him he'd have to wait because I was going to be off for a couple of days. And then that stretched, and I was in a hurry when I got back so didn't return his messages."

Julian glanced at Suzanne. "I feel as guilty as hell, too. What was on his mind, Suzanne?"

Suzanne was sitting in an odd, tense pose. "Nothing, Julian He . . . he was just upset and wanted somebody to talk to."

"Well, you were there."

"We . . ." She looked at Toby, spooning up the last of his dessert, his gray eyes on his mother. "Run along upstairs, darling," she said. "I want to talk to Cousin Julian."

"About Daddy?"

"About our affairs, Mr. Nosy. Now go!"

Toby grinned and slid out of the chair. A couple of hours before he had been informed that his father was dead. But there was nothing whatever in his manner to indicate that he had suffered any kind of major blow. Something made me say, "Aren't you sorry about your father, Toby?"

For the first time since I'd met him, I saw his cheeks stain pink.

"'Course," he said gruffly.

Julian spoke. "Did you care for your father, Toby?"

"I told you, of course. It's just that—"

"He's been away an awful lot in the last couple of

185

years," Suzanne said. "And before that he was busy a large part of the time."

"Anyway," Toby said. "He didn't like me much. The way Mummy doesn't like Michelle."

Suzanne swung around on him. "How dare you say that, Toby? It's wicked."

"No, it isn't. It's true. I know it is. I heard you and Daddy talking about it."

"Go to your room at once," Suzanne said.

"—and you said that if you hadn't been forced to take—"

"That's enough!" Julian snapped. "Do as your mother says."

"Take what, who?" I asked.

There was a queer silence that lasted about fifteen seconds, which can seem a very long time. "He's simply saying the first thing that comes into his head," Suzanne said. She glanced at Toby, who was looking mulish. "Now go to your room or I will punish you."

"You can't do that," Toby replied. "You can't punish me just after my father's died."

For the first time since the beginning of dinner Aunt Ginevra spoke. "I'm afraid that justification comes a little strangely from you, Toby. You have shown us how little you care."

"I told you—"

Abruptly Suzanne got up, reached her son in one stride, whirled him around and pushed him out of the room, closing the door as she did so. Then she came and sat down again.

Aunt Ginevra rose. "Why don't you have coffee in the living room? Jessie can bring it in. I'm very tired and I'm going to bed."

She looked worse than tired, I thought. She looked ill.

"I'll come up with you, Aunt," I said.

"No. Thank you, Avril. You're a good child. But I'd rather be by myself." Gathering up her shawl with a hand that shook, she said, "I never knew George well
186

or was close to him. But it is a terrible thing that has happened to him. Terrible."

Julian moved to the door. "Good night, Cousin Ginevra. Please try to sleep."

Aunt Ginevra stopped. "You've always been very indulgent towards me, Julian. I don't know why. But I love you for it." And she kissed his cheek, receiving his kiss in exchange.

When she left, the three of us were looking at each other, waiting for the first to make some move or remark, when Jessie marched in with a huge tray.

"Coffee in the lounge," she said dourly.

"We can have it in here, Jessie," I said. "If that would be easier."

"It would not. I want to get the table cleared. Have it in the sittin' room."

We followed Jessie upstairs into the living room, looking, I thought, for a moment like three sulky teenagers.

"I don't know why I'm drinking this," Suzanne said, taking a sip out of her demitasse. "I'll never get to sleep at this rate."

Julian stirred his coffee, took a swallow, and then sat looking down at it. "George was in trouble, wasn't he, Suzanne?"

"I don't know what—"

"Don't be disingenuous, Suzanne. We've known each other far too long. George had got himself into some kind of trouble and was being blackmailed. I'm pretty sure of that much. But I'm willing not to tell the police if I can be sure that it's not necessary."

There was another silence. Then Suzanne said, "If you're sure of that, why didn't you make more of an effort to see him? Maybe he would still be alive."

Spoken like the old Suzanne, I thought. She had always been expert at deflecting responsibility.

"If you really think that," Julian said, putting down his cup, "then you don't believe your own assertion about George's attacker being your run-of-the-mill

187

mugger. You believe there's a connection between his being blackmailed and his death."

Suzanne stood up. "I really don't feel like discussing this today. After all, it was only a few hours ago that . . . I think I'm going to bed."

Julian stood up, too. "Suzanne, stop playing games."

She spun around. "What do you mean by that?"

"I mean that the only person who is really grieving over George—poor bastard—is Michelle. There hasn't been much between you for some time now. That his death is a shock, I can believe. That it is a terrible emotional blow to you, I don't. If we don't talk about it now, then you're going to have to talk about it to the police. George is—or was—a prominent man. They're going to have to dig. Do you want everything to come out?"

"Won't it anyway?" I was astonished at the bitterness in her voice.

"Not necessarily. But you're going to have to be candid with me."

"Why you, Julian?"

"Because I'm your family lawyer, because I was here when the police were, and because I think I know something of what was going on."

They faced each other. Finally, Suzanne's body seemed to go less rigid. She sat down again. There was a short silence. Julian looked at Suzanne, and in his usually hard gray eyes there was both pity and kindness.

It was hard for me to get up and say what I knew I had to, but I managed it. "Shall I go? Suzanne, would you rather talk to Julian alone?"

She looked up and across at me. "Since you've always hated me, you might as well stay and get your enjoyment out of it."

"Enjoyment?"

"Yes. How-are-the-mighty-fallen kind of enjoyment."

"Schadenfreude."

"German's never been one of my languages."

"It means pleasure in somebody else's misery."

188

Suzanne looked down at her hands. She was now thirty-four years old. Her hair owed some of its silvery lightness to art, but her figure was as slim as ever, her eyes as blue, her face as firm and smooth as when we were ten and fifteen years younger. She had been the success, I the failure. She was right about one thing, I had always crowed whenever she had stubbed her foot. But, curiously, I felt no pleasure now, no spiteful justification for all the years when she was the golden girl and I was the lump of lead. "You know, Suzanne, I really don't feel satisfaction at your problems. Quite why, I don't know. I'm sorry—whatever they were. What was it? Did old George have a girl on the side?"

She gave me a bitter smile. "You're pretty naïve, aren't you? Just as I was. Not a girl, Avril. A boy. Several, in fact."

It took me a minute to know what she was talking about. "*George?* You mean George was a homosexual?"

"Yes. I mean just that."

"And you knew this when you married him?"

"Of course not. I wouldn't have married him if I'd known, or had any idea. He always seemed to me your fourteen-karat all-American business boy on the rise."

I sat down this time.

Julian spoke. "Did George know about himself when you were married?"

Wearily Suzanne shook her head. "No. At least not consciously. Any ... any experiences he may have had along that line he put down to adolescent confusion. Something every boy went through—particularly if he went to one of those all-boy prep schools. We really only talked about it once, I mean discussed it rationally. I'm afraid there were times when I flung it at his head ..." And Suzanne put her hands up to her face and began to cry.

Julian got up and went over to her, sitting on the arm of the chair she was in. He put his arm around her. "Self-reproaches aren't going to do you or anybody else any good. It can't have been easy for you."

Suzanne took her hands away and pulled a hand-

189

kerchief out of her sleeve. "Thanks, Julian. It wasn't. I just wish I hadn't—but as you say, it's no use."

"I'm sorry to have to talk about all this, but it is important. When did you discover all this?"

"When we were in Cairo. And by the oldest, tritest of methods. Somebody—I could never find out who—dropped an envelope by our house addressed to me. In it were a snapshot of George and a terribly attractive young boy, dark, Arab-looking—obviously a Middle Easterner of some kind. They weren't *doing* anything...but by the way they were looking at each other, it was just obvious. And in case I had missed the point, a typewritten sheet of paper said that if George didn't do as he had been asked to, this would be sent to one of the local papers that was bitterly opposed to American interests..." Suzanne blew her nose and stared down at her handkerchief.

"Did you talk to George about it?"

"Yes, but not for a while. You see...when I first saw...saw the picture, and read the paper, two quite opposite things happened immediately. One was, a lot of the things in the marriage were explained, and the other was I was quite sure that it couldn't possibly be true. I know it sounds crazy..."

"Not entirely...wasn't it the Red Queen who said she could believe twelve impossible things before breakfast?"

In a funny way, Julian was trying to help Suzanne, and his quip did wring a wry smile from her. "Well," she went on, "for about four days I had myself absolutely convinced that it was impossible. The thing is, we *looked* such a perfect couple...I can't tell you the number of women who were quite open about their envy, and equally open in trying to attract George. And he adored playing up to the them. I mean he was *the* cavalier, and in a very virile, macho way. So what that wretched communication said had to be a lie...And then four days later, for no reason whatsoever that I could think of, I suddenly knew it was not a lie. It was as though I had blotted one side of my mind out, and then done a switch. And now the fact that it was impossible was blotted out. I say nothing happened. Actually what happened had happened so often that I didn't think of it as anything special. George came home from a trip and slept in the spare bedroom. He was given to migraine headaches... or anyway, he said he was given to migraine headaches... or he had a touch of the bug, or the tourista or Egypt tummy, or something. And I never questioned it because..." Suzanne unfolded the wet handkerchief and looked at it, then folded it again.

"Because there was somebody else for you," Julian said, not questioning but stating.

"Yes. You see"—she looked up at both of us—"it was very hard to take... George's... well... lack of interest."

"So you did your thing and he did his, and neither of you inquired too closely into what the other was doing."

"Yes."

Julian got up and walked around the room for a minute or two. I was too stunned to make any comment, and I was also terribly sorry for Suzanne. The golden girl who married the golden boy—and then this. I looked across at her and she looked back at me: two sisters, their defenses, for the moment, down. It was probably the first time in our lives together that we looked at each other without a barrage of those defenses, expectations, angers and resentments standing in the way. Expectations... the word stuck in my mind. Was that what went wrong with everybody, everywhere? My expectations of my father? His of me? Suzanne's of George?

In the silence of that stripped-down moment between us, I said, "Were you in love with George when you married him?"

"I thought I was." She gave me an ironic look. "That was nineteen sixty-eight. Do you remember nineteen sixty-eight, Avril? You were busy making your personal political statement that year, in Chicago, among other places, where you were raising the clenched fist and going to jail. Our cousin, Charles Carteret, heir to one of the West Coast's richest fortunes, was kidnapped that year, and never heard from afterwards. So I, too, made a statement, only it was so lost in white satin and orange blossoms that it didn't look like a statement. It looked like the society wedding of the year."

"Are you trying to tell me that you married George because of me? I won't buy that."

"No, I'm not trying to tell you that. But George Petersen, young businessman of the year, combined what our father admired most—executive ability along with a family of the same blue-blooded strain as the Marchingtons. If you and Father had ever had a normal conversation, you would have learned that for all his romantic feelings over, quote, old family, close quote, he found most of them, the male members, from a business point of view, an inept lot. Then along came George, trailing his quarterings and rising in the business world as though he were some pushy type from the boondocks. And George was paying attention to me, so Father pushed his suit whenever he got a chance. But no, I was not falling down dead in a faint love with George. He was a terrific escort and bright and funny. But even then his lovemaking lacked a certain conviction. And I was still thinking it over when our family made the front pages on two counts—you and Cousin Charles. At the end of that week Father looked about ten years older. So I accepted George's proposal. I don't mean," Suzanne said a little bitterly, "that I did this as a personal sacrifice. I told you, I liked George. But I did do it after that week."

"'Though I give my body to be burned and have not love...'" Julian murmured.

"I did love him," Suzanne said. "I just meant I wasn't madly in love with him. There's a difference. And even then, it might... but after that... and anyway there was the business in Cairo... But I wondered then, if things had been different... maybe George... maybe he wouldn't have..."

192

"What do you mean, Suzanne?" I asked. "What are you talking about?"

Julian suddenly stood up from the arm of Suzanne's chair and faced her. "Are you quite sure you want to go on with this conversation?"

"Yes," Suzanne said. And all of a sudden I could see she was shaking. I thought for a minute that fear or distress had overcome her. But it wasn't either. Suzanne was shaking with anger. She stood up. "I've tried, God knows I've tried. The marriage could have worked. I could have made him happy. But then Father came along with that huge hunk of money. And, of course, we were in debt. We were always in debt. But he would pay everything, plus a big lump sum, if we would just do this one thing for him . . . I told George not to accept. I begged him not to . . ."

"Suzanne, wait," Julian said. "Think about it first."

"No. I'm not going to think about it. You know what that money was for, Avril? Guess!"

I knew even before the words came out of her mouth.

"To adopt your bastard child. George made me take her. So we took her, and we got the money, and things have been getting worse ever since."

CHAPTER 9

Curiously, the first thought that occurred to me was wonder that I hadn't guessed myself long before. The signs could hardly have been more obvious.

I let out my breath in a long sigh.

"Michelle," I said.

"Yes, Michelle." Suzanne gave a funny laugh. "I somehow thought that if I gave her a name like that and brought her up abroad, I could turn her into somebody who would have been my daughter."

"Delicate and stylish, instead of a lump with glasses." I was now the one who was shaking with anger. I had gone to so much trouble to bury my father, to push him and the memory of him out of my life forever. And now there he was, back. The mess that we were all in, his handiwork. No child of his must be permitted to have and bring up an illegitimate child. But then it would not suit him to have the child put anonymously up for adoption, so that he would not be able to keep tabs on her. What would Michelle have been like if I had brought her up?

"Oh, my God!" I said. I went to the chimneypiece and put my elbows on it and my face in my hands. Poor Michelle, with her self-loathing and her vulnerability and her spiky defenses and frequent disagreeableness. Might all of that have been different? In my ever ready mind's eye another version of Michelle took shape: short, still, but slender, the square face softened to an oval, the glasses removed, the churlishness absent.

"Before you go into an orgy of might-have-been, Avril," Julian said, with an accuracy of reading my mind that made me jump, "just remember that if your father had not taken your baby away, you might be

194

dead by now of an overdose, and your child with you, or be living some kind of a zombie life in a West Coast commune with Michelle already smoking pot with her peers. Your father didn't mean well by you at all, but he may have saved your life and your reason—and Michelle—by doing what he did. His abduction of Michelle gave you what you needed to break out of that disastrous rut you were in. All that rage and adrenaline in your system had the healthy effect of sending you on a long search and chase, for which you had to remain rational, and finally put you in a good sanitarium where you finally recovered. I think it's a moot point whether the joys and gratifications of unhampered motherhood would have done the same. Michelle may not have lived the best possible life, but it's a fifty-fifty bet that the life she has had was a better one than the one she would have had with you, at least at that point in your career."

The anger was like a great animal inside me, clawing and tearing to get out. At that moment I would, if I could, have been happy to kill Julian. Of all the things thronging and pushing in my mind, I managed to get out only one: "You knew."

"Yes, I knew."

"So you lied to me. You told me you had no idea what happened to my child."

"Technically, I didn't lie. I never said I didn't know what happened to your child. I said your father never told me, which was true. George told me shortly after the adoption when I visited him and Suzanne in Europe. But although I thought that the way your father carried out his scheme was brutal, it seemed to me at the time the best thing to do, for the sake of everybody concerned. I could have been wrong. Perhaps I was. But I had to consider not only you, but Michelle herself and Suzanne here. There was also the little matter of my promise to your father. When he discovered I knew what had happened to Michelle, he asked me to promise not to tell you—again for your sake as much as hers."

I was having a reaction I hadn't experienced in

years. My heart was pounding in my chest, I had broken out in a sweat on my body. And I was afraid I would lose control and pick up the nearest heavy object and crack Julian's skull with it. "All this time, through all my pain, you could have told me, and you didn't."

"No, I didn't. And given the same circumstances, I'd probably make the same decision again." He and I looked at each other. "When your father went out to the coast and brought the child back, nobody had any idea that you would break free of drugs. On the whole, and given the statistics of other young pill addicts, you probably wouldn't. Addicted mothers have been known to addict their own children. For all we know, Michelle could have been affected when you were carrying her. If she was adopted by people nobody knew, whose identification was protected, they could have discovered that she was the child of an addicted mother, and they might have decided to return her to the adoption agency. Your father thought of that angle. He was tyrannical and domineering, and he manipulated everyone according to his will. But he was not inhumane. He thought he was doing the best possible thing for your child. But he also thought that if you had any knowledge of where she was, you'd not only make your sister and brother-in-law's life miserable, but your own child's as well. You weren't exactly in a state to be a fit mother. And Suzanne was."

I walked over to the window and stared out into the night, trying, somehow, to encompass and contain my anger.

"And George was very sweet with her," Suzanne said in anticlimax. "He was probably the only person who just liked her for herself."

"And not for the money Daddy paid him to take her?"

"No. George wasn't mercenary. He got into debt because he wasn't thrifty either. He liked to gamble. He liked not to count the cost. By adopting Michelle he was able to pay off the debt. But you're being unfair to him if you think this affected how he felt. And then, later, Michelle was the only one who showed him any

196

affection. It wasn't all a waste." There was almost a pleading note in her voice.

I started to go out of the room.

"Where are you going?" Julian asked.

"I'm going up to see Michelle, my daughter." The words "my daughter" had strange power. It had been so long since I had said them aloud.

"To tell her that she is your daughter? And that the one person in the family she thought really loved her—her father—took her in for money?"

I stopped, halfway to the door.

"Before you go up and spill the beans and have a tearful mother-daughter reunion, think about something. Everything you've ever done has been a reaction. That whole political nonsense that you were involved in did not, I'm certain now and was then, spring from profound ideological principles. You were getting back at your socially aspiring father. You never did anything entirely for its own sake until you started to paint. Even that long quest for your daughter was partly to undo what your father had done. If you go up now and tell Michelle the whole miserable story, it'll be out of more of the same motive. Michelle's good will not be a high priority. She's not happy now. She's been yanked out of whatever she's known and been put down over here. She's just lost her father, who may have taken her for money, but who really cared for her. But do you think in the present state of affairs she'll remember that? Avril, you've always been pigheaded and self-centered. For once in your life try and see something from someone else's point of view before you go and carelessly destroy her life."

I continued walking out of the room. Even to answer Julian would have given some credence to what he said. When I started upstairs I was already planning how I would break the news to Michelle that I was her mother. By the time I reached the hall outside Michelle's bedroom I knew that I was not—at least right now—going to tell her. Behind my fury over what Julian had said, some small voice was trying to tell me that, dreadful as he was, he might, by some accident, have been telling the truth.

Instead I went on up to my own room and started walking around it. After a while—I don't know how long—I knew I could not bear the terrible confusion of thoughts that poured in and out of my head. So I turned on a small television set I had and proceeded to watch it numbly, hour after hour. Vaguely I was waiting for the endless news shows to finish so I could settle mindlessly into an old-fashioned chase or whodunnit—the kind of movies that were made in the thirties, forties and fifties and are now shown for insomniacs at two, three, and even four in the morning. I had always found such films a reliable narcotic for pain, or, when I had something to work out and chew over, enough of a distraction to engage the upper surface of my mind and leave the rest of my brain free to work out my puzzle. But tonight my search for a distracting film seemed doomed to failure. Changing channels did no good. They all were completely preoccupied with the historic treaty signing in Washington. Getting up for the second and third times I changed stations only to find a different newscaster with the same story: ". . . . the culmination of weeks and months of negotiations and hopes, the signing of which tomorrow will bring peace that generations of Middle Easterners have sought. . . ." I switched to another channel. ". . . The Arab leaders arrived in New York late tonight, and the Israeli prime minister will come up from Washington tomorrow for the celebration at the UN. Our correspondent at the UN—"

Unwillingly, a captive audience, I watched the preliminaries of the Big Event, knowing that anything was better than being alone with myself. The screen was filled with crowds pressing around tall Arab representatives, their cloth headdresses rising above the heads of many around them, police holding back crowds, angry demonstrators across the street, placards held up to the camera: *The Land Belongs to the Palestinians* . . . Suddenly there was a scuffle, other demonstrators who had been out of range of the camera burst through a line of police and threw themselves at the Palestine supporters. There were shouts and shrieks. The police waded in ...

It all seemed weirdly familiar. Julian, whom (I told myself) I would never forgive as long as I lived, I conceded to be right about one thing: Politics had for me been a useful vehicle for my resentment. When I finally learned that, my political activism was over. But how the milling around on the television screen brought those days back!

"That angry feelings are far from appeased," intoned the anchorman, "is obvious. Yet there is belief that following one failure after another, one summit meeting after another, after Camp David One and Camp David Two, the four men who among them control peace or war along the eastern littoral of the Mediterranean have achieved more progress than any of us dreamed could be possible ..."

The Arabs were a picturesque bunch, I thought, as the robed men, their dark profiles turned to the camera, walked majestically into their hotel. A shriek and what sounded like the backfiring of a truck somewhere off camera brought the swathed heads around. Somehow all that headgear made them look alike ... or did it? Hadn't I seen that young-looking man before somewhere? That powerful curved nose, the dark eyes under heavy brows?

Because I was a portraitist, my ability to recognize faces I had seen only once was usually good. Yet my talents were letting me down when it came to the youngest-looking of the Arab entourage. I watched him turn back and sweep under the canopy of the hotel. Frustrated, I decided I'd probably seen his picture in the newspaper.

Eventually I found the movie I was looking for—an old friend from the thirties called *The Man Who Knew Too Much*—and turned to it with a sense of relief. But even then the commercial breaks showed news clips featuring easily identifiable Arabs, and less identifiable members of the Israeli delegation, looking like any Western diplomats in ordinary suits, minus head-dress. And I sat there, exhausted, mesmerized, unable to sleep, a surrealistic montage of the movie and the current news going through my head: Arab headdress, a man being shot during the loudest part of Beethoven's Ninth Symphony, the face of the Israeli prime minister, numerous television reporters, each one sounding more pompous than the last, some kind of a cops-and-robbers chase in England—all without sense or sequence tumbling across the same mental screen in my head.

Disgusted, I finally got up and went to bed and lay staring at the ceiling, where the reflection of street-lights outside shining through the trees made strange patterns as the wind moved the branches of the trees in front of the lights.

The strange, unsettling part was that I thought I would feel different about Michelle because she was my daughter. I expected some tremendous emotional resolution of all the things I didn't understand about myself, about Michelle and about Suzanne. But every-thing was exactly the way it had been. She was still a lumpy, demanding, difficult child. I rolled over once, trying to envision the Michelle that would have been if she hadn't been given to Suzanne and George. But the image that emerged, though much prettier, had no reality. Michelle, whatever her faults and assets, was powerfully real, and I was dismayed to find how much, within my head, she remained stubbornly herself.

I heard my little clock strike five. Then I drifted off to sleep and was awakened by the alarm an hour later. I should have felt tired and sleepy. But I was as fresh and full of energy as if I had had ten hours of sleep.

Warning myself that the reckoning, however post-poned, would come sooner or later and I would feel like hell, I got out of bed, bathed, dressed and started down the stairs. At Michelle's door I paused. Then, after a minute, I turned the knob and walked in.

Her dark hair spread over the pillow, Michelle was sound asleep. Without glasses she looked younger and more vulnerable. Beside her, his ginger head also on the pillow, was Clancy. He opened his yellow eyes and yawned, showing an excellent set of incisors. He raised his head. The sound of a deep, rumbling purr filled the room. Surely, I thought, there was no greater compliment than that involuntary statement of pleasure and affection. An animal was both too innocent and too savage to turn it on and off for profit. A line I remembered from long in the past when I had been part of a school choir ran through my mind:

"For I am possessed of a cat, surpassing in beauty, from whom I take occasion to bless Almight God." Thus wrote the eighteenth-century poet Christopher Smart, in his *Jubilate Agno.* Clancy, I thought, was worthy of such a line and sentiment. As though he could read my mind and was responding, Clancy purred more loudly.

"Good boy," I said softly.

Getting up, he padded to the edge of the bed. I walked over and rubbed him between his ears. His purr got so loud it rattled. Standing on his hind legs he put his forepaws above my waist. As I ran my hands down his supple body, I watched Michelle, wondering if she would wake up. Michelle, my daughter. No wonder she looked so much like me and, behind me, like my father. And that's where all the trouble had started, my almost ludicrously close resemblance to my father. Everything in his life was following his carefully laid pattern until I arrived. What was it Julian had said in the attic, when he was talking about my father? In almost total recall my mind produced Julian's words: *"He had married a Marchington and sired a daughter who in looks and manner displayed, par excellence, what he obsessively called the Marchington Inheritance. His feelings about that amounted to idolatry."*

I frowned. What had come after that? Still staring at my sleeping daughter I prodded my memory. *"And then came you,"* Julian had continued. *"Every time he looked at you, it was like looking at the part of himself that he wanted to forget..."*

And because, on some level, I knew that, because as

201

far back as I could remember I felt my father's rejection and resented it to the marrow of my bones, I was fertile soil for rebellion. And how more completely could a female child rebel than to give birth to a fatherless, illegitimate child? I myself had been, in one sense, fatherless. I produced a fatherless child...And the whole thing started because, at the age of ten or eleven, I looked very like the small replica of myself now sleeping. I leaned over Michelle and a great sadness and tenderness filled me. Did I want to wake her up at this early hour—I glanced at the small clock on the bureau across from me; it was not yet a quarter to seven—to tell her about herself and me?

For more than ten years, a thousand times a year, I had fantasized the meeting with my daughter. Our joy, our arms around one another. Why was I hesitating? Why didn't she wake up of her own accord and save me having to take the step to wake her? Why was I standing here as though I couldn't make up my mind? Bending, I put my lips against her cheek. She stirred, made small, sleepy noises, then turned over on her stomach. Clancy, feeling left out, butted his head against me. I picked him up, a soft, strong, bundle of fur, and put my face against his side. His purr rose loud and rhythmic. Then I put him back down on the bed. But he'd had enough sleep. Padding over to the door, he sat down and looked at me, yawned and licked his whiskers.

Yet still I stood there. All I had to do to wake Michelle was to shake her gently. Then we would talk. She'd be pleased to know that I was her mother...or would she? Suddenly I remembered the eager look that would sometimes flash across her face when she was talking to Suzanne, her mother...her mother.

Turning, I walked to the door, opened it and followed Clancy out and down the stairs. "All right, Clancy, I'll feed you," I said.

Opening a can of cat food, I put it in his dish and put his dish on the floor. Then I made myself some coffee.

Something was bothering me very much, but I couldn't quite pin down what it was. Suddenly Randy popped into my mind. I wondered if, after his adventures, he'd be in school today. If I were his mother, I knew I wouldn't let him near that school.

I paused, the quart of milk in my hand as I lightened my coffee. Why did I feel that strongly? Stirring the coffee, I watched Clancy attack his breakfast. He didn't so much eat it, I thought, as inhale it. One minute it was there. About three bites later and it wasn't. Poor Clancy, he must have had a hard life since Joseph died. I was glad he was now living with us.

"I can't understand myself," I said aloud. The words echoed in the small room off the kitchen that, in the old days, used to be called a pantry, but now was a general snacking room, with an electric coffeepot, jars and packages of cookies and a jar of peanut butter. Clancy's gourmet dinners were also stored here. At the sound of my words, Clancy looked up at me, and then went back to his main objective, finishing his plate.

Why was I so reluctant, after all these years of thinking I had been deprived of my life's greatest treasure, my child, to claim her? Was it because that, in spite of the state of tension between them, I felt there was an affection—more than affection, a powerful bond—between Suzanne and Michelle that I shouldn't tamper with? Not to mention her feeling for her dead father that would certainly be affected by what I would have to reveal?

If true, such restraint would be startlingly uncharacteristic of me. I had never been guilty of self-punishing unselfishness in practice, and all the theory I had learned in adulthood militated in favor of my developing a clear concept of my own limits and rights.

"Oh, hell," I said. I washed out my cup and decided to go to the school even though it wasn't my day to be there. It was at that moment that I remembered that it was the day the children were to sing at the UN in honor of the Arab and Israeli chiefs of state. Perhaps, with all the inevitable excitement, I could help out.

"Thank heaven you're here," Miss Gales said, as I walked in shortly before eight. "Ginny's come down with some kind of bug. She was going to take the singers—twenty-seven of them—down to the UN for their rehearsal and keep them there until the performance itself at the reception when Miss Sutherland will take over. What with Ginny not being here and Mrs. Ferris on the phone threatening us with the police, I feel like going to bed myself."

"Why was Mrs. Ferris up in arms?"

"Well, she blames us for letting Randy get down into the basement in the first place. And, of course, she's right. I try and train the staff to count heads every ten minutes. But until they've had their first crisis, faced their first enraged parent, they just think we're being fussbudgets. And Miss Sutherland herself—oh, well, that's understandable. Can you hear the oldest bunch through their songs? I'll hear the rest."

"Sure. But by this time they must be able to sing those songs backwards and standing on their heads."

"You'd think so, wouldn't you? If I never hear an ethnic, or national, song again as long as I live, I won't mind at all. But you can't run them through too often. The last time we did something like this, one half of the children forgot the songs and the other half had to go to the bathroom. Miss Hurd will play. She knows the songs well."

I grinned. Then I asked, feeling oddly concerned, "But *is* Randy going to be here?"

"Oh, yes. I think his mother would have been delighted to tell us that she was taking him out of our school. But, of course, that would mean that either she'd stay home from work herself, or, at the last minute, find someplace for him to stay—if she could. And then she'd have to scout for another school. Frustration that she couldn't—or wouldn't—really do any of those things was what was behind her rage as much as anything. So, after telling us what she thought of our careless ways for fifteen minutes, she said she'd be bringing him around."

"Oh." My feeling of unease was uncomfortably strong.

"Don't you like Randy?"

"Very much. He's so impossible he's kind of winning." What I wished, though, I discovered, was that his mother had suddenly decided to take him to Acapulco or California or Hawaii or Paris. I told myself not to be silly.

"Okay," I said, "I'll take the older lot through their songs. Would it add to your burdens if I told you that I have no sense of pitch?"

"Not much. Those who are good at singing lead the others. And nobody will care. All those Middle Easterners, to say nothing of the rest of the world, won't care if they can't sing a note. They'll just look at all those little faces and sentimentalize over their role as innocence leading experience into the hills of peace, if you follow me."

"Sort of." When she said the words "Middle Easterners" something had jogged loose in my mind and was trying to come to the surface. "Did you see all those news accounts last night?" I asked idly. "What a hubbub!"

"Impressive, wasn't it?"

I turned. Janet Sutherland was coming down the stairs leading to the second floor. "The arrival of the peace-treaty signers, I mean," she said, arriving at the bottom. Today she had on a skirt under the familiar tweed jacket.

Who was it Aunt Ginevra had said Miss Sutherland resembled? Louise Carteret... Louise Carteret, mother of Charles, who had been kidnapped, who had, herself, died after a year of anguish and several times having her hopes raised for nothing. Surely if anyone had ever died of a broken heart, she had.

I suddenly became aware that Miss Sutherland was looking at me, her brows raised, her mouth smiling, her brilliant blue eyes as hard as glass.

"Yes, very impressive," I stammered. "I'm sorry. You must think I'm an idiot. I haven't had a chance to tell you . . . My brother-in-law was killed yesterday. We've all had rather a difficult time and not much sleep."

"I'm terribly sorry," Miss Gales said. "How on earth did it happen?"

"I'm afraid it was a mugger in the park."

"How awful! I wish they'd do something. It's dreadful not to feel safe in our own park!"

"Yes."

"There's no reason for you to be here," Miss Sutherland said. "It's not even your regular day."

"Oh, she must," Miss Gales wailed. "Ginny just called. She's sick, and I've just asked Miss Marchington to take the kids to the UN."

"That would indeed be nice of you." The words were conventionally polite, but spoken without expression.

I heard myself say nervously, "If you think I could do it. Or I could stay here with the kids while Miss Gales took them."

Miss Gales's face lit up. She looked for a minute like an excited child. "Perhaps that would be best. And I can—"

"No." The headmistress's voice cut across her associate's like a knife. Miss Gales's cheeks flushed. Miss Sutherland smiled at her. "We can't spare you here, Lucy. My own peace of mind when I go to the reception wouldn't stand for it. We have more than twice as many children staying back here—most of them three- and four-year-olds, and three news ones arriving." She smiled at me. "So, if you don't mind taking our young choristers to the UN for their rehearsal, I'd be most grateful. I'd do it myself, but unfortunately I have an important business appointment this morning that cannot be postponed."

"I don't mind," I said, sounding in my own ears like an adolescent seized with a crush on the magnetic headmistress. There was no question but that when Janet Sutherland turned her fiery blue gaze on someone it

206

had a compelling effect. Fiery, my inner censor amended, but it was the fieriness of dry ice.

"You're sure you don't mind?" she was saying now. "Those six- and seven-year-olds can be wild. The last time Ginny took them out she mislaid two. Luckily, they turned up after she got back."

"I'm sure," I said, wondering if I was. "How am I going to get them there? Bus? School bus? And how many are going?"

"Twenty-seven, and we've hired a school bus. Do you know the songs?"

I grinned. "Very well by this time. There are seven." I ticked them off on my fingers. "One Russian, one Chinese, one Hebrew, one French, one Norwegian, one Spanish and one Irish—all translated into English."

Miss Gales said, "Teaching them at all was difficult enough. If they'd had to struggle with the original languages, the project would never have got off the ground. English may not be the mother tongue of all of them, but they do all know it."

"When do we go?" I asked. "Whom do we meet and are they expecting us? I mean, I know they are," I added hastily, "but whom do I see?"

Miss Sutherland smiled. "The school bus will be here in"—she checked her watch—"half an hour, at nine. Even allowing for traffic you should get there by nine-forty-five. You'll rehearse at ten-thirty in one of the meeting rooms with the guest conductor and a piano accompanist. I'll be there at a quarter to twelve to take them to the delegates' lounge, where they will join a small older choir and sing for the reception guests at twelve. Now, as to whom you see, you won't have to worry about that. A friend, John—you'll never be able to pronounce his last name so I won't bother you with it—will meet you in the main UN lobby—that is the lobby of the Assembly Building—and he'll be in charge of steering you to the right rooms from there. All the right people are expecting you—"

"Right people?"

"Guards, police, guides, staff, etcetera. The UN

watches everyone who comes in and goes out pretty carefully. Especially at a time like this."

Miss Gales looked at me and gave me her toothy smile, which I had come to find pleasant and reassuring. "You'll be all right," she said.

"We'll pack the books in three or four book bags," Miss Sutherland said, "and the oldest children can carry them, so you can reserve all your attention for counting heads and keeping everybody in order."

"Books?" I said. "What books?"

"The songbooks," Miss Gales replied.

"But I thought they were singing from memory. They surely know those songs by now. Even I could sing them by rote."

"I'm sure you could," the headmistress said, glancing at her watch again. "We all could. The songbooks are really for moral support and in case the conductor wants to check the words. The English words to the songs are short and simple so the children can read them if they have to. But I'm sure they won't have to."

"Oh, I see," I said with some relief. The thought of keeping count of three or four book bags plus twenty-seven children was beginning to sound formidable. "So if they're mislaid it's not a dire tragedy, I mean," I added hastily, "it's not that important." There was a flat, hard expression on the headmistress's face that brought back my nervousness.

"It *is* that important," she said sharply. Then her smile appeared. "Don't worry. Go and hear the songs now. Miss Hurd will play for them here, and of course, the children will go through them again with the conductor and the pianist at the UN. The older children will carry the books. There'll be no problem."

"Fine." I had a strong inclination to add "Sir." There was a brisk, military precision about all this that was catching. I glanced at Miss Sutherland. The fine blue eyes were chilling. Perhaps it was because, for all her smiles and pleasant manner, the headmistress was more worried and keyed up than she wanted anyone to know. There was a tautness, a hardness about her that came through her obvious effort to appear at ease.

"Miss Marchington will do beautifully," Miss Gales said soothingly. "The children like her."

"And I like them." It was a fairly pedestrian statement, yet to be able to make it suddenly filled me with an unexpected joy. I had spent so many years avoiding children, and avoiding the pain that the sight of them brought me. What had effected the change? The answer was obvious: Michelle. More specifically, the knowledge that she was my daughter. But that was a situation I didn't want to have to deal with now—even in my mind.

"Okay," I said. "Are there any particular problems with the kids, or any one of them, that I should be aware of?"

"Just that they must go to the bathroom before they leave, the moment they arrive, and when they finish before coming back. And don't believe them when they say they don't want to go. Ten minutes later they'll tell you that if they don't go immediately the worst will happen, and it often does."

An hour afterwards I was counting heads for the third or fourth time as the six- and seven-year-olds were piling into the bus. With his red hair and either the same or an identical green T-shirt, Randy Ferris stood out a mile. He was quiet, but his sky-blue eyes sparkled. Four of the older children were carrying tan book bags containing the little songbooks.

Armed with a whistle, a baggie of cookies and one or two pieces of candy—the latter for purposes of bribery—I was sitting at the back of the bus, keeping an eye on my charges. But, given their age and excitement, they were remarkably well behaved. The bus trundled uneventfully down Second Avenue, and in the Forties crossed over to First Avenue, turned up beside the fluttering flags of the UN, and stopped at the gate. The sidewalk, the steps leading up to the plaza enclosing the buildings, and the plaza itself were thick with police and UN guards. Across First Avenue two sets of demonstrators were marching and shouting.

Quickly, and before the doors opened I went to the front of the bus.

"Okay, kids," I said. "This is the United Nations, the place where you'll be singing your songs. Has anyone seen these buildings before?" I waved at the low, curving assembly building and the Secretariat beside it. Mimi Townsend, Randy Ferris and the Schlegel twins all put up their hands.

"All right, Mimi," I said. "You've been here. What's this building for?"

"It's for all the countries where they talk and make peace."

I glanced at one of the twins. "Boopie, anything else?"

Every syllable meticulous, Boopie said, "The World Health Organization." His rhythmic speech pattern reminded me of stage Welsh.

"That's right," I said. "And UNESCO and so on. And why are we singing today? What's going to be happening? Randy?"

"They're signing a treaty not to fight anymore."

"Right. Okay, now. Let all get out, slowly and one at a time."

I went first, hesitating on the step of the bus, taking in the lovely sight: the graceful, curved white building, the tall Secretariat beside it, the multicolored flags, the blue-tunicked police and gray-uniformed UN guards, the crowds of people and, barely visible, a blue strip of river and the buildings and warehouses on the farther bank. It all made a brilliant picture.

Then I stepped down on the pavement and stood aside as the children started tumbling out of the bus.

"One at a time," I said. "Twenty-five, twenty-six, twenty-seven."

"When do you want me back?" the driver said.

I paused. Curiously, for all her specific instructions, Janet Sutherland had not said what time we'd be leaving. Hastily, I did some mental calculation. If the concert were at twelve . . . "How about one-thirty?"

"See you then."

My eyes strayed over the group. A little higher than the others, Mimi's dark, intelligent face looked up at me.

"Mimi, I want you to keep an eye on the younger kids for me. Will you do that?"

"Sure, Miss Match."

"Thank you very much. Will you go in front and lead the way? We have to meet someone in the lobby there."

Mimi had on a brown skirt and red blouse, white socks and sneakers. Dignified and responsible and carrying her bag of music books, she went to the head of the ragged knot of children and took a hand of one of the Schlegel twins, who were walking hand in hand with each other. Each wore neat short trousers, white shirts and knee socks.

Red hair above green shirt, Randy Ferris was streaking up the flight of steps leading to the broad promenade in front of the Assembly Building, his bag of books bumping beside him.

Feeling every kind of fool, I took out my whistle and blew. Randy looked back. "Wait, Randy! Don't go ahead. Wait for the rest of us!"

I had no confidence that he would obey, but to my astonishment, he stayed put.

"All right, Randy," I said. "Now I want you to stick close beside me."

"Why?"

"Because you have some of the books and because I need your help."

Randy regarded me out of cynical eyes. "That's what Mom always says when she wants me to do something I don't want to do."

"Please," I said.

A look of gratified machismo came over the urchin face. "Okay."

"First off, please help me keep the younger kids from getting lost."

Since the younger ones were, by this time, huddled

at the top of the steps chattering like sparrows, it was obviously not a job of immediate urgency.

"They all have to go to the bathroom before we start rehearsing," I explained.

"I've already peed," Randy said loftily.

"Yes, but you're older. The younger ones have to go at every chance so they won't have to go in the middle of singing."

"Or wet their pants," Randy finished.

"Or wet their pants," I agreed, profoundly aware of several guards enjoying our conversation.

Still counting, I got them across the plaza and fed the herd through the revolving door of the Assembly Building past a friendly guard. He glanced at the book bags. "What's in those?" he asked.

"Books," Mimi said, holding hers up.

"For our concert," Randy joined in, his voice full of importance.

The guard, a fatherly-looking man, smiled into the little faces. "Okay, kids, put on a good show. We'll be listening."

I collected them all and counted them again, wondering what John Something would look like.

"Miss Marchington?" a male voice spoke beside me.

"That's right. Are you John?" I said, and then stopped. That same nagging sense of familiarity, of having been through this before, was once more bedeviling me as it had several times of late.

He smiled. My uncomfortable feeling lightened and almost went away. When he smiled he looked totally unfamiliar. I could well believe Miss Sutherland's statement that I would not be able to pronounce this young man's name. It was not only that his foreign accent was apparent in the two words he had spoken. There was something about him that bespoke distant cultures.

"This way," he said.

"What I need first is a cloakroom, a ladies' room." I glanced over twenty-seven heads. "A large one."

212

John Something, who had appeared as though he might be going in one direction, smiled, glanced over my horde and led the way down a flight of stairs and across a wide concourse beneath.

"This is the largest," he said, pointing to a door.

I counted heads again, as well as I could for all the moving and shoving. "Now be still, all of you. We can't go in until I know everyone's here." Once again I counted them. Twenty-seven. "Okay, in with you."

John Something pointed to Randy. "Him? Men's room over there." And he waved down the hall. I turned and looked. There, indeed, was a door marked "Men."

"I'll go to the men's room," Randy said, sounding all puffed up.

"Us, too," the Schlegel twins chorused.

"Everybody's going in here," I said firmly.

"Not me. I'm going to the men's room and you can't go in." And my limb of Satan ran down the hall and into the men's room. I looked at John Something. I really didn't want to ask his help, but he was there for our use, and Randy was right: I couldn't chase him into the men's room. "Can you go in and make sure he's back here waiting for us?" I asked.

All smiles and white teeth, John Something followed Randy into the men's room. I realized immediately that I was going to have trouble with the rest of the boys, all of whom were younger and smaller than Randy, but who felt that their masculinity had been affronted by my forcing them into the ladies' room after Randy's stand of male solidarity. "I don't care how you feel," I said to Boopie Schlegel, ignoring the women whose raised brows indicated their strong feeling that the male presence, however small, in the ladies' room was not to be encouraged. "I want you to go in there and pee. We won't get to our rehearsal until everybody has gone. And I mean *everyone*."

"It's not fair," muttered Oojima, struggling with his zipper as he emerged from a cubicle. "Miss Match, my zipper's stuck."

I bent over. It was indeed stuck. Trying to unstick it took about three heavy-breathing minutes, while doors opened, toilets flushed and the general noise level rose.

"Be quiet," I said in exasperation, rising up and absentmindedly taking the zipper fastener with me.

"Ouch!" yelled poor Oojima.

"Sorry, Oojima. Now, I want all of you to stand there quietly, while I fix Oojima's zipper." I bent down again.

Finally it was done. As I got off one knee and stood up a woman stalked out of the ladies' room. "Really!" she said.

"And yours, too," I muttered.

"What did you say, Miss Match?" An angelic little creature with gold curls and a pinafore, with, I remembered, a mother to match, looked up at me.

"Nothing, Deirdre. I was just clearing my throat. All right. Did everybody go?"

"I couldn't, miss. I tried. But I couldn't." I looked down. Brown eyes, brown hair, missing front teeth. Betsy. Betsy Leboutillier.

"If you tell me you have to go in the middle the rehearsal, Betsy..." I started, and then stopped. If I threatened her, however jokingly, she might take me seriously, and instead of telling me she wanted to go, she'd just go. Right there. "I'll take you to a ladies' room on the other floor," I said.

"Can I go too?" three little girls cried.

I suddenly understood why the staff were so willing to let the children yell and scream to their hearts' content in the playground. This was the first time I had had them all to myself and was completely responsible for them. It occurred to me that the rehearsal had hardly started and I was fading fast.

"Come along now."

When I got them all outside I saw Randy and John Something standing and talking with great cordiality. Until I saw Randy, I hadn't realized how worried I was to have him out of my sight. "Okay, now I'm going to count you again. Stand still."

"But you just counted them," John Something said.

"Count them with me. There are supposed to be

twenty-seven. And I have to count them every time we go anywhere, and at least once in between. Those are my orders."

He shrugged, looking all of a sudden very Latin, although something about him did not seem to me either Spanish or Italian, or even Greek. But I was not concerned with him.

"Twenty-seven," I said finally. "Does everyone who was carrying a bag still have it?"

"Yes, Miss Match."

I glanced over at the four holding their bags.

"They're heavy," Mimi said.

"No, they're not," Randy contradicted.

"Yes they—"

"Never mind," I said. "You can soon distribute the books."

"They must practice without them," John Something said. "Miss Sutherland said the books were to be put in the anteroom behind the rehearsal room."

I didn't fully relish his telling me my business. Evidently Miss Sutherland was no mean slouch at manipulating people. She was taking no chances that I might forget her orders.

"Yes, I know," I said, ruffled, to John.

"I get twenty-seven, too," he said. "Shall we go up to the hall now?" He led the way to a bank of elevators. "We have to go in several elevators," he said. "It's the third floor."

"All right."

I glanced over them as John pushed the button between two elevators. "Mimi, I'm going to send one bunch with you and Randy." It was a risk, I knew, including Randy in my instructions, but I thought an appeal to his sense of responsibility would keep him from taking off at that moment. "John," I looked at the swarthy young man, "would you go first and take the first lot?"

An expression flickered over John's face that reminded me strongly of Randy's when he refused to use the ladies' room. It gave me a certain grim pleasure to reflect that I was affronting his sense of masculine machismo and leadership as well. Then John shrugged. "Very well."

One elevator door opened. "Come along, children," he said. Eight went inside with him.

I sent another ten with Mimi and Randy and took nine up with me. When I arrived at the top Mimi and Randy were counting and recounting heads in full voice, noisily assisted by all the rest.

"We're all here, Miss Match," the chorus assured me. A great wave of affection went over me as I looked at them. I counted again and confirmed that there were indeed twenty-seven. "Yes, you are all here, and I think you're all wonderful!"

They giggled with gratification.

"You can put your bags and any coats or sweaters here," John said, opening a door down a short hall and revealing what appeared to be a large cloakroom divided into a lounge in one room and toilets and wash basins beyond.

"Okay," I said. "Bags over here on this table. Anyone want to go to the bathroom?"

"We've just been," said an indignant chorus.

"I wanna go."

It was Betsy Leboutillier. "I couldn't go before, Miss Match. Remember?"

I remembered. Five minutes later, counting them once more, I ushered them out of the cloakroom into the rehearsal room.

"The guard in there wants to talk to you," John said, as he held the door of the rehearsal hall open.

The room was large and high-ceilinged. On the other side was a piano. Standing by the piano were three men, one in uniform. The man in uniform turned, showing himself to be about forty-five, with a heavy face and quick, intelligent eyes.

"Miss Stevenson?" he asked.

My eyes were moving over my charges. "Twenty-seven," I intoned ritualistically, and with some relief.

"What did you say?" the policeman asked.

"She was just counting us," Mimi said. "She does that all the time. When we were in the ladies' room—"

"Yes, all right, Mimi. You wanted to ask me something, officer?"

There was a twitch at the side of his mouth. "You remind me of my wife," he said. "She teaches kindergarten and even counts in her sleep."

"I already have a feeling that I'll be counting up to twenty-seven for the rest of the year. Are you here to guard us?"

"Yes, and to make sure I know you. You're Miss Stevenson?"

"No, she's Miss Match," several of the children chirruped helpfully.

"Match?" The officer frowned, looking suddenly much more formidable. "I was told a Miss Stevenson or possibly a Miss Gales."

"Miss Stevenson is ill and at home, and Miss Gales had to stay at the school. My name is Marchington. Match is what the children call me. I'm the art teacher."

"I see. You don't mind if I check, do you?"

"Not at all." As the officer lifted the receiver off the wall phone, I saw out of the corner of my eye a green shirt disappearing across the polished floor to the other end of the room.

"Come back here this minute, Randy."

John Something took off and in a few minutes brought Randy back, a firm hand clutching his T-shirt. "Tell him," John Something said, looking fairly grim himself, "that he is not to leave the group, this is to be understood."

"I'll be delighted to tell him. Randy, did you hear that?"

"And I'll add my piece," the officer said turning away from the phone. "Young man, if you leave the group I'm going to put you in protective custody."

"What's that?"

"Jail."

"You wouldn't! My mother would be mad at you. You'd be sorry."

Randy spoke with such confidence that I had a fleeting moment of sympathy with Mr. Ferris, whoever he might be.

"Unless you promise me, Randy," I said, "you won't be able to sing at the concert. The school will ask your mother to take you home."

"Pooh! You wouldn't!" But despite himself, he looked impressed.

"Yes, I would."

We eyed each other.

"That's not fair. I—"

"BE QUIET!" the police officer boomed.

Even I jumped. There was a silence.

"Now," the police officer said. "Do we have your promise?"

Randy opened his mouth very wide. I braced myself. Then he closed it part way. "Okay," he said.

"Thank you. If Miss . . . Miss Match says you're trustworthy, then I'll accept that. Now," he turned towards me. "I'm Captain Connelly. I'm in charge of the inside security today. I checked and Miss Sutherland confirms everything you say. She says she will be here herself just before noon and will take the children into the reception room. So I'll just stick around and listen. Here is the man who's going to play, and the maestro who will conduct."

I found myself looking at one of the more famous symphony orchestra conductors.

"And here is my young chorus," he said genially. "Now let's see, what are some of your names?" He spoke with an accent, but of what origin I couldn't decide. A youngish man, he had a lot of hair and a nice smile. I had seen him often on television.

The children, invited to speak, promptly lapsed into silence.

I introduced the twenty-seven names, counting them as I went.

"Splendid!" the maestro said, consulting a small list.

218

"Now we will begin with the Russian song, and our good friend Roger, here, will play for us."

Miss Gales was quite right, I thought, as I returned from a brief trip of my own to the ladies' room and sat down to listen. It didn't matter that out of the twenty-seven the strength and accuracy of the singing rested with about ten. Under the leadership of those ten and aided by the almost charismatic spell cast by the handsome conductor, the children were creating quite a lot of extremely pleasant sound. There, in front, the tiniest and the youngest of the children, was six-year-old Virginia Wu in a gray skirt and dark red blouse. Lost in her singing, with her small, pretty mouth open, and her tilted eyes and black hair, she looked like something out of an oriental tapestry. Then there was Dojima. I had forgotten from which African country he came. But baby-faced as he was, the hint of high cheekbones and clearly crafted mouth made me think of the statues I'd seen of the young pharaohs. Beside him, Deirdre Lang was something out of a Gainsborough painting. And the fact that her profoundly determined mother did everything she could to produce just this effect did not detract from the fact that little Deirdre could have stepped out of one of the master's portraits. As a matter of fact, she was a nice child, and if she could just be judiciously separated from her parent for reasonable intervals, might well show some initiative and dash.

Like a robot permanently wound up, I counted them all again, which was difficult, because I kept having to peer around the conductor, who kept moving. Twenty four, twenty-five, twenty-six. Twenty-six. Come on, Avril, I said to myself. You know there are twenty-seven. Even though I had counted them just before the maestro stood up and took over, nevertheless, I had to count them again. Trying to keep all the heads straight, not to count anyone twice, and to keep dodging the conductor took a lot of attention. But I managed. Twenty-four, twenty-five, twenty-six . . .

All of a sudden panic gripped me. I stood up and

walked over to the side where I had an unimpeded view of the children. The latter, who had been gazing fixedly at the conductor, followed me with their eyes. Their voices faltered. The conductor turned and glared at me. It didn't matter. I was busy counting the little heads that were now still. There were twenty-six. Even before I looked I knew who was missing.

"Just a minute," I said. "Stop the music immediately!"

"What on earth—this is outrageous!" The conductor was plainly unused to such cavalier behavior.

The children gaped at me. I stared at the back row, where the tallest had been placed, and from where Randy was missing. My eyes swept past Mimi and then stopped. She was not only one of the older ones, she was bright and observant.

"Mimi, where did Randy go?"

"He said he had to go to the bathroom, Miss Match."

"May we continue?" The conductor, no longer a bunch of charismatic charm, said icily. "I am willing for an occasion of outstanding importance to interrupt my work with the philharmonic in order to make my small contribution to world peace, but this interference over nothing more than a child's ... er ... need of the bathroom ..."

I didn't listen to the rest. Twenty-six children, the conductor, the accompanist and the guard—where was the guard?

"Where did the guard go?" I said. "Captain Connelly?"

"Perhaps he, too, wished to use the facilities."

"Mimi? Did Randy go with the police captain?" I trusted Mimi's intelligence more than I did that of the talented bag of wind standing in front, lashing his baton back and forth against his leg.

"No, Miss Match. I think Randy went with John—you know, who brought us in here."

"If we may continue?" The conductor seemed to speak between locked teeth, as though holding his rage behind them.

I stared at him, thinking as hard as I could. Somehow, I didn't worry as much about the other children. My main concern about them at the moment was that in all the excitement, and while I was looking for Randy, nature would start calling in imperative terms. But I couldn't help that. I said, still staring at the conductor, "My orders were to keep track of all the children. I have to find Randy. I am holding you responsible for keeping every one of the others in here till I get back. If they have to go to the bathroom"— my eyes swept to the accompanist, a chinless, vague-looking young man, and onto Mimi—"then Mimi Townsend, there on the back row in a red shirt, will be in charge of taking them and bringing them back. Do you hear that, Mimi?"

"Yes, Miss Match," she said proudly.

The conductor, unable to do justice to his feelings in English, had gone into a language that sounded like iron bars falling downstairs. Quickly I left the room. Whether or not I was right to do so, I didn't know. Perhaps I should have used the wall phone that the police captain had used. But Randy had been locked in the school basement. Whatever Julian's motives were in coaching the child in a lie and permitting him to go back to the school, I had never been happy about it. Where was John Something? Checking first the cloakroom on the third floor, I plunged into the elevator and went down to the concourse. John wasn't loitering outside either of the cloakrooms. I didn't think for one minute that Randy would use the ladies' room, but I burst in there anyway.

"Randy?" I yelled. Two women who were washing their hands and three who were combing their hair turned. "Did you see a little boy in a green T-shirt and with red hair?" I asked.

"Hardly here," one woman said, carefully combing her long hair into the washbowl, in direct defiance of a nicely worded request immediately above.

"I haven't seen any little boy," another woman said.

I didn't have time to be delicate. Three of the cubicles

were being used. Looking below the bottom of the door I took in two pairs of high heels and one pair of rubber-soled moccasins, about size nine, and above them a nyloned and obviously female pair of ankles. Nevertheless, I stood and yelled, "Randy, are you anywhere here?"

A white-coated attendant burst in. "What's the matter?" she said, looking at me.

"I've lost a little boy who said he was going to the bathroom."

"Oh. Have you looked in the men's room?"

"No. Can you look for me?"

"Well, all right. Come along. I'll see what I can do."

"Perhaps you should have trained him better in the first place," said the young woman still combing her hair over the sink.

"Perhaps you should get help in remedial reading," I said. And when she favored me with her arrogant stare, pointed to the sign and to the spidery black lines of hair in the sink. "So nice for everybody else," I said.

"Please clean that up, miss," the attendant said. "And step back when you comb your hair."

"Disgusting," an older woman said.

"I'll have you know—"

The door slammed on the conversation. I led the way at a trot. "Can you go in?" I asked when we arrived.

She took out a key and knocked on the door with it. "Anyone in there? We have to come in to clean."

There was no reply.

"Coming in," she said, and opened the door.

In the glimpse of white tile I had through the open door, something else hit my eye. There, vivid green on the white, was a discarded T-shirt. With a cry I went in. Fortunately there seemed to be no one in there. But I was beyond caring. I picked up the T-shirt and stood with it, shaken by an overwhelming desire to cry. Somehow Randy had been brought down here and the highly identifying green shirt taken away. Tears blinded me for a minute. It was incredible how fond of him I'd become in such a short time. But what was like

222

steel pincers inside me was the thought of what might be happening to him, of his terror and fear and pain. That brave, obstinate, wonderful little boy . . .

I became aware of the attendant patting me on the shoulder and offering me some water to drink.

"It is your son?"

I shook my head and suddenly woke up to the urgency. There was no time to explain anything. "I must find a telephone," I said.

"Out here. Just behind the stairs."

It was only when I heard Julian's voice at the other end that I remembered how much I hated him, and my reason for it. But it seemed far away, as though it no longer mattered. Much nearer was the fact that he was at fault in not telling Randy's mother everything, so she could take him away. But even admitting that, I knew that it was Julian I should call, and not the school.

"Julian," I said. "I'm at the UN with the children. We came to rehearse before the performance. Randy's disappeared. And somebody must have taken him, because his green T-shirt is lying on the men's room floor. Please come right away. I can't leave the other kids who are upstairs, but I need help."

Julian went straight to the point. "Where are you?"

"I'll be on the third floor of the Assembly Building in one of the meeting rooms." I told him how to get to the room.

"Okay," he said. "Don't tell anyone he's gone. Pretend you sent him home—say he had a stomachache or something."

"We should call the police."

"No, Avril. That really would be the end of him. Trust me."

I stood there, the receiver against my ear, not saying anything.

"Trust me," he repeated.

"I see no reason why I should," I said finally. "But I don't suppose I have much choice."

223

CHAPTER 10

Going back upstairs, it took all the control I had to pretend nothing worrying had happened. I could hear the voices singing away as I got off the elevator and was reluctantly grateful to the wretched conductor for keeping them occupied. Twenty-six children not doing anything could raise twenty-six problems in no time at all. If there were still twenty-six . . . But somehow I knew there were; only Randy was in danger.

Opening the door as quietly as possible, I stood and watched the children trying to regain some calm. But my mind had lost the habit of serenity. Before I had listened to two bars of music I was worrying over how Julian would get in. The children and I had had no trouble. But the guards had been expecting us. The whole thing had been set up and arranged before. What about Randy's disappearance? Had that been set up? And by whom? It was then I remembered something that by some freak had slipped out of my mind: Mimi Townsend had said that Randy had gone off with John Something. And where was John Something now? Was he part of the kidnapping of Randy? Was he also a victim?

Everything in me said no to that. Whatever he was or wasn't, John Something was not a victim. Why was I so sure? Again, in my mind, I saw the brows drawn over dark eyes, the powerful curving nose . . . And then another picture slid over that, a picture on a television screen. It had been the previous night during the endless news broadcasts about the arrival of the Arab and Israeli delegations. The reason I had such a hard time recognizing John Something was because today he was not wearing the colorful Arab headdress.

I must have made a sound because I saw the conductor glance at me. Walking quietly I went over to the window. So John Something was a member of one of the Arab delegations. That by itself did not argue anything. He could be posted here on permanent assignment in something quite innocent—such as their press office. If they had a press office, which they must have because everybody did . . . He could be on the staff of the Secretariat. After all, this great international institution sitting on its eighteen acres of international territory was staffed by citizens of all the member nations. Janet Sutherland could have met him anywhere. She certainly could have met him through the school. Although the school—our school—had no official ties with the United Nations, it was undeniably true that some of the parents of the children worked for or in connection with the UN. He could be a boyfriend. Why did I have the total conviction that that was not true? That it could not be true . . .

Where was Julian? How on earth would he get in? Glancing out the window I could see there were even more police and guards than there had been and there were at least five police cars in sight. One of the protest groups had been moved several blocks farther north and was surrounded by still more police.

Where was Julian? The question hammered in my mind like a drill. I glanced at my watch and was surprised to see it was only twenty past eleven. It was true, of course, that the school bus had made excellent time and we had started rehearsing early.

Why didn't Julian come? What could be keeping him?

I dragged my mind away from that and tried to concentrate on what was going on immediately around me. The children had stopped singing for the moment, and the conductor, his charm back in full force, was complimenting them. I turned and looked at the enraptured young faces. But instead of finding pleasure in them as I had before, as though they were so many little stars or upturned flowers, all I could think of was

Randy. Where was he? What was happening to him? A feeling that was both sickness and fury seized me and I turned back to the window. I saw Julian there. He was at the gate, talking to the guard. After a few seconds his hand went into an inner pocket and came out with something. The guard looked at it and nodded, then he waved in the direction of the entrance to the assembly building, as though telling Julian how to get up to the third floor. If I could have, I would have opened the window in front of me and shouted. But aside from the fact that it was impossible, it would have been unwise. Some inner caution was telling me to keep our problem as quiet as possible.

I watched Julian's dark and gray head as he came to the revolving door and disappeared. Expecting him to appear on the third floor in a matter of seconds, I was let down and irritated when he didn't. What could he be doing? It seemed a long time, but was probably no more than five or seven minutes until he did show up. As always, he looked what he was: a conservative lawyer with an old blue-ribbon, conservative firm, dressed in a blue-gray pin-striped suit with a striped tie. What on earth was he doing here, and why was I looking to such a total denizen of the ivory tower to untangle this mess and find Randy?

Something of all this must have showed on my face. Julian came over quickly. "Are you all right?" he asked.

It struck me as such a ludicrous and irrelevant question that I was exasperated.

"Of course I'm all right, Julian. It's Randy who's missing. And the whole proceedings are going to start in about half an hour. How can we possibly find him before then? The Arabs and Israelis are going to arrive any minute, and then there'll be the reception."

"Is that going to be in this room?"

"I don't know."

I saw his eyebrows shoot up.

"Julian, all I know is that Janet Sutherland is coming here to collect the children and take them to wherever they're going to sing, but I don't think it's here.

What's worrying me is *Randy*. Why won't you let me call the police?"

"Because I'm reasonably sure we're going to find him somewhere in the four UN buildings—probably this one. They can't have smuggled him out."

"How do you know?"

"Because I have friends among the city and security police plus the intelligence agencies on temporary duty here. And they're watching every possible exit."

"Are you trying to tell me that you're really with the CIA or the FBI or the Secret Service?"

"None of those—although I've done work in liaison with them. I was once in army intelligence, you know, and am still a reserve officer. But that's not important. What's important is stopping what I think—what I'm afraid—is going to happen."

"What is important is Randy."

He looked at me. "Yes, he is important. So is the safety of the Mideast representatives who are about to arrive. The only possible reason Randy's missing is that somebody's afraid he'll say something—probably by accident—that will give them away. Crazy and incredible as it may sound, the safety of those august gentlemen who are about to arrive and that of Randy Ferris may be connected, and both are related to whatever's going to happen in the next hour."

"The Mideast representatives? The next hour? What on earth are you talking about?"

He looked at me for a minute, frowning, his brows drawn down over his eyes, as though coming to some kind of decision.

As he hesitated, my anxiety peaked and snapped. "Let me tell you my attitude, Julian. After all my years of political activism, I've arrived at the point where I think Voltaire was right: The only thing of ultimate importance is *Travailler dans votre jardin*—to work in your garden—and Randy is my garden. As far as I'm concerned he's worth more than all the diplomatic moguls that ever signed a treaty."

There was a wry look on Julian's face. "I'm glad I've

lived long enough to hear you say that. But it's not that simple. Behind the peace treaty, behind the moguls, behind the staffs and the diplomats and the ambassadors and the aides, are more little boys, just like Randy. They live in villages all over the Middle East and when there's bombing and shelling they die. On both sides, they die. And they're probably just as mischievous and just as endearing to their mothers and aunts, cousins and friends as Randy is to you. If this peace effort goes through, there's just a chance they all might grow up in peace. If it doesn't—and there are extremists on both sides who don't want it to—then many of them will be bombed and burned and mutilated and killed. And what happens in the next hour can decide—at least for a time—which way it's going to go."

As though on cue, a particularly joyous snatch of song came from the children.

My sick feeling was back. I had been pushing away the full meaning of what he was saying, but could keep it at bay no longer. "What are you talking about?" I said again.

"We've had a tip that something may happen at this reception—we don't know what. That's why all the police are out there."

"Wouldn't they be out there anyway? With the prime minister and the others arriving?" I wanted desperately not to believe what he was saying.

"Not as many. They've tripled the number within the last few hours. Everybody who has come in has been checked and rechecked. Unless they were expected and their credentials okayed, they weren't allowed in."

My brain seemed to be moving in slow motion, but the next question was so obvious that I wondered why I hadn't asked it before. "What is the connection between Randy and those VIPs?"

"Remember the drawing he made and you finished?" I nodded.

"I thought I recognized it and one of our brighter

minds confirmed my hunch that the drawing probably represented the symbol of the PRA—the People's Revolutionary Army: two intertwined snakes with flames coming out of their mouths."

"You mean the terrorist group?"

"Yes."

"And that was what Randy saw in the basement of the school?"

"We think so. And maybe he saw—or half saw—some person, someone who may have locked him in. That door may not have slammed by itself."

The chill was all through my body now. "Oh, my God," I said. "Then we should have called the police, Julian, the way I wanted to. If you knew then what you just told me, it was criminal to let Randy come here."

"At that time, I didn't connect the basement and its contents or Randy with the tip about what might happen this morning. I'm sorry, I blame myself for that."

"Did you know about the tip—the one you had concerning the meeting today?"

He hesitated. "We had been told—by George, incidentally—that something was planned. But he didn't know exactly when or where. He may have found out after we talked—which is why he was killed."

"George?"

"Avril—there isn't time now. I'll explain later. In the meantime the police and security guards are alerted about Randy and are looking for him as well as they can in view of the fact that their main priority is the safety of the delegates and representatives—to say nothing of the two prime ministers."

"Why don't you just call off the whole stupid ceremony right now?"

"Because it's important. It's a public symbol. After years of wrangling it's almost as important as the signing itself. All the parties have been notified about this threat, and they all agreed that the reception had to go forward. Three quarters of the security police are down there checking every person who comes in."

"Yes, I know," I said. "My bag was checked. Just like the airport." Into my mind at that moment sprang the picture of Mimi holding up her bag of books, and despite everything, I smiled.

"Why the smile?"

"I was just thinking about one of the kids . . . If everyone's checked and every one who comes in is known, then who . . . ?"

Julian accepted my implied question. "I don't know," he said tiredly. "Neither does anyone else."

We were silent for a minute. The children's voices rose again. I glanced over. There at the back, singing with all her heart, her dark eyes shining, was Mimi. Directly in front of her were the Schlegel twins. Next to Boopie Schlegel was Betsy, with her missing front teeth, and Deirdre, looking like the angel on top of a Christmas tree, and Oojima, his strong voice making him one of the leaders. In front of everyone was Virginia Wu, a tiny gem of a Chinese doll. All of a sudden I was overwhelmed with the truth of what Julian had just said: everything would be safe. Perhaps that was the whole reason for having the children there to sing: so the delegates, as they argued and negotiated and gave a little here and there, would remember the children they had all left at home.

"Maybe that's why Janet arranged to have the children sing," I said, "so the potentates would know what they're here for—for all those children back home who deserve not to be blown up."

"Somebody arranged it," Julian said. "I wonder whether it was your headmistress."

"You can ask Miss Sutherland yourself. Here she is," I said, and went forward. As I walked across the parquet floor, it occurred to me that today was the first time I had seen the young headmistress in a skirt, and that she was, on the whole, wise in usually wearing slacks. She was good-looking enough to look well in anything, but her legs, with their prominent ankles, were not her best feature. And under the skirt her thighs seemed heavier than I would have thought. Like

230

all females everywhere, she had obviously dressed up for the occasion, even to having a stylish raincoat over her arm. And she had had her hair coloring retouched. There were no gray roots. She was a striking-looking woman with those blazing blue eyes and strong bone structure.

"Everything all right?" she said. Her eyes slid towards the chorus. Anxious as I was, I was amused to note that she, too, seemed to be counting heads. Finally she asked, "Where's Randy?"

"He went to the bathroom with that young man, John. The one who met us and brought us here. And now we can't find either one. I'm terribly sorry and worried."

"Well, John must have abandoned the search, because I saw him outside with the rest of his delegation." Janet Sutherland looked dismayed. "That's the first of his duties, and on a day like this, I wish you'd gone to the bathroom with him, Avril."

More guilt went through me. "I was in the ladies' room myself and didn't see him leave. Mimi, who was standing next to him, said he suddenly had to go to the bathroom and John said he'd take him."

"And you didn't see them go?" If she had spelled it out in neon letters, the headmistress couldn't have made it more obvious that she considered me derelict in my job.

"I'm sorry to say, no. As I said, I was in the ladies' room."

At this point the children's song came to an end with a flourish and a slightly squeaky high note. The conductor turned. "Ah, Miss Sutherland, you and your staff have trained them well"—his eyes traveled towards me and his smile stiffened a little—"at least as far as the singing is concerned."

"I'm very sorry," I said loudly and defiantly. Somehow the whole thing had become my fault. And the awful part was, there was a Judas in me that agreed with Janet and the maestro: if I had just stayed in the room as I was supposed to, I would have seen Randy

231

go off with John Something and would have speeded to take him myself.

"And this is—?" Janet said, looking at Julian.

"Julian Demarest, my cousin." I opened my mouth to go on when I felt fingers pinching my elbow with such power that all I could think about was the pain.

"How do you do?" Julian said to her with a slight bow. He glanced at the conductor, who was standing nearby. "Maestro," he said.

Faintly, because the walls and windows were thick, we heard a commotion outside.

"The prime ministers must be arriving," Julian said.

Janet frowned. "I suppose we'll just have to look for Randy later."

"I shouldn't worry," Julian said. "He'd never get through the guards and police. We'll find him here after the concert."

"Very well, I'll go and get the books." She started to move off.

"But these children are letter and word perfect," the maestro said. "Aren't you, little ones?"

The little ones giggled and shuffled and crowded around the tall conductor, sounding, once again, like sparrows.

"Nevertheless, they're going to have their books," Janet said. "They might be so overawed by all the distinguished people they're going to sing to that every word might fly out of their heads, mightn't it children?"

"Oh, no, Miss Sutherland, we really know the songs. Don't we, Miss Match?"

"It's true, they do. Maybe they don't need them."

"Never take anything for granted," Janet said gaily and went towards the anteroom where the bags were stashed.

"A woman of great determination," the maestro commented, in a tone somewhere between caution and admiration. "One would not care to cross her."

No, I thought. One would not.

"Is the singing going to be in here?" Julian asked the conductor.

"Oh, no. It's going to be in the delegates' lounge two floors below. It's much bigger. The adult male chorus can stand at the western end with the children in front. The guests will be gathered in the rest of the room."

"Strange," Julian said. "To have both children and a men's chorus. It's not a combination I would have thought of."

"No, neither would I," the conductor agreed. "But it's another example of Miss Sutherland's ability and imagination. She said it would have a little the effect of the great boys' and men's choirs in England. She was, perhaps, a bit optimistic about the children here. They do not have anywhere near the musical training of some of those boys' choirs—the King's College and the Canterbury. And, of course, the effect here is much lighter. Still, the singing is very pleasant. We must all be grateful to her."

Julian was looking at him in an odd way. "Of course," he said.

Janet came back in carrying all four book bags, and the raincoat over her shoulder. "Come along, children. Zero hour has come. I know you know the songs but I'm taking these down just in case. Now, right down the hall is a cloakroom, and Miss Marchington and I will take you there first."

Leaving the cloakrooms, we went down a short stairway, with Janet Sutherland leading the way, carrying the book bags and raincoat. I brought up the rear. Julian had gone down ahead of us.

"Quiet, children, quiet," Janet said over her shoulder, and the sparrow chatter quieted down. I had to admire her, I thought. I could tell them to be quiet until the cows came home, but nine times out of ten it would have little or no effect on them whatsoever. But Janet Sutherland had a magnetic grip on them. When she ordered, they followed.

At one point she stopped. "Now," she said, "around that corner you will be passing one of the most beautiful and valuable gifts the United Nations has ever received. It's an ivory carving showing a railroad winding through mountains and over bridges in China. It's a gift from the People's Republic of China and was made from pieces of eight elephant tusks. We can't stay and look at it, but you can see it as we pass."

It was indeed an incredible treasure, carved in minute detail. The children slowed as they walked past, their heads turning.

"It's extraordinary, isn't it?" Miss Sutherland said, standing in front of the down escalator. "Come along, now."

"Miss Sutherland," Mimi said, stepping onto the escalator. "Did those elephants have to die so people could use their tusks?"

Janet turned back. "Now don't get sentimental, Mimi. That's a work of art."

"I bet nobody asked the elephants," Mimi said, *sotto voce.*

"I bet you're right," I said quietly.

She looked back at me and grinned. I grinned back. I liked Mimi.

Finally we were all gathered outside the delegates' lounge. There was no door. The lounge itself formed the longer arm of an L of which the hall where we stood was the short arm. All we had to do was go around the corner and the lounge would stretch to our right, eastwards to the East River.

But at the moment we were huddled outside. Brilliant lighting lit up the western end of the lounge, which we were facing and where we would sing. What looked like a temporary dais fanned out from the western wall over which stretched a modernistic tapestry. The male chorus, some ten men in dark red jackets, were already on the dais. A piano had been placed on the other side, and Roger, the chinless young man, was seated at it.

"All right, children," Miss Sutherland said, "we're going in now." And she stood aside. "Mimi, you lead the way. Just go onto the dais and stand in front of the men, the smallest at the front. Virginia, that's you. Do you understand?"

234

"Yeth, Mith Thutherland," Virginia said, her lisp, in her general excitement, quite pronounced.

Roger, at the piano, struck up a cheerful marching tune. Giggling, chattering a little and looking, suddenly, quite angelic, the children filed in led by Virginia Wu. I hoped her parents were at the reception to see her. She was such a little flower, it was almost heart-breaking to watch her. For some illogical reason (and not because he was like her), this sent my mind back to Randy. As pain went through me I said a prayer for his safety.

Janet Sutherland and I were still out in the hall, but as the children mounted the dais, I could hear a rising murmur of appreciation followed by a burst of applause.

When Janet and I entered the room I saw the delegates and the VIPs standing in twos and threes and groups, stretching the length of the splendid room. Among them were some of the most famous faces of world politics. Tall, austere, unsmiling, the Israeli ambassador stood beside his prime minister, a shorter, stockier and younger man. There was John Something, standing well behind another famous face, this one under a cloth headdress. Probably nowhere else in the world did one man's power rest on so much oil and money. He looked the personification of feudal arrogance. yet I knew that the fanatics of his own country considered him a dangerous liberal, a man who had sold out both Islam and the Arab peoples by trying to drag them into the industrialized twentieth century. Curiously, I felt sorry for him. And there was the American secretary of state, for once off his shuttle and, other ambassadors, many of them from Africa in gorgeous robes. Just the sight of all those people standing, talking peacefully, should have made me feel better. But all I could think of was Randy. Who had taken him? What did John Something have to do with it? Why was I so sure that he had a lot if not everything to do with it?

I suddenly became aware that Janet Sutherland was saying something to me.

"What?" I asked.

"Go over to the other side by the windows," she said. "There's more room."

"I can't. It's too late."

The conductor, looking impressively handsome, stalked past us, took the baton from the piano, smiled at the children, then turned and made a few graceful introductory remarks expressing his pleasure at being a part—however unimportant (as he put it)—of proceedings that would bring peace to the world.

They all clapped, their eyes on the children. Janet Sutherland and I were standing just inside the big room. Opposite, the north wall, a long succession of windows, showed the gardens, the East River, the Queens Bridge and Roosevelt Island beyond. On the south wall over our right shoulders stretched a huge, very green tapestry, depicting the Great Wall of China from an aerial view. The greens, I noted, were extremely vivid, lending the tapestry considerable power.

"That's quite a tapestry," I said to Janet Sutherland. She was still, I noticed, carrying the book bags and the raincoat, which was now over one arm. "Would you like me to take those?" I asked.

"No!" The word snapped out. "They're no trouble," she added quickly and turned and smiled. I had never been this close to her before, and was a little surprised at the heaviness of her makeup. Everything else about her seemed so spare and tailored. Yet I could see the heavy matte finish on the skin of her cheeks. Maybe, I thought idly, she wanted to tone down the bony and muscular strength of that jaw. And perhaps, I thought, striving to be charitable, I was picking up such flaws only because of the brilliant lighting overhead.

"There's your cousin across there," she said suddenly, as the pianist trilled an introduction. "He looks as though he'd like you to join him."

"I can't run across there now," I said, nevertheless aware that I'd like nothing better than to be next to

Julian's reassuring presence. "They're going to begin," I added.

"Off with you." With one hand she gave me a slight push. The two book bags slung over her arm thumped against me, surprising me with their heaviness. I was unprepared for her shove and thrown off balance. Reaching out, I grabbed at her arm.

"Go *on,*" she said.

The guests were startled, but I made it across before the children actually started to sing and took my place beside Julian as the first note of the first song started. As I watched the children I found my mind preoccupied with the incident that had just taken place. My fingers could still feel the hard muscle under Janet's jacket sleeve. She was athletic, of course. Anyone looking at her could see that. I suddenly heard myself whisper to Julian, "She's pretty strong."

Some of the prominent guests standing a few feet away glanced at me, frowning. The Israeli prime minister and the Arab leader were standing together, one thin and dark-skinned, with strong nose and a short black beard, the other stocky, square and fair, with a balding head and small blue eyes. My gaze shifted to John Something. His hand started to reach inside his jacket. Perhaps it was the gesture, one I knew I had seen before, but suddenly I remembered the first time I had encountered him. It was not on the television screen. It was coming down the steps of the school. What did Miss Gales say? Was it Miss Gales or one of the other teachers? Whoever it was said he had come to check the meter. That was the day—yesterday, although it seemed a week—that Randy was locked in the basement . . .

"Julian—" I said abruptly, my voice fortunately drowned out by the crescendo of the song in which the male chorus joined.

"What?" he said. And then, without turning his head, went on, "Hurry while they're singing loud. Keep your voice as quiet as possible, but don't whisper."

"That man, the one who came to the school yesterday

237

when Randy was locked in the basement, he's over there, behind the Arab leader, in a gray suit."

But Julian's eyes were fixed on Janet. "What's in those bags?" he asked.

"The children's songbooks."

"But they're not using them."

"No." And furthermore, I thought, she didn't make the slightest attempt to give them to the children when they marched in. The men's voices, like bass instruments, were providing a powerful ground under the soaring sopranos of the children. My head, I thought, distractedly, felt like a computer into which too much information was, all of a sudden, being fed. I stared across at Janet Sutherland. The powerful overhead light picked up the thick sheen of her makeup, the brilliant blue of her eyes, the fine aquiline nose—the Marchington Inheritance, I thought ironically. An inheritance so valued by my poor father that he attached the Marchington name to his own, in the best socially aspiring English tradition. But he couldn't attach the looks he prized, the genes that produced those could not be bought. Aunt Ginevra had them. Suzanne and Toby inherited them as did Louise Carteret, and her son, Charles...

The music was getting louder. Roger, pounding at the piano, was visibly perspiring. There flickered into my mind the old movie I had seen in my long vigil the night before, those sleepless hours when I wrestled with and tried to forget what I had been told: that Michelle was my daughter. Hastily I wrenched my mind away from that area. What was the movie about? The scene drifted again across the screen in my mind, a pistol firing in a concert hall, the noise of the shot drowned in the crash of the cymbals...

Charles Carteret. My mind shifted back to Cousin Charles, who had been kidnapped by the PRA and never found...I stared at Janet Sutherland, at the dark hair, or the hair that had recently been darkened, because I remembered the broad white streak...white or blond. The Marchingtons were always blond, it went with the bones and the eyes...The dark hair could almost be a wig...Quite suddenly I knew that it *was* a wig...The music and voices grew louder, the children were really wonderful, the male voices powerful...

"Julian!" I said, and gripped his arm. "Charles— that's Charles—"

Julian leaped at that moment, but just before he did I saw the pistol glinting in Janet's hand, half hidden by the raincoat, a long piece on the muzzle, trained on the two prime ministers.

Julian was then in front of the pistol. I screamed. Janet's hand, still holding the gun, was thrust in the air. There was a popping sound. With a twist she was gone, out through the entrance. All this took less than a few seconds. Then bedlam broke loose.

Security guards were streaming out of the door, running after Janet. Julian had gone after her, too. People were milling about, there were shouts and loud voices. The children, still on the dais, were huddled together looking frightened, most of them with their mouths open. I was about to go to them when something made me look towards the prime ministers, who were standing, both of them quite calm, where they had been standing all the time. I saw a movement behind them. An arm in a gray sleeve went into a breast pocket. My eyes met those of John Something. A curious smile curved his mouth. His hand came out of his jacket cradling a heavy pistol. Deliberately he took aim, not at the prime ministers near him, but at the huddle of children. He looked as though he were giving himself some extraordinary pleasure, and it was the most terrible sight I had ever seen.

"No," I screamed. "Stop him!" And I plunged into the room towards him, knowing that I could not reach him in time.

It was the Israeli prime minister, a guerilla fighter himself once, who lunged at the arm holding the pistol, and it was the Arab leader who helped him struggle with the terrorist. Those shots were not silenced, and they roared into the decorated ceiling of the handsome lounge.

Randy was found, savagely and spiritedly kicking the door of a private toilet where he had been left, his arms bound and a gag in his mouth. Julian and one of the security guards located him, while I waited with the rest of the children and several more guards inside the lounge. The conductor, whom I had mentally stigmatized as something of a conceited oaf, came magnificently to the rescue and went soaring up in my opinion by insisting that the children continue through their songs and repeat one or two special favorites. It was a stroke of genius because it kept them occupied and reassured as the center of admiring attention past the period when they gave every sign of wanting to collapse in hysterical chaos. Other than taking them in relays to the nearest cloakroom, conducted this time by several of the guards, I had nothing to do but worry about Randy and Julian and admire the children.

The two former turned up in a surprisingly short time, Randy once again in his green T-shirt, looking somewhat the worse for wear but immensely pleased with himself.

"They heard me, Miss Match," he said proudly. "I knew they would so I got myself where I could kick the door."

"You were wonderful, darling," I said, and kissed him. He looked intensely embarrassed for a minute, then nearly undid me by reaching up, pulling me down and kissing me in return.

"Where's Janet—Charles?" I asked Julian.

"The police have him."

"I wish I could have seen her—him. I still can't believe it."

"Did you ever see Charles before the kidnapping?"

"Yes. But years before, when we were both children. Did you?"

"Yes. Not long before he was kidnapped. He was

about fifteen then, and just sixteen when the PRA took him."

"I suppose he was completely brainwashed, radicalized, whatever you call it. He wouldn't be the first to identify with his captors."

"No, it's now a recognized syndrome. The longer prisoners stay with those who capture them, the more they identify with them. That was the problem during the Korean War. And why the pilots during the Vietnam War went through so much training beforehand. It was to enable them to resist systematic indoctrination or brainwashing. Charles Carteret, at sixteen, didn't have a chance."

"Poor Charles. But it's hard for me to sympathize, considering what he was trying to do." I remembered the man who tried to shoot the children, and told Julian, "That's something that's beyond me. How on earth could anything or anyone that calls himself human do that?"

"If his secondary object—the first having been stymied—was to create chaos, then to shoot the children would do it."

"But it could hardly bring much sympathy for his cause."

"I doubt if he would think of it that way. That particular fanatic fringe of revolutionaries don't think of people as human beings. They're pawns in a grand scheme to establish perfect justice. That can only be done by destroying everything now in existence, especially present established authority. If it can be demonstrated that present authority cannot protect a group of helpless and appealing children, then that authority will be undermined. It may be horrible, but to them it's logical."

I shivered.

One of the guards came up and said the school bus was outside and the children, well protected, should get in and go.

The area outside the UN itself looked like an ordered battle scene. Police blocks had been set up as far as I could see up and down First Avenue, so that any spectators were far across the Avenue and farther uptown. There were more police cars than I could count, and the police themselves, some of them armed with shotguns, were standing one every few yards. Back, behind a cordon, were television cameras and reporters. There were shouts. Orders rang out, but other than that there was a queer, tense silence everywhere. The bus was pulled up next to the pavement, and more police were standing by that.

Julian was walking ahead of the children. I was behind, and there were several police in between. Silent and subdued by the sight of so many police and arms, the children filed quietly into the bus. I was just about to follow them when there was a flurry of noise and steps. I turned.

Coming down the steps by the gate was Charles Carteret. He had been handcuffed and was between two policemen, with others around. Catching sight of me, he stopped for a minute, perforce stopping his retinue.

How on earth could I have missed the resemblance? I wondered. Much of the makeup had streaked off his face. His hair was in a thick blond crew cut. He had on trousers, and it took me only a second to realize that the oddly wide thighs under the skirt had simply been the pants legs rolled up. He had arrived with wig and skirt, emphasizing the fact that Janet Sutherland was a woman. In his getaway, he had thrown away the wig and simply rolled down his trousers, throwing the skirt aside. In view of the fact that he had so successfully played the role of a woman, he now looked incredibly masculine. His coloring, of course, helped with the masquerade, I thought, staring dumbly at him. If he had been dark, it would have been much harder if not impossible to hide that stubble that now glinted blond on his cheeks. And what I had thought carelessness in letting his hair grow out white or fair—as I now knew— was calculated. He was letting it grow to a short blond skullcap over which he could wear a discardable wig.

242

Suddenly I said to him, "How could you do it, Charles?" and became aware of the television cameras set as near as the police would allow. "How could you use those children?"

"You always were a stupid sentimentalist, Avril," he said. "Running around making noises like some genteel radical just to get even with your father."

"Well, it was the genteel ex-radical who foiled you," Julian put in dryly. "So one up to her."

The police jerked Charles's arm and forced him down the steps. Without another glance, he got into a police car and was driven away. I thought perhaps I should feel something because this terrorist who had so nearly succeeded in destroying the carefully built peace was my cousin—but I could feel nothing but disbelief and astonishment that this slender young man with the killer's eyes was the headmistress, Janet Sutherland. I couldn't, in my mind, put the two together.

"Have they got them all?" I asked, just before getting into the bus.

"They think so," Julian said. "But they have to be sure. There was also a related bomb scare, which they think now was a hoax, but they can't leave anything unchecked. That's why this whole section of the city is cordoned off. People in this area have been told to stay indoors for a while, but that will probably be lifted before too long."

"It's so big to be so fragile," I said, getting on the first step of the bus. "I mean the city."

Julian smiled, and the contrast made me realize how strained his face had been. "Unfortunately, given modern weaponry, a few people in strategic areas armed with explosives can just about paralyze as well as terrorize any modern city. In fact, it doesn't have to be a few. One man—or woman—can do it."

"Anyway," I said. "Thanks." I hovered on the step. "I thought there for a minute you were going to be killed."

"Would it have made any difference to you?"

I glanced up quickly.

It was that moment the bus driver chose to say, "Come on, lady. The cops said they wanted this bus out of here. Let's go." He slammed the doors shut and the bus moved off through the tense, strangely silent streets.

Several hours later, after the children had been returned to the school, soothed, calmed, rested and sent home, I found myself up in my studio with Julian, who had turned up after his own tiring day. "Did you know?" I asked him.

"Did I know Janet Sutherland was Charles Carteret?"

I nodded. I had put a large sketching pad up on the easel and was drawing vague lines on it with a piece of charcoal. It was nothing but doodling, but it settled my nerves.

"No. If I had known I would have stopped her/him somehow before she got to the delegates' lounge." He paused. "Now that we know Janet was Charles, it seems unbelievable we—I— didn't guess immediately, but at the same time such an outlandish charade simply didn't occur to me. I console myself for that lack of imagination by the fact that the one time I did see him, not long before the kidnapping, he was a remarkably underdeveloped fifteen—skinny and at least three inches shorter than he is now. There are boys that do a lot of growing after sixteen and he was obviously one. But I forgot that and the height threw me off. For a woman, Janet was very tall, and my mind was fixed on that." He sighed. "Still, there's no real excuse. The eyes—those Marchington eyes—should have tipped me off. Instead of which I remained dumb while you dropped one hint after another: Aunt Ginevra's statement that Sutherland reminded her of Louise Carteret—the old girl was on the ball even though she didn't know she was—and your describing Janet as having a color job over white hair."

"Did you know Charles was alive and acting as a terrorist?"

244

"We—some old buddies in intelligence and I—knew who had taken him. There was never any secret about that. But we weren't sure whether he was still alive. Since no one had seen him for years we assumed he was dead or had slipped out of the country. I think we were right about the latter, although none of our friends overseas seemed to have gotten wind of him. I suspect he was trained in his role abroad. He was certainly adept at it. Aside from any nagging feeling you may have had about his Marchington looks, did it remotely dawn on you he might be a man?"

"None. The only time I came anywhere near it was when I wondered if her—his—revolutionary colleague—John Something or other—were a boyfriend. I knew instantly that wasn't true. But I didn't stop to analyze why I was so sure. When did you suspect the school was connected to terrorist goings on? Ye gods that sounds funny!" I said. "A day-care and primary school connected with terrorists!"

"That was its genius. Who would make a connection there?" Julian sat down on the window seat and put one knee up, resting one arm on it. "It was the drawing you and Randy produced. My visual sense is terrible. And, of course, even with your help, the sketch from memory of a seven-year-old boy is hardly reliable. But I thought it looked like the PRA symbol, and a colleague, or rather former colleague of mine in intelligence, nailed it immediately. So I did some digging. You remember when I told you the house had been bought by the Smith-Penfield from the Carterets?"

I nodded.

"Well, I dug around and talked to a few people and did some checking in old files. Smith-Penfield was a respectable-sounding name picked out of nowhere by an old organization that benefited mightily from the bad old witch-hunting fifties. When I say benefited I mean nobody would have known about it or cared if some eager and idiotic soul on the un-American activities committee hadn't decided it was subversive. And overnight it became another noble victim of wicked tyranny. Prominent liberals who wouldn't have bothered with it promptly joined and had their names engraved on the letterhead. In the turnaround of the sixties it really didn't have to *do* anything. Its old symbolic importance was enough, and it became a sort of gathering place and haven for well-known people who simply wanted to lend their names and contribute money to liberal-sounding causes. And there's no question but that the foundation did a lot of good—particularly in the areas of homes for homeless children, schools for handicapped children and so on. To buy the old Carteret house for a school went right along with everything else they'd been doing. And so this respectable-sounding front for the PRA approached the Carteret heirs with an offer to buy the house, into which they put a perfectly genuine day-care school. But it was a setup for Janet's emergence. I don't know which of Charles-Janet's PRA friends in high and diplomatic places made the suggestion that the children should sing at the Arab-Israeli reception, but it was a stroke of genius. The moment it was set, the kind of situation for which Charles must have been trained and groomed was put into effect."

"Were any of the other teachers involved?"

"No. They were all quite as innocent as you." He glanced at me. "Didn't they seem horrified when you got the children back?"

"Horrified hardly describes it. They'd been watching the thing on television along with the children who remained at the school—mostly the younger ones. And all of them, but especially Miss Gales, were just about in shock. You know," I said after a minute, "the more I think of the mechanics of Charles's masquerade, the more I wonder that he didn't slip. Little things, like . . . well, like going to the bathroom."

"Aren't there a lot of private bathrooms all over the house? Surely there aren't just multiple cubicles as in public schools."

"No, you're right."

"Did all the teachers live there?"

"No, only Miss Gales and...and Charles. There again...with only two of them there in the evenings ...women are terribly prone to drop in on one another—at least they were in school."

"Yes, but Charles—Janet could easily neutralize that by giving out that he didn't want to be disturbed after a certain hour or before such and such a time in the morning, and you can be sure he slept behind locked doors. Also, was he around that much?"

I thought for a while. "Not really. Not consecutively. She...he...went away a lot. Do you think that made a difference?"

"Of course. It lowered the risk. Because it was still a risk. Anything could have happened. One of the teachers could have fallen and grabbed him to stop herself. If that had happened, if she'd grabbed, say a muscular arm—"

"That's what happened to me," I said suddenly. "I clutched her arm there in the lounge, and it was one of the things that dropped into place and made me suspicious. It was not only terribly muscular, but it didn't feel like a woman's arm...I mean it was sinewy."

Julian nodded. "I once talked to an agent who had to pass as a woman over an extended period, and he said unexpected accidents like that were the real hazard. Plus other things you wouldn't think of. Such as smell. Not everybody is aware of this—at least consciously—but men and women smell different. So anybody of one sex trying to pretend he or she is another, would have to be careful to be freshly bathed at all times, and never to get too hot. If Charles had turned up at the school twenty-four hours away from a bath having had some vigorous exercise, I don't mean one of the teachers would sniff the air and say, Ah, that's a man, but I think they'd all be aware on some subliminal level that she didn't smell right—that there was something funny going on. The same is true vice versa. And, of course, there was the matter of a beard. He couldn't have carried it off if he'd been dark."

"No, even I thought of that. What an irony! It was the Marchington looks, what poor besotted Father called the Marchington Inheritance, that made it possible."

"There's cosmic justice in that somewhere, considering your father's worship for the established order."

"But to go back to the masquerade. Charles . . . Janet . . . whatever you want to call him, was an attractive person, male or female. Good-looking, terrific bones, good build. Bright. Yet I never felt warmed by her. There was something about her that chilled me and, I think also the others at school, and I realized, as I watched Charles when he was being taken off by the police, that it was his eyes. They belonged to a person who could kill anything."

"That's right. He has been as totally programmed as a dog that has been trained as an attack killer."

"I'm glad Cousin Louise, his mother, is dead." I thought for a minute. "Do you really suppose Randy was *locked* in the cellar, and didn't just lock himself in?"

"Possibly either Charles—Janet or her colleague, that John Whatever who came to the house pretending to read the meter, could have done it. Charles may have told him to go there and nose out the situation. Randy, by his drawing, had revealed that he had been in the cellar and had seen some incriminating stuff—mainly posters. Randy's drawing had been taken away, of course. And the chances are that Charles and her friend John would have let the situation alone, since it would have been more dangerous to do something to Randy than not—especially with their big day coming so soon. But by chance Randy had gone down for another look at just the time that John was there, or maybe it was before Charles—Janet left. We may never know. But one of them, finding Randy once more in the cellar—even without the incriminating posters—may have succumbed to the temptation to put him out of communication until at least the reception was over. After that, it didn't matter."

"You'd have thought they would realize the fuss that would be raised over a missing child would do them far more damage than anything Randy would say."

"You would think so. But just because people are terrorists doesn't mean they don't make mistakes—from their own point of view."

"Did Randy tell you why John tried to get rid of him again?"

"Apparently John, still trying to find out what he knew, took advantage of Randy's having to go to the bathroom again and teased him into betraying himself. He somehow brought up the subject of the drawing and then taunted him for inventing the calico cat. Randy got so mad he forgot our instructions and said he had so seen the cat, and what's more he'd seen those funny drawings. Which, of course, was what John Whatever was fishing for, and sealed Randy's fate. He would have to be disposed of in the melee following the murders of the Israeli prime minister and Arab chief."

"Poor Randy!"

"Poor Randy nothing! He'll be the hero of his peers for years to come. He'll be even more insufferable than he already is."

"He's not insufferable," I said indignantly. "He's a darling."

Julian grinned.

After a while I asked, "Where did George come into all this?"

"Blackmail. If he had stuck in Europe he would have been all right. I think. But being transferred to the Middle East and North Africa proved his undoing. He and Suzanne weren't getting on too well. He traveled a lot, drank a lot and one day when he was in or around Tunis, he was approached by an Arab boy on the make." Julian sighed. "Whether it was a trial balloon tried on any American official just to see if he would bite, or whether somebody somewhere had an idea that George was deeply strapped in a closet, I don't know.

249

It isn't even important at this moment. Poor George fell. After that it was the usual story, incriminating photographs, threats of exposure and so on. What the blackmailers probably wanted more than any national secrets, which George didn't have, were industrial ones. And he was a prominent officer of a big corporation with expensive tastes. They may have mostly wanted somebody on their payroll, so to speak, who would be sitting in on boardroom decisions and throwing his influence, such as it was, in their directions. Evidently he stumbled on information about the terrorists, who may or may not have been connected with those who held the incriminating pictures. Weak as George was, he found he had reached his limit and resigned. Poor bastard, he must have known or guessed he didn't have long to live. Politics in that area of the world can get very rough.

"His resignation was his act of courage and rebellion. He did it before they could stop him. And since he'd been less than an effective executive for some years previous, his employers accepted his resignation with alacrity. It couldn't be reversed. Then, when he got home he insisted on seeing me. He knew that I'd been in army intelligence. But since I was the family lawyer, I think he felt he could see me without running the risk of getting a bullet in his back. Any meeting with me would be innocent-seeming . . . And I was too stupid and too unsympathetic to pick up his signals. He wouldn't talk in my office, he wouldn't talk on the street, and by then I'd already made a date at the lunch place I told you about, thinking I might do him some employment good. So he didn't get to talk much to me there. By the time my glad-handing friend had gone and we'd eaten lunch, the place was fairly deserted, and he didn't want for us to be seen loitering. He was a very scared guy, Avril, and I don't blame him. Those people play for keeps. As he found out. I should have put him in a taxi and taken him then and there down to a friend of mine in intelligence work, who could have arranged some protection. But he only told me a little:

that he thought some kind of blowup was arranged when the Israeli prime minister and the Arab leader were to meet here. But, of course, we'd already had dozens of those, and I thought this was just one more. So I said I'd get in touch with a friend and would call him. Then he got that phone call you and Suzanne talked about, and although we'll never know, he probably talked to somebody who said they'd talked to me and the three of us were to meet in Central Park early the next morning. Hell, he may have talked to a perfect mimic imitating me. There are such people, expert at voices, who could fool anyone. If he thought it was I, then he'd accept without question a meeting the next morning."

"Poor George," I said.

"When is he going to be buried?"

"On Tuesday. At St. Andrew's. Suzanne is making the arrangements."

After a minute, I asked, "Are you actually in intelligence now?"

"No. I'm a reserve officer, as I told you. But once in you're never entirely out. And my talents, such as they are, are sometimes co-opted." He looked at me. "Do you remember once, about ten years ago, on Lexington Avenue, you saw me?"

"I was right then. I asked Father's secretary if you were in town and she swore up and down that you were in a hospital out in the Pacific somewhere."

"You were indeed right. I was in town. I've never moved so fast from a corner in my life. It was essential that everyone who knew me thought me to be in a hospital in the Pacific."

"I don't know why I feel so delighted about having been right—being justified after all this time. But I am."

Julian smiled again. "What are you going to do about Michelle?"

A curious stab that was both pain and pleasure went through me.

I stopped doodling and went over towards the win-

251

dow and sat down on the window seat. "If you had told me that I could have found the daughter I spent so much time and agony looking for, and then not know the answer to your question, I wouldn't have believed you."

"Did you tell her?"

"That I knew she was my daughter? No. I almost woke her and told her, but I didn't."

"Are you going to?"

"I don't think it's for me to tell her. It's for Suzanne."

"Well, will you pressure Suzanne?"

"I don't know. I can hardly believe myself saying that, but I don't know. Somehow . . ."

"Yes?" Julian said helpfully. He reached out and took my hand. "Yes?"

"I think my lost daughter became a sort of symbol of all the things my father took away from me. I felt that he'd torn away part of my being, and that I could never live without finding it. And then it turns out to be Michelle. And she's not a symbol, she's herself. It's not me she loves, it's Suzanne, who has never really been that fond of her, or at least Michelle thinks she hasn't. But maybe Michelle was part of Suzanne's resentment against George because George forced her to take Michelle. And now, with George gone . . . I don't know what's best for Michelle or what's best for Suzanne, or what's best for me. We'll just have to see."

"How do you feel about her?"

For some reason his question shook me more than what had gone before. I could feel the tears slipping down my cheeks and put my hands up. "I always imagined that there would be this tremendous gush of mother-feeling if and when I ever found her. I like Michelle. I'm sorry for her. I guess I love her, I certainly understand some of her problems more than Suzanne ever will. But I don't feel the titanic wave the way I expected too."

Julian took out his handkerchief and handed it to me. "No romantic agony."

I shook my head and then blew my nose. "And what's

252

more," I said, through a stopped up nose, "I can't get rid of the feeling that what poor Michelle wants is for her mother—Suzanne—to love her. And with George gone, maybe Suzanne will. At best, I'd be a sort of substitute."

"Well, it's not a thing you have to decide in the next half hour. By the way, I have some news of my own."

I looked up. "What?"

"Marjory astonished me by asking me for a divorce."

I lowered the handkerchief. My heart had started an odd thumping. "What did you say to her?"

"I said yes I would give it to her, and tried hard not to show indecent alacrity. She even said I could have custody of the boys."

"I didn't know you wanted it."

"I know you didn't. You never asked."

"No. I didn't, did I?" I paused. "I've never been exactly fair to you, Julian."

"That could easily be called the understatement of the year." He glanced at me in the late-afternoon light. "I even had a suggestion I thought I might put to you."

I was having a curiously hard time breathing. I noticed that either I was gripping Julian's hand very tightly or he was squeezing mine. Or we were squeezing each other's. I looked up at him. He leaned forward and pulled me into his arms. I put my own up around him. We had a long, satisfying and delicious kiss. Then he held his cheek against mine for a while and then I kissed it. "What is your suggestion?" I asked rather breathlessly.

He leaned back, still gripping one of my hands. "I hate to spoil the unblemished drama of your life, but I was thinking of something middle-aged and unexciting, a triumph of middle-class values over the romantic anguish you've always favored."

"Like?"

"Like marriage."

"I accept," I said, and put my arms around him again. "I'm no longer young and even today with liberation

253

exploding around us on all sides, a girl has to look after herself."

"Woman," Julian corrected. "You mustn't let your terminology drag behind."

Then we kissed again.

Get Your
Coventry Romances
Home Subscription NOW

And Get These
4 Best-Selling Novels
FREE:

LACEY
by Claudette Williams

THE ROMANTIC WIDOW
by Mollie Chappell

HELENE
by Leonora Blythe

THE HEARTBREAK TRIANGLE
by Nora Hampton

Stranger in the Night

Suddenly the bat fluttered its wings extra fast. Everything went kind of hazy. I felt dizzy. I don't know what happened next exactly. I only remember that I heard a sound like a cork popping out of a champagne bottle.

When I could focus again, a tall, pale man was standing beside my bed. A thin mist swirled around his feet. A long black cape hung from his shoulders, and his jet black hair was slicked back from his pale face. "Good evening," he said, raising one elegant black eyebrow. "You are Michael McGraw, are you not?"

I nodded, wondering when he was going to bite my neck.

"Don't vorry—I am not going to bite your neck," he said as if he had read my mind. He had a deep voice and a funny accent that put the stress on the wrong syllable half the time. "I am here to enter your contest. . . ."

Books by Bruce Coville

Camp Haunted Hills:

How I Survived My Summer Vacation
Some of My Best Friends Are Monsters

The Monster's Ring

My Teacher is an Alien

Monster of the Year

Available from MINSTREL Books

Monster
of the
Year

by
Bruce Coville

Illustrated by
Harvey Kurtzman

A GLC Book

A MINSTREL® BOOK

PUBLISHED BY POCKET BOOKS

New York   London   Toronto   Sydney   Tokyo

For Troy

This book is a work of fiction. Names, characters, places and incidents are either the product of the author's imagination or are used fictitiously. Any resemblance to actual events or locales or persons, living or dead, is entirely coincidental.

A MINSTREL PAPERBACK *ORIGINAL*

 A Minstrel Book published by
POCKET BOOKS, a division of Simon & Schuster Inc.
1230 Avenue of the Americas, New York, NY 10020

Copyright © 1989 by General Licensing Company, Inc.
Cover artwork copyright © 1989 by General Licensing Company, Inc.

Special thanks to Rich Hubeny of Penn Advertising for allowing me to visit his shop and for sharing his expertise in outdoor advertising, and to Pat MacDonald for her generous support.

Cover painting by Steve Fastner
Book Design by Alex Jay/Studio J
Typesetting by Jackson Typesetting
Editor: Tisha Hamilton

ISBN: 0-671-69667-X

First Minstrel Books printing October 1989

10 9 8 7 6 5 4 3 2 1

A MINSTREL BOOK and colophon are registered trademarks of Simon & Schuster Inc.

Printed in the U.S.A.

Table of Contents

Chapter One

My Slightly Strange Family

THUD! That was me, falling off the couch.

"Something wrong, Mike?" asked my mother, without moving her eyes from her laptop computer.

I moaned softly. That got her to look up, so I crossed my eyes and let my tongue hang out.

Mom sighed. She knew what was coming, but now that I had her attention, she figured she had to ask anyway.

"What is it, Michael?"

"I'm bored. If I don't find something to do I'll die."

"So, go clean your room. Or are the junk-piles too high for you to get through the door?"

"Very funny," I said. "I mean it, Mom. Syracuse dies in August. I haven't been able to play baseball for a week because of the rain. I've read so many comic books my eyes are crossing. I'm going out of my mind!"

1

"The boy needs a job, Elsa," said a third voice. The words drifted out of a heat register at the base of the wall. "I say put him to work. Then the two of us can take a vacation."

My mother pushed aside her computer and went to kneel by the register. "Jeff, either come down and join us or stop eavesdropping."

"I wasn't eavesdropping," said my stepfather as he stepped through the living room door.

Mom glanced at the register, then back at my stepfather. "I thought you were upstairs, tearing out a wall."

"I was," said Jeff. "But I got tired." Curling his fingers, he used them to comb some flakes of plaster out of his brown beard. I could tell from his smirk that he had tiptoed down the stairs as fast as he could after he first spoke into the register. He loves doing that kind of thing, which should tell you a lot about him. "Besides," he continued, "this conversation sounded interesting."

"Well I'm glad *someone* has found *something* interesting around here," I said from the floor. "I'd feel bad if you were both as bored as I am."

"Boredom is a sign of mental deficiency," replied Jeff, wiping the plaster dust from his bald head. "The solution to this pathetic condition is to learn something. For example, you could learn about your mother's business."

2

"Thanks a lot, motor-mouth," said Mom.

"I'm serious," said Jeff. He stepped over me to sit on the couch. "It would be good for him. Better than lying here like a footstool," he added, placing his feet on my chest.

I shoved aside Jeff's boots and scrambled to my feet. "What a great idea!" I said. I love my mother's office—mostly because the people she hires are all a little strange.

"It would be a bad idea for Mike to hang around the house the rest of the summer," continued Jeff. "Just because I work at home doesn't mean I can keep an eye on him all the time. He could get in all kinds of trouble while I'm wrapped up in a story idea."

Jeff is a science-fiction writer. He's also kind of weird. (I think the two things probably go together.) But I like him a lot. In fact, when he adopted me I had my last name changed to McGraw, to match his. He meant more to me than a father I hadn't seen since I was six months old.

The funny thing is, my mother didn't change *her* name when they got married. She said she had changed it the first time she got married, and changed it back after the divorce, and that was enough. She planned to stay Elsa Adams for the rest of her life. This confuses outsiders, since

3

they can't figure out who I really belong to, but it suits the three of us just fine.

What didn't suit Mom was the idea of me working for her. "Adams Billboard and Outdoor Advertising does not need a sixth grader hanging around the office all day," she said firmly.

"Adams B.O. Advertising needs all the help it can get," replied Jeff. "And what difference does sixth grade make? He starts seventh grade next month. And just last week you told me you needed a new gofer. So why not Mike?"

"If I'm going to be an animal, I'd rather be a gorilla."

"A gofer is an errand person," said Jeff. "Known as such because someone is always telling him to 'go fer' something. As, for example, right now I want you to 'go fer' a soda for me."

What Jeff really meant was "Get out of the room so I can work on your mother." So I headed for the kitchen.

I like our kitchen. It's a big old room with huge wooden cabinets and a blue tile floor. It may be kind of grungy, but it has "character," as my mother likes to say.

"Going downstairs for more soda!" I yelled, without checking the fridge. I figured that would give Jeff more time to convince Mom she should give me a job.

4

Our cellar is cool and deep and dark. But I never turn on the light before I start down the creaky wooden stairs. It's a little game I play— seeing how well I can get around down there in the dark. It's trickier than it sounds, because for some reason the previous owner put up rough wood walls that divide the cellar into sections.

Of course, it's usually not all that dark during the day. But on that particular afternoon the thunderclouds had darkened the sky and the cellar was too dim for me to see more than a few feet ahead of myself.

I moved slowly, groping my way along the rough wood of the cubicles. I was almost to the root cellar when a cold hand reached out of the darkness and grabbed the back of my neck.

Chapter Two

Kevver

Kevver Smith was laughing so hard he could barely stand up. "You should see the look on your face!" he gasped, leaning against a post and pointing a small flashlight at me. "It's great."

I leaned against another post and glared at him. I wasn't mad at him for scaring me. After all, we've been playing "Gotcha!" for years now. I was mad because this put him several points ahead of me.

Kevver and I started sitting together in the cafeteria in first grade because we both had Frankenstein lunchboxes. When we discovered we were both born on the twenty-ninth of August that cemented things. We've been best friends ever since. We spend so much time together that we call each others' mother "Mom"—which gets us some funny looks when we're out in public, since Kevver is black and I'm white.

"How long have you been down here?" I asked.

"About three hours."

"Didn't you get bored?"

Kevver shrugged. "I brought some comics and my flashlight. Were you doing anything better than that?"

I shook my head. The rain was pounding against the tiny windows. Kevver followed me to the root cellar. We found a six-pack of cream soda, then clumped back up the stairs.

"Make a lot of noise," I said. "I want to make sure my folks know I'm coming."

"How come?"

I explained about the job idea, and how Jeff was trying to talk Mom into it.

"Man," said Kevver, "you are soooo lucky! That place is great. I wish I could work there."

"That's a good idea. If Mom says yes, let's see if we can get her to take you, too."

"Well, how did it go?" asked Jeff when we walked back into the living room. Kevver gave him the thumbs-up sign, and I realized that Jeff must have helped him hide in the cellar. The rat.

"So what about it?" I asked. "Do I get the job?"

My mother sighed. "We might as well give it a try," she said, reaching for a cream soda. She took a sip then leaned back against the couch and said, "I ought to have my head examined."

Jeff leaned over and stared into her hair. "It looks fine to me," he said. "In fact, I think it's quite lovely."

My mother snorted, and I decided to wait until supper to bring up the idea of having Kevver work at the shop. Her response was not encouraging. In fact, her exact words were, "You have got to be kidding!"

"I think it's a good plan," said Jeff, reaching for the mu shu pork.

We eat mu shu pork a lot. Mom claims she can run a business, make a house sparkle, and cook like Betty Crocker. She also says she has no interest in trying to do all three at the same time. So unless Jeff or I cook, which isn't very often, we eat take-out from the Chinese restaurant down the street. That's fine with me; I like the stuff.

"And just why is it a good plan?" asked my mother.

"Well, for one thing," said Jeff, scooping a pile of brown glop out of the carton, "young Kevver has excellent taste."

Mom rolled her eyes. "The fact that Kevver Smith thinks you're the world's greatest science-fiction writer does not mean I can use him at my office."

Jeff turned to pass me the carton. He gave me a

9

wink and said, "People who make billboards for a living need all the good taste they can get."

Mom started to growl, so I decided to wait until morning to bring the subject up again.

To my surprise, she brought it up first. "I thought about Kevver last night," she said, slathering cream cheese on her Sunday bagel. "Jeff is right. If the two of you are at the office and there's nothing to do, you can keep each other company—and stay out of my hair. But the first time I hear the words *I'm bored*, you're fired. Both of you!"

Jeff flashed me a grin. I decided to forgive him for letting Kevver in the cellar the day before.

Kevver stayed overnight. In the morning the three of us piled into Mom's car. I turned on the radio, so we could listen to our favorite DJ, "Skip" Toomaloo. He was singing one of his "morning songs."

> Oh, I know a girl, her name is Sue
> She's got lips like Superglue

My mother snapped off the radio, killing Skip's voice in mid-warble. "How can you listen to that moron?" she asked.

"Because he's more on than off," said Kevver.

I ignored the pun—Kevver makes them all the

time—and said to my mother, "Everybody listens to Skip. He's the most popular DJ in Syracuse."

"Well, I think he's disgusting," she said. "They never should have let him back on the air after that cat thing."

Everyone in Syracuse has an opinion on how station WERD should have handled the now infamous "Thirty Ways to Cook Your Cat" episode. Skip claimed he was just trying to find out if anyone else was really awake at five o'clock on Monday mornings. He said later that the way the studio switchboard lit up with protest calls showed the problem wasn't that people weren't awake, but that their sense of humor was still asleep.

After a flood of letters and newspaper editorials, the station banned Skip from the air for a week.

When he came back, his audience had tripled.

I was trying to decide what to say to my mother about all that when we pulled into the parking lot.

"Now remember," she said as we walked to the building, "this is an experiment. If it doesn't work out, I don't want any complaints. The first time—"

She didn't finish her sentence, because just then she tripped over a woman who was lying on the floor, moaning.

It was Wendy Moon, the company's billboard artist.

Wendy was young, and except for the fact that her nose pointed a little sideways, she was very pretty. She was dressed in black jeans and a black T-shirt. She had a black headband wrapped around her wispy blond hair, and a large piece of cardboard pinned to her chest. Written on it in huge, black letters were the words, *Art is Dead*.

Chapter Three

Wendy Moon

"Wendy, get up and stop blocking the doorway," snapped my mother. "And take off that ridiculous sign! I have some new employees I want you to meet and you're giving them a bad impression."

"A bad impression!" cried Wendy, climbing to her feet. "How can we give anyone a good impression, when we have clients like Ed the Plumber?" She darted behind the counter and held up a piece of stiff cardboard. A flap of tissue paper covered the front of it. "Have you seen this? Have you seen what this man wants to do to my design?"

We gathered around the drawing, which showed a man standing next to a maze of pipes. It was labeled, "Let the Amazing Mr. Ed Solve Your Plumbing Problems."

"Sounds like a laxative ad," said Kevver.

The drawing was very funny. I knew it was Wendy's work by the style. Unfortunately, the tissue paper overlay was filled with corrections and changes. The revised design was as dull as a pair of kindergarten scissors.

"It's pretty bad," agreed my mother. "On the other hand, it's Ed's billboard. If he wants a disaster, that's his choice."

"Agggh!" shrieked Wendy. She dropped her head against the counter. "Arrrgggh, aaaggggh, errrrgggh!"

She stood up, stomped into her office, and slammed the door. Two seconds later her hand reappeared to hang the Art is Dead sign on the doorknob.

"I knew this was going to be fun," whispered Kevver.

My mother sighed. "I do so love working with creative people," she said. "Well, I'll deal with Wendy later. Come on, boys. I'll show you where you're going to be stationed."

We followed her through a large double door into the shop, which is this huge area filled with the stuff they use to make billboards: metal panels for the painted boards, racks to hang them on, paint, brushes, the projector that blows up artwork to billboard size. Just tons of neat stuff.

Just inside of the doors to the right was a box as big as a room. Actually, it *was* a room. But in that huge space, it looked like a box. From other visits I knew this was a staff room. The shop crew gathered there in the morning for coffee, ate lunch there, and so on. Before Mom even opened the door I knew I would see a table, a coffee pot, and a wall covered with flyers, announcements, and small versions of her billboards.

What I didn't expect to see was the big man sitting at the table. He was wearing a grubby T-shirt. His muscular arms were about as thick as my legs. He had a gold tooth.

"Peter," said my mother, "I want you to meet our new gofers, Kevver and Michael."

The big man looked up and squinted at us. "Kids," he said, crushing his coffee cup. "I hate kids!" The cup was only cardboard, but the movement made Peter's bicep bulge like a softball.

"I take that back about this being fun," whispered Kevver.

But by late afternoon Kevver and I were feeling fairly comfortable with our job. The staff room had an intercom that people used to call us when they wanted something. We spent a lot of time delivering messages, sharpening pencils, and fetching fresh coffee.

The week went by in its own weird way. Wendy took to leaving little drawings for us to discover when we first arrived each day. Pete got friendly enough to growl hello each morning. We started to see how the business really worked.

Friday afternoon Kevver and I helped unload a shipment of paint. By the time we finished my arms were throbbing. "No wonder Pete looks the way he does," I whispered to Kevver.

He nodded. "If we keep this up, our muscles will be so big we can be superheroes for Halloween."

I smiled at the thought. Then I rubbed my aching shoulders. I wondered if it would be worth it.

We were heading back to the staff room when we heard a burst of angry voices explode from the front office. Without saying a word, we changed course and headed out the double doors.

It was Wendy again. At least, she was involved. But she wasn't making much noise this time. She was just standing in the corner, banging her head against the wall.

Chapter Four

Brainstorms

"I knew (*thump, thump*) this (*thump, thump*) was going to (*thump*) happen," moaned Wendy. "I just (*thump*) knew it."

"Now Wendy," said my mother, "settle down and get back over here. Let's see if we can work this out."

She was standing at the front counter, holding a billboard design. Next to her was a short, fierce-looking woman. She was dressed all in black, except for a large, round button that said, "BAM!" She looked familiar, though I couldn't figure out why.

Standing next to the woman in black was a man who could only be Ed the Plumber.

"That's amazing," whispered Kevver. "He looks just like the cartoon Wendy drew."

I nodded, but didn't say anything. I was trying to figure out what was going on.

"So you see, Mrs. Adams," said Ed, spreading his hands, "once Mrs. Smud talked to me, I decided not to go ahead with the billboard. I want to cancel."

"There *will* be a cancellation fee," said my mother sharply.

"No matter," snapped the woman in black. "BAM! will cover that cost."

She turned and stalked out of the office. Ed followed, looking sheepish. He paused at the door. "Do you think I should try television?" he asked. "I was talking to—"

"Out!" cried my mother. "Out, out, O-U-T OUT!"

Ed ducked through the door and disappeared.

"What was that all about?" I asked.

"Nothing much," she said softly. "Just Ed, coming to cancel his contract."

"Aaarrrghh!" cried Wendy, banging her head against the wall again.

"Didn't like the new design?" asked Kevver.

"He loved it," said my mother. "Only he's not going to do billboards anymore."

"Why not?"

Mom held up a button identical to the one Mrs. Smud had been wearing. "BAM! stands for 'Billboards Are Monstrous!' Myrna Smud wants to ban outdoor advertising, and she's starting with us because she thinks we make the most offensive billboards in town."

"What's wrong with them?" asked Kevver.

"According to Myrna, they're too imaginative. She says stimulating the imagination leads to crime."

"Sheesh!" said Kevver. "Next thing you know she'll want to ban fairy tales."

"She's working on it," said Mom grimly.

Suddenly I realized why Mrs. Smud had looked familiar to me. I had seen her hanging around our school last spring. "She's the one who was trying to ban all those books from our library!" I shouted.

I was really mad now. This woman wanted to shut down both my mother and my brain. I wanted to strike back. But it wasn't until the next morning that I figured out how to do it.

It was one of those ideas that grows slowly, then suddenly explodes. It started at breakfast. It was Saturday, and Kevver had stayed overnight. Jeff decided to make bacon and pancakes for breakfast. Mom joined us in the kitchen. When the four of us sat down to eat together we were still complaining about Myrna.

"Can we change the topic?" asked Jeff. "Talking about censorship while I eat gives me indigestion." He paused for a moment, then brightened.

"You guys have a birthday coming up. What do you want?"

"A billboard," I said, without even thinking about it.

"That's ridiculous," said my mother. "Do you know how much a billboard is worth?"

"No."

She told me. I almost choked on my pancake. But I didn't give up. "What's an empty billboard worth?" I asked.

"Nothing," she said. "It's just a drain on the company. When I think about what Ed did yesterday—" She stopped in the middle of her sentence, but it was too late.

I smiled sweetly. "Ed the Plumber's contract for that billboard was supposed to start on my birthday. Don't you see, Mother—this is fate! It's like it was planned. We can't resist it."

Kevver picked up the battle. "I think it's a neat idea. I'd like one, too."

"We could share!" I cried, trying to give my mother the idea that this would save money.

She looked at me with a puzzled expression. "What would you do with a billboard if you had one?"

"Let me think about it," I said.

Mom smirked, which I did not take to be a good sign.

After breakfast Kevver and I examined one of Mom's media kits. These are folders she uses to show clients the kinds of signs we make. I figured it might give us some ideas.

"How about a public service billboard?" asked Kevver. "This says the company donates a few billboards to good causes every year. If we can convince your Mom we're doing something worthwhile, she might say yes."

"Sounds pretty dull to me," I said.

"Wait!" cried Kevver. "I've got it! Let's tell her it will be educational."

I made a face. "That sounds even duller than a public service billboard."

"No, you don't understand. We tell her it's going to be educational for *us*. We'll do the look-how-much-we'll-learn-from-this number on her."

"I like it!" I said. "Do you think we'd be pressing it if I tell her I want to learn the family business?" I frowned. "Of course, if that old bat Myrna Smud has her way, there won't be a family business much longer."

That was when it hit me. I've heard about inspiration, but this was the first time I ever experienced it. I felt as if a bolt of lightning had just sizzled through my skull.

"Oh, wait!" I cried. "What if we use the billboard to take a shot at BAM? Mom ought to like that. After all, Myrna and BAM! are the reason the billboard is empty anyway."

Kevver was immediately caught by the idea. Listen, BAM! stands for 'Billboards are Monstrous!' right? So why not make a *monster* billboard?"

It took another two days, and a lot of help from Jeff, but we finally wore my mother down.

"All right," she said. "You win. You can have the sign for one month. But here are the conditions."

And then she handed me a contract.

I couldn't believe it. A contract from my own mother!

"Hey," she said. "You want to get involved with the business? Then do it in a businesslike way."

The contract was pretty official looking; Mom had even written it on company paper. It had some gobbledygook in it, but most of the important parts were right to the point.

For this sign, Adams Billboard and Outdoor Advertising will provide:
* paint and other necessary supplies
* two days of staff time
* one month of display on the structure adjacent to Erie Boulevard and Tanner Avenue
Michael McGraw and Kevver Smith will provide:
* concept for the sign

* labor and talent necessary to finish the sign
Sign concept and design to be approved by Elsa
Adams before work commences.

"What does this mean?" I asked, pointing to
the part about what Kevver and I would supply.

"It means I expect you to do your share. Wendy
will help with the design, and Peter will set you up
for the painting. But I can only afford to give you
two days of their time. So be careful how you
use it."

"So what kind of sign do you guys want?"
asked Wendy, after my mother had explained to
her what was going on.

"Something with monsters," I replied.

Wendy pulled a BAM! button out of her cork-
board wall. "Billboards Are Monstrous," she said,
pointing to the letters. "You guys wouldn't be
trying to rattle Myrna Smud's cage, would you?"

Kevver and I smiled.

"That's cool," said Wendy. "This should be fun."

We started brainstorming. Let me tell you, thinking can be hard work. But it was fun, too. We
threw around a million stupid ideas, kept a few,
put parts of different ideas together. Wendy
sketched like mad all the time we were talking,
tossing sheet after sheet of paper into her waste-

basket. It took almost six hours, but we finally settled on a billboard announcing a Monster of the Year contest.

The design showed Frankenstein's monster, with Dracula and the Wolfman peering over his shoulders. All three were staring at the Bride of Frankenstein. Along the base of the drawing eerie black letters proclaimed, "ENTER THE MONSTER OF THE YEAR CONTEST TODAY!"

We thought it was pretty funny. How could we guess anyone would take it seriously?

Chapter Five

Sign Up

"Kids," snorted Pete when he saw our design the next morning.

Shaking his head, he stomped over to a stack of tall, thin metal panels standing against the wall. His muscles bulged as he lifted a panel and carried it over to the rack. Hoisting the panel a little higher, he set the hooks on the back over the rack's crossbars. *Snap!* The panel clicked into place. "No one told me I was going to have to work with kids," he muttered as he headed back to get the next panel.

"Ignore him," said Wendy. "He's terrified he might have a pleasant thought before he gets his listing for 'Longest Bad Mood in the History of the World' in the *Guinness Book of Records*."

Snap! Another panel clicked into place.

"Back soon," said Wendy and headed for the door.

"Hey, you two!" yelled Pete. "You're big enough to help with this. Grab a panel and start moving."

The panels were twelve feet high and just over two feet wide. When they were all in place we would paint our sign on them.

By working together, Kevver and I were able to slide a panel over the floor to the rack. With me standing at one edge and Kevver at the other, we managed to heave it off the floor. It took a couple of tries to catch the hooks onto the crossbars.

"Good,' said Pete, when he saw that we could do it. "I've got other work to do. You can finish this yourselves."

Wendy came back just as we were putting up the last panel. She was carrying the final artwork, which she had done with transparent inks on a sheet of clear plastic. She put the artwork on the tray of a projector. When she switched on the machine, a twelve-foot-high image of the Bride of Frankenstein appeared on the panels.

"All right!" I cried.

"Your mom told me to remind you that you've only got six hours of my time left," said Wendy, as she opened a can of paint. "So pay attention while I show you what to do. You'll have to do most of this on your own."

Three days, seven paint spills, and one near fall

from a ladder later, our sign was ready to face the world.

On the morning of the big day, Pete and his crew took apart the metal panels and loaded them onto one of the company lift trucks. Kevver and I followed in a pick-up truck, with Wendy driving. It took about twenty minutes to get to the "structure," which is what you call the frame that holds a billboard.

Pete handed me a pair of work gloves. "Climb in," he said, pointing to a big metal bucket on the back of the lift truck. "We're going up."

I did as he told me. Pete got in beside me. Then somebody flipped a switch, and the bucket started going up. I wasn't about to let Pete see how nervous I was, so I gripped the edge of the bucket and smiled as we floated into the air. I guess maybe it showed anyway, because when I got back to earth Kevver told me I was as green as the monster on the billboard.

My mother showed up just as we were maneuvering the last two strips of metal into place. "Not bad, boys," she said after staring at the sign for a while.

"Not bad?" cried Kevver. "It's gorgeous!"

I agreed. Twelve feet high, forty-eight feet long, and all monster, our sign was the most beautiful thing I had ever seen.

Even so, I wasn't prepared for what happened when we started driving home that night. Mom had the radio on to get the report from the traffic helicopter. Most of it sounded like it does every night. The big difference was the last bit, when the pilot said, "The only unexpected problem is the big curve on the boulevard. Westbound traffic there is running a little slow because people are still gawking at that new billboard—the one with all the monsters."

I looked at Kevver. He looked at me. My mother made a funny sound. "I can't believe it," she said. "I just can't believe it."

"Oh, come on, Mom," said Kevver. "If you really believe in your business, it shouldn't surprise you when people pay attention to a billboard."

"It doesn't surprise me," she said. "It annoys me. I've been trying to get that kind of reaction to a billboard for twenty years!"

The next morning it seemed like every radio station in town was talking about the sign. We even got mentioned on the Skip Toomaloo show, which Mom let us listen to for a change.

As it turned out, part of what made the sign so fascinating was that no one could figure out what we were trying to sell. (No one even guessed that we weren't trying to sell anything; that was too unbelievable for words.) Most people figured it was a stunt to drum up interest in some new product or film that would be announced in the fall. But they were dying to know what it was— partly because they loved our sign so much.

We knew they loved it because when one of the local TV stations covered the story (another shock for my mother) the people they talked to were all laughing and smiling; well, all except one. The last interview was with Myrna Smud, and when she talked about the sign she looked like she had just been chewing on a lemon.

"This monster mania is terrible for our children," she fumed. "It stimulates their imagination, excites their minds. It could give them . . . *ideas*!"

"Now there's a terrible thought," said Jeff when he heard Myrna on the news. "Children getting ideas. Another sign of the decline of western civilization."

We hadn't set out to keep the sign's origin a secret, so any good reporter could have followed our trail. Several did, and three days after the sign went up Kevver and I had our pictures on the front page of the morning paper. That was exciting in itself. But what came next was even more thrilling.

We were sitting in the staff room, waiting for someone to ask us to do an errand when it happened. Mom's secretary buzzed us on the intercom. "Phone call for you boys," she said.

"Both of us?" I asked.

"That's what the man said."

We headed for the front desk. When I took the phone a familiar voice said, "Michael McGraw? I want you and your friend to be on my show tomorrow morning." I almost fell over. It was Skip Toomaloo! We were going to be ON the Skip Toomaloo Show.

To celebrate, Kevver and I got Jeff to drive us out to the billboard that night. It seemed especially appropriate to go in his car because he drives an old hearse—a funeral car. Jeff loves that car; he says its part of his image. Mom doesn't like it so much. She says if he considers it part of his image he must use a fun-house mirror when he shaves.

Anyway, we piled into the hearse and Jeff took us for ice cream, then drove us over to admire our billboard.

The sun was setting behind it when we arrived. I sat there, licking my butter brickle ice cream and admiring our beautiful monsters. As the light faded, I thought I saw something begin flapping around the sign. Then I saw another, and another. Before I knew it there were dozens.

"What kind of birds are those?" I asked, motioning with my ice cream cone.

Jeff squinted at the sign. "Those aren't birds."

"Well what are they?" asked Kevver.

Jeff hesitated. He looked at the sign, and then at us. "They're bats," he said at last.

I felt myself shiver—and it wasn't from the ice cream.

And still the bats kept coming—more and more, until there were thousands of them flying around the sign. The sound of their wings was like distant thunder. Suddenly, as if they had heard some kind of signal, they all flew away at once. All except one.

The last bat fluttered over to the hearse. It circled us three or four times, flapping at the windows, before it flew off to join the others.

Chapter Six

Telegram from Transylvania

Skip was on the air when we arrived at the radio station the next morning. I could see him through the glass wall of the booth. He was tall and slender, with a long, pointy moustache. While we were waiting for him, someone came up behind us and said, "Are you the guys that made the sign?"

We turned around and found ourselves facing a *very* pudgy girl.

"Well, are you?" she demanded.

I nodded, wondering what this kid was doing here.

"That's neat," she said. "I love monsters. Mostly because I am one."

"That's nice," I said. I glanced back through the window. I hoped Skip would come out soon. I didn't want to have to listen to this kid much longer.

"So, you like my father's show?"

I looked at her. "Your father?" I asked.

Just then the door to the soundbooth opened and Skip skipped out. (I mean it!) "Hello, boys," he said cheerfully, reaching out to shake our hands. "I see you've already met my daughter, Lulu."

As I shook his hand I was thinking, *What kind of a man would name his own daughter Lulu Toomaloo?*

But Skip seemed nice enough. He bought us a couple of sodas and told us what to expect when we went on the air.

"There's nothing to be nervous about," he said several times. "Pretend we're having a conversation in your living room. I'll just ask you about the billboard—how you got the idea, that kind of thing." He glanced at his watch. "News break is nearly over," he said. "Come on—let's go."

We followed him into the sound booth. He sat down, slipped on his earphones, and took a sip of coffee.

Instantly, a horrible look crossed his face. He spit the coffee back into his cup. Covering the microphone, he turned to his daughter and said, "Lulu, did you do this?"

Lulu Toomaloo returned her father's look with wide, innocent eyes. I'm not a kid for nothing. I could tell everything that was going on between them. Of course she had done it. He knew that. She knew that he knew. And he knew that she knew that he knew.

But admitting any of that would spoil the fun. So Lulu placed a pudgy hand against her face and let a single tear spill out of her right eye. It rolled slowly down her round, red cheek. "I guess maybe I did, Daddy Dear," she simpered.

I thought I was going to throw up. I don't think Skip took it much better, because I noticed that his right eye started to twitch. He began fiddling with the ends of his moustache.

"Now, Lulu," he said, "you know it's not nice to put salt in Daddy's coffee. It makes Daddy very unhappy."

Lulu smiled up at him, which almost caused her blue eyes to disappear behind her fat cheeks. "But, Daddy," she said, "I love to see the funny face you make. That face makes Lulu happy!"

We learned later that Lulu put something in her father's coffee once a week. To make things worse, she always did it at different times. This meant that Skip never knew *when* it was going to happen—or *what* it was going to be. In the past six months Lulu had spiced his coffee with vanilla, hair oil, and tabasco sauce. But those were for variety. Usually it was just salt, which worked well for Lulu's purposes, since it dissolved quickly and didn't smell.

What made all this especially cruel was that Skip really loved his coffee. As a morning DJ, it was the fuel that made his life possible. But the first sip of each new cup had become an adventure in anticipation. When would Lulu strike next?

Actually, from what Skip told Kevver later, that was only one of the questions that burned in his brain. The others included: Where did this kid come from? Is she really mine? Why is she doing this to me?

The answers to those questions were all very simple. Lulu had come from the same place all babies come from. She was indeed his. And she was doing this because she had a permanent, unending grudge against her parents for naming her Lulu Toomaloo. While some kids might have learned to laugh off the name, Lulu figured she had been permanently wronged. She had every intention of making her parents pay for what they had done.

Of course, things might not have been so bad if Lulu's parents hadn't spoiled her rotten before she ever understood how remarkably silly her name was. But as a baby, whatever Lulu wanted, Lulu got. I guess her parents figured it was better than hearing her scream.

Unfortunately for Lulu, most of what she wanted was edible, which was why she looked like she was in training as a replacement for the Goodyear Blimp.

But those were all things that we learned later. The only thing we learned about her that day at the station was that she was the most spoiled kid we had ever seen.

So who would have guessed that she would have been part of the great thing that happened next?

I first found out about it a few mornings later, when my mother called me and Kevver into her office. She had a funny look on her face—kind of like she had just seen a flying saucer or something.

"You OK, Mom?" I asked.

She nodded.

"What's going on?" asked Kevver

"Station WERD just called. They want to sponsor the contest."

"What contest?" I asked, ignoring the obvious answer. It was so ridiculous it never even crossed my mind.

"The Monster of the Year Contest," she said. "I told them I was going to take down the billboard in three weeks, and they said they'd pay to keep it up." She shook her head as thought she was in a daze. "They plan to buy space on other

37

structures, too. They want to build their whole fall promotion around your idea."

Kevver and I let out a whoop.

We were interrupted by Mom's secretary. "Telegram, Ms. Adams," she said from the doorway.

Mom looked startled. She took the yellow envelope and opened it. She grinned. "Listen to this. 'Monster of the Year Contest is great idea. Stop. Will be in touch. Stop. The Count.' "

"How could someone know about the contest already?" I asked.

"Oh, I'm sure it's from the station," said Mom. "Just a way of saying, 'Welcome aboard.' "

But I thought about the bats we had seen flying around the billboard, and I wasn't so sure. What I was thinking seemed too silly to say out loud, so I kept it to myself. But I was beginning to get a little nervous.

Over the next few weeks the Monster of the Year Contest took on a life of its own. Once my mother got over her shock she started to work out ways to take advantage of the situation.

She also gave me and Kevver a bonus. She said letting us have a billboard was the best investment she'd ever made. I realized then that it might be possible to make money doing something I liked.

Jeff felt pretty smug about the whole thing. I

could tell he was having trouble not teasing my mother about what a good idea it had been to hire us—especially when the story was picked up by the international wire services.

The first entries came from local people. Some announced the monsters they would be impersonating. Others began to stretch the term. A teacher entered one of her former students. Secretaries sent in entries for their bosses. People began talking about entering the mayor.

Kevver and I had fun going through the entry forms, even if we did have to put up with Lulu while we did it.

Then we got another telegram. It was from Transylvania.

Greetings. Stop. Will arrive Syracuse in two days. Stop. Bringing entrant for M.O.T.Y. contest. Stop. Please arrange accommodations. Stop. Igor.

Chapter Seven

Waiting for Igor

"Is this a gag?" I asked.

"It must be," said Kevver. "Transylvania is a made-up place."

"Not so," said Jeff. He ran a hand over his shiny head. "Transylvania was absorbed into Rumania decades ago, so people don't talk about it much anymore. But it's a real place."

He reached for the telegram. "We might find out something about this by calling Western Union. I'm guessing it's just a joke. You should consider it a compliment. Someone else is playing the kind of reality game you two started when you put up a sign for a contest that didn't exist."

"But now it does exist," I said.

Jeff looked at me. "What are you saying?" he asked.

I stopped. What was I saying? That what we did changed the way things really were? That seemed silly. I shrugged. "I don't know," I said. "Just talking, I guess."

"Well, stop talking and come eat," yelled my mother from the kitchen. "I don't plan to cook supper again for at least a month, so I want you to pay proper attention to this one."

My mother's claim that she can cook like Betty Crocker isn't far off. If she wasn't running a business, and my stepfather wasn't a truly weird science fiction writer, we could have a normal home, like on "Leave It to Beaver."

I mentioned that to Jeff once. He just looked at me and said, "If pigs had wings, they could fly." I wasn't exactly sure what he meant by that, but it didn't matter. I wasn't complaining. I pretty much like things the way they are.

When I went to bed that night I took the telegram up to my room and hung it over my desk. It was cool having a telegram from Transylvania.

But it got a little spooky when the second one arrived.

Greetings. Stop. Arriving at airport 9:30 PM, EST, October 15. Stop. Please secure accommodations and arrange to meet us. Stop. Igor.

We were at the radio station, sorting through

the mail that had come in about the contest. We could have sorted through it at home, of course, but Lulu always wanted to be involved. Since it turned out that one reason the station had decided to support the contest was that she had offered her father various threats about what would happen if they didn't, we could hardly refuse to let her help. But we weren't happy about it.

I suppose we sound kind of stuck-up. But you know how it is—little kids always want to hang around with big kids, and big kids always want little kids to leave them alone. That's just the way it is. We didn't hold the fact that Lulu was a girl against her that much. What we had against her—besides her being a little kid—was that she was obnoxious. I mean, would you want to be friends with a kid whose idea of fun was pushing up the end of her nose and making piggy noises at you? A kid who thought dropping ice cubes down your back was a sign of affection? A kid who liked to stuff a whole candy bar in her mouth, chew it for thirty seconds, and then stick out her tongue?

The more I saw of Lulu, the sorrier I felt for Skip. That bothered me. Skip had been a kind of hero for me. But it's hard to look up to someone you feel sorry for.

Anyway, we did most of our work on the contest at the station after school. Jeff drove us in twice a week to look at entries and discuss details for the big night.

Halloween was on a Monday. The plan was for the station to throw a huge party the Friday before that. Anyone who wanted to take part had to show up in costume or display whatever it was that made them monstrous. People who had nominated their boss or some local politician would be allowed to explain why they thought their candidate should win—though we didn't figure too many folks would try that. "Good way to get fired" was the way Jeff put it.

Then Kevver and I would do the judging, and give out the trophy.

We had billboards all over the city now. And every kid in school was talking about the contest. (And were they ever jealous of Kevver and me.) So things were rolling along pretty well.

At least until the fifteenth of October.

Jeff decided we should go to the airport, just in case someone named Igor really did show up. Mom wouldn't come—she thought we were just being silly. Lulu, on the other hand, insisted on going.

We drove over in Jeff's hearse, which seemed appropriate. Because it had only one seat, Kevver and I got to ride in back, far away from Lulu. Of

43

course Jeff had to put up with her, but we figured it wouldn't hurt him. Besides, he could always use her in his next book.

The airport was nearly deserted when we arrived, which wasn't surprising. Not many flights come into Syracuse on Saturday evening.

We checked the big flight board. The only thing coming in at nine-thirty was a Baltic Air Transport flight. But it was listed as coming from New York City.

"Well, no flights from Transylvania," I joked, feeling a little nervous.

Jeff shrugged. "You wouldn't expect a direct flight here from Rumania. Anyone flying in would probably have to make several stopovers."

He talked as if he actually expected someone to show up. Maybe he did. We had discussed the telegram over and over, again, and our current theory was that if it wasn't a joke, it was from a film company trying for free publicity. That was OK with us. It would make the contest all that much more fun.

We decided to go to the indoor observation deck to wait for the plane. A large glass wall looked out over the airfield. The night was dark and moonless—soon it started to rain. A flash of lightning streaked through the sky. Thunder rumbled.

"Baltic Air Transport flight number one has been delayed," announced the loudspeaker. "Arrival is now anticipated at ten o'clock."

Half an hour later the flight was delayed again. I wasn't surprised. The weather was really awful.

Jeff glanced at his watch. "I hope we're not waiting here for nothing," he said.

"I'm bored," whined Lulu. She had been saying that off and on after the first five minutes. Jeff gave her some money and told her to go get herself a snack.

No wonder she was so fat. I bet people gave her money and told her to go get food a lot.

Time dragged, and I fell asleep for a while. I'm not sure why we didn't just go home. I suppose it was because we had spent so much time there already. You know how it is—you start something, and then decide you're going to finish it, No Matter What.

Finally I heard the announcement: "Baltic Air Transport flight number one will land in exactly five minutes."

I looked at the clock.

It was five minutes to midnight.

Chapter Eight

The Mysterious Crate

At midnight the biggest bolt of lightning I had ever seen split the sky.

Then the rain stopped—just stopped, as if someone had turned off a faucet. Puddles gleamed on the runways as a plane came in for a landing. The four of us stood with our faces pressed against the glass of the observation window, staring at it. All was silent, until Lulu found that she could make rude noises by blowing on the glass.

A shiver whispered down my spine when the plane landed. It was small and black, with wings shaped like a bat's.

Jeff laughed. "That settles it. It has to be a film company. Come on, kids. This should be fun."

"Wait a second," said Kevver. "Let's watch."

Even after the passengers got off the plane we would have plenty of time to get to the meeting area. So we decided to wait.

Soon two men wheeled a ramp up to the plane. The door opened and we waited for the passengers.

There was only one—a short, hump-backed man, wearing a white lab coat.

I shivered again, and we headed for the escalator. We were waiting when the man came shuffling through the gate—Kevver and I close together, Lulu behind us. I don't think she was scared. She just liked to check out a situation before she made up her mind what kind of damage she was going to cause.

"Igor"—or whoever he was—came shuffling down the corridor, dragging one foot behind him. He had long, dark hair. One eye was half-closed in a kind of squint. One arm swung freely, and he kept the other tight against him.

Jeff stepped forward to greet him. "Igor, I presume?" he said with a smile on his face.

Remembering the movie *Young Frankenstein*, I almost expected him to say, "It's *Eye*-gore." But he didn't. Neither did he take Jeff's hand. Instead he grabbed Jeff's arm. "We have no time to lose!" he said desperately. "We must get to the baggage claim."

When no one moved right away he said, "Is there something wrong with you? Hurry!"

Kevver swung into action. "It's this way," he said. He started down the hall. The rest of us trailed after him.

47

Igor clumped along beside me. "Let's hope the tranquilizer doesn't wear off before we get there," he said. Then he gave me the weirdest smile I had ever seen.

"I'm hungry," said Lulu. We ignored her.

The baggage claim area was empty.

"Good," said Igor. "We're in time." He sounded almost disappointed.

The luggage carriers were moving. After a few moments several large black bags came sliding out from behind the wall.

"Grab them!" cried Igor. He lurched forward and snatched the first two off the conveyor belt himself. I dived for the next one. Kevver got the two after that.

"Well, here I am, stuck with a couple of old bags," he said.

"Don't mind him," Jeff told Igor. "He has an uncontrollable urge to make bad puns. Aside from that, he's a good kid."

"Remarks about kids really get my goat!" said Kevver happily. I could see he was just getting started. But before he could come up with another groaner a door at the side of the baggage area opened. A man came through, pushing a hand cart ahead of him. On the cart was a huge wooden crate. It was covered with red signs that said, "FRAGILE! HANDLE WITH CARE!"

"Package for a Mr. Eye-gore!" yelled the man.

"That's Ee-gore!" we all yelled. The man shrugged. Something thumped inside the crate.

"Quick," cried Igor, "help him get it off the cart." He thumped over to the man. Jeff joined him. Kevver and I put down the bags we were holding and ran over, too.

"I'm hungry," said Lulu.

The crate was at least eight feet tall. And was it ever heavy! But between the five of us we managed to wrestle it to the floor. As we did, I heard something start thumping inside of it.

"We're too late!" yelled Igor. "Stand back."

Before I could move, a huge green fist smashed up through the boards. Splinters flew in all directions.

The man who had brought the crate screamed and ran back through the doors.

A rumbling roar came from inside the crate as another fist smashed up through the wood.

"This is great!" cried Jeff.

I wasn't so sure I agreed.

"Reeooarrrr!"

The hands disappeared. I heard a horrible creaking noise—as if nails were being ripped out of wood. They were. The lid of the crate started to lift into the air.

Igor spun around and snatched one of the black

49

bags. "Don't let him out!" he cried, rummaging through the bag. "Don't let him out!"

Kevver and I looked at each other, uncertain of what to do. While we dithered, Lulu went and sat on the top of the crate.

"Reeaaooorrr!" rumbled the deep voice.

"Calm down!" snapped Igor. He scurried back to the crate, carrying a hypodermic needle in his right hand.

"What's that?" asked Jeff.

"Elephant tranquilizer. Now, if the young lady would kindly move."

"I'm hungry," said Lulu, getting off the end of the crate.

Immediately the lid wrenched away from the rest of the box. Igor jabbed forward with the needle. An outraged cry rang through the empty baggage area. It echoed for a time, fading finally to an eerie silence.

With a thump, the lid fell back into place.

Chapter Nine

Guess Who's Coming to Breakfast?

"You may take us to our hotel now," said Igor.

"Aren't you going to let your friend out?" asked Jeff.

Igor shook his head. "Flying makes him airsick. He will not calm down for another day or so. Until then—well, it is best that he stay where he is."

He took a hammer from one of his bags and started to pound the nails back into the crate. Of course, that still left two big holes in the top. I was dying to peek through one of them to see what was inside. But I had a terrible vision of those hands thrusting out again. If that happened I could get the biggest black eye in the history of the world. Either that, or lose my head altogether.

"I have to get the car," said Jeff. "Kids, why don't you come with me?"

We followed him down the hall. When I looked

back, Igor was sitting on the crate, pounding one last nail back into place.

"Well, what do you think?" asked Jeff when we were far enough away that Igor couldn't hear us.

"I think I'm hungry," said Lulu.

"I think they're great," said Kevver. "Or at least, Igor is. Who knows if there's anyone in the box or not?"

I started to ask what he meant, then figured it out for myself. All it would take for someone to create the effect we had just seen would be a sound box, a remote control and a couple of mechanical arms.

"That Igor guy must really want to win the contest," I said. I wasn't about to admit that I thought Igor and the box were for real. It made me feel pretty silly.

Lulu didn't worry about feeling silly. "I think they're real," she said. "By the way, I'm still hungry."

We happened to be passing a candy machine, so we took up a collection. Between Jeff, Kevver, and me we had enough change to get something for Lulu to stuff into her mouth.

She was happy. But I wasn't, not until I had an explanation that made sense of all this. "Why

would anyone want to win the contest this much?"
I asked.

"I can think of half a dozen reasons," said Jeff.
He started to tick them off on his fingers. "One:
it's someone who (a) has money and (b) loves
monsters—sort of how you and Kevver might turn
out if you ever get rich. Two: some film company
is taking advantage of your contest to get some
extra publicity. Fair enough. This whole thing is
about publicity. Three: some company is going to
use the contest to introduce a new product. You
know, one of those monstery breakfast cereals or
something. Four: some nut has decided—"

"OK, OK," I said, holding up my hands to stop
him. "You've convinced me."

"Good," said Jeff. "Because I'd hate to have you
think those guys are for real. This *is* just a joke."

I didn't know if he was trying to convince me,
or himself.

I tried another question. "If they're fakes, why
did you ask Igor if he was going to let his friend
out of the box?"

"I was just playing the game," said Jeff. He
took out his keys and unlocked the hearse. "Good
thing we decided to bring this baby," he said as
we climbed into the long, black car. "Otherwise
Igor would have needed to rent a van to get that
crate of his to the hotel."

"Mom will be amazed that this thing actually turned out to be useful," said Kevver. He knew how my mother felt about the hearse.

Igor was waiting for us at the front of the airport. With a lot of dragging and thumping, we managed to get the crate into the back of the hearse. It slid into the spot where coffins used to ride as if it had been made for it.

"My wife made reservations for you at the Karloff Hotel," said Jeff when Igor climbed into the front seat. "I hope that will be satisfactory."

"We shall see," said Igor. He slammed the door and we drove away with Lulu, Kevver, and me keeping the crate company in the back.

"I'm hungry," said Lulu. She crossed her eyes, pushed up the end of her nose, and started to make snorting noises.

The rain started again. Jagged bolts of lightning flashed all around us. The thunder sounded like exploding bombs. And then the thing in the crate began to moan.

It was still pouring when we pulled up in front of the hotel. "You kids wait here," said Jeff before he and Igor climbed out of the hearse.

I glanced down at the moaning crate. Jeff read the look on my face. " Don't be silly," he said. He hesitated, then added, "Look, if you have any problems, come and get me."

Then he slipped out of the car and disappeared into the rain.

We waited. Five minutes went by, and then ten. Other than a few thumps and moans, the box was quiet. I pressed my face against the cold glass of the passenger window to see if I could spot Jeff. Lightning sizzled down to my right through the thick rain. The clap of thunder that followed made me jump. It seemed to scare whatever was in the box, too. It thumped the sides and began to moan louder.

"I'm hungry," said Lulu nervously. "I think I'll go inside to get some food."

"I could use a candy bar myself," said Kevver. "Besides, this is the wrong time of the day for 'Good Moaning.'"

I didn't bother to groan at the pun. The box was doing enough groaning for all of us.

I opened the back door and we stepped into the rain. Drops the size of quarters spattered against us. We were soaked before we'd gone five feet from the hearse.

We bolted through the revolving door and into the hotel. I was peeling my soaked shirt away from my skin when I heard Igor shout, "This is an outrage!"

I turned and saw him banging his fist against the desk. Then he climbed on a chair, so that he could look the desk clerk in the eye. "It's an outrage!" he cried again.

"I'm sorry, sir," said the clerk. He looked pretty frightened. "But there is nothing I can do about it. Perhaps if you come back tomorrow?"

Jeff sighed. "Come on," he said to Igor. "We won't get anywhere with this guy. I'll take you to our place for the night. Maybe we can work this out in the morning."

Our place? Jeff was going to bring this nut home? I shook my head and reminded myself that it was all just some kind of stunt.

But if this guy was here from some movie company, what was the problem? Why wouldn't the hotel let him in?

"They won't accept his money," explained Jeff as we drove off through the pelting rain.

"An outrage!" muttered Igor. "An offense to my homeland. "I shall report them to the embassy!" He paused. "Better yet, I shall have a press conference!"

Well, there it was—a press conference. Must be Jeff was right after all. This was just a publicity stunt.

We dropped Lulu off at her place. Her parents were waiting up for her. As she ran to the door I heard her shout, "I'm home! What's to eat?"

We waited until Lulu was inside before driving away.

"A most strange little girl," said Igor, nodding back at the Toomaloo house.

He was the first person I had ever met who seemed too weird to call Lulu strange.

Mom was asleep when we got home. We had called her several times from the airport, so she knew about all the delays. About the fourth call she said she was going to bed, and we could tell her all about it in the morning.

Boy, was she in for a surprise.

"Do you think the crate will be all right out here for the night?" asked Jeff when we pulled into the driveway.

Igor looked as though we had just suggested that we sell one of his children. "Are *you* trying to insult us, too?" he asked.

"Of course not," said Jeff hastily. "I just thought—"

"We take him inside with us," said Igor. "Or else I stay out here—a fact I shall mention in my press conference tomorrow."

"Hey, it's OK," said Jeff. "We'll take it—him— inside."

Inside wasn't good enough. Igor insisted that the crate had to go up to the spare room with him. So we started dragging it up the stairs. The noise woke my mother. When she came into the hall to see what was going on, she just shook her head and said, "I can't believe I married that man."

Without another word, she turned and went back to bed.

Igor was incredibly strong, so it wasn't as hard as I had thought it would be to get the crate upstairs. Even so, by the time we had both Igor and the crate settled, Kevver and I were so exhausted we could hardly see straight.

"Good night, boys," said Igor as he closed the door to his room. "Sleep well. And don't be afraid. Nothing is going to happen—*tonight.*" Then he gave us a weird laugh and closed his door.

"That guy is major strange," said Kevver.

I nodded. But I was too tired to think about it right then. I don't even remember getting into bed. I just know sleep felt awfully good.

When I woke up, I wondered if the whole thing had been a dream. Kevver said if it was, we had been having the same dream.

We went downstairs for our usual Sunday morning breakfast. "Morning, Mom!" I said. I was trying to be cheerful, so I was kind of insulted when she started to scream.

Kevver tugged on my sleeve and pointed behind us.

I turned around and found myself nose to navel with a guy who had to be at least seven feet tall.

I looked up and swallowed. He looked down and smiled. He had green skin. Two large bolts stuck out of his neck. His face looked as if it had been stitched together by a drunken tailor.

He reached toward me with the biggest hand I had ever seen.

Chapter Ten

Igor and Sigmund Fred

My brain felt as if it had blown a fuse. My muscles refused to move. I could only stare at that huge hand, waiting for it to close around my neck.

Suddenly Igor pushed through the door and was standing next to me. His head barely reached my shoulder.

"For heaven's sake, don't be rude!" he hissed. "Shake hands with him, or there's no telling what might happen."

I swallowed hard and held out my hand. It was trembling like Jell-O in an earthquake. The tall, green man started to smile again. He took my hand, which disappeared inside his huge fist. "Good morning," he said.

His voice reminded me of last night's thunderstorm.

"Good morning," I managed to squeak.

"Michael," said my mother, "what is going on here?"

I blinked. How should I know what was going on? All I knew was that life was getting weirder by the minute. I swallowed and said, "This is Igor—you saw him last night—and his friend."

If Igor's "friend" had walked up behind me on a dark night, I would have screamed and run for my life. But the fact that we were in our kitchen, and that it was a bright, sunny morning helped to keep me in place.

Besides—it was all just an act.

Right?

My mother rose to the occasion. "So pleased to meet you," she said graciously. "Won't you both join us for breakfast?"

The thing standing behind Igor rumbled, which I took to mean yes. Igor rubbed his hands and clumped forward.

We made room for them at the table. The chair creaked under the creature's weight, but didn't break.

I wasn't sure what to call the tall green man. He sure looked like Frankenstein's monster. But I didn't want to call him "Frank." As a monster lover, I knew "Frankenstein" wasn't the name of

62

the monster. It was the name of the scientist who made him. The correct title for the creature itself is "Frankenstein's Monster."

But that's not really a name. I mean, you wouldn't say, "Pass the butter, please, Frankenstein's monster." At least, I wouldn't—not under those circumstances.

Finally I got up my courage and said, "Aren't you going to introduce us to your friend, Igor?"

Igor looked at me as if I was out of my mind. "You mean you don't know who this is?" he asked.

"I know!" I said. "I just wasn't sure what I should call him."

Igor sighed. "That's a delicate subject," he said, slathering cream cheese on a bagel.

We all waited. Igor put down the bagel. "It's like this," he said. "The man who made my friend named him Sigmund. But he used a brain that had once belonged to a man named Fred. So sometimes we call him Sigmund. And sometimes we call him Fred. And sometimes we call him Sigmund Fred."

Kevver snorted. "That's what you get when you let some psycho analyze things."

I knew there was a joke in there somewhere, but I didn't have time to figure it out. The monster was starting to growl.

Igor looked a little nervous. "So usually I don't

call him anything," he continued quickly, "since it just upsets him."

"Just make sure you call me for dinner," rumbled the monster.

And then he smiled. The sight made me nervous. I was afraid he was going to rip out some of his stitches.

My mother laughed her business laugh—the one she uses when she doesn't want to offend a client who's just told a joke she doesn't think is very funny.

"You two are quite delightful," she said. "Now, why don't you tell us what this is all about."

Igor raised one bushy black eyebrow. "I beg your pardon?"

"Who are you working for?" she asked. "I can't believe you went to all this trouble just for the fun of it. Those costumes are terrific. Come on—you can tell us. It's not against the rules or anything. Who put you up to this?"

Igor's nostrils flared, and he raised his other eyebrow to the level of the first. "Madame," he said, in dignified tones, "We have come to enter the Monster of the Year Contest. We have come in good faith. I do not like to have our sincerity questioned."

"Well, where do you live?" asked Jeff. I had the impression he was trying to humor Igor.

"We have a cozy little castle in Transylvania."

It was my mother's turn to raise an eyebrow. "Transylvania?" she asked slyly. "I thought that was where the Count lived."

"That arrogant booby!" cried Igor. "I, too, was born and raised in Transylvania. But I had dreams, ambitions. So I moved on. After much wandering, I met—the doctor." He placed his hand over his heart. "The doctor. Ah, now there was a man."

Sigmund Fred put out one huge hand and tipped it back and forth. It was clear he didn't think as much of "the doctor" as Igor did.

"With the doctor, I scaled the heights of success. When we retired, I took Sigmund Fred back to Transylvania with me, where I bought the very castle my parents had worked in when I was a child."

My mother rolled her eyes. She thought Igor was full of baloney, and she was getting tired of it. Fortunately, the conversation was interrupted by the doorbell.

It was Skip and Lulu. When Skip saw the tall, green man sitting at our breakfast table sipping tea, the ends of his moustache began to twitch.

"See, Daddy," said Lulu. "I told you they were interesting."

"How do you do," said Skip, when we introduced our visitors. He looked so nervous when he shook hands with Fred that I almost laughed. Then I realized that I must have looked about the same way myself a few minutes back.

"Coffee?" asked my mother.

"I'd love some!" said Skip.

When Mom went to get the coffee, Skip turned to Igor and Sigmund Fred. "How would you two like to be on my show tomorrow?" he asked.

"Can we talk about the rude way we were treated at the hotel last night?" asked Igor.

"Sounds good to me," said Skip.

Mom set a cup of coffee next to him. He smiled at her and took a sip. I realized it must have been a relief to him to get a cup of coffee and be sure that Lulu hadn't had a crack at it. Unfortunately he was so interested in our visitors that he failed to keep an eye on his daughter.

"How long does it take you to do your makeup?" he asked Sigmund Fred.

"Why do we need makeup for radio?" asked Igor.

"Well, you don't," said Skip. "But I want to have a photographer there. I'd like to get you just the way you are now. You look great."

"But we are not wearing makeup," said Igor angrily.

Skip smiled and took a sip of his coffee. "Phh-auugh!" he cried, spitting it back into the cup.

Lulu covered her face with her hands and made loud, piggy laughing noises.

Igor and the monster looked confused.

"Come on, Lulu, we're going home," said Skip angrily.

I expected Lulu to complain. But I guess she figured she had had her fun for the morning, so she didn't care what happened next.

"Skip and those two were made for each other," said my mother after the Toomaloos had left.

I didn't think she meant it in a nice way. She went in the kitchen and started dragging out her cookbooks. Jeff went out to help her. Even so, I knew she was going to be in a bad mood for the rest of the day. She hates cooking—especially on Sundays. But as long as we had company, she felt she had to.

Kevver and I stayed in the living room with Igor and Sigmund Fred.

"So what did happen at the hotel last night?" I asked.

Igor frowned. "They would not accept my money," he said.

"Why not?"

He pulled a bag out of his coat. "They say it is not good," he said, emptying the bag on to the coffee table.

I could feel my eyes getting rounder. The bag was filled with gold coins.

"Are these real?" I asked.

"Of course they are real!" said Igor. "Genuine Transylvanian gold coins. But that fool clerk said he had never seen any such thing, and he couldn't accept them. So I took my credit card. But they didn't accept Transylvanian Express either."

Igor talked all about that on Skip's show the next morning. Later Skip helped him organize a press conference, and he repeated the story for the local papers. They loved it—especially since he had Fred with him. The seven-foot-tall green monster made a great "photo op." (That's newspaper talk for photo opportunity—the chance to get a good picture.)

I wasn't surprised when the local newspapers carried the story. They had been having a lot of fun with the Monster of the Year Contest. What I didn't expect was that the national news would pick it up. But they did, and the next day Igor and Fred were featured in newspapers, coast to coast.

That night we got a second telegram from the person who called himself the Count. He claimed to be outraged at "Fred" for traveling to America to try to pick up the Monster of the Year Award.

"Tell Igor this means war" were the last words of the telegram.

Jeff was still convinced that this was all some big publicity stunt. I wasn't so sure now. But when I woke up that night and found the biggest bat I'd ever seen in my life hovering at the foot of my bed, I made up my mind.

This was for real.

Chapter Eleven

Life Gets Weirder

I had never been so scared in my life. I lay beneath the sheets, staring out at that big bat and thinking: *This is it; I'm about to become one of the living dead.*

I also thought: *Why is it you never have a chunk of garlic when you need it?*

Suddenly the bat fluttered its wings extra fast. Everything went kind of hazy. I felt dizzy. I don't know what happened next exactly. I only remember that I heard a sound like a cork popping out of a champagne bottle.

When I could focus again, a tall, pale man was standing beside my bed. A thin mist swirled around his feet. A long black cape hung from his shoulders, and his jet black hair was slicked back from his pale face. "Good evening," he said, raising one elegant black eyebrow. "You are Michael McGraw, are you not?"

I nodded, wondering when he was going to bite my neck.

"Don't vorry—I am not going to bite your neck," he said as if he had read my mind. He had a deep voice and a funny accent that put the stress on the wrong syllable half the time. "I am here to enter your contest—and to teach those upstarts Igor and Sigmund Fred a lesson in manners. I assume you have a place for me to stay?"

"I don't know," I said. "I'll have to check with my mother."

All right: so I was too cowardly to tell him no on my own. At least I didn't tell *him* to go ask my mother.

"I assume it vill be settled quickly," he said. "I read in the news that you have offered Igor and Sigmund Fred your hospitality. If this is so, it vould not be good to refuse me. It vould make the contest appear—unfair! Especially as I contacted you *before* they did."

"You did?"

He looked at me scornfully. "You did receive my telegram, did you not?"

I remembered the telegram that arrived the day WERD had told Mom they wanted to sponsor the contest—the one signed, the Count. I swallowed. "We got it. But we didn't think it was for real."

My visitor looked offended. "Not real?" he asked in a low, dangerous voice.

"Well, no," I said. "We thought it was a joke. After all, how could you have known about the contest so early?"

"I have my sources," he said. Then I remembered the bats we had seen circling the billboard. I swallowed nervously. "What do you want me to do?" I asked.

"Tell your mother the Count has arrived," he said. "I vill avait her response."

Then he swirled his cape in front of his face. I heard the champagne cork noise again. A sudden puff of smoke hid him from view. When the air had cleared, the Count was gone and the bat was back. It fluttered into the corner, and hung upside down from the edge of my bookcase.

Keeping one eye on the bat, I slipped out of bed. I grabbed my robe, headed for the door, and ran down the hall to my parents' room.

"Mom!" I yelled. "Jeff! We've got company!"

Jeff came to the door, tying on his robe and looking groggy.

"Michael, what in heavens' name is going on?" he growled.

I swallowed. How was I going to explain this one? Finally I just said, "The Count is here."

Jeff sighed. "This is too much," he said. "I don't mind these people—whoever they are—taking advantage of your contest for a little self-promotion, but what makes them think they can disturb us in the middle of the night? This is too weird."

"Jeff, this may be weirder than you think."

"What do you mean?"

I swallowed, then said cautiously, "I think this guy is for real."

Jeff put his hands over his face. That's the gesture he makes when he's trying to figure out an important plot point. It means he's thinking really hard.

"All right," he said at last. "Let's head for the kitchen."

"Jeff, I don't think you understand. There's a vampire in my bedroom!"

"That's why we're going to the kitchen. I want to get some garlic."

"You mean you believe me?" I said in surprise.

"Let's just say that I'm keeping an open mind," he replied. "Obviously, if I was in my right mind, I would say that you were out of yours. But since I make my living by trying to believe six impossi-

73

ble things before breakfast, I can't just brush you off. So let's get some garlic. Then we'll see what's up."

To my surprise, we had a whole string of fresh garlic. "Lucky thing Mom went shopping this week," I said.

"Luck had nothing to do with it," said Jeff. "I bought that garlic myself."

I looked at him. He shrugged. "I told you, I make my living by taking the impossible seriously." He cut the rope of garlic in the middle and handed me half of it. "I also believe in being prepared. Now—tell me a little more about what happened."

I think the look on Jeff's face was even more frightening than the arrival of the Count. He didn't act as if he thought I had had a bad dream. He was taking me seriously, and he looked pretty nervous.

I don't like it when adults get scared. It makes the world seem out of control.

"Did he seem friendly?" asked Jeff when I had finished my story.

"Well, he didn't seem mean," I said. "But that doesn't necessarily tell you anything."

He nodded. We both knew plenty of people who acted nice but were really mean—and vice versa.

"He did say I didn't have to worry," I continued.

"The government says something like that every year when they send out the tax forms," replied Jeff. "Better hold on to your garlic."

And with that we started back up the stairs.

The Count had changed back into his human form. "Greetings," he said when I introduced him to Jeff. "I am so pleased to meet you." He glanced at the garlic. "I see you are feeling cautious," he added.

Jeff smiled. "It never hurts to be careful," he said.

"I disagree," replied the Count. "Sometimes diving right in is the only vay to avoid real pain. But that is neither here nor there. I vas inquiring about a place for me to stay."

Jeff scratched his head. "Don't you have a—well, a coffin, or something?" he said.

The Count nodded. "But of course. It should be delivered any moment now. I vould appreciate a room below ground, if you do not mind. The sunlight—hurts my eyes."

The doorbell rang. "Ah," said the Count. "That vill be my coffin."

Jeff looked at his watch. "A vampire I can almost believe. But deliverymen who come at three in the morning? That's the strangest thing I've heard yet."

As we followed the Count down the stairs I got the feeling that his feet were not actually touching the steps. But his cape was in the way, so I couldn't tell for certain.

We opened the door.

"Ah," said the Count, rubbing his hands together. "My home away from home."

Resting on the sidewalk was a polished wooden box, the deliverymen nowhere to be seen.

"Give me a hand, will you?" said the Count.

The coffin was lighter than it looked. I realized that was because it was empty. Working together, the three of us carried it into the cellar.

The Count was delighted when he found that the cellar had been divided into sections. "Do you have guests down here often?" he asked.

"Not really," said Jeff.

The Count poked his head into the cubicles until he found one that he liked. "Vell, it's not the Plaza," he said. "But I guess it vill do for now." He glanced around. "Vould you mind terribly finding something to cover those windows?"

Jeff found some burlap sacks and we tacked them up over the windows.

"Thank you kindly," said the Count. He lifted the lid of his coffin. "Such a cozy spot," he said, looking into it. "If you vill forgive me, I am exhausted from my journey. I vill visit vith you more tomorrow."

"But not before sunset, eh?" asked Jeff.

The count lifted one long eyebrow. "Vhat do you think?" he asked with a smile.

The curve of his lip revealed a pair of gleaming fangs.

Chapter Twelve

And Weirder!

"Well, what *do* you think?" I asked Jeff when we were back upstairs.

"I think life is weirder than anyone can imagine."

"Come on, Jeff. You know what I mean. Is he for real?"

Jeff laughed. "You're the one who saw him turn into a bat," he said.

That was true. But I was beginning to wonder if it had been some kind of trick. I was pretty groggy when he first woke me up. Maybe he had hypnotized me, or something. It didn't seem likely. But then, how likely was it that we just helped a vampire drag his coffin into our cellar?

I didn't sleep very well that night. It was a big relief when morning came.

The relief didn't last long. As I came down to breakfast I heard an angry voice in the kitchen.

"Here?" cried Igor in astonishment. "You let him come here?"

I came through the door in time to see my mother smack a large spoon against the table. The noise made Sigmund Fred flinch.

"Now you listen here, Mr. Igor," said Mom. "This is *our* house, and it is *our* business who we let stay here."

"But we are enemies," said Igor. "We are having a feud."

"Well, have your feud somewhere else," said Mom.

Good old Mom. She wasn't taking any nonsense from these monsters. Sometimes it pays to have a hard-nosed advertising executive around the house.

I slipped into a chair beside Sigmund Fred. "Have some cereal," he rumbled, passing me a box of flakes. The box looked tiny inside his giant green hand. It was almost empty. That was because the monster had already taken most of it. He was eating out of a mixing bowl, and using one of Mom's big cooking spoons to shovel the cereal into his mouth. I noticed the bolts at the side of his head moving up and down as he chewed. I hoped one of them would fall off. At least that would prove he was a fake.

But they stayed right in place.

It was a relief when two guys from the radio station arrived to pick up Igor and Sigmund Fred. Since we could count on the Count to sleep until sunset—or at least, to pretend to do so—we could stop worrying about the monsters until after supper.

The Count appeared about five minutes after sunset, looking for V-8 juice.

I found a can at the back of the pantry.

"Sorry it's not cold," I said.

The Count shivered. "That vould be terrible," he replied. "I much prefer it varm."

He watched as I rummaged in the drawer for a can opener. "That tool is much like a big fang, isn't it?" he said as I poked a hole in the top of the can.

"I hadn't noticed that until you mentioned it," I said. I poured some of the thick, red juice into a glass and passed it to him.

He licked his lips. "Vould you happen to have a straw?" he asked. "It seems more natural if I can —suck it."

I found a straw, and the Count went into the living room. Unfortunately, the guys from WERD chose that moment to bring Igor and Sigmund Fred back to the house.

"Ah, I see the peasants have returned," said the

Count, who was leaning against the fireplace, sucking on his V-8 juice. "How charming."

"This is America," snapped Igor. "Everyone is a peasant here. So being a Count doesn't count for a thing."

"So clever!" purred the Count. "And so short!"

Fred started to rumble about then. The noise started somewhere deep inside him. It began to get louder and louder, like an approaching jet airplane.

"Why doesn't everyone come to dinner!" said my mother, desperately trying to sound cheerful.

Igor and the Count managed to avoid an actual fight during the meal. Mostly they just sneered at each other.

"Look," said my mother. "Are we being filmed or something? Is this like some big joke?"

Igor, Fred, and the Count looked offended. But before anyone could answer, the doorbell rang.

By this time that was getting to be pretty frightening in and of itself.

For a minute no one said a thing.

The bell rang again.

"Oh, go answer it," said my mother. But she didn't sound happy.

When I opened the door, I knew her mood was only going to get worse.

Standing on the front step was a tall creature

H. Kurtzr

covered with green scales. He had webbed hands, and gills at the side of his head. A puddle of water had collected around his big, flat feet.

"Hi," he said with a nervous smile. "I'm the Creature from the Yuccky Lagoon. Have I come to the right place?"

I hesitated for a moment, then invited the creature in. By this point, I thought, what difference did it make?

The creature spotted the aquarium on the other side of the room and said, "Oh, do you raise your own food?"

"Actually, those are just to look at," I said.

The creature glanced at me like I was out of my mind. But he shrugged and said, "I'm so excited about your contest. I think it may be just the break I need to get back into the business."

"You'll never get back into the business," said a voice behind me. "You've got no talent."

It was Igor. He was crouched in the doorway leading to the kitchen. Fred and the Count loomed large behind him.

"That's not true!" cried the scaly creature. He sounded hurt. "I had lousy scripts. I had bad directors and low budgets. But that doesn't mean I got no talent. All I needed was a good agent."

At the mention of the word *agent* the other three made a series of gestures with their hands, crossing them in front of their faces a couple of times, then spitting between their fingers.

"What was that all about?" I asked.

"It's a protective ritual," said Igor.

Before I could figure out what he was talking about, someone knocked on the door.

I hesitated. Did I really want to answer it?

"Oh, go ahead," said Jeff, who had elbowed his way through the monsters. "We might as well see what happens next."

That's one of the neat things about having a science-fiction writer for a father; he tends to look at life as a kind of story.

I was almost disappointed when the person who knocked on the door seemed so normal. He was a bit taller than average, with sandy brown hair. The only thing that looked a little odd were his eyebrows, which were so thick and bushy that they merged into a single long brow stretching right across his forhead.

"Is this the place to come for the monster contest?" he asked. He sounded kind of nervous.

"It seems to be be," I said. "Come on in."

He stepped into the living room.

"Vell, I suppose it vas about time for one of his kind to show up," said the Count.

"I don't understand," I said. "What are you doing here? You don't look like a monster."

"Just wait," grumbled Igor. "We've got a few more nights until the moon is full.

Suddenly everything clicked. I remembered what I had read about people who had the kind of long, thick eyebrow this guy had.

"You!" I cried. "You're a werewolf!"

Chapter Thirteen

Judge Not, Lest Ye Be Clobbered!

The man nodded and bobbed his head. "That's all right, isn't it? I mean, werewolves do get to enter your contest, don't they?"

"I suppose it depends on whether or not the moon is full the night of the contest," I said. He was so gentle and—well, nervous, I guess—that it was hard to imagine him in a monster contest. But then, who knew what he would be like once the moon was full?

"Now look, fellows," said my mother, who had followed Jeff into the living room. "I want to know why you've all come here. I'm not prejudiced or anything. But I really don't want my house full of monsters. Surely with the careers you've had, you have enough money to go to a hotel or something."

"They don't want us," said the Frankenstein monster sadly.

"That's right," said Igor. "They do not . . ."

Suddenly he seemed to sag. "Oh, let's be honest," he said. "Most of us aren't very well off these days. The business has changed. Fifty years ago we were the kings. The greatest ever. We had heart. People loved us even when they were afraid of us. But it's not that way anymore. The new guys are different. Guys like Jason and Freddy Krueger have taken over the business. Siggie and I were hoping this contest might change things a little. I guess the others all had the same idea."

It made me sad to hear him talk like that. I mean, I loved these guys. I thought they were they greatest.

"Ve have been tossed into the trashbin of pop culture," said the Count gloomily.

"It's not true," I cried. "Lots of people still love you!"

The Count's lower lip started to tremble. For a second, I thought he was going to cry. I hoped he wouldn't; then I wondered if he could. It seemed like one of those things that vampires couldn't do—like casting a reflection in a mirror.

The mirror! I glanced at the one which hung in the hall. Sigmund Fred and Igor were standing right beside it, their reflections clear in the slightly dusty glass. But the Count had positioned himself so that he was nowhere near it.

Had he done that on purpose? I still couldn't tell if these guys were for real or not.

"I suppose we can put you all up for the time being," said Jeff. He sounded a little nervous. I wondered if he was worried about sleeping in a house with all these monsters—or about what my mother was going to say when she got him alone.

She didn't wait to get him alone. "Now just hold on," she said. "Before we invite them to stay here, I want to know who these people really are."

Igor drew himself up to his full four and a half feet. "Madam, we are just what we say we are: monsters—or in my case, a friend of a monster —who happen to be down on our luck."

"No, I mean who are you *really*," persisted my mother. She turned to the Creature from the Yuccky Lagoon. "You, take off your mask so I can see what's underneath."

The creature looked worried. "I'm not wearing a mask," he said.

My mother put on her no-nonsense face and went over to examine him. "There must be a zipper here someplace," she said. "I've seen those movies. You can always see the zipper in one of these costumes."

"They used to put on a fake zipper, so people

would think I wasn't real," said the creature. "The director thought it was more believable that way."

"Directors!" cried the others in disgust. They made that series of hand gestures again, ending with a "P-tooie" between their fingers. It was a good thing they were doing a dry-spit. Otherwise Mom would have been very angry.

"Jeff," said my mother nervously, "you're the specialist in weirdness. You handle this."

"All right. Look, guys," said Jeff. "All I want is a promise that we'll be safe with you around."

"I never bite my hosts!" cried the Count, sounding terribly offended.

"Well, we don't want you biting anyone else in the area, either," I said.

The Count nodded. "Medical science has made great strides regarding my—condition. If you will simply provide me with plenty of the elixir of life, I can guarantee my behavior."

"The elixir of life?" said my mother nervously. "You mean you want us to get you *blood*?"

"No," said The Count. "V-8 juice. I need lots of V-8 juice."

Now, I ask you—what do you do with a vampire like that?

My mother had much the same question, which

is why she hauled us to the radio station the next morning.

When we got there, Skip was skipping. I mean it. He was holding the morning paper, which had another front page article about the contest, and he was hopping around outside the sound booth singing, "This is great. This is incredible. This is wo-o-o-o-nderful."

"This is annoying," said my mother. "Look, Skip, I have a demented dwarf and his seven-foot friend sleeping in my spare bedroom, a gill man soaking in my bathtub, a vampire in the cellar, and a werewolf in my attic. At least, that was the total when we left his morning. Who knows how many there may be when we get back?"

Kevver started to speak up. I nudged him into silence. This was *not* the time to mention the Mummy that had showed up at midnight, asking for a place to "rest his weary bones."

Skip stopped and looked at my mother. "Aren't you having fun?" he asked.

"Fun?" my mother exploded. "Fun! Skip, I have a business to run. I have a child to raise. I can't cope with any more monsters."

"You should try raising Lulu," said Skip ruefully.

"Lulu is your problem!" cried my mother. She grabbed the front of Skip's jacket and pulled him forward until their noses were almost touching.

"Listen, Toomaloo: I can't spend all my time feeding monsters."

The tips of Skip's moustache started to twitch. "I'll see if I can get the station to help out," he said.

Which was the beginning of the night I still think of as The Great Restaurant Disaster.

It started out well enough. At Skip's urging, Station WERD decided to treat the monsters to dinner at a fancy French restaurant called Chez Stadium. The management was a little hazy about exactly who they were, but as long as they were getting good publicity out of it, they didn't mind.

My mother was jealous. Chez Stadium was one of her favorite restaurants. She was also a little nervous, since she sometimes took her clients there.

"Please don't embarrass me, boys," she said as we were getting ready to leave. "This is a very high-tone establishment." She straightened my tie, which I had been told I MUST wear, and used a little spit to slick down my hair.

"Oh, calm down," said Jeff. "It'll do those stiffs good to have someone a little different come to dinner."

I looked around at our crew. Different was hardly the word. At seven-thirty a stretch limousine pulled up outside the house. Nine of us climbed into the car: me, Kevver, the six monsters who had already been there, plus a hunchback named Quasimodo. "Quaz," as he suggested we call him, had arrived just after sunset. At first he and Igor had stared at each other suspiciously. But when Quaz found out that Igor was not going to be a contestant, he seemed to relax.

Mom and Jeff stood on the porch and waved as we drove off. They were holding hands. I think they were looking forward to an evening alone.

Skip and Lulu met us at the restaurant. It was a good thing Skip had warned the management ahead of time. Otherwise I don't think we would have gotten in.

The restaurant wasn't the only place Skip had warned. Several of the local TV stations had sent camera crews.

"How do you think I got them to let us come?" whispered Skip when I asked about it. "Chez Stadium was *not* interested in having a group of monsters come to dinner. But when I explained the publicity angle, they changed their minds."

Publicity again. Everyone wanted publicity.

The TV crews had attracted a crowd. Everybody was waving and cheering as we made our way into the restaurant. A tall man in a tuxedo greeted us at the door.

"Walk this way," he said and sniffed.

As we followed him into the dining room I noticed that Kevver was holding his shoulders very straight. He had his nose in the air.

"What are you doing?" I asked.

"The waiter said, 'Walk this way,'" said Kevver.

I poked him in the ribs and reminded him that my mother wanted us to behave.

As it turned out, it wasn't Kevver I needed to worry about.

The maître d' (that's what they called the guy in the tux who took us to our seats) showed us to a large round table under a huge chandelier. A starched white cloth covered the table.

When I sat down and looked at my plate I got nervous. It was surrounded by more silverware than I usually use in a day. I remembered the rule my mother gave me: Start at the outside, and work your way in. That was good as far as it went. But what was I supposed to do with the fork at the top of my plate?

"Get a load of that," said Kevver, pointing behind us with his thumb.

I glanced over my shoulder. In the center of the room was a two-level table. It was loaded with more fancy desserts that I had ever seen in my life—thick pies, cream puffs, cakes with so many layers I couldn't even count them. I would have been glad to skip supper and just have dessert.

Dinner started with appetizers. The Count ordered V-8 juice. The lagoon man asked for raw clams. The Mummy wanted some dry toast. Quasimodo did what I really wanted to do, and asked for a French pastry.

As for Lulu, she ordered some of everything.

When everyone had settled in, Skip raised his water glass. "I'd like to propose a toast," he said. "Here's to the judges of the first Monster of the Year Contest: Kevver Smith and Michael McGraw."

A deathly silence fell over the table. Every one of those monsters turned toward me and Kevver. Suddenly I realized just what we'd gotten ourselves into. We were going to have to pick one of them to win the contest.

That meant we were going to make one monster very happy.

It also meant we were going to make the rest of them very, very angry.

Chapter Fourteen

Disaster at Dinner

It was Lulu who broke the awful silence. "I'm sure glad I'm not you guys," she said.

She sounded really happy.

I decided silence would have been better.

Suddenly I noticed that the lagoon creature was weeping. His tears were green, as if they had algae in them. They rolled down his scaly cheeks and fell into his raw clams.

"What's wrong?" I asked, putting a hand on his arm. I could feel the muscles move and shift under his leathery green skin. It was kind of frightening. But it was hard to be too frightened of someone who was so unhappy.

"I don't have a chance," he cried. "I shouldn't even be here. The others don't like me. They never have. They say I'm just an upstart, not a classic like them."

It was meant to be a quiet conversation between the two of us. But Lulu had ears that the government should study for use in spy planes. When she heard what the creature said, she decided to help, in her own revolting way.

"Is that true?" she demanded. "Have you guys been picking on Swamp Lips here?"

The other monsters looked embarrassed. They stared at their plates and poked their food around.

"It's not really him," said the Count at last. "It's just that he made so many lousy movies he started giving monsters a bad name."

"It wasn't my fault," blubbered the creature. "It was the scripts. I had lousy writers."

"Writers!" cried the others in disgust. They made that complicated gesture, and spit through their fingers again. I was glad Jeff wasn't here to see *that*.

A passing waiter did happen to notice. I thought for a minute he was going to throw us out of the restaurant. But we were a pretty big group, and I guess he decided he didn't want to lose the tip. Or maybe it was the thought of what might happen to someone who tried to throw us out. The idea would have made me think twice!

The lagoon creature's bad feelings seemed to loosen something up in the other monsters. They all started to talk about the past.

"We've each had our share of hard times," said

Quaz, in his gravelly voice. "Remember when the Mummy and I had that fight over a girl we were both in love with?"

"I remember!" roared Fred. "You grabbed his bandages and started to run. It's a good thing you can't run very fast, or there would have been nothing left of him." He started to laugh, which made the whole table shake.

"I didn't think it was funny," said the Mummy dryly. "I was dizzy for a month."

The Count started to chuckle. "How about the time Igor put the starch in your hairspray, Volfie? I haven't laughed that hard in years."

"That wasn't funny either," replied the Wolfman stiffly. "In fact, I thought it was quite disrespectful."

"Ooo," said the Count, shaking his fingers daintily "Aren't ve la-di-da all of a sudden?"

"Well, what makes you think you're so great?" Lulu asked the Count. "I've seen your old movies. I think you should have gone to acting school."

Sigmund Fred start to snort and pound the table. "She got you, Count," he wheezed happily. The rest of us snatched our glasses, which were wildly bouncing around from the whacking he was giving the table.

"And I suppose you call vhat you did acting, Siggie?" replied the Count. "All that grunting and groaning! You sounded like you vere doing barnyard imitations."

"Now, boys," said Skip.

The monsters ignored him.

Lulu ignored him, too, which was unfortunate, since she was the one who got things stirred up. "I always liked the Mummy best, anyway," she said. I doubt she had even seen a film with the Mummy. She just wanted to annoy the others.

The Mummy smiled gratefully.

"That stuffed shirt!" cried Igor. "He couldn't scare up ten cents to make a phone call."

"Hey!" cried the Mummy.

"Being scary isn't the only thing in life," interrupted Quasimodo. "I touched people's hearts."

"Yeah, and I've got a hunch that's why you only got one story," said Igor. "They couldn't figure out what to do with you so they kept making the same film over and over. *Ding dong, ding dong!* All those bells in that old church. If you had been versatile, like me, you might have been in lots of films."

"Lots of *cheap* films," said Quasimodo. "Rip-offs of rip-offs. You aren't a character. You're a cliche!"

"Now, boys," said Skip again. Everyone ignored him. So he took a sip of coffee. Then he spit it back in his cup and glared at Lulu, who was trying to look innocent.

"A cliche?" cried Igor. "Look, Buster, there's room for only one hunchback in this monster business, and I'm it."

And then he hit him with his spoon.

At that point I expected Quasimodo to pick Igor up and throw him across the room. Instead he started to cry, which made two of them, since the Creature from the Yucky Lagoon was still leaking tears, too.

The lagoon creature was sympathetic to Quasimodo. I think it had something to do with them both feeling like second class monsters. Anyway, while Quaz didn't respond, Goony did. He stood up and flicked Igor on the ear. "You leave him alone!" he said sternly.

"Did you see that?" cried Igor. "Did you see what he did?"

"No, I missed it," said Lulu, an evil twinkle in her eyes. "What did he do?"

"Are you out of your mind?" I hissed at her. "What are you trying to do, cause a riot?"

"It is one of my life's goals," she said. Her voice was so sincere I couldn't help but believe her. I didn't know what to say. It didn't matter, because about that time war broke out.

"Don't you touch my friend!" roared the Franken-

stein monster. He grabbed a ketchup bottle and shook it at Quasimodo.

Now you know as well as I do that shaking a ketchup bottle is usually about as effective as kicking a rock. But you have to remember who was shaking it. With a loud *kuh-loop* a huge glob of ketchup went flying across the table. It splattered across Quasimodo's tunic.

"Yum!" cried the Count when he saw the red smear. Leaping to his feet, he dived for the Quaz. Then he caught himself. "Excuse me," he said, looking truly embarrassed. "I got carried away."

Quasimodo had also gotten carried away, because he picked up his French pastry, pointed it at Fred, and squashed it between his hands. This caused a great chunk of white cream to go flying across the table. However it missed Fred completely. In fact, it missed everyone at our table. Instead it landed on the throat of an elegant lady sitting a table away and began dripping down the front of her dress.

"Oh!" she shrieked. "Oh, oh, oh!"

Lulu was laughing so hard she nearly fell off her chair.

The woman's husband (or her boyfriend, or whatever) glared at us. Then he picked up his soupbowl. Carrying it over to our table, he poured it into Quasimodo's lap.

"You can't do that!" shouted the lagoon creature. "He's my friend." He grabbed his raw clams and started stuffing them down the man's neck.

"Go, Goony!" cried Lulu. By this time she was laughing so hard she couldn't control herself. I watched in astonishment as she really did fall off her chair.

The excitement was too much for the Wolfman. Even though he was still in human form, he climbed on his chair and started to howl. The woman sitting behind him began to scream. He turned toward her and began clacking his teeth together.

"Now, boys!" said Skip. "I think you'd better—"

But before he could tell us what he thought, a flying chicken breast hit him in the face. *Sploop!* The meat fell to the floor, leaving Skip with gooey sauce dripping from this moustache. "Stop it!" he ordered, wiping away the sauce. "Stop it right now!"

It was about then that someone discovered the dessert cart. When the first lemon meringue pie took flight, I knew we were in for a rough time. It sailed across the room and hit the snooty maître d' in the face.

"*Sacre bleu!*" he cried. But his fake French accent disappeared as he ran for the fire extinguisher.

"You want foam!" he shrieked. "I'll give you foam!"

He turned the canister upside down and shook it. A stream of white foam flooded the floor. People were slipping and sliding all over the place. Next to me a beautiful lady in a red strapless gown fell face-down into her onion soup.

"Stop this!" cried the Frankenstein monster. He stood up—a seven-foot tower of green muscle— and smashed his hand into the table for silence.

The main effect of this action was to smash the table into the floor.

By now the air was thick with pies. Suddenly a cream puff went sailing past my ear. I looked up and saw Igor swinging from the crystal chandelier. He had an armful of cream puffs, and he was lobbing them across the room like hand grenades: *Splat! Splat! Splat!* Gobs of cream were erupting all around us.

As the chandelier hit the peak of its swing a well-dressed lady with raspberries in her hair went screaming past the table. That was more than the Wolfman could stand. He went bounding after her, snapping at her heels—which looked pretty strange, since he was still completely human.

"This is the best night of my life!" cried Lulu. She was rolling around on the floor, holding her sides and shrieking with laughter.

Suddenly I heard a noise like the pop of a champagne cork. The Count had disappeared.

"Oh, my God!" cried a lady on the other side of the room. "There's a bat in here! A bat! A bat!"

People started screaming. Women in fancy dresses covered their heads and ran for the door. Unfortunately the police arrived before any of them could get out. The screaming got louder. Kevver and I crawled under a table to watch what happened next.

We might have escaped the police roundup if Sigmund Fred hadn't decided to join us.

With the table floating two feet in the air, it was easy for the cops to find us.

Chapter Fifteen

Gadzinga!

My mother had to come down to the police station to get us out. She was not amused. She was even less happy when she saw the morning paper. Actually, *disgusted* was the word she used—as in, "I'm disgusted with all of you."

This was her first statement at breakfast the next morning. Her second was: "I can't believe you acted so childishly."

Mothers must have some secret power to instill guilt. Only two sentences, and she had those monsters hanging their heads in shame. I was feeling guilty, and I hadn't even done anything.

"We're sorry, Ms. Adams," everyone muttered. Well, everyone except the lagoon creature. He had taken to calling my mother "Mom." He looked up at her and said, "It won't happen again, Mom." He sounded miserable.

My mother looked uncomfortable. She was still

trying to figure out how to deal with Goony. "Well, I should hope not," she said at last. "You may be even sorrier when you see the effect of your actions. Listen to *this* headline: 'Smud Renames BAM! Vows All Out War on Monsters.'"

It turned out that Myrna Smud had been having dinner at Chez Stadium when the pie fight broke out. My theory is she only showed up to keep an eye on us. Well, she got an eyeful all right—an eyeful of lemon meringue pie. She had been so offended by the whole thing that she called the newspapers to announce BAM! had been changed from "Billboards Are Monstrous!" to "Ban All Monsters!" She was starting a petition to have the city council outlaw monsters in Syracuse.

"She can't do that!" cried Igor. "It's discrimination!"

"Never underestimate the power of a small mind," said Jeff sadly.

"What are we going to do?" moaned the wolfman. He was holding an ice pack against a large lump on his head, which he had gotten when someone bonked him during the battle in the restaurant.

"I'd suggest you start by trying to behave," said my mother. "I have a feeling things are going to get worse before they get better. Here's the third article I wanted you to hear."

And then she read a ridiculous item about rumors that a radioactive dinosaurlike creature was swimming his way up the Great Lakes, and was scheduled to arrive in town the next morning.

"Gadzinga!" cried the lagoon creature happily. "He's my hero!"

"That's absurd!" said Igor. "This isn't his kind of contest."

"That doesn't make any difference," said Mom. "When people get upset, rumors start to fly. But I would like to get my hands on the idiot who started this rumor. We've got enough troubles as it is."

A nervous look twitched across Jeff's face, and I got a pretty good idea where the rumor had come from. I figured he had been having a little fun at the newspapers' expense. But I wasn't about to blow the whistle on him. He's kept his mouth shut for my sake plenty of times in the past.

I forgot about the rumor until that evening when the doorbell rang. We all looked at one another nervously. Over the last week and a half answering the door had become a real adventure.

"I vill get it," said the Count at last.

We all crowded in behind him. I didn't know what to expect: another monster, a policeman, an angry BAMmer. It might have been anyone.

But it was just the UPS man. "Package for Michael McGraw," he said. "Signature required."

I pushed past the Count and signed my name on the deliveryman's clipboard. He handed me a cardboard box—a cube, about a foot and a half on each side.

"What is it?" cried everyone.

"I don't know," I said. "I haven't opened it yet!"

I carried the box into the kitchen and set it on the table. Jeff handed me a knife.

I was about to cut the packing tape when something began pounding on the sides of the box—from the inside.

I put down the knife.

"I'm not sure I want to open this," I said.

"Oh, please," cried Goony. "My curiosity is killing me."

I looked at my mother. She looked at Jeff. He just shrugged. "You've got plenty of friends here to protect you," he said. "Besides, maybe it's just a little bunny or something."

"The way things are going, it'll be a killer rabbit from Mars," I said.

But I cut the package open. As I was pulling back the flaps something leapt through the top of the box. It landed on the table, legs flexed, ready to jump again. I looked, blinked, and looked again.

A teeny-tiny *Tyrannosaurus rex* was stomping across our table. "Oh, dat better!" it growled in a

H. Kurtz

voice ten times too big for such a little creature. "Gadzinga didn't like dat box!"

Jeff gulped. "Gadzinga?" he said nervously. "I thought you were just a rumor."

"Do I look like a rumor, baldy?" roared the little monster.

Jeff blushed, and not because Gadzinga had called him baldy. I was sure now that he had started the rumor about Gadzinga—and gotten caught in the kind of reality game he had warned me about earlier.

"What are you doing in a box?" I asked. "I heard you were going to swim your way here."

"What are you, nuts?" cried the little monster. "That would take years."

Goony stared at the newcomer in horror. "Gadzinga?" he whispered. "That little thing is Gadzinga?"

"Yah, me Gadzinga. You got a problem with dat?"

"But you're so—so small," said Goony. He turned away, and I heard him whisper, "All my life I've looked up to Gadzinga. And now I find out he's only eighteen inches tall!" He sounded crushed.

"It's what's inside dat counts," roared Gadzinga. Stomping across the table, he opened his mouth and shot out a heat ray.

"Ouch!" cried Igor.

The Quaz patted Goony's back consolingly.

The Count was less sympathetic. "You should have known they always use miniatures in those movies," he said.

"Excuse me," said Goony. "I think I need to go upstairs and soak in the bathtub for a while." Shoulders drooping, he trudged out of the room.

"Another dream crushed by reality," said the Quaz. "The world is full of heartbreak."

"Heartbreak, schmeartbreak." said Igor. "He'll get over it. In the meantime we've got to figure out some way to get people around here on our side."

"What we need is a public relations campaign," I said. "You know about that stuff, Mom. Can't we figure out some way to get people to be glad the monsters are in town?"

My mother can't resist a professional challenge. "That's not a bad idea, Mike. If we can get people to think positively about the guys, it might take care of the whole situation."

"Maybe you could get them a Broadway show," said a tall, masked phantomlike figure who had arrived late the night before. "It worked for me."

My mother waved her hand. "That takes years," she said.

"How about endorsements?" asked Kevver. "One

111

of the car dealers is advertising 'monstrous savings.' Maybe the guys could do some image building that way."

"Kevver, that's brilliant!" said Mom.

"You want us to do commercials?" cried Igor. His voice sounded like he was in pain. "You want us to sell out?"

"Sell out what?" asked the Count. "A commercial couldn't be any worse than your last three movies."

"You could go the education route," said Jeff.

We all looked at him.

He shrugged and spread jam on his toast. Before he could raise it to his mouth, Gadzinga stomped over and took a bite. "Yum!" he roared. Jeff looked startled, but he kept his cool. "Look," he said, "if you really want to change the way people think, you've got to start young. So why not have the gang make guest appearances in some of the local schools?"

Chapter Sixteen

Monsters in the Classroom

My mother called the principal of the junior high where Kevver and I go, and asked if he would be interested in having the monsters visit.

"Are you kidding?" he cried. "I've got four hundred monsters in this school already. Why would I want any more?"

Fortunately, Miss Shelley, principal of our old elementary school, was more interested. So the next morning Frankenstein's monster, the Wolfman, the Creature from the Yucky Lagoon, Gadzinga, and the rest headed over to give an assembly.

The only one who didn't come was the Count; he still refused to appear before dark.

Most of the monsters were excited. Goony, however, was a nervous wreck.

"Kids make me nervous," he explained while we walked. "They're very frightening."

"Hey," I said. "*I'm* a kid!"

"But there's only one of you. Bunches of kids terrify me. Especially live ones!"

"Don't worry," said Igor. "They won't be living long once you start to talk. You'll bore them to death in the first ten minutes."

Goony turned to me. "See what I mean," he said, his lip quivering. "I don't get no respect. No never."

"Well, this is your chance to start building a new reputation," said Kevver. "If you let them in-spect you today, maybe they will re-spect you tomorrow."

The monsters groaned. Luckily, we reached the school before Kevver could make another bad joke.

"Look!" cried Goony happily. "They want us!"

He was pointing to a huge banner that hung over the front door. "Welcome to Bram Stoker Elementary," it said, in bright red letters.

Miss Shelley was waiting to greet us. "it's nice to have you back for a visit," she said to Kevver and me. "I'm very glad that you were able to bring your friends with you."

She didn't seem at all startled by the sight of the monsters. But then, as Jeff had pointed out the night before, there probably wasn't much that *could* surprise the principal of an elementary school.

"I've worked up a complete schedule for the day," said Miss Shelley, patting a stray hair back in place. "We'll start with an all-student assembly in the auditorium. I'd like each of you to talk a little bit about your career. You know, explain what you do and how you got involved in it."

The monsters looked a little uncomfortable. Miss Shelley didn't seem to notice.

"After that, we'll be sending you to individual classrooms," she continued.

Miss Shelley had everything worked out. Sigmund Fred was supposed to make a presentation on what it was like to live in a castle. The Mummy was to give a lecture an ancient history. She had assigned Goony to talk to some kids who were studying swamp life. The others were just supposed to go from class to class, doing question-and-answer sessions.

The assembly started out fairly well. Sigmund Fred titled his talk "A Patchwork Life." The Mummy told some pharaoh jokes. ("He certainly has a dry sense of humor," said Kevver.) Goony trembled and stammered, but managed to tell the story of how he was discovered by some people making a travel movie about the Yuccky Lagoon. In fact, everything went fine, until it was Gadzinga's turn. The tiny Tyrannosaurus stomped to the front the stage, jumped onto the desk next to the microphone and roared, "Me Gadzinga. Me the greatest!"

Then he offered to wrestle "any teacher in the joint."

Miss Shelley decided it was time to end the assembly. As the kids filed out, she gave each of the monsters their schedules. I should have realized that splitting them up was a mistake; it was going to make it that much harder for Kevver and I to keep things under control. When Miss Shelley told us she had invited one of the local TV stations to come in and tape part of the day for the evening news, I should have recognized that we had all the ingredients we needed for a master disaster.

Goony was still pretty nervous, so he asked me to stick with him. His speech was going pretty well when the Quaz came shuffling through the door shouting, "Trouble. Trouble in one-thirteen!"

Without waiting for Goony, I shot out of the room and raced down the hall after the Quaz. Kevver was just ahead of me. We burst into the room to find fifty third graders shouting, "I-gor! I-gor! Igor!"

Igor was standing on top of the teacher's desk, trying to fend off the kids, who were grabbing at him and holding out papers for him to autograph. He looked terrified.

"I-gor! they shouted, waving their papers at him I-gor! I-gor!"

"Get me outta here!" cried Igor when he saw me.

The kids started grabbing at him as if he were some kind of rock star. Suddenly Igor panicked. He leaped from the teacher's desk to the blackboard. Then he scrambled up the board and jumped from there to one of the support beams that ran across the ceiling.

The kids began to shout and cheer.

Grabbing the beam with his stubby hands, Igor swung his feet up, then he hung from the ceiling, quaking in terror until the teacher got the kids back in their seats.

When he climbed back down I noticed that he had left his footprint on the ceiling.

I also noticed that the newsmen had captured the whole thing on film.

Miss Shelley decided it was time for us to leave.

When the Count heard how our day had gone he laughed so hard he nearly choked on his V-8 juice. Unfortunately, Myrna Smud wasn't nearly so amused. The television cameras had captured the disaster, and they showed plenty of footage on the news that night. Naturally, they asked Myrna for her reaction.

Her response was true to form. "These terrible people are warping the minds of our young people!" she declared "They are twisting the very fabric of American society. They must be banned!"

"Vhy does that voman hate us so much?" asked the Count.

"Maybe she was scared by a monster movie when she was a little kid," said Kevver.

"I was scared by a monster movie when I was a little kid," I said. "I loved it."

My mother couldn't decide whether she was appalled or ecstatic to have her company connected to all this madness. "There's no such thing as bad publicity," she kept whispering to herself.

"Shhh!" hissed Jeff. "I want to hear what Myrna's saying."

We turned out attention back to the screen.

"I have decided that we must take vigorous action to end this menace," said Myrna. "Therefore, I am announcing that BAM! will lead an anti-monster parade past city hall tomorrow night. All concerned citizens are welcome to join us to help root this menace from our society."

"Just what is it about the monsters that bothers you so much, Mrs. Smud?" asked the interviewer.

Myrna's features puckered into her lemon-eating

look. "They overstimulate children's imaginations," she said. "This causes them to think too much, which is not healthy at a young age."

We looked at one another in astonishment. The Count rose to his feet, trembling with anger. He stood in front of the television.

"This," he said, "means var!"

Chapter Seventeen

What a Riot!

Myrna scheduled her parade for the same time as the Monster of the Year Contest. Fortunately, I didn't have time to worry about it, since both events were less than twenty-four hours away.

By six o'clock the next night it was clear that we were going to have perfect Halloween weather —cool, but not too cold; clear, with a few wispy clouds. A soft breeze was scratching the dry leaves along the sidewalks, whispering through those leaves still clinging to the trees.

We began gathering for the parade at seven-thirty. Skip had invited Jeff to lead the parade in his hearse. Kevver and I were riding in a Station WERD car close behind. It was a black convertible. The top was down, and Skip told us to sit on top of the backseat, so that we could wave to the crowds. We were real excited, until he told us Lulu was going to ride with us.

"What can I do?" said Skip apologetically. "Lulu thinks you two are wonderful." He shifted the bullhorn he was using to organize the parade from one hand to the other, then looked at it as if he might find something to say written inside its bell. "Last night she threatened to hold her breath and turn blue unless we adopted both of you. I had to call a lawyer and get him to tell her why it was impossible before she would settle down."

What could we say? I mean, how do you tell a man that his child is revolting?

Besides, he already knew.

The plan was to have the parade go south on Salina Street, turn and pass City Hall and then move on up to the War Memorial Building, where WERD was sponsoring a giant party for anyone who wanted to come. Skip had booked a pair of local bands—Squashed Spider and the Pink Punks—to play. Admission was free, but you had to pay for your own cider and doughnuts.

At the end of the night we would have the contest.

And then Kevver and I would have to make our dangerous decision. As Jeff said, the idea "was not a pretty prospect."

It wasn't just the idea of having a dozen or so monsters mad at us that bothered me. (Though that was pretty frightening.)

It was that I had gotten so fond of all of them that I couldn't stand the thought of hurting their feelings. I knew Goony would cry buckets if he lost. Quaz wouldn't cry, but his lip would tremble, and I would know that he felt terribly rejected. The Mummy would cough dryly and say, "Oh, don't mind me."

The others might hold it inside, but they would be just as upset

"What are we going to do?" I asked as we climbed into the parade car.

"I don't know," said Kevver. He looked as worried as I felt.

"I'm really scared," I said.

He nodded. "Me, too."

Then we stopped talking, because Lulu pushed in and sat between us. "Hi, guys!" she said cheerfully. "Isn't this fun? Did you bring anything to eat?"

"Sorry, Lulu," I said. "I lost my appetite two days ago."

It was the first time I ever saw sympathy in that round, red face. I guess from Lulu's point of view, losing your appetite was the worst thing that could possibly happen to you. "Oh, that's really sad," she said.

Except for Igor and Sigmund Fred, who were riding together, each monster had a convertible to himself. Several of them stopped to say hello to us as they took their places. I could tell by the look in their eyes that they were wondering if we had already made up our minds who was going to be the Monster of the Year.

If only I knew!

The parade started. The sidewalks were crammed with people, most of them in costume. It was neat seeing all those wolfmen, vampires and Frankenstein monsters when we had the real thing riding behind us.

By this time our picture had been in the paper so much that, in Syracuse at least, Kevver and I were real celebrities. Everyone cheered as we rode by.

"Wow!" I said. "They like us!"

"I'm bored," said Lulu.

I should have known enough to get scared right then. But I was too busy enjoying the parade, and worrying about what was going to happen next.

What happened next was that Myrna Smud showed up. Or, more accurately, we got to where Myrna and her crowd were waiting. They had gathered on the steps of city hall, where Myrna was making a speech.

"People of Syracuse!" she cried, "awake to the monsters in your midst!"

She was yelling through a megaphone. Her voice could be heard even above the music of our parade.

"Now I know why they call those things bull-horns," muttered Kevver.

The parade stopped. We were face to face with about a thousand people carrying signs that said, "BAM! BAM! Ban All Monsters!" and "Monsters Go Home!" and even "Frankenstein, Frankenstein. He is not a friend of mine."

"Monsters go home!" they shouted.

"That's right!" cried Myrna. "Save our children's imaginations. Drive these creatures from our midst!"

"Excuse me," said Lulu, squeezing past me. "I gotta go do something."

I was too worried about Myrna and the Bammers to realize that it was Lulu I should really be worrying about.

Suddenly the Count was standing next to the car. "I have never been so insulted in my life!" he declared. "I vill lodge a complaint with the Transylvanian Embassy first thing tomorrow morning."

"Does she mean us?" asked another voice. It was Goony. He was standing on the other side of the car. He was crying again.

"No more monsters! No more monsters!" chanted Myrna.

"No more monsters!" chanted the crowd on the steps.

Suddenly I heard another voice, also using a bullhorn. "Two bits, four bits, six bits, a dollar! If you love monsters, stand up and holler!"

It was Lulu! She had grabbed her father's megaphone, and was leading *our* crowd in a cheer. The people behind us began to shout and applaud.

"No more monsters!" cried Myrna.

"No more monsters!" shouted her followers.

"We love monsters!" screamed Lulu.

"We love monsters!" shouted our followers.

Then the voices all got kind of mixed up. "No More We Love Monsters Monsters Monsters!" screamed the mob.

Now Lulu was walking up the steps of City Hall. "Give me an *M*!"

"*M!*" roared the crowd.

"Give me an *O*!"

"*O!*" they screamed.

"*N-S-T-E-R*! Monster! Monster! *Monster*!"

The crowd went nuts—and so did Myrna. She hit Lulu over the head with her sign.

That was it—the battle was on. Most of the crowd didn't know that Lulu had spent her entire life doing things that made people want to hit her over the head. They only saw an overweight adult woman who should have known better bopping a little kid with a sign.

"Lulu!" cried Skip, racing up the steps of city hall.

"Lulu!" cried the crowd.

People were surging forward. Even the police lines couldn't hold them back. BAM! signs were going bam all around.

Then the moon slipped over the horizon. It looked huge behind the city towers.

I heard a horrible howl behind me. I turned and saw the Wolfman shaking and snarling as his big eyebrow seemed to spread over his entire face. His hands were getting hairy. His nails turned black, stretching out into sharp claws.

An instant later the Count vanished in a flash of smoke and a big black bat appeared in front of our car. Sigmund Fred was growling ominously. Quasimodo was leaping from car to car. The Mummy had started to moan. Steam was curling from Godzonga's mouth, and the little creature was bouncing up and down, waving its paws menacingly.

The monsters were basically nice guys. But if they got too excited I could see we would have a real problem on our hands.

What we needed was something to distract everyone.

I knew of one thing that might do the trick.

"Come on," I said to Kevver. "Time to bring out our surprise."

"I thought we were going to save it for the party," he protested.

"If we don't bring it out now, there might not be a party!" I said.

He nodded. We grabbed the keys out of the ignition. We climbed over the back of the car and opened the trunk. Inside was the package we had worked up with Wendy Moon over the last few weekends.

It took both of us to carry it. But we couldn't get anywhere. The crowd surging around us was too thick to make any progress. "Igor!" I cried. "Siggie! Give us a hand!"

Sigmund Fred came plowing through the crowd. Even in the grip of the riot, people cowered from the huge green monster. Igor was riding on Siggie's shoulders, shaking his fists and screaming at the people below.

Without even asking what we needed, Sigmund Fred stooped down and scooped up the device.

"Up on the steps!" I shouted in his ear.

He nodded and plunged back into the crowd. Kevver and I tried to follow, but we couldn't get anywhere. For a minute I thought everything was lost. Then the rest of the monsters appeared. They gathered around us in a V-formation, and plowed through the crowd after Sigmund Fred. Kevver and I were protected inside the wedge.

We got to the steps faster than I would have thought possible. Once we got onto the steps we were out of the worst of the riot. I looked back and shivered. I think I'd rather face a monster than a mob any day.

Sigmund put down the device. With the monsters clearing the way, Kevver went left and I went right. We stretched the device to its full length.

Then I pulled the trigger.

Familiar music began to blare. I turned it up. It still wasn't loud enough. I turned it up again.

People in the crowd began to notice that something new was happening. When they turned toward the music they saw it: a forty-eight foot long flag, rising from the steps of city hall.

What could they do?

With the speakers playing The Star Spangled Banner so loud you could hear it in the next county, everyone had to stop.

They all put their hands over their hearts and started to sing.

When you think about it, that's not a bad way to stop a riot.

Chapter Eighteen

The Monster of the Year

The police were not amused. So everyone who seemed to be involved in this mess—including me, Kevver, Myrna, Lulu, the monsters, and a half dozen of the top Bammers—was whisked off for questioning. The only one who escaped was the Count. He just flew away.

He headed straight for my house, which was how my mother knew what was going on even before we even had a chance to call her. She was not happy when she had to come to the police station to bail us out again.

The WERD party was going full swing when we finally arrived. Everyone seemed to be having a good time. Kevver and I were more nervous than ever. No matter who won, it seemed that we were going to be in trouble.

Then I got brilliant again. I guess desperation can do that for you. I whispered my idea to Kevver, and he nodded eagerly. We found Jeff and told him our plan. He agreed and even helped me write a little speech.

The contest began at midnight. Skip was the host. Kevver and I sat on the stage as a parade of monsters made their way past us, growling and snarling at the crowd. Our friends were all there, of course, as well as a lot of local people who had entered the contest just for the fun of it. Some of them had costumes so good I might have believed they were for real—if I hadn't already met the real thing.

Finally the parade was over. Kevver and I conferred for a few minutes. But that was just for show. We had already made up our minds.

We walked to the front of the stage.

"Have the judges made their decision?" asked Skip.

I nodded.

He handed me the microphone.

I looked out at that sea of masks and faces, a wonderful stew of monsters and humans. My hands began to tremble. I had never made a speech before.

Kevver was standing beside me, holding the prize. Siggie, the Count, and the other monsters were gathered on the stage behind me.

I tried to speak, but my throat seemed to have closed in on itself. I swallowed and tried again.

"Being the judge of the first Monster of the Year Contest was a great responsibility," I said. "We have been lucky enough to have some of the most popular monsters of all time participate. It has been a great privilege to meet and talk with these wonderful characters. We hope that they have enjoyed their stay in Syracuse as much as we have enjoyed having them."

I paused and everyone applauded politely.

The monsters smiled. But you could feel the nervous tension crackling between them. Who was going to be the winner?

I knew the answer, but I was still pretty tense. I had another question on my mind. Would I survive announcing the winner?

"Look at these great faces!" I cried, gesturing behind me.

The monsters all growled and snarled. People shrieked in appreciation.

I smiled. This was going better than I had expected. I realized that once you get over being nervous, talking to so many people is fun.

I held up my hands for silence.

"We want to thank these monsters for their participation. However, wonderful as they are, we all know that ugliness is only skin deep. So

the judges have decided that the first Monster of the Year prize should go to someone who has demonstrated what it really means to be a monster. Someone who wants to squeeze the human spirit, stifle imagination, and hold our hearts in bondage. Someone who wants to control what we think, what we see, what we hear, what we read. Someone who represents the tradition of the cruelest, most frightening monsters of all time—those who would bind not only our hands, but our hearts. Yes, ladies and gentlemen, the monster of the year is none other than— Myrna Smud!"

The crowd roared its approval.

I looked behind me nervously. At first the monsters looked confused.

Then they began to smile.

When the Count gave me a thumbs-up sign, I knew I was home free.

And that was about the end of it.

Oh, we still had some messy legal business to deal with. For a while it seemed like everyone was suing everyone. ("Lawyers!" cried the monsters. Then they all made that complicated hand gesture and spit through their finger *three* times.] But finally everyone agreed to drop charges against everyone else. It just seemed easier that way.

Actually, the monsters were gone by that time.

After all, as the count said, "Halloveen is almost here. Ve have vork to do!"

We do get an occasional letter from the gang. The publicity seems to have done them good. Some of them have been picking up extra money endorsing products and so on. They all seem happy.

Skip has kept in touch, too. I think he likes me and Kevver because we're almost normal.

One last thing. I should tell you that before the monsters left, they decided that getting together had been so much fun they wanted to have a convention every year.

So maybe you'd better keep a string of garlic in your kitchen just in case.

After all—next year they just might come to your town!

About the Author and Illustrator

Bruce Coville has written dozens of books for young readers, including, *My Teacher is an Alien*, *Sarah's Unicorn*, *The Monster's Ring*, and the Camp Haunted Hills books, *How I Survived My Summer Vacation* and *Some of My Best Friends Are Monsters*. He grew up in central New York, where he's lived most of his life. "My grandfather was a farmer, but also served as caretaker of the local cemetery and I spent a lot of time helping him there when I was growing up," he says. "Not only that, my school colors were orange and black. And my favorite holiday has always been Halloween. So sometimes I think I can't *help* writing monster stories." Before becoming a full-time writer, Bruce Coville worked as a magazine editor, a teacher, a toymaker, and a gravedigger.

Harvey Kurtzman invented *MAD* magazine, serving as editor for its first 28 issues. His art and humor have inspired comic book artists for over two decades, and have made millions of people laugh. He is also the author of *My Life as a Cartoonist*, available from Minstrel Books.